THE ETERNAL THRONE CHRONICLES
CONTINUE WITH...

BOOK TWO: JUDGE OF ISRAEL

Coming Soon to
http://stores.lulu.com/timothywilkinson

Prophet
of Israel

Timothy S. Wilkinson

Book One of the
Eternal Throne
Chronicles

Prophet of Israel

Available for purchase at:

http://stores.lulu.com/timothywilkinson

Published by Lulu.com
860 Aviation Parkway
Suite 300
Morrisville, NC 27560
U.S.A.

First Edition
December 2007

All Rights Reserved
Copyright 2007 by Timothy Wilkinson
Cover design by Jordan Avery
Cover art by Brian Kawal
Maps and Diagrams by Jordan Avery and Timothy Wilkinson

This book, or parts thereof, may not be reproduced in any form without permission.

ISBN 978-1-4357-5478-2

PRINTED IN THE UNITED STATES OF AMERICA

ACKNOWLEDGMENTS

My sincere and too-oft unexpressed gratitude to all those who have supported me through the long years of the development of this project:

- to my students, who fill me with an endless wonder;
- to everyone who courteously read early (and often appallingly bad) drafts or sat patiently through story sessions;
- To my editor, Kate Goschen, for her encouragement, her selfless, invaluable editing, for understanding the power of language properly wielded, and for supporting me in my ongoing battle with commas;
- To Tyler Avery, for punctuation, positivity, and a perspective uniquely his own;
- to Corey and Rebecca, always reliable sounding boards;
- to Leif, for writing and reading honestly, and for *Wing Riders*;
- to Terin, LeAna, Isaac, and Amira Gloor, for reading even when reading was a chore;
- to Daniel Bauguess, for always being there in the effortlessly generous way of a true friend, and to Cora, for an enthusiasm for my work that helped me fill the blankest of pages;
- to Jordan, my partner in this endeavor, whose writing is his promise to me that drives me to better my own;
- to my mother, Darlene, for loving even writing that had a face only a mother could love;
- to Axel, for being so much more than a reader and editor (and without whom so many of my favorite elements of this story would not exist);
- and to Chelsey, for being the brave and beautiful heroine in every tale I weave.

For the princes of our tribe:
Jordan and Tyler,
Brendan and Colton,
Tavish and Finian,
and Colin;
And for Circe, our princess

PRIESTS OF ISRAEL

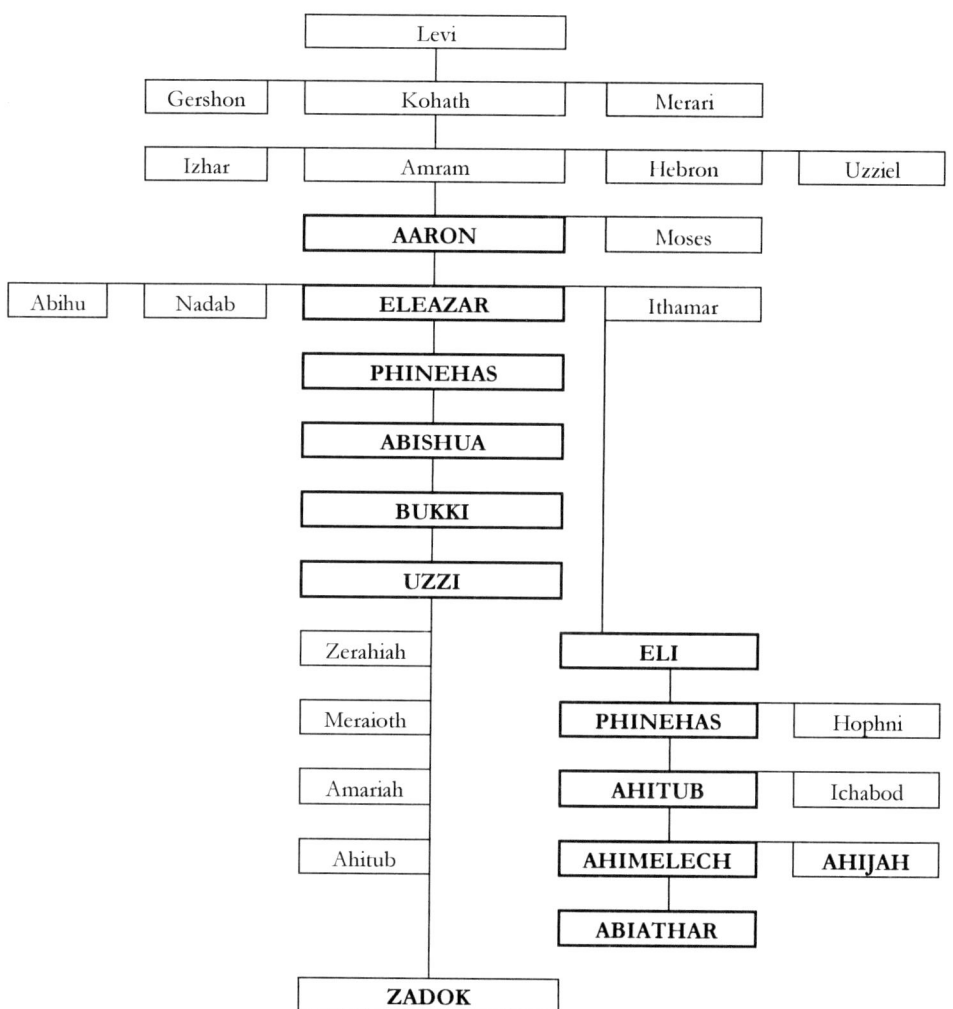

*Names in bold capitals served as High Priest

The Tribes of Israel

Asher
Benjamin
Dan
Ephraim
Gad
Issachar
Judah
Manasseh
Naphtali
Reuben
Simeon
Zebulun

Levi, the Priestly Tribe

Author's Note

The following book is a work of fiction. The historical account from which it is drawn, found in the Holy Bible in the book of 1 Samuel, Chapters 1 through 7, is factual. Any similarities between the two are intentional and deliberate.

As Appendix A will explain in greater detail, this story is written on the premise that the Biblical account of Israel's transformation to a monarchy in the days of Samuel and David is the origin of the famous stories of King Arthur and the Knights of the Round Table. If the story of King David did transmogrify into the story of King Arthur, it might have gone through many gradual changes in the centuries between the writing of the two accounts. This book does not claim to tell the story of what really happened in Palestine in the 10th century, but to present what the author imagines could have been one of those early renditions of the account as it slowly changed from history to literature. Therefore, while I tried to never contradict any known Biblical fact, the details with which I fleshed out the story came from historical research, the demands of the story, AND the tone, themes, and narrative elements of the Arthurian tales.

This is the story of a war fought in Palestine at the dawn of the Iron Age. In describing this war, I have attempted, for the edification of my readers, to capture the grisly reality of Iron Age warfare without resorting to the inclusion of gratuitous violence or gruesome descriptions. It has been my intent to use as a guideline for my own writing the descriptions of battle, war, and violence in the Bible itself.[1] Such details are meant to educate and illuminate.

---

[1] Such as Deuteronomy 28 and 32, Numbers 25, Judges 3, 4, 9:53, 16:21, 19, 1 Samuel 15:33, 2 Samuel 2:23, 3:22-30, 8:2, 16:22, 18:14-17, 20:10-13, 2 Chronicles 21, or Acts 1:18.

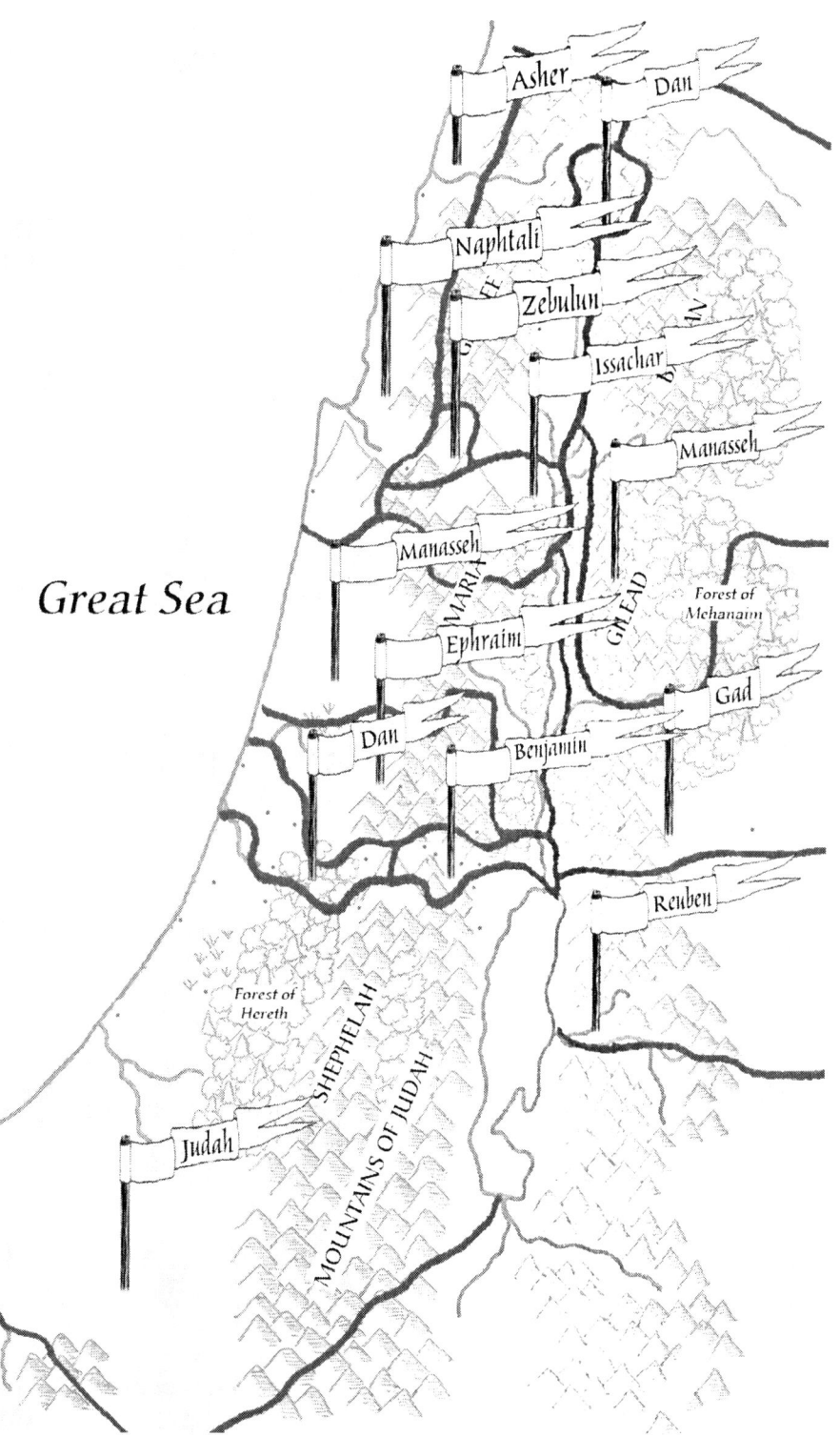

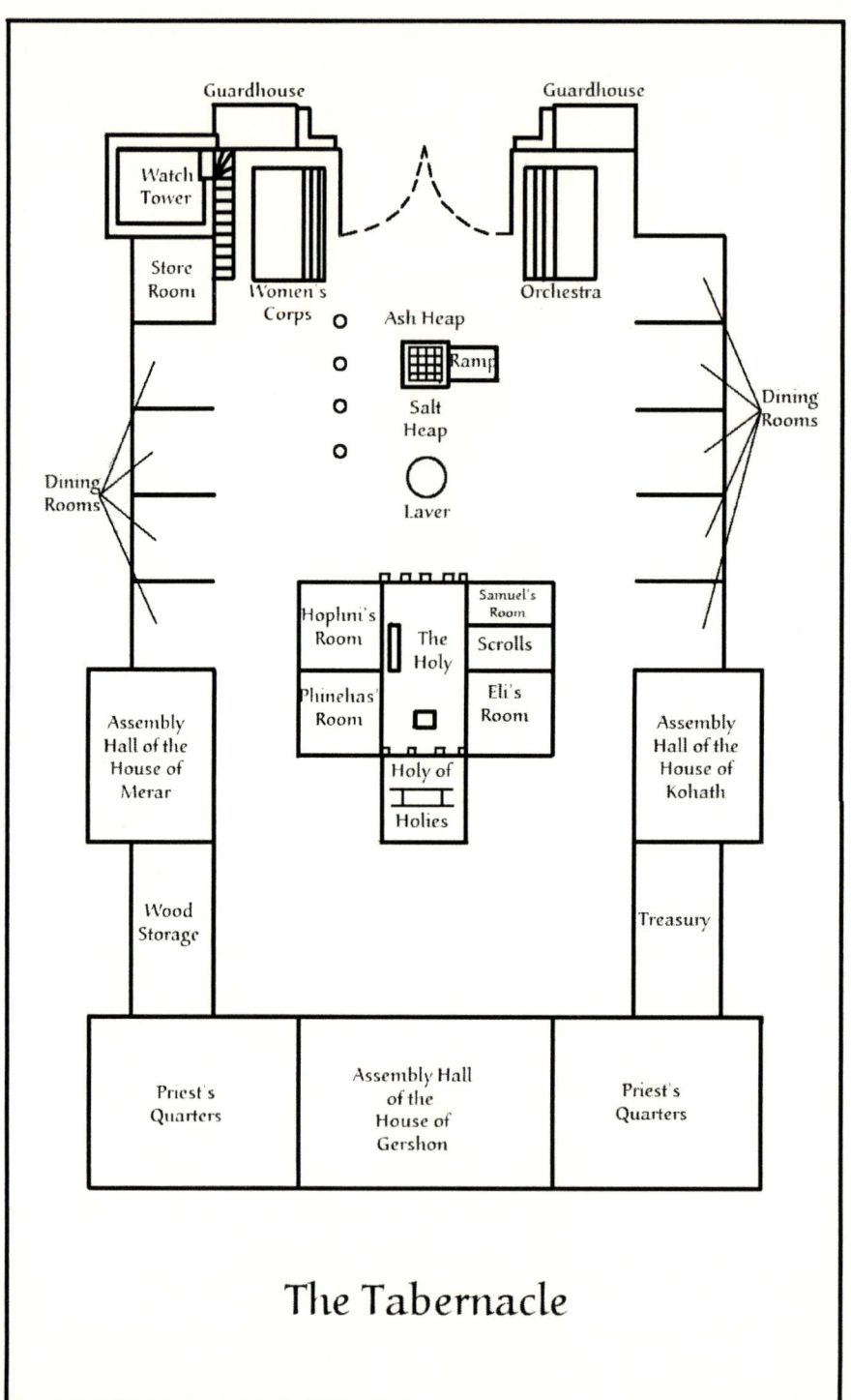

"Jehovah summons death and quickens life;
He brings down to the grave, and He resurrects
Jehovah impoverishes and enriches;
He abases and He exalts.
He raises the poor from the dust
And lifts the needy from the ash heap;
To seat them with nobles
And bestow on them a throne of glory."

The Prayer of Hannah,
1 Samuel 2:6-8

1

Samuel awoke in fear, wrenched from sleep in the unsettled hour before sunrise by the hiss and moan of a storm blowing in from the west. The tempest was flailing water and wind with such force that the wood-framed, cloth walls of his room alongside the sacred Tabernacle creaked with the strain of holding themselves together.

He sat and pushed free of his thin blanket, closing his eyes against the utter blackness to try to force his ears to work harder. All but lost in the gale's discordant song, he could just make out the cries of panicked voices and the slap of bare feet on wet flagstones outside his room.

He opened his eyes, revealing nothing more of the room around him, crawled from his bed and pushed aside the wool curtain that served as his door. Icy raindrops spattered on his forehead as he squinted across the dark Tabernacle Courtyard. Instantly, he found words for the sense of dread that had torn him, gasping, from nightmared sleep.

In the attack of wind and rain, the sacred Altar's Eternal Flame was in danger of being extinguished.

The storm had stripped the sky of stars and moon—the only light a pale grey dimly silhouetting the Curtain Wall surrounding the Courtyard. Through the haze of wind-swept rain, he saw the shadowy outlines of Priests and their acolytes, the Levites, scurrying around the Courtyard, their pale, linen robes soaked through and clinging to their bodies.

"Bring those skins!"

"Hang on to it!"

The bitter wind bit through his own thin tunic, already damp from the rain, and he wrapped the bottom portion of his woolen door around his lean body; the coarse material scratched against his bare shins. The wool warmed his skin, but the icy pit of fear in his stomach did not abate. He searched the Courtyard for his mentor and friend Priest Ahitub but cowled robes and sheets of stinging rain shrouded the men's faces.

A great muscle of cloud flexed somewhere above them, allowing dusky moonlight through to paint details on the shadowy shapes Samuel was watching. He saw a knot of people clustered around the burnished-copper Altar of Burnt Offering, mantled shoulders hunched against the assault of the storm. To the south of the Altar a ramp ascended, the means by which Priests and Levites bore the animal offerings to the copper grating on its top. A waist-high heap of rock salt slouched to its west, dissolving in the rain. Men knelt in front of the firebox door on the east side, trying to re-awaken the flame. Four others were attempting to stretch a mottled-grey sealskin oilcloth over the top of the Altar; it whipped and jerked in their hands like a thing possessed.

"Hold it!
"Pull your corner tight!"
"Farther down! Farther down!"

A snarl of wind ripped the oilcloth from their fingers and hurled it, fluttering like an autumn leaf, over the Courtyard wall and into the dark city of Shiloh.

Samuel ducked back into his room, whispered a quick prayer, and tugged his *me'il* on over his tunic; his mother, Hannah, had woven the linen sleeveless coat for him to wear whenever he was serving, but that had been nearly a year ago, and it no longer fit him properly. He wished he could wear something else, but to do so felt like a rejection of his mother's gift. As he pulled it over his head and its musty smell filled his nostrils, he saw her face. He saw her the way he saw all people, registering each detail of expression and body, compiling the elements to uncover whatever truths might be hiding behind the masks and postures they wore for the world. His mother's face, even in memory, was easy to read: *mouth hovering between a smile and a frown; wide, soft eyes characteristically downcast but full of the expectation of an unspoken hunger she waited for her firstborn to satisfy.*

He remembered that he had been dreaming of her before the storm wakened him, dreaming about the day she had given him to Tabernacle service. Moments before she and his father, Elkanah, had left the holy city of Shiloh without him, she had knelt within sight of the Altar and offered a prayer that still haunted his waking and sleeping. "My heart does exult in You, O Jehovah" she had said, her gentle voice quavering. "By Your power, even the barren woman has given birth."

The unbidden memory supplanted his fear of the storm's fury. He tied his apron-like *ephod* of white linen around his waist, threw his tattered cloak over his shoulders and stepped outside.

The wind buffeted him and the rain stung his face and bare arms. He struggled forward toward the center of the Courtyard, toward the Altar. The Levites and Gibeonites were huddled around it, shoulders hunched and robed arms spread to shield it from the downpour. Three or four of them cupped palm-sized clay lamps to their chests as if they were holding injured doves; tiny, useless wisps of flame guttered at the end of reed wicks.

When Samuel had struggled against the wind to within a few feet of the men, his eyes adjusted and he saw Priest Ahitub, kneeling in front of the firebox. Bits of the charred carcass of the last evening's sacrifice still rested, dark, shapeless, and sodden atop the Altar's grating. While other Priests spread outstretched cloaks and sealskins like shiny, black bat-wings over him, Ahitub was placing dry slivers of wood onto the coals in the firebox. The flickering lamps turned streaks of rainwater on the Altar's sides into lines of burnished gold. In the dim light, Samuel could just make out the color and grain pattern of the wood chips: *Cypress. A good choice.*

He glanced around at the anxious faces of the other Priests and Levites. Where was Chief Priest Phinehas? He was the one who was supposed to be tending the flame this night. Of course, Phinehas rarely did what he was supposed to do. Phinehas and his brother Hophni were the kind of men who disobeyed the Torah just to demonstrate their own sense of superiority.

His unspoken criticisms of the Chief Priests made him think of his mother again, this time of the horror she would feel if she knew he entertained such disrespectful thoughts. He pushed the condemnation from his mind and eased nearer to the Altar. Ahitub was leaning in close to the firebox, blowing gently on the bed of ashes.

"Is it out?" a young Levite asked, but he was not answered.

Samuel leaned to one side to see past the Priest's head, glimpsed the ashes, and spider's legs of cold fingered his skin, chilling him as though all his clothes had been stripped away and he stood naked before the fury of the storm.

Samuel knew fire. For as long as he could remember, it had fascinated him. He had served at the Tabernacle for nine years now, and in all that time, he had never tired of seeing the Altar's flames writhe upward to the waiting skies, of watching their darting tongues lick at the offerings placed on the grating.

Dirty white ash filled the firebox. Samuel narrowed his eyes and read it the way he read a person's face: *not the black of ash newly-formed, nor the drab grey of cooling ash—the dirty white of ash whose energy is spilled already into the flame.* The top layer, in fact, was the peculiar, sullen grey of damp ash; Ahitub had scraped some of this aside and was laying his cypress slivers onto the powdery bed beneath. Samuel could hear almost nothing beyond the noise of the storm enveloping him, but he could feel the tension, the stilled inhalations of everyone gathered around the Altar.

Ahitub turned to look back at the Levites and Priests. Rain dripped from his turban to his wild, jutting eyebrows and trickled down the deep creases in his weathered, brown face. He noticed Samuel and for a brief moment their eyes met. Samuel took a mental inventory of what he saw: *knots in the clenched jaw beneath the full, grey beard, eyes wide, the almost imperceptible flaring of nostrils in the long, straight nose.* He saw what the Priest wanted to hide from the eyes of those watching: his mentor was haunted by desperation.

"Is it out?" Voice cracking, the young Levite again asked the question on all of their minds.

Ahitub did not answer. Instead, he brushed water from his dripping turban, turned again to the firebox and leaned in close to the powdery ashes. They stirred and rose fitfully in the tendrils of wind that slipped past the cloaks and oilskins raised all around him. Adjusting the chips of dry wood, Ahitub blew gently into them. Samuel was struck by the irony of it: the Priest's controlled sigh of air was indiscernible amidst the howl of the gale. In response, the ashes rose and roiled like mist, then swirled and settled atop the wood like a fine dusting of snow.

No flame appeared.

"Is it out?" the young Levite asked again, the panic in his voice discernible even amidst the cacophony of the storm. "Should we re-light it with the lamps?"

"Hush, Eliab!" someone answered him.

"It is an Eternal Flame, Eliab," someone else added, with the emphatic tone people use when they want someone to know they are being foolish.

"It cannot be out," one of the Priests said, as if saying the words could make them true.

"The guilt is in Phinehas' hands," another Priest responded. "He was supposed to be tending the Flame this night!"

"Laying blame will not resurrect the fire," Ahitub said.

"What do we do if it's out?" Eliab asked, his voice cracking again. This time, everyone ignored him. Jehovah God Himself had lit the Eternal Flame. There was no procedure for re-igniting it if it were truly extinguished.

Samuel saw the taut muscles in Ahitub's neck lurch as the Priest swallowed once, hard, and Samuel wondered how much of what he swallowed was pride and how much was fear; and Samuel felt fear forming into a lump in his own throat.

Still, Ahitub did not speak. Instead, he grasped one of the copper shovels used for cleaning the firebox and stirred the ashes with it, the cautious probing of a man searching for some tiny, fragile treasure that has been lost. Samuel watched his apprehensive movements, and in those moments forgot the raging wind and the cold rain dripping from the hood of his cloak onto his forehead and nose. Only the dull, white ashes and the rhythmic sweep of the copper shovel remained.

The shovel continued its rhythmic sweep, and Samuel's eyes followed it as though mesmerized by its movements.

And then he saw it.

Something appeared in the patch of ash over which the shovel passed, nothing more than a lump among the rough embers. The shovel brushed it and scraped past, still searching.

But Samuel knew fire. He reached out without thinking and grasped Ahitub's forearm.

The shovel stopped moving.

Samuel leaned closer to the firebox, forgetting for a moment that he was the youngest person present, and the least qualified for so solemn a task.

The Altar was only as high as his chest when he stood upright. Now, he knelt on the wet flagstones and placed his face right at the firebox's door, as if he were going to climb into the tiny opening head-first. His mother's *me'il*, too tight to let him bend freely, caught on his knees and he tugged at it irritably.

"Hand me that lamp," Ahitub said to someone, and a moment later the Priest was holding one of the guttering flames next to the firebox door.

Samuel reached slowly inside, the flared sleeve of his linen undershirt dragging across the powdered ash. With the nail of one finger, he uncovered the tiny patch he had seen.

It was an ember. At first glance, it looked no different from the dust and cinders all around it. One side of the ember, no larger than the tip of Samuel's middle finger, was still dark—not black, but darker grey than the spent ash that coated it. As he rolled it over, Samuel saw a faint glimmer of crimson.

Cupping his hand around the ember, he blew as Ahitub had blown, the faintest breath he could muster. From behind him, he heard the anxious voice of one of the Priests. "What did you find, Samuel?"

He could not take the time to answer him. Instead he breathed at the ember again; this time, in response, a tiny crimson bud glowed on one side of it. Hardly daring to move, he reached slowly for the collar of the *me'il* his mother had made him. Keeping his eyes focused on the ember, he felt for a section of unraveled cloth at his neck, and his fingers told him that it was still dry.

He pulled a wad of threads free and dropped it onto the ember. He breathed onto it again, feeling the air flow from his lungs and out past his dry lips, a part of himself given to the flame. He thought suddenly of the creation of man, of the Creator breathing life into Adam, the father of all.

He could almost see his exhalation brush the ember, and when it did so, the crimson bud blossomed into a tiny flame that pounced on the loose tangle of wool.

The Priests and Levites gasped as the light of the resurrected Flame glimmered on his face. He scrambled back from his crouched position and Ahitub knelt in his place, extending his hand into the firebox and sprinkling it with slivers of dry cypress chips. The flame licked at them hungrily; more slivers followed, then aromatic cedar kindling, and the fire began to crackle and pop. Ahitub reached for larger pieces of seasoned oak.

The crimson tongues streamed skyward, slipping through the grating and around the charred remnants of the offering with the effortless grace of fish sliding upstream. They hissed and spat defiance at the rain, and threw fierce sparks upwards amidst the blue-grey smoke, scattering into the darkness like stars whirling back to their places in the heavens. The previous evening's sacrifice smoked and steamed, and the sweet smell of roasting meat filled the area immediately around the Altar.

The storm began to abate then. Defeated and ready to search for less intrepid prey, the wind spun off toward the brightening horizon. The sound of the re-awakened fire grew louder, and Samuel found himself staring into the flames as he had so many times before.

He felt Ahitub's hand on his shoulder, and turned to find the aging Priest smiling down at him, the wrinkles around his eyes carved deeper by the expression. "Jehovah bless you, Samuel."

Samuel realized that many of the Priests and Levites were likewise standing still, smiling at him. Embarrassment burned his cheeks, and he shrugged. "My hands did nothing, my lord. Jehovah will not let the Flame be extinguished."

Ahitub cocked his head sideways. "We who serve at the Tabernacle are Jehovah's means of keeping it alive. This morning, I am even more grateful than usual that you are among us."

The first light of morning glowed on the horizon, barely visible through the darkness. The rain graduated from drizzle to mist, and then stopped falling as the somber clouds overhead began to break. Samuel glanced around the Courtyard, searching for an escape from the awkwardness of accepting Ahitub's compliment. The warm light of the Altar fire cast dancing shadows off the Levites scurrying to clean the storm's debris from the Courtyard. The light gleamed off the copper laver the Priests used for washing, and off the five polished, golden pillars aligned across the entrance to the Tabernacle itself. Everything looked clean and bright, bathed by rain and burnished by firelight. Nothing hinted at the corruption that remained within the sacred walls, the disease that had been growing in Shiloh ever since High Priest Eli had become too old to keep his sons, Phinehas and Hophni, in check.

The storm outside is easing, Samuel thought. *The storm inside is still raging.*

Ahitub's voice interrupted his musing. "Let all who have washed gather for the casting of lots!" he called, and the Priests who were on duty started toward him.

At that moment, the door of one of the rooms attached to the Tabernacle swung open, and Chief Priest Phinehas stepped out into the waxing light. Samuel, and everyone else in the Courtyard, froze.

Phinehas' stained robe stretched over his broad shoulders and huge stomach. Six decades had clawed a bitter story onto the skin of his wide, fleshy face. One meaty fist gripped the arm of a slender girl whose head lolled forward so that her limp hair obscured her features; she slouched as if all that kept her from collapsing were the thick fingers clenched over her upper arm. Samuel could not tell if it was a pose of exhaustion or shame.

Phinehas scanned the scene before him, white eyebrows knitted over his veined, bulbous nose. His gaze lingered a moment on Samuel. Under that baleful stare, Samuel felt the urge to escape, to run as far from Shiloh as roads or paths would carry him. Then the Chief Priest's eyes flicked toward the debris scattered across the Courtyard, and settled on the face of his son, Ahitub.

"What is going on here?" he growled, not in query, but in accusation.

Samuel saw the mixture of indignation and shame that swept across Ahitub's features. For an instant, it looked like a mask, or veil, that Samuel's mentor had donned to face his father, a mask that Ahitub was not comfortable wearing. In that moment, Samuel wondered if in one way or another, everyone had to wear something their parents had made for them, whether it fit anymore or not.

2

Ahitub's voice was ice. "We are about to cast lots, Father."

"And is that not my job, as heir to the High Priest?" Phinehas asked.

Ahitub remained very still. "The time for the morning's rites had come, and I had not seen you—."

"Don't lecture me!" Phinehas glanced at the Altar, where Gibeonites were stacking wood. "I heard the commotion earlier. You let the Flame go out, didn't you?"

"Samuel reawakened it. It did not go out."

"Samuel!" Phinehas spat the name like a curse, but did not look toward him. "I should have known the Nazirite child was a part of this mess."

"It was not Samuel's duty to tend the flame this night, Father. Nor was it mine."

"How dare you!" Phinehas bellowed. He released the girl's arm; she collapsed, as though her joints had all come unhinged, in an unmoving heap onto the flagstones. Phinehas took two threatening steps toward his son, his face reddening and his hands clenching into fists. "Are you accusing me...?"

Abruptly, he paused, as though noticing for the first time all those watching. He raised his nose and pushed his shoulders back. "I was indisposed. I trusted that my son would willingly care for things in my place—and not resent the opportunity to handle so sacred a duty."

Indisposed! Samuel thought. The night before, Phinehas had sent his pregnant wife, Mara, away to sleep with her relatives in the city. He had then taken this girl who served at the gate, barely more than a child, off to his bed. It was a surprise to no one; he did the same thing nearly every night with a different girl. Samuel often heard his drunken laughter, and sounds like muffled cries of pain, from across the Courtyard as he fell asleep.

Ahitub opened his mouth to respond, then closed it again and turned his back to his father, facing the Priests who had gathered. Phinehas watched him a moment. "Go on, then, my son. My hands bestow upon you the privilege of caring for these duties in my stead."

Phinehas bent, grabbed the girl's bruised arm again and lifted her as if she were a sacrificial corpse; Samuel winced at her quiet gasp of pain. "Go back to your duties as well, my sweet," Phinehas breathed into her ear. "I have already given you something more than a blessing."

For a moment, the girl looked up and Samuel saw her face through a veil of stringy hair. Bruises purpled her mouth and neck, and her eyes were as empty as the maw of a cave. Gathering her torn skirts, she fled without a word toward the gate.

Phinehas disappeared back into his home as the Priests formed a circle around Ahitub. Samuel wanted to scream, wanted to stand atop the Tabernacle and shout condemnation down on the Chief Priest. However, the morning ritual would not wait; the sun was about to rise. Somehow, Ahitub continued with the ceremony, but his face was grim.

Ahitub assigned responsibilities by lot, so that all Priests serving had an equal opportunity for each privilege. The Priests each stretched one arm toward the center of the circle they had formed, extending however many fingers they chose. Ahitub paused a moment, closed his eyes, and chose a number at random: "Thirty-three."

Aloud, eyes open, he began counting outstretched fingers until he arrived at the number he had chosen. The man on whom the count had ended stepped from the circle and bowed. "Clean and prepare the Altar," Ahitub commanded, and the Priest left to perform his task.

Ahitub turned to the next man in the circle. "Go, and look for the dawn."

The Priest nodded and ran to climb the stone steps that ascended to a squat watchtower built into the Curtain Wall's northeast corner. When he reached the top, he glanced eastward, then turned back to face the gathered Priests. "The sky is lit, as far as Jerusalem!"

At that signal, Priests led the morning offering forward with a short, flaxen rope around its neck: a young ram, its mottled brown-and-white wool matted and streaked in dark patches from the rain, hooves clicking on the flagstones. Behind it, another Priest carried a copper pot of flour, moistened with olive oil, and a small jug of wine. Samuel felt himself relaxing, only then realizing how taut the muscles in his shoulders were. Watching the morning rites comforted him, a reminder that in the midst of the maelstrom that Shiloh had become, some things remained the same, customs that invisibly bound them to their past, to times when the heartbeat of Israel's traditions was steady and sure.

"Samuel!" Ahitub's voice pulled him from his reverie. "It is nearly dawn."

Samuel nodded and hurried across the Courtyard toward the gate. Behind him, he heard Ahitub begin the second lot, to choose which priest would slaughter the ram. Ahead he saw Tirzah, Judge Jephthah's daughter, gathering the Women's Corps and lining them up on their low risers opposite the Levite orchestra.

When Samuel reached the gates, old High Priest Eli was already there, as he was every morning, his immense girth wrapped in the white robe, blue *me'il*, and purple *ephod* of his office. He supported his massive bulk by leaning heavily on a polished acacia staff, his sightless eyes staring toward the east. As Samuel drew near, the orange morning light softened the lines of the old Priest's face, melting away a few of the myriad wrinkles that creased it. The light glimmered off the golden headband that encircled his white turban, inscribed with the words "Holiness Belongs to Jehovah," and off the square, gold breastplate decorated with twelve precious stones in four rows, each one engraved with the name of one of the tribes of Israel. It hung from his shoulders and hips by slender, gold chains and blue cords, its simple elegance inconsistent with the obese body that swayed ponderously beneath it. With each movement he made, the hem of his robe, fringed with alternating golden bells and golden pomegranates, softly tinkled and chimed.

Eli's ears had borrowed his eyes' strength when his vision failed; he heard Samuel's barefoot approach. "May peace be with you, my son." The High Priest's voice, deep and warm, had grown no less powerful in his twilight years.

"May peace be with you, my lord," Samuel responded.

Eli looked toward him with milky eyes that seemed to be functioning still, but focused on something that lay beyond the power of ordinary men to see. "May Jehovah bless you for your faithfulness in caring for this duty," Eli said, folds of wrinkled flesh on his jowls and neck quivering as he spoke. He turned his face again toward the sunrise, shifting his great bulk and gripping the acacia staff tightly. "These gates were once tended by the grandson of Aaron himself, a faithful and zealous priest named Phinehas…"

The High Priest trailed off, but Samuel had heard the story many times before. Eli told it to him at least once every other week, his aging mind sometimes losing its way as he sought to remember which words he had already spoken, which deeds he had already done. Phinehas, son of Eleazar, son of Aaron, was a legend among Israelites, held up as an example of what a Priest of Jehovah should be.

Eli was speaking again, softly, as though to himself. "I named my own son after him, with the hopes that he, too, would…"

His voice faded again to silence. Samuel took a step forward and grasped the High Priest's forearm. "Dawn is near, my lord."

A smile whispered across Eli's face, then disappeared. "Tend to your duty, my son." He clasped Samuel's hand with one of his own—it was warm but shook with palsy. "You have not betrayed my trust."

The compliment was more of a condemnation against Hophni and Phinehas than Samuel had ever heard the High Priest make, and the thrill of hope prickled the back of his neck. Was Eli going to, at last, take action against his sons?

When the High Priest released his hand, Samuel walked to the wooden gate and grasped its copper handles; they were cold and damp from the rain. He could hear the sounds of the people gathered outside, waiting for dawn. He bowed his head until his brow rested on the worn wood of the gates and let the sounds wash over him: the bleating of sheep, the gentle murmur of early-morning conversation. A cow lowed in the distance, and a woman's voice sprinkled the air with quiet laughter. "Please, Jehovah," he whispered. "Let these gates open on a new day in Israel, the day when reproach and corruption are cleansed from Your house."

From the Courtyard behind him, a Levite sang:

"Out of the depths I call to You,
O Jehovah, hear my voice!
My soul has longed for You
More than watchmen for the dawn!"

A Priest standing beside the Altar raised a crimson flag atop a long, intricately carved pole. Near the gate the conductor, willowy, white-haired Benarza, lifted his arms, and the Levite orchestra struck their cymbals and blew three blasts on silver trumpets, clear and hard, shattering the morning's stillness. The sun had crested the mountains to the east. Samuel swung the gates open and stood off to one side. The mass of waiting people surged forward a few steps, crowding into the gateway, eyes focused on the Altar.

On the other side of the Altar, through the rising flames, Samuel watched two Priests disappear into the Tabernacle itself while another led a young ram forward to the Altar. Once there, he positioned its neck over a U-shaped slaughtering stone. A groove in the stone led to a niche in which he placed a copper pan. The Priest chosen by lot reached down and slit its throat in a single, swift movement. It collapsed, and the pan filled and then overran with crimson. When the blood had stopped flowing, the Priests hefted the ram's limp carcass and hung it from a hook on one of the six posts sunk through the flagstones nearby. They flayed and butchered it deftly, salting the skin and setting it aside. The offal was removed, the intestines and shanks washed with water from the Laver, and the head and flesh carried up the ramp to be salted and laid just outside the grate of the Altar.

Samuel watched the firelight flushing Ahitub's face even as the brightening dawn reddened the face of his grandfather, Eli. At that moment, it looked as if the blush of shame darkened both, and a hollow, aching sadness opened within Samuel. Grandfather and grandson stood disgraced by the same men, by the selfish betrayal of Phinehas and Hophni. But while Ahitub could do nothing but endure, the High Priest, the most powerful man in Israel, *chose* to ignore his sons' rebellion. In a tribal nation without a king, only the High Priest had the power to appoint and remove Priests and Judges. In Samuel's opinion, this High Priest had let his love of his children overtake his good judgment.

Levites loaded the offal, steaming in the brisk air, onto a two-wheeled cart and hauled it from the Courtyard while Ahitub gathered the Priests into a circle yet again. They raised their eyes and arms heavenward as Ahitub prayed loudly so that the people gathered at the gate could hear: "With great love You have loved us, O Jehovah our God, and with overflowing pity You have pitied us. Our Father and our King, for the sake of our forefathers who trusted in You, and whom You taught the Torah, have mercy on us, and enlighten our eyes, that we in love may praise You. Blessed be Jehovah, who in love chose His people Israel."

Samuel raised his voice with all the Priests and Levites in chorus, reciting the *Shema*, Israel's declaration of faith: "Hear, O Israel: Jehovah our God is One."

The gathered Priests stretched their arms toward Ahitub again, and he chose numbers and counted fingers twice more to select two more Priests for duty. The first selected went immediately to the Altar, gathered fig-wood coals from the firebox in a golden bowl, and filled a golden censer with incense. Then, he disappeared into the Tabernacle, striking a gong beside the door as he entered. At the solemn sound, all the assembly stilled.

A few moments later, the Priest emerged again, the incense on the golden censer having burned. As the smoke from both altars ascended, Ahitub again raised his arms heavenward and led the people in prayer: "Be pleased, Jehovah our God, with Your people, Israel, and with their prayer. Accept, please, the burnt offerings of Israel and their prayers; let their service be always pleasing to You. Bless us, O our Father, with the light of Your face. For in the light of Your countenance You, Jehovah our God, have given us the life-giving Torah, and righteousness, and blessing, and compassion. Blessed are You, Jehovah, who bless Your people Israel with peace."

The supplicants spread their hands and offered their own private prayers as the Priest chosen by the final count walked solemnly up the ramp to the Altar. He had just reached the top of the ramp and was leaning down to place the pieces of the ram onto the fire when a shout interrupted the ceremony.

"Wait!"

All turned toward the voice. Chief Priest Phinehas had come forth from his rooms again, still pulling on his formal Priestly garments. He strode across the Courtyard to the Altar and pointed at the Priest standing with the sacrifice in his hands. "Come down from there. My hands will offer the sacrifice this morning."

The crowd murmured at the interruption of the services, and Samuel saw the young Priest's brow furrow in stunned disappointment. But no one in Shiloh dared defy Phinehas, and the Priest quickly descended the ramp. Phinehas took his place, tossing the gobbets of flesh onto the grating and then pouring the flour and wine, hissing and steaming, onto the flames. Samuel watched his thick, blunt hands, and an image flashed through his mind of young women subjected to the brutal caresses of those hands…

He turned away from the hypocritical Chief Priest and craned his neck upward to watch as the smoke roiled from the sacrifice. He wanted to believe what Ahitub taught him: that Jehovah could still accept the sacrifices in behalf of the people, even if the one presiding at the offering was not pure in heart. But at that moment, the smoke did not look like a pathway that prayers could follow to heaven. It just looked like smoke.

The chorus sang a different Psalm each day of the week; the Priests blew their silver trumpets and the orchestra clashed their cymbals, signaling the Levite chorus and the Women's Corps.

> *"Jehovah is great and worthy of praise,*
>   *In the city of God, on this holy mountain.*
> *We have considered Your love, O God,*
>   *Within the walls of Your Tabernacle.*
> *Like Your name, O God, so Your praise is*
>   *To the ends of the earth*
> *Your Hands are filled with Righteousness.*
> *For this God is our God for all eternity,*
>   *He will guide us until we die."*

After each verse, the silver trumpets blared, and the people knelt or bowed their heads in prayer. When they completed their supplications, they entered the Courtyard, leading their sacrificial animals and delivering seasonal offerings of grapes, dates, figs, and carob pods to the waiting Priests.

Samuel watched them as they passed, letting his eyes tell him a story about each of them. Fathers walked forward: *long strides, heels landing hard with purpose, focused on their own thoughts, not noticing wives and children falling behind.* Wives and mothers glanced sidelong at the Women's Corps: *swift, anxious looks, eyes moving up and down, weighing another's beauty against their own.* Some men walked more slowly: *steps steady and measured, eyes wandering surreptitiously over everyone around them, wanting someone to see them fulfilling their sacred duty.* Grandfathers hobbled by: *gnarled hands clenched tightly around worn staffs, eyes fixed on the smoke rising from the Altar.* Like blind Eli, Samuel thought, they perceived something there that young eyes could not see.

As the crowd entered, the High Priest raised his shaking arms as if to encompass all of them and boomed out the Priest's Benediction: "May Jehovah bless you and keep you. Make Jehovah make His face shine toward you, and may He favor you. May Jehovah lift up His face toward you, and assign peace to you."

Samuel loved to hear him recite the Benediction, even though it was Eli's ritual and not commanded by the Torah. It made Samuel recall a question that had plagued him for weeks now; he chose his words carefully before he spoke. "My lord?"

Eli faced the dawn again. "Yes, my son?"

"My lord...Why do you still come out to greet the sun each morning, when it has been...hidden from your sight?"

Eli shifted his weight and the shadows on his face slid into wrinkles and creases in his age-spotted skin. "Hear me, my son, and remember. No one can hide the dawn."

He turned, then, and Samuel felt chilled staring into his milky eyes. "I can feel the sunrise in my bones."

Samuel was about to ask him to explain his answer, but the High Priest extended one trembling hand toward him. "Come, my son—be my eyes."

Samuel took the Priest's hand and placed it on his own shoulder; Eli squeezed it affectionately. "Lead me to the gatepost, please."

With short, slow steps, Samuel guided the High Priest to a stone bench built into the wall next to the gate; the tiny, golden bells on the hem of Eli's robe tinkled as he shuffled along. When he was settled, Eli said, "Now gather the Priests, and send men to summon the Elders —all of the Elders of Israel who are present in the city today. Have them come to me here. And then bring my sons, Hophni and Phinehas."

He coughed, the phlegm rattling in his lungs. When he spoke again, emotion choked his voice. "It is time for my hands to take up a task I have tried to put off for far too long."

For the second time that morning, a thrill prickled Samuel's spine. "Yes, my lord! Just as you have said, so I will do!"

It took the better part of an hour to fulfill Eli's request. Samuel sent Levite messengers into the city to find and bring any tribal Elders they could find. The messengers looked at him strangely, puzzled that the High Priest had charged so young a boy with so weighty a task, but they did as he asked. When the High Priest of Israel made a request, everyone listened, no matter how lofty their position in the nation. Samuel enlisted the help of several other Levites to spread the word among all the Priests serving that day in the Tabernacle.

Samuel brought the summons to Ahitub himself. He found his mentor laboring at the Altar, rearranging the sacrifices on the grate with a copper fork, droplets of sweat glimmering on his forehead below his turban. Samuel watched him for a few moments in silence before Ahitub glanced over and saw him waiting. "Samuel! What is it, my son?"

"High Priest Eli has summoned all the Priests of Israel to the gates of the Tabernacle."

Ahitub stopped what he was doing and hung the fork on its prong alongside the Altar. "I will come, and bring the Priests on duty with me."

Samuel watched anxiously for Ahitub's reaction to his next words. "He asked me to summon also his sons. My lord—he told me that he is going to do something that he should have done long ago!"

Samuel saw the muscle in Ahitub's jaw bulge as the Priest gritted his teeth. His bearded chin sank to his chest and he stared into the flames enveloping the sacrifice.

"My lord?" Samuel stepped nearer the Altar. "What is wrong, my lord? Is this not the answer to our prayers?"

Ahitub looked up then and smiled. *Corners of his mouth hard. Smile not touching his eyes.* "Perhaps," he said, nodding. "Do as my grandfather told you, Samuel. I will come shortly."

"Yes, my lord." Samuel turned and wended through the crowd, back toward the gate. Ahitub's reaction was not what he expected. He had thought he would be joyful that Hophni and Phinehas were about to be expelled from the Priesthood. The brazen apostasy of his father and uncle affected Ahitub more than any other person in Shiloh. He also stood to gain more than anyone else did, since with their rejection he would become…

Abruptly Samuel knew why Ahitub had reacted the way he had. With his father and uncle expelled, Ahitub would become the next High Priest of Israel. In his humility, Ahitub was feeling unworthy of the honor and probably concerned that he would have to begin serving at a young age for a High Priest since Eli could not live many more years. Besides, Samuel realized, even though Ahitub hated the reproach and shame that Phinehas and Hophni brought upon Israel and upon the Priesthood, they were still his family. The condemnation of the father left its mark on the son, no matter how faithful that son was. And Ahitub would have to see his mother disgraced as well, a good woman who was now stained forever by the unfaithfulness of her husband.

Even a denunciation of his father and uncle, necessary though it was, was a two-edged sword for Ahitub, and would not erase the memory of the corrupt Priesthood of Hophni and Phinehas or the terrible effects this had visited upon the nation.

Still, in his heart Samuel believed that Ahitub's reaction meant something more. He thought back to the look on the Priest's face: *jaw tightening beneath his beard; shoulders sagging; eyes hollow.* Ahitub had acted more defeated than nervous, more distressed than sad. Ahitub loved Jehovah and longed for a clean Tabernacle—it was his zeal for true worship and steadfast opposition to the corruption in Shiloh that had fostered the same feelings in Samuel.

Despite his mentor's reaction, the possibility that Ahitub could someday become High Priest was enough to resurrect hope in Samuel's heart. Samuel thought again of his mother's prayer: *You raise the lowly one from the dust, and the poor one from a pit of mourning, to make them sit with nobles.* Jehovah could change the fortunes of the nation. It was the people who suffered when the Priesthood was corrupt. Jehovah had withdrawn His blessing from the land, and something had taken its place, a malignancy that was killing Israel. Blind though he was, Eli had to see it, too. The offerings coming in were paltry, the animals sickly, the people hopeless and resigned. Eli may have tolerated his sons due to a father's love, but he could not forever ignore the suffering of the people he served. Even if he did, Jehovah could not overlook it for much longer—and putting Ahitub in the position of High Priest could be the True God's way of handling the situation.

He found Phinehas and his brother Hophni in one of the dining booths attached to the Curtain Wall. Samuel tried to read their faces as he approached, although he knew already what he was likely to find there: pride, anger, and disdain were the only emotions at home on the brothers' features. He studied Hophni a moment before they noticed him: he looked dramatically different from Phinehas. Both were big men, but while Phinehas' size was intimidating, Hophni's was comical. His large, bald head rested on his bony shoulders with no neck to separate them. His stomach, swollen by gluttony and drink, bulged beneath a sunken chest and spindly shoulders. He was eating as he listened to his brother, his bulbous eyes staring at the food in front of him, blinking in his slow way that reminded Samuel of a toad. The two men were alone, talking in low voices as they ate. A platter of cold mutton and fresh bread sat on the table; Samuel could hear the crackle of tearing cartilage as they gnawed on the bones, wiping grease from their mouths with the backs of their hands.

They quieted when they saw him, frowning in unison. "So! It is the little disciple of my rebellious son, Ahitub," Phinehas said.

Samuel stopped, forcing himself to breathe slowly. He was emboldened by Eli's words to him that morning, enough to respond, "I am a disciple of the Torah, as is your son."

Phinehas slid his plate across the table and his eyes narrowed. "Do not dare to correct me, child! Do not think for a moment that I cannot send you back to that cluster of huts your family calls a town. What would they think of you then? The 'Nazirite for life' who failed to fulfill his vows—their local hero returned in shame to his hovel?"

Samuel went cold and spoke before thinking about his words. "You cannot…Only the High Priest has the power to revoke my mother's vow."

Hophni snorted in disdain and shook his head.

"And do you think my father would not support me if I decided to declare you *shammata,* eternally banished from the Tabernacle?" Phinehas asked. "Cut off from all spiritual help, unable to have your sins atoned for by sacrifice, and all the house of your father become a stench in Israel?"

"You would be better off as a leper!" Hophni said, smacking his wide, thick lips. "At least then you might get thrown a few scraps of food now and again."

Samuel's heart raced and the room seemed to spin around him. "I was sent by the High Priest," he said, seeking to escape the conversation as quickly as possible. "He has summoned both of you to the Tabernacle Gates."

"And he sends the little gatekeeper with the message, eh?" Phinehas asked. "Tell my father we will come when we are ready, boy."

The Priest turned back to his brother dismissively, and Samuel bowed and hurried out of the dining hall, his ears burning. His mind raced, wondering what he had possibly done to earn the ire of the Chief Priests, and how many people they had told their opinions of him. He replayed in his mind the conversation in the dining booth, and then tried to recall everything Hophni or Phinehas had said to him over the course of the last several weeks. Were they turning other people at the Tabernacle against him?

He did not stop until he was once again at the gates, where he took up his position alongside the High Priest. Ahitub and the last of the Priests were gathering as he did so, and he looked around at their faces. One or two of them were looking in his direction, and he imagined that he could see hatred etched on their faces. He shook his head, forcing the thoughts from his mind, telling himself he was seeing only what he was afraid he would see. Trying to focus, he leaned down and whispered in Eli's ear that all were present except for Hophni and Phinehas.

Eli reached out and found his shoulder with one hand. "Help me to rise, my son."

Samuel shifted himself nearer, and the High Priest rocked forward, resting his weight briefly on Samuel's shoulder and his staff. When he got to his feet, he stood for a few moments, breathing heavily, leaning on the polished stick. Samuel looked across at Ahitub's face, but his expression was unreadable, a careful, emotionless mask. Then the arrival of Hophni and Phinehas caught Samuel's eye, and he saw that the brothers took their places with arms crossed over their chests, smug and confident. Hophni stood with his peculiar loose-jointed stance next to his brother. Phinehas saw Samuel staring and smirked back at him, eyebrows raised. Neither fear nor humility were in the look; realizing at once what was about to happen, Samuel felt as if the world beneath his feet had disappeared and he was falling into an endless abyss.

"Hear me, O Israel," Eli intoned. "For forty years I have served you as High Priest and Judge. From my father, a son of Ithamar, a son of Aaron, I received the anointing oil. In this office I should have served for all my days, since that is the way among the High Priests of Israel.

"But now I am a son of ninety-eight years. My eyes have set so that I cannot go out or come in without the hand of another. In seven days, the children of Israel will celebrate the solemnest of our festivals: the Day of Atonement. On that day, the High Priest must assume his most sacred duty, to enter alone into the Holy of Holies, where the *Shekinah*, everlasting light of Jehovah's presence, burns above the Ark of the Covenant. There, he must make atonement for the sins of the Priesthood, and of all the people, that Jehovah's Hand may not come to be heavy upon us, and that He may not remember our sins for all time."

Eli paused, and Samuel saw his knuckles whiten as his grip on the staff tightened. His voice rasped as he continued, "And so this day I must ensure that the Day of Atonement takes place. I must anoint a new High Priest, a Priest who can find his way alone into the Holy of Holies, and atone for Israel in my stead."

A communal gasp whispered through the crowd as they comprehended what was about to happen. Eli stretched out one arm in a gesture that encompassed them all. "Phinehas, step forward."

Phinehas glanced once at his brother and took three long steps toward his father, unable to wipe the smirk from his lips. "I am here, O High Priest."

Eli lowered his arm. "Kneel before me."

Phinehas went down on one knee. Eli reached into a fold of his robes and drew forth a pale, yellow phial of Egyptian glass. He removed the stopper and poured a pool of golden oil onto his shaking palm. "Samuel!"

he whispered, holding out the phial; Samuel reached woodenly and took it from his hand.

The old Priest dipped his fingers in the oil and slowly reached forward to draw an "X" on his son's forehead. The rest of the oil he poured from his palm over Phinehas' thinning, grey hair; it ran in pale, golden lines down his veined cheeks and dripped into his beard.

"Rise," Eli intoned. "Rise, Phinehas, son of our forefather, Ithamar, son of Aaron, chosen one of God. Rise, High Priest of Israel."

3

Cackling like a man gone mad, the Prophet Rohgah fled, his shuffling feet whisking the paper-dry leaves carpeting the forest floor. From behind him, he heard the Philistine soldiers getting closer: the tramp of heavy footsteps, the clink of armor, and the thump of bronze swords hacking at the brush that barred their way.

His lungs burned, and he cursed his age. Years ago, he would have considered the passage of eight decades interminable, but it had fled so quickly, stealing his strength without affording him sufficient opportunity to get used to the idea. He hobbled through the forest like a cripple, driven on by the fate he knew awaited if the Philistines caught him. His bald head and wrinkled skin would waken no mercy in them—he had seen them crush the skulls of more than one old man in the years since they had begun encroaching on the borders of Canaan. And most of their victims had done nothing to deserve their wrath. The Philistines needed no reason to slaughter and pillage, beyond their desire for whatever food stores one might have secreted away. Crops had been so poor in recent seasons, flocks and herds failing, ancient vineyards and orchards withering and desiccated—and the fertile plains of Philistia had been affected just as Israel's land had. A darkness was slipping over Israel, a darkness that whispered at Rohgah in his dreams. It had a name, but he did not say it, even to himself.

Behind him, he heard a triumphant shout and his heart pounded in his chest as he realized that his pursuers had caught sight of their quarry. He tried to quicken his pace, but his joints ached with every movement. Of course, he reflected, smiling even as he panted, they might be chasing him for some other reason than to steal his food. It could be because they had heard about the speeches he made in every town he visited, inciting his fellow Israelites to rise up and drive the Philistines out of Canaan. Alternatively, it could be because he had set fire to one of their sacred groves and taken a hammer to their stone idols of Dagon, Baal, and Ashtoreth, smashing them to powder. He cackled again at the memory, but his lungs failed him and the laugh came out as more of a wheezing cough.

Just ahead of him, a narrow wash ascended to a cluster of willows, terebinth, and acacia, grown so thickly that they hid the gathering of boulders behind them. An arrow whispered past his left ear and glanced off a tree just ahead of him. He gritted his remaining teeth and clambered up the wash, grasping at rocks and trees to steady him as he climbed.

When he arrived at the cluster of trunks, he allowed himself a quick glance over his shoulder. Another arrow whizzed past, but flew wide of its mark and clattered into the boulders behind him. The Philistines, four of them, were several hundred paces down the slope, but the distance was narrowing quickly. "Sons of Belial!" he cursed at them, and then dove into the broom and willow trees.

A flock of doves scattered, flapping through the yellow-leafed branches. He pushed his way through the dense brush until he reached a massive, pitted boulder, its surface a mottled patchwork of forest colors. Knees aching, he lowered himself to the sandy, leaf-strewn ground and squirmed forward on his belly into a narrow crevice beneath the rock, a shadowed opening that was invisible until he was lying on the ground next to it. The crevice became a tiny, cramped tunnel as he used his elbows to pull himself farther along. The sharp, dry smell of mold filled his nostrils, mingling with the pungency of the sandy soil and the decaying leaf skeletons that clung to his wool robes. For several feet the darkness around him was complete; then the tunnel began to lighten again, and widen as well, so that he could see a black, spongy growth that clung to the rock at either shoulder. He did not remember it being there the last time he had hidden in the cave, and found himself annoyed by its presence without really understanding why.

At last, the tunnel spilled him into a broad cavern, lit by shafts of dim light spearing down from cracks in its stone ceiling. He grasped the rough walls and gingerly raised himself to his feet. It took him three attempts to straighten his back; pain stabbed through his muscles as he pulled himself upright. A well-worn, wooden club leaned against the wall where he had left it; he hefted it and hovered over the mouth of the tunnel, waiting and listening, his breathing harsh in the echoing silence.

From outside he heard the poignant lament of the doves—their cry ached with loneliness. He could feel the bones of his hips and elbows as sharply as if someone had struck them with a hammer.

Bones! They were all he was anymore: a tattered bag of a robe wrapping arms and legs as thin and hard as sticks. He looked like a skeleton even to himself, but it did not bother him. He lived every day with the nearness of death and was not afraid of its coming. He flattered himself that he was not afraid of anything anymore. Thoughts of his own mortality were his constant companions now—Philistine raiders had killed his children, and his wife had poured her life, teardrop by teardrop, onto the packed earth floor of their home. It was one of the reasons he kept coming back to this cave: it had the feel of a tomb. He had written his epitaph on a scrap of leather and tucked it into a hole in the wall behind where he now stood. One day, when he felt life at last ebbing from his veins, he would come here to lay his bones down one final time. Far in the future, perhaps someone would find his skeleton, picked clean by insects and scavengers, read his message and know that here had died a Prophet of the True God.

Hearing nothing of the pursuing soldiers, he relaxed his grip on the club and leaned against the cold, stone wall. The dove outside cooed again, and he realized that it likely would have flown away if men were approaching the cave. He grinned, pinching his tongue between his teeth to keep from giggling aloud. How he must irritate them, he thought. They rode their chariots over Israel's western roads unhindered, their bronze spears spreading fear ahead of them like storm clouds, but they could not stop one crazy old man from opposing them! "Israel lives yet!" he whispered, and his voice sounded hollow and frightening in the stillness of the cave.

But his own words betrayed him, and he was suddenly awash in thoughts of the malignancy that gripped his people. Israel lived, but for how much longer? He was old enough to remember when the Tabernacle in Shiloh had been a place of wonder and joy, the house of God on earth, the heart of the nation since its construction and dedication four and a half centuries before. He had lived to see the children of Israel fall from the great people they had started to become: a military power that had conquered Canaan and driven out the demon-worshipping savages that had possessed it. God had given them the land! All enemies fell before their swords; kingdoms all around them had learned to fear Israel's name, from the Great Sea to the barren desert, from the forested mountains of Lebanon in the north to the wastelands of Edom in the south. Jehovah had promised them an eternal kingdom, if only they would listen to his voice.

And they had. For a time.

Then, with the land all but conquered, the nation had collapsed into a morass of bickering tribal chieftains, seduced by the twisted worship of pathetic nature gods until the stain of corruption and sin blackened even Shiloh. Like the black mold growing on the walls of his tunnel, a glooming shadow had infested their land, their spirits, and their worship. Eli should have seen it and taken action, but he was weak and vacillating, too enamored of his own foul offspring to do what was required.

Israel was dying, the traditions, beliefs and faith that had held her together for five centuries slipping away, withering—even as the land itself wasted away. The word of Jehovah had become rare. And now, all the Prophets were gone. All except him.

He eased himself down to the cave's sandy floor, hearing his joints creaking in complaint. "Prophet of God!" he mocked himself aloud. "What do you see now, O Seer?"

Somewhere outside the cave, the dove made its plaintive response. Rohgah shook his head, trying to drag his mind from the desolate pathways it so often wandered these days. At times, everything in the world that defined him seemed to have died, or be dying. It was the real reason that he lived now as he did—here, in the hills of Gilead, owning nothing, far away from the futile lives and petty conflicts of his countrymen. His eyes had turned inward, to memories of better times, and to his vision of the future day when Jehovah called him from the grave to a healed world.

Bitterness welled up within him and he stared at the dust-motes sparkling in the shafts of sunlight. "Why, Jehovah?" he prayed. "Will You continue ignoring the plight of Your people? What of those who are trying to obey Your law? Will You abandon them because of the evil of other men?"

A chill chased goose-pimples across his skin, and he rose to his feet without even noticing the pain of his joints. A resonance filled him, an awe that was not fear, a comforting sense of purpose, of being caught up in something much greater than himself. The air in the cave silently hummed with Power.

He knew this feeling.

It had been a long time since he had felt it, since the last time he had borne a message to Judge Jephthah during the war with Ammon.

It was the feeling of the Presence of the True God.

The once-familiar Voice, when it came, enveloped him in power and warmth, a sureness of who he was and of his place in the world. He could not tell if he heard it with his ears or only in his mind, but its gentle resonance, tones of kindness and wisdom, drove all other thoughts from his head.

—I have heard the entreaties of My people…I will not forsake them for the sake of My great Name—

Rohgah let the Voice fill him, wash through him like a flood that hinted of the burning of coals, the purity of spring water, the inexorable tides endlessly washing the shores of the Great Sea.

—Hear and remember O Prophet of Israel…carry My words to My house in Shiloh and speak them in the ears of High Priest Eli—

Rohgah pressed his back against the rough, stone wall of the cave, feeling every breath that swelled his lungs, his skin tingling as though he were chilled. The Voice continued speaking, and the words entered Rohgah's ears like a torrent that filled him to overflowing, a message of condemnation and judgment against the House of Eli.

When Jehovah stopped speaking, the message complete, Rohgah felt his heart pounding in his chest and throat. He wondered briefly what would be done to the man who brought such a message to the corrupt sons of Eli. The cave before him blurred as his eyes filled with tears. He blinked them away, searching for words with which to respond to his God. But before he could think of anything appropriate, the Voice echoed in his mind again.

—*Hear and remember, O Prophet of Israel: the corruption that is in Shiloh must be cleansed, or the Malediction that I warned my servant Moses about will descend on the land. See—*

A spasm jerked Rohgah's body, and for a moment he felt weightless and looked down quickly to make sure his feet were still resting on the sandy ground. But even as he looked, the floor and the walls around him dissolved. He was wrapped in a cradling force, held as gently as one cups a baby bird in one's hands, and as the cave disappeared, he had the sensation of flying, or rather, being carried, safe and secure, through the sky.

He looked down again, and now he saw a soaring eagle's view of the land of Israel spread beneath his feet. He flew with breathtaking speed, swooping over the black-basalt homes of Galilee and down to the white limestone houses of Judea. Snaking caravans of traders wended their way along the roads, and hard-working Israelites picked olives or turned dark-stained, stone presses to extract the fruit's golden oil. The Jordan squirmed down its broad, green valley from the hazel waters of the Sea of Galilee to the white and turquoise of the Dead Sea, a shining strip of river slicing through fields and jungles. To the west, the Great Sea glittered in the sunlight, while white-sailed ships plied the waters off Joppa and Ashkelon. The scattered cities of Israel looked like stacked blocks of pale stone, their streets as busy as anthills. Tendrils of smoke rose from hidden villages beneath the canopy of the deadly Forest of Ephraim, spiraling up through the mighty oaks of Bashan and Gilead. A haze or fog hung over the swamplands soaking up the runoff from the highlands of the Shephelah, dissipating where the winds off the coastlands of Philistia caught it and spun it into invisibility.

At first, he remained high above the land, so that all below him appeared as a beautiful patchwork of tended fields, forests, and vineyards. But then he was carried closer, and he watched in growing horror as an enormous black mass began to envelop the land below him, like clouds of smoke. As if dragged by the clawed wings of some dark angel, it swept over

Israel and clung, wispy and ethereal, to every tree, every animal, every person and home that it brushed, though they did not see it or feel it. But as Rohgah watched, the blackness began to transform everything that it touched, staining it, withering it, and before his eyes the land began to die.

"Malediction..." he whispered.

—See what will be, Prophet—

He watched, sickened but unable to turn away, as pestilence ravaged man and animal. Sweat-streaked women and children lay, pale as new wool, in their beds and coughed blood-flecked foam onto their blankets. Men stumbled behind their plows or collapsed among the tangled roots of the olive trees, covered from head to foot in pustulant boils. Boys careened through the streets of deserted towns, their mouths frothing, their bloodshot eyes wide with madness.

Cattle withered until their bones stretched and distended their scabby skin; entire flocks of sheep lay rotting on grassless hills while crows, dark as twilight-born shadows, pecked at their eyes. Color drained from the sky all around Rohgah and hardened the heavens to the dull hue of aged copper. Beneath it, the soil dried, withdrawing like the skin on a decaying corpse, until it wrinkled and cracked in a myriad of moistureless fractures. He saw Israelites worshipping at stone altars to Baal, dancing and slashing themselves with flint knives in an effort to bring forth rain, but only red dust sifted from the cloudless sky to mingle with the blood at their feet.

Roiling swarms of locusts ravaged what was left of the fields of grain; worms infested vineyards and orchards until even ancient trees crumbled and collapsed under their own weight. Tawny lions and great black bears emerged from the shadows of the withering forests and, made fearless by hunger, menaced the countryside, ribs obtruding through their hides, and people fled and hid from them or died under their razor claws.

Then, when it seemed the land could handle no more, Rohgah saw raptor-prowed ships beaching along the lip of the Great Sea. Swarthy, sharp featured foreigners with black-bladed swords swarmed ashore and raged against the cities of Israel. They slaughtered wide-eyed old men, raped weeping women in the streets, and dashed the heads of screaming children against the rocks of the walls.

The people of Israel tried to gather to defend themselves, but the dark armies encircled and besieged their cities until starvation and madness overwhelmed the defenders and Rohgah saw rawboned men hiding in darkness, furtively eating the flesh of their own children. Emaciated, pregnant mothers delivered cold corpse-infants and slurped down their afterbirth in secrecy...

Abruptly, the vision vanished, and Rohgah was once more in the cave, kneeling on the cool sand. He felt tears bleeding down his cheeks, and he curled into a ball, his stomach churning. The images were gone, but the

Voice continued, intoning the fearful description of Israel's future until he thought he would die with the pain of it.

—*You will build, with the power of your own hands, a home, but you will not dwell in it. You will plant a vineyard, but you will drink none of its fruitage. You will become engaged to the woman you love, but will watch as another man rapes her. Your sons and your daughters will be captured and taken into slavery with your eyes looking on and your heart in desperate yearning for them always...but your hands will be without power. And you must become one who is only defrauded and crushed always—*

—*And the sight of these things that your eyes will see will certainly drive you mad—*

—*And you will return by ship to Egypt, to the shores of your ancient enemies, and in your desperation you will try to sell yourselves there to your foes as slaves, but there will be no buyer—*

Rohgah gagged, trying to clear his throat and mouth of the bitter taste of bile. For several long moments he knelt in the sand, wondering if he was going to be sick. He realized that he had been wrong. There remained things that could frighten him.

The air in the cave hummed, still charged with power. He raised his head and looked around for some visual sign of Jehovah's presence. "Is this to be my message, then? You send me to the lion's den, to put myself within reach of the arms of Hophni and Phinehas with a message of doom?"

Jehovah spoke again, but it was not an answer to the Prophet's bitter question.

—*All these things will overtake My people Israel...the Malediction about which I spoke to My servant, Moses, if the badness is not cleansed from My house—*

"And who will lead this wayward people out of their badness? Me—a half-mad old man? High Priest Eli? Blind, fat, and even older than I am?"

—*The arms of one house I shall cut off, but another I will raise up, a child in Shiloh, and I will fill his hand with power...Go...speak My words to Eli—*

The Voice went silent, and Rohgah was engulfed in a smothering solitude, as startling after the vision as being dropped from a great height. "What will happen to me?" he yelled at the silence, heedless now of the danger of being overheard by the Philistines who could still be searching for him outside. "Will I die here, in the place I have prepared for myself?"

No answer came. Jehovah had spoken. And already Rohgah knew that he would, indeed, travel to Shiloh and deliver the True God's message. The commission gnawed at him from deep in his heart like a terrible hunger, urgent, insistent, impossible to ignore. It had always been this way for him when Jehovah called him to serve as a Prophet. The message yearned for release; he would have no peace until he had fulfilled his charge.

He covered his mouth with one wrinkled hand and allowed himself a cackle of pure glee. Eli's debauched house was ending! But in the midst of this condemnation was hope: a child, living in the heart of diseased Shiloh, a child who could save them all...

He let the longing that Jehovah had awakened within him draw him back down to the cave's entrance. Once again he crawled, knees pushing, elbows pulling, into the dank blackness of the tunnel. Hope awoke the mischief in him, and as he crabbed his way along he tore the spongy, black mold off of the rock walls. Dust or spores powdered from it, and he coughed. "Do your worst!" he snapped back at the mold, scraping off the last of it. "Your time is over!"

Coughing and cackling, he pulled himself out of the tunnel and back to his feet. Through the sparsely leaved willows, he saw a towering wall of clouds massing on the far western horizon, green and grey-blue, like bruises.

He wondered if the Philistine soldiers were still about somewhere, then decided he did not care. Turning to the east, he began hobbling toward Shiloh. Shadows shimmered through the branches overhead, and he glanced upward to find storm crows winging east as well, pacing him. Aching with every step, he shuffled through the carpet of dead leaves, pulled by the yearning of his commission, pushed by the crest of the storm.

4

Among Samuel's earliest memories were stories of the Eternal Flame. He remembered huddling around an evening fire with other children in the village square of Ramathaim, where he had been born. While shadows danced and hovered at their backs, Samuel's grandfather Jeroham had wrapped them in the subtle warmth of tales from Israel's past: the feats of their heroes, the chanted psalms of their celebrated poets, the miracles performed by their God, Jehovah, on their behalf. Many times Samuel had heard them describe the day, four and a half centuries ago, in the time of Moses and Aaron, in the time when God gave them the Torah, that Jehovah Himself had sent a whirling torrent of fire from heaven to ignite the Altar.

When as a child he had first come to the Tabernacle, Ahitub and others had gently teased him about his fascination. His mentor would come upon Samuel in the evening hours and find him standing, still and silent, beside the Altar or a cooking fire, head pushed forward, fixed eyes reflecting the dancing, amber light. Once, when he was only four years old, the Priest had discovered him in such a pose and approached him laughing. "What are you doing, Samuel?" he had asked.

Without thinking, Samuel had answered: "Dreaming the fire." To this day he did not know what the phrase meant, only that the childish expression described what he did better than any words he had come up with since.

Ahitub had laughed again, but his laughter, like everything about him, was warm—it did for Samuel's insides what a hug from his mother did for his outsides. Putting one arm around Samuel, he had pulled him close. "Keep dreaming, Samuel. Your dreams no man can take from you. And who knows? Always your eyes have seen more than other children. One day you may find a great truth staring back at you from out of the flames."

Centuries of tending and sustaining the flame through war and storm had only made the Flame more sacrosanct, the spark of spiritual life eternally smoldering at the heart of the nation. Samuel had spent nine of his twelve years in the Tabernacle, and among his other duties he assisted in gathering wood and making charcoal to feed the Flame's endless hunger. It could not—must not—be allowed to go out.

He had often gone with the Gibeonite acolytes into the forest just outside the city to collect dead wood and haul it back to the Tabernacle storehouse. He found out early on that he had a gift for the simple task, a memory that retained every detail of fire's subtle dance and what fuels it craved. He could tell by weight and brittleness if a piece was dry enough for the flames; he learned quickly that the wood of the white broom tree, if placed in a pit, ignited, then covered with earth and allowed to smolder for several days, produced the best charcoal. He could identify acacia by its oily-spicy smell, even with his eyes covered, and he knew that it burned with incredible heat, unmatched by any other wood. Dead, but sound, branches of fig sycamore burned in one corner of the Great Altar, withering into the soft coals used to ignite the golden Censer inside the Tabernacle itself.

He had watched countless times as the sacred flames transformed the fuel beneath a sacrificial offering. The fire's first flickering kisses just darkened the wood's surface; moments later deep brown turned to black and then gradually lightened again, a patch at a time, to storm grey. Like the night sky creeping toward dawn, the fuel drained of color, releasing it into the ascending smoke. When grey gave way to the dirty white of spent ash, Samuel knew that the wood's life was exhausted. The only thing that remained was for a Priest, dressed in his official robes, to gather the ashes from the firebox, change out of his linen garments, and transport the ash on a two-wheeled cart outside the city walls, where Eli used it in making holy water.

Neither Phinehas nor Hophni seemed to understand the real significance of the Flame, nor of any of the sacred accoutrements of worship in the Tabernacle. Thinking about the Chief Priest and his brother sent an unpleasant chill down Samuel's spine. Since the day that Eli had anointed Phinehas, Samuel had been unable to stop worrying over what the Priest had said to him on that day, of his threat to declare Samuel *shammata*, and revoke his mother's vow. Now that Eli had given up the authority to stop Phinehas' hand, it was anyone's guess what Phinehas would do.

He tried to imagine himself, expelled from Shiloh, returning to Ramathaim. He tried to picture the look on his mother's face: *eyes wide with horror, wet with tears, lips opened in a silent moan, muscles slack in disbelief; head turning away in shame.* Something deep inside him, some protective, mental barrier he had erected without even knowing it pushed the image out of his mind. It would not allow him to think on so painful an outcome. It would not allow him even to consider the possibility.

He had heard stories of Israelites whom the Priests had declared *shammata*. Some disappeared into foreign lands and were never heard from again. Others took their own lives in a final, desperate act of sacrifice, hoping their own spilled blood might atone for their sins in some way. It was not something that Samuel had been able to understand before, but he thought that perhaps he did now. There was a kind of life so filled with pain that it made the stillness of death welcome. There were things worse than dying. He saw shadows of some of those things in Phinehas' cold eyes.

He shook himself to break free of his dark thoughts, and looked around at the activities in the Tabernacle Courtyard all around him. Penitents and supplicants were bringing their sacrificial animals and other offerings toward the Altar. The air filled with the bleating of sheep, the staccato beat of hooves against the flagstones, murmured prayers and benedictions. He stood still for a few moments and let the sounds wash over him, waiting for his heart to accept and believe the normality that his eyes were seeing.

But the Tabernacle was somehow different this morning, changed in a way that he recognized but could not put his finger on. It was as if everything around him, Wall and buildings, Altar and Laver, Pillars and Tabernacle shroud, people and animals—all were somehow dulled, less real, less defined than it had been the day before. To Samuel, it had the look of a dream, as though he were seeing everything through a fog that lay upon his eyes.

Like wood that is turning to ash, he realized. *Like fuel that has exhausted its life into the smoke. The color has faded.* He felt suddenly chilled and wrapped his arms around his chest. Something was being drained from Shiloh—something that could not be seen, at least not by young eyes. He wondered if Eli saw it, or the old men who came to Shiloh, their watery gaze fixed on something beyond Samuel's vision.

He could not help but feel that whatever was leaching away was somehow like the Eternal Flame—when it was gone, there was no procedure for reigniting it. When it was gone, it would mean the end of all that was good and sacred in the Land of the Promise. It would mean, for the nation of Israel, something worse than dying.

5

Grey skies lowered as a hundred raptor-prowed ships battled wind and foaming waves in their approach to the quays of the Philistine seaport Ashkelon. The ships were long enough for a score of oarsmen, a navigator, steersman, and a tiny, covered cabin for the captain. The weather-stained sails, hastily furled onto the yards, released a shower of drops onto the rowers' heads with each creaking pull at the oars. In the cabin of the foremost ship, General Sarnam of Caphtor stood beneath the tiny, peaked roof that kept him out of the weather and scowled out the open door at the approaching shoreline. He let his body roll with the undulations of the ship, balancing with the steady sureness of years spent at sea. Sighing, he turned his head, studying for a moment the man hunched beside him in the cabin: the priest swathed in black, woolen robes and a cowl that shrouded his face in shadow.

"Is there no other way, Sihphil?" General Sarnam asked, voice raised over the moan of the wind and the wash of the waves.

The priest did not turn to face him. "There iss alwayss another way, my lord. But thiss iss the path the godss have chosen for you."

Sarnam looked back to the shoreline where the quays led across the beach to the stacked blocks of whitewashed houses within Ashkelon's walls. The wind moaned through the ships' shrouds, and date palms onshore writhed as if in agony. A handful of ships were beached or tied to the quays already—two of them Phoenician, the rest Philistine, from the looks of them. No one moved along the waterfront; the weather or the celebration had drawn everyone indoors. Greasy smoke streamed in parallel lines from rooftop altars atop several houses. "I am Dagon's servant," Sarnam responded. "But I do not claim to understand his ways. Or to have your confidence that we know his will clearly."

"Hsssss!" Now Sihphil turned, and Sarnam felt a chill as the dark priest's cold, flat eyes bored into him from beneath their heavy lids. "I have sseen it in the livers of ssix sheep, in the flight of the birdss, in the ssmoke of incenssse, in the sswirl of human fat melted onto water," he answered, with the peculiar sibilance of the magician-priests of Canaan. "If you are to ssatissfy the will of Dagon, Father of All, and of Baal, Lord of Heaven--."

"Dagon's will is going to be bought with the spilled blood of his own worshippers!" Sarnam interrupted him. A large wave crawled beneath the boat and both of them grabbed the sides of the cabin to keep from falling. "With the blood of our people!"

Sihphil spit onto the foam-splashed floorboards. "It iss lesss than a drop in the ocean of blood you have sspilled in your life!"

The dark priest sidled closer. "You cannot allow two heartss to beat in your chesst, my lord. Ssss, shsss! Thiss iss the path that the godss have put you on. There iss no sswerving from it now."

Sarnam refused to look at him, staring instead across the heads of the rowers bent at their tasks, to where the shoreline rapidly approached. He had nothing to say in response. It was, indeed, the path that the gods had chosen for him, a path that his father's fathers had started down before he was even born. It was his destiny to one day conquer Egypt for his people.

Six generations of Philistines had lived and died to put him in position to achieve that victory. His great-grandfather had waded in blood up to his knees at the gates of Troy, and had left that city leading wagons burdened with the wealth of Trojan storehouses. His grandfather had pillaged Ugarit and had sailed away with the smoke of its burning palaces rising behind the wake of his ships, and with their holds bearing its greatest, most secret treasure. From there he had led their people in a wild sweep down the coast of the Great Sea like a horde of demons, and whatever tribal peoples opposed them had been defeated, their cities razed: Anatolia, Phoenicia, Edom, Hattusas.

But Egypt's military was the mightiest in the world. Sarnam's father had convinced Egypt's ancient enemies, the Libyans, to fight alongside them, and they had struck the Nile delta by land and sea. Pharaoh Ramses lined the shore with row upon row of archers; their arrows had darkened the skies and prevented the ships from landing. Then, Ramses had launched his own navy, and the Egyptian sailors had attacked the Philistine ships with spears and grappling hooks.

The Philistines and their allies had been forced to flee. Sarnam, still a young man, had watched his father die on an Egyptian spear, writhing and screaming until blood swallowed his voice. The archers had ignited their ship, and Sarnam had nearly drowned amidst its burning wreckage. He had washed ashore somewhere in Libya, wounded and weak. He would have died there if Sihphil had not found him.

"You were ssaved for a purpossse," Sihphil whispered, as if reading his mind. "The godss have given you Canaan as a meanss to Egypt. Ssss. It is a necessary ssidetrack, my lord."

"I know," Sarnam said, and breathed the damp, sea air deeply. "So you have told me many times."

Sihphil blinked his heavy lidded eyes slowly. "And yet today, when the godss have delivered your fleet ssafely to Ashkelon, sstil you doubt."

"Our armies were not sent from Caphtor to capture Canaan, priest! They were sent to Egypt!"

"The wealth of Egypt flowsss like blood from Aram, Caphtor, Babylon—even from far Iberia and beyond. But all of it passess through Canaan! Control the blood that flowss into Egypt, hssss, and you will ssstrangle her into ssubmission!"

Without thinking Sarnam shook his head in frustration, and the priest reached out and grabbed his arm; the strange man's thick, yellow nails dug into Sarnam's flesh. "Ssss! To control the trade route, you mussst expel the Hebrewsss who ssquat in the land! To do thisss, you must command an army!"

"I have an army!" Sarnam snapped, gesturing vaguely toward the boats following them.

At that moment the pilot, standing at the prow, looked back over his shoulder. "Ship oars!" he yelled, and Sarnam heard the clatter of oarlocks as the rowers obeyed. The ship glided silently alongside one of the quays. A dock guard, wrapped in a woolen cloak and hood, walked from the shelter of a cluster of date palms down the slick, wooden surface toward them.

"I have ssseen the army of the Hebrewss in vision, my lord!" Sihphil hissed urgently. "They sserve a mighty god! Remember what he did to the hostss of Egypt in the Red Sssea? If you are to defeat thisss god, you must listen to the messengersss of Dagon, sss!

Sarnam ground his teeth. "Egypt is what I care about, priest! Egypt! And vengeance for my father's death."

Sihphil let go of his arm and his hands disappeared into the folds of his black robes. "Thiss iss the circuitouss path that will take uss to Egypt, my lord. The godss have ssspoken."

Wood gunnels ground against wet, wood dock joists, and his men jumped onto the slick boards of the quay, pulling taut the dock lines and tying them off. Seconds later, the next ship tied up on the opposite side of the quay and Sarnam saw its captain disembark. He turned toward Sarnam, a predatory look on his twisted, young face, a mass of inflamed scar tissue where his nose should have been, the wind tossing his shock of blonde hair. Two battle hounds followed and ran to the nearest pilings, soaking them with steaming urine.

"General!" The young man, his voice a nasal rasp, addressed Sarnam, pointing down the dock at the watchman who approached.

"I see him, Phicol," Sarnam responded. He climbed over the slick gunwales and onto the dock, pulling his cloak tighter around his body. Sihphil followed him, a pendulous, sealskin bag slung across his robed back.

The watchman's weather-lined face had probably seen more than five decades. A wave crested next to the dock just as he arrived, sending a massive splash of foam and spray across them all. The dogs shook themselves off in a cloud of mist.

The watchman scanned the arriving fleet. "These are Philistine ships?"

Sarnam nodded. "We come, after many trials, from the failed attack on Egypt."

"State your name and your business in Ashkelon," the watchman growled.

Sarnam glanced around. The rest of the ships were beaching or tying to other quays. From Phicol's ship, two dozen black-clad soldiers disembarked, scanning the shoreline and the nearby houses for any sign of danger or defense. They had fought with him for many years—they knew their business. They had been tempered on the brutal battlefields of Egypt, battling impossible odds on the burning sands of the desert and under the steaming, green canopy of the jungle. They were the ones who had been strong enough to survive everything war and circumstance could throw at them. He called them his Gedhudhra, his death-troops.

"I am General Sarnam of Caphtor," he answered the watchman. "I have an urgent message for Pugnit, Axis Lord of Ashkelon."

The guard looked up and down the beach. "You bring a host of men just to deliver a message. Already, the captains of Ashkelon have been alerted and are ready to oppose you should you—."

"I bring this army for the service of Philistia. Your troops can stand down. But I must speak to Lord Ashkelon."

"Lord Ashkelon is—."

"Is at the celebration," Sarnam finished for him. "The message is, as I said, urgent. Get him from the celebration and bring him to me here."

Still, the watchman hesitated. "Can I give him some details of the nature of the message?"

Phicol sprang toward the guard like a cat and they tumbled to the wet dock. Phicol came to his feet with his arm around the watchman's neck, his dagger pressing into the man's ear. He forced the watchman's head to turn back and forth, as if scanning the beach and harbor. "The details are that an army has landed at Ashkelon," Phicol rasped. "That, you miserable coward, should be enough to bring him here."

He released the watchman, who stumbled to his knees and looked up at Phicol, then Sarnam, teeth gritted in anger. He stood slowly and straightened his cloak. "I will take your message to Lord Ashkelon. Do not enter the city until I return."

"As you say," Sarnam responded, and the watchman loped back down the quay to disappear through the city gates. A moment afterward, soldiers within pulled the gates closed, and Sarnam heard the heavy thud of the crossbar being dropped into place.

It was several minutes before they returned; by the time they did, the shore was lined with beached ships and crawling with soldiers and war hounds. Philistine guards from inside the city appeared along the seawall and above the gate. "They don't trust you," Phicol said.

"They have no reason to, yet," Sarnam answered. "They do not know that I am sent by the gods."

6

Sarnam, Sihphil, and Phicol were still waiting at the end of the quay when the watchman reappeared. Behind him marched a small delegation of men. Sarnam recognized Axis Lord Pugnit Ashkelon by his embroidered, ceremonial robes and purple cloak; his stumpy legs pumped furiously to keep up with the willowy woman who walked beside him, her blonde curls held in place by a slender, silver circlet across her fair brow. The hem of her flowing, white dress, dragging on the wet dock, nearly tripped a young boy, maybe ten years of age, who held her hand. Sarnam smiled when he saw that the boy was a miniature version of Pugnit, dressed in matching clothes. The fact that Pugnit had brought his wife and son suggested that he was intending to extend hospitality to his unexpected guests; Philistine tradition placed the responsibility for a visitor's welfare in the hands of a leader's wife. Behind them were a handful of officials and two dozen or so guards, swinging spears like walking staves, swords hanging from their hips, and oiled leather shields gleaming dully in the grey light.

Pugnit arrived out of breath, his round cheeks flushed. "What is the meaning of this? I do not appreciate being taken from the festival. On whose authority do you bring this army to my city?"

Sihphil answered, his sibilant hiss sending chills down even Sarnam's spine. "On Dagon'sss authority. Hsss!"

Pugnit took a step backwards from the priest and wrinkled his stubby, turned-up nose. "Explain yourself."

Sarnam nodded. "Forgive me for any inconvenience I have caused you, Lord Ashkelon. The matter is urgent."

"Then get to it!" Pugnit demanded, stamping one foot like an angry child.

"I have come to ask for command of the armies of Philistia in order to capture the Hebrew city of Aphek," Sarnam said.

For several long moments, Axis Lord Pugnit just stared at him, his round mouth hanging open. "What?" He snorted with laughter. "Who are you?"

Sarnam took a deep breath. "I am General Sarnam of Caphtor. I have come here under the direction of the god Dagon to request command of the Philistine armies in order to capture the city of Aphek."

Pugnit glanced at the watchman, and his eyes said that he was already planning the man's execution. He looked up and down the shore at the waiting ships. "Clearly, you have an army already. Take them to Aphek, if you want."

Sarnam forced himself to smile. "That was not what Dagon instructed me to do, my lord."

"You're mad!" Pugnit responded.

Sarnam turned toward Sihphil and nodded slowly. "You were right. There is no other way." Immediately, Phicol and the Gedhudhra launched themselves at the delegation. Sarnam drew his swords and slaughtered an astonished Pugnit, running one blade through his stomach and cutting off his head with the other.

In seconds, it was over. Other than Pugnit's wife and child, the entire delegation lay dead on the docks; Sarnam's soldiers rolled the bodies off into the water, and the dark stain of their blood spread like storm clouds under the waves. Phicol knelt next to one body and hacked it to pieces with his hand-axes, laughing maniacally. Sarnam saw the woman watching him, hiding her son's eyes in her skirts. Her chin trembled but she did not flinch, even when the blood spattered the boy's hair.

Some kind of alarm had been set in the city, and the guards were again closing the gate. Ignoring it for the moment, Sarnam raised his arms skyward. "Look down, O Dagon, and see who today fought with courage and bravery. Gather their souls to your bosom. They were men."

He dropped his hands and looked at Pugnit's wife. "Take me to the festival and the rest of the Axis Lords gathered there."

She stiffened. "I do not take orders from murderers."

Sarnam smiled again. It was comforting to see a woman with inner strength. She was a fitting wife for an Axis Lord of Philistia. Not for that fool, Pugnit, of course. For a true leader. "I suspect that you do," he answered her.

"What?" She forced herself to look only at him, and he could see that she was trying to ignore the grisly sounds Phicol was making behind her.

"I suspect that you do take orders from murderers, when they tell you that if you do not take them to the Axis Lords of Philistia, they will give your son to Phicol, here."

She shuddered and put one hand over her mouth, pulling her son closer with the other.

"If you require a few moments to compose yourself, I will happily give them to you," Sarnam said.

She straightened, her face white and set. "I will take you there now."

"Excellent." Sarnam turned back toward the beach. "Phicol and his Gedhudhra come with me. The rest of you know what to do."

Cries of "aye" echoed back to him. He rinsed his sword in the seawater, sheathed it, and followed the woman and child up the quay. The wood planking gave way to a hard-packed, gravel road that led to the main seaside gate of the city, nestled between two sets of towers with a guardhouse on either side. Just outside the gate a golden shrine glistened, shining with droplets of fog or sea spray. When they reached it, Sarnam saw that it was dedicated to Dagon and he stopped a moment and knelt outside its narrow opening.

"May your blessing be upon us, O Father of all," he whispered.

Sihphil hissed behind him. "Hhhhh. The power of the godsss iss sstrong in thiss place"

Sarnam stood. "I pray that you are correct. We will need their help if this errand is to succeed."

Sarnam looked up at the guardsmen who watched from atop the towers on either side of the gate. "I request audience with the other Axis Lords of Philistia," he said.

After a moment of murmured conversation, a voice responded, "You wish to enter into negotiations?"

"No negotiations are necessary," Sarnam answered. "I surrender myself and my armies to the will of the Axis Lords."

The murmured conversation went on longer this time. Then: "You can enter the city alone."

Sarnam shook his head. "I will bring only my priest, and my personal bodyguard."

"So be it," came the response a moment later, and the gate ground open. A mass of troops stood, spears at the ready, guarding the opening. "My soldiers are clearly not attempting an attack," Sarnam called to them, gesturing to the men and dogs scattered across the beaches and docks.

He turned to Lord Pugnit's widow, still standing beside him, her wide-eyed son clinging to her skirts. "Shall we, lady?" he asked.

Her jaw clenched, but she started forward into the city and the guards parted to let them enter. Sarnam ignored them, even though several dozen followed them as they ascended through the square. One of the guards guided them up a series of spiraling streets that wound past sprawling, yellow sandstone homes with elaborate bronze gates. Dogs wandered among the houses, well groomed, sleek, and dangerous looking. The road led them past rows of vintner's shops, storefronts piled with casks or with dark mounds of the dates from which they brewed their nectar. A bazaar spread haphazardly through one section of the city, rows of garish shops and drab administrative buildings, most of them closed for the holiday. Brightly painted limestone sculptures and solemn, granite obelisks loomed at some of their entrances. Sarnam noticed the Egyptian textiles and jewelry offered at many of the stores, as well as some displaying gold and silver treasures obviously stolen from Egyptian tombs.

They continued onward to the city center, where a hill rose above the houses all around it. Following the woman and child up the hill, Sarnam saw at last the city's largest temple, a squat, vaguely pyramidal structure built of cut, white stone. A series of steep steps led them to the antechamber entrance; the wind built in violent gusts as they climbed above the protection of buildings and walls.

When they reached the temple entrance, Sarnam paused a moment and looked behind him. The door of the temple faced east; far across the coastal dunes and green plains of Philistia, he could see the mountains rising in the land now claimed by the Hebrews.

"I have done as you asked," the woman said to him. She was trembling, but trying not to let him see it. "The Axis Lords of Philistia are inside."

Her courage impressed him, and Sarnam felt proud to belong to her race. "You have done well, and under difficult circumstances. Take your child and go home."

Her nostrils flared in anger and for a moment he thought she was going to respond. Instead, she turned in a swirl of white skirts and strode back down the steep steps, child in tow. The city guards, now arrayed up the steps, parted to let her pass.

A pair of temple guards stood at either side of the antechamber entrance, looking nervously at the feral Gedhudhra. Music and shouting echoed from within. "We are loyal Philistines," Sarnam assured the guards. "I must speak to the Axis Lords, but we will not disrespect the ceremony."

One of the guards planted the butt of his spear in front of him, clutching its polished shaft in both hands. "I can allow only two of you inside."

Sarnam had expected this. "The priest and I will go in." He turned to Phicol. "Wait for me."

Phicol smiled; the expression grotesquely stretched his scarred face. "We will wait."

Sarnam passed through the antechamber and into the temple proper, flanked by half a dozen guards. The people inside swayed and rocked to the explosion of music that met their ears as they entered. Orange lamplight flickered everywhere in the long hall, lined on either side with graceful wooden pillars supporting polished oak beams on their carved capitals. Lattices screened off smaller rooms on either side of the main hall; behind some of them Sarnam glimpsed furtive movements.

At the far end of the hall stood a row of incense burners, and on a low dais, a stone altar with a sloped top. Casting dancing shadows in the lamplight, three small, cast-bronze idols stood atop the altar: Baal, raised arm wielding a lightning bolt; Ashtoreth, arms cupping her own pendulous breasts; and Dagon, his human body terminating not in legs, but in a broad fish's tail. In front of the altar, flames flickered through a bronze grate.

The guards stopped Sarnam and Sihphil at the back edge of the throng of sweating, chanting worshippers. Next to the stone altar, a handful of priests and priestesses swayed. The highest ranking, the Baru-priest, oiled body gleaming golden in the lamplight, was chanting out the ritual as the worshippers writhed and danced, splashing wine from a pitcher onto their mouths and bodies. "O Baal, leave off your work on your beautiful palace, we implore you! Cursed Mot, open-mouthed god of death, holds captive Shapshur, light of days, and the ground withers under his endless burning. Turn your eyes away from your palace and look upon us, O Baal, and raise your mighty arm that we may have rains!"

Two nubile priestesses in sheer linen shifts, poured wine offerings out at the base of the altar into wide-mouthed, sacred vessels. The music swelled and the dancing of the worshipers grew more ecstatic while the priests leading the ceremony slashed their torsos with flint knives, screaming out their devotion to the gods. Rivulets of crimson trickled from the wounds and dribbled down their ribs.

Sweating men and women began to pull off their clothes, writhing against each other in their dance.

"Yes!" screamed the Baru-priest. "Let the magic of our unions bring fertility back to the land!"

Abruptly, Sihphil lurched forward into the crowd, arms flailing into the dancers around him. The guards attempted to stop him, but before they could touch him, he was amongst the worshippers. He screamed, rolling his head, spitting and coughing. The sealskin bundle across his back swung and bounced with every movement. The worshipers drew back, recognizing the throes of divine ecstasy.

Sihphil whirled and twitched, eyes rolling back in his head. "Hssss! Hssss! I am sssent with a messsage from Dagon, father of all!"

The crowd quieted. One of the Axis Lords, broad-shouldered and thick as a boar, pushed his way forward, noticing Sarnam for the first time. "Who are you? Where is Lord Ashkelon?"

Sarnam saw the threat in the man's squinty eyes and smiled. "I am Sarnam of Caphtor, coming from our people's failed attack on Egypt. I bring an offering for this celebration, and a message from the gods."

Sihphil lurched forward with wide steps, pendulating as he neared the altar fire. He pulled the bundle from his back and unwrapped it. Sarnam edged toward the altar as well; at a gesture from the Axis Lord, the guards let him go. Sarnam took the object from Sihphil and lifted it for all to see.

It was a child—an infant, really, dangling limp and pale, its skin translucent and tinged with blue, one tiny ankle clutched in Sarnam's fist. Sarnam took the final steps toward the altar fire. The worshipers parted before him. "I offer to Baal, Rider of the Clouds, Lord of Heaven, my son!"

He dropped the child onto the bronze grate. Its shriek pierced the temple, then grew weaker, and a moment later it was silent.

Sarnam watched the tiny corpse burning. It was not his son, of course—just a child the Gedhudhra had taken from some woman at their last stop along the coast. His greatest worry had been that it would die before he could make the offering, but Sihphil had given it a green paste to keep it alive long enough to get the attention of the crowd with its screams. They had seen people offer their children to Baal before, of course—in fact, some of those gathered for the festival had burned their firstborn children in years past in order to assure a good harvest. However, it was still the greatest sacrifice a person could offer, and since the harvests had begun to fail, fewer children were being born.

He turned back to face the crowd. All eyes were upon him now, as he had known they would be.

"I bring a message to you from the gods of Canaan!" he said.

Sihphil lurched forward, twitching; he fell to the ground and rolled across the tiled floor. Other priests in the room began to hiss and moan, carried along with him in his ecstasy. Sihphil pulled himself upright and slowly spun, his wide, glassy eyes gathering everyone in the room to him. "Dagon hass ssent Shapshur, torch of the godsss, to me with a word for you, O Priestsssss and Lordssss of Philisstia! Yamm, god of watersss, hass brought usss ssafely to your shoressss!"

He flung one yellow-clawed hand out toward Sarnam, arm stretched and shaking. "Ssssss! Thiss man iss chosen by the godsss to sspread their glory!" His sibilant voice rose to a fever pitch. "He isss chosen by Dagon to lead you in battle!"

The Axis Lord who had spoken earlier stepped forward again, crossing his arms across his thick chest. "I am Axis Lord of Gath. It is we five Axis Lords who command the armies of Philistia, whatever this priest may say."

Sihphil and some of the other priests hissed at him, but Sarnam held out one hand to silence them. "What you say is true. That is why I was forced to become Axis Lord of Ashkelon."

A confused murmur rippled through the crowd. "What has become of Pugnit?" Lord Gath asked.

Sarnam stared back at him. "Pugnit is dead."

Before the crowd could react, Sihphil wailed, and then began to spin and twitch his way around the room, yellow claws reaching out toward the awed faces of any he neared. "Hsss! I have sseen it in the liverss of ssix sheep! Sssss! I have read it in the oil, and heard it whisssspered by the ssmoke of holy incense! I have ssseen with my own eyessss the sssignss that thiss man issss called by Dagon to lead you!"

The clawed fingers curled, gesturing Sarnam closer. Sarnam stepped to his side and slowly drew his two swords from their gilded sheaths. The long, black blades rasped dangerously, and then cleared the sheaths with a quiet ring. He held them above his head, arms spread wide. "These are the magic swords Chaser and Driver, forged of the black metal of heaven by the smith-god Chousor for Baal himself!"

He swung one of the blades toward the stones of the altar; the glancing blow sent a shower of sparks slithering across the room, and the sword rang loudly, like no bronze sword did, like no sword those gathered in the temple had ever heard.

Sihphil opened his mouth wide and bared his teeth. "Hhhhh! The sword sssspeakssss!"

The Axis Lords looked wide-eyed to their own priests, who now began to murmur and hum. The Baru-priest leading the celebration bowed toward Sihphil. "The swords of Chousor! The gods have sent us a great sign!"

Sarnam held the swords up again. "Baal came to me in a dream! He told me of my destiny—he sent this priest to be my guide. And when I woke, his swords, the swords of the gods themselves, lay at my side!"

Another priest stepped forward. "Last night, as I stood upon my roof, the gulls flew in rows from the sea, winging towards the territory of the Hebrews! I watched in wonderment, not knowing what it meant—until now!"

A withered, old priest hobbled forth, leaning on a gnarled staff. "At midnight, five bright stars streaked across the heavens toward the east, toward the land occupied by the Hebrews! It is a sign!"

The crowd murmured in response. "It is a sign!"

The scowl had still not left Lord Gath's face, but he looked with awe on the magic blades. "I am not one to question the will of the gods.

But your two swords and the army you bring with you will not be enough to assure us of victory."

Sarnam let himself smile. He knew he had them now. "Come with me. Withhold your judgment a little longer, and I will show you the secret that will give us the power to take Canaan from the Hebrews."

7

Within an hour of leaving his cave, Rohgah the Prophet had decided that he was going to need help to deliver his message to Shiloh. For one thing, the land was crawling with Philistines, some of whom might be searching for him. For another, some Israelites held him responsible for stirring up trouble, and it was possible that, if these men found him, they would deliver him to the Philistines in the hope of winning some favor with their powerful neighbors. He had no doubt that Jehovah would watch over him on his journey, but that did not relieve him of the need to take practical steps to do what he could to protect himself. To expose himself needlessly to danger would be tantamount to testing God. He was obligated to take whatever precautions he could to make sure he carried out his commission successfully, and Jehovah would bless his efforts.

Therefore, he decided to travel first to the city of Gibbethon. It was the nearest city to his cave, and he hoped to find someone there who might accompany him on the remainder of his journey and provide him with some measure of protection. Maybe they would even give him a donkey to ride or a wagon to ride in—at times the ache of his joints made him question whether he could physically manage the journey to Shiloh if he had to travel the entire distance on foot.

Jehovah had allocated Gibbethon centuries before to the tribe of Levi, acolytes to the Priests. Since they as a tribe had received no land inheritance of their own, cities throughout the territories of the other tribes were given to them, and they lived off the produce of those cities and their dependent towns, as well as from their share of the offerings given to the Priesthood. Gibbethon lay within the boundaries of the land given to the tribe of Dan, and many of its inhabitants were Danites who had been battling the Philistines on their borders for centuries. Some had lost their ancestral lands to Philistine raids. He hoped that someone among them would be willing to aid an old man whose mission could bring Jehovah's blessing back to Israel—a blessing that brought with it protection from their foreign enemies.

He traveled the first several hours through the forested foothills that descended from the highlands of the Shephelah to the broad, yellow plains of Philistia. Sunset found him still beneath the trees, and he curled up atop a pile of crackling leaves between the encircling roots of a mighty oak, wrapped in his travel cloak. Sheer exhaustion allowed him to sleep in spite of the aching of his muscles, though he woke the next morning so stiff he thought for a time he would never get to his feet again. After several prayers and an equal number of colorful, pain-inspired outbursts, he managed to straighten his back and get his legs beneath him, leaning heavily against the oak's rough bark. He remembered the feeling of freedom and lightness when he had flown over this same territory in vision. The crows from the night before had long since left him behind, and for a moment he was envious of their wings.

"Old fool!" he chided himself aloud, tightening his grip on the staff he had picked up the day before. "And if you were a crow, would you lay eggs, too, and eat carrion?"

By mid-morning, his muscles began to limber and the stabbing pains in his joints eased to a dull ache. The trees thinned until the land he crossed was grassy hills with only a few clusters of sycamores or palms dotting the lowlands. The plains spread out before him, and beyond them, the ashen grey and slate blue shades of the Great Sea. Clouds rolled inland as the day progressed, the sky darkening and then completely shrouding the sun by noon. Shortly thereafter, he found a stunted palm tree with sparse clusters of withered dates still hanging below its ragged leaves. He knocked some to the ground with his staff and gulped them down, wishing he had a handful of grain, or water, to offset their sweet stickiness.

Nevertheless, the dates revived him, and he set off with new vigor toward the sea. Within a few minutes he clambered onto the dusty, rutted traders' road that wound toward Gibbethon like a brown snake lying motionless on a blanket of yellowed fields. Murmuring a quick prayer of thanks, he headed immediately down it, hoping to meet up with a merchant's caravan and be offered a ride on one of their wagons.

But the only travelers he encountered were going east, and few even greeted him. People were on edge, suspicious, frightened of something that they could not name. They plodded past woodenly, faces pale with exhaustion and empty eyes fixed on the dusty road. Some coughed phlegmy coughs; others were pockmarked by boils or swathed in stained, linen bandages. Even those who were not ill slumped exhaustedly atop their donkeys or wagons and stole sideways glances at him as he passed.

The road took Rohgah through once-fruitful orchards, vineyards, and fields—all of them dry now, and withered. The shadows of the clouds overhead settled in his heart, and for the first time in years, he questioned his decision to isolate himself from the activities of the rest of the nation. He still wanted no part of their foolish inclination to turn to false gods at the first sign of trouble or of their stubborn disregard for whatever dictates of the Torah that they found inconvenient. But in his eagerness to distance himself from their unfaithfulness, he had also crippled his ability to see what was happening to his own people and the extent to which it had progressed. Would this child in Shiloh be able to act in time to undo what had been done? Or was it too late already for the children of Israel?

It was not too late, he told himself. Jehovah had chosen to give him the message when He did — Jehovah had chosen to empower this child in Shiloh now, when the time was right. Jehovah would not have waited too long.

When the gates of Gibbethon came into view, the sun had melted into an orange smear of cloud just above the Great Sea, and a stiff wind was whipping across the fields and orchards, stinging Rohgah's face with dust. He shaded his eyes with his hand and scanned the horizon beyond the city. At this time of year, rain clouds usually blew in with these storms, ending the drought of summer and sprouting the seeds farmers had sown in the fall. But though the skies to the west were dark with cloud, he could see no sign of the vertical grey streaks that should have hung below them if rain were falling somewhere over the Sea.

As he neared the walls, the traffic on the road grew heavier with traders coming and going, most of them simply passing Gibbethon by on the road that ran from Egypt far to the south, through the full length of Israel, and on to Phoenicia and Aram to the north. He was forced to wait for several minutes while a long train of wagons rolled by, laden with red clay urns of thick grape syrup bound for Tyre. From that port, Phoenician distributors conveyed it by ship to a dozen countries, where it would be used as a sweetener for baked goods, fruit juices, candy, and wines.

Many merchants and shop-owners had already gone home for the day when Rohgah arrived at the gates of the city, though a handful of the city's Elders, identified by their vermilion staffs, hunkered in the shelter of the gatehouses, handling the legal transactions or adjudicating cases brought to them by the citizens of Gibbethon's dependent towns. A few tenacious merchants hawked their wares to passing travelers and townsfolk: bread, wine, date-cakes, pottery, leather harnesses, ointments, perfumes, or spices. Rohgah saw shop after shop displaying the crimson and purple woolen cloths that were the primary export of the region. Behind the displays, dyers labored to drape their newly pigmented ribbons of material from the high, wooden railings that towered over the perimeter of the courtyard; they hung, vivid splashes of color against the grey sky, swinging and curling in the wind. Looking at the drying bolts of cloth fluttering around the courtyard, Rohgah smiled, thinking that princes of Mycenae, Egypt, and Aram, even far Babylon, were draped in the secretions of the insects and mollusks of Israel. Craftsmen in the shops on one side of the square, their hands stained blue-black from their labors, boiled the tiny eggs of the qirmiz, an insect that nested in the bark of oak trees. The eggs, round and dark as ant segments, were the source of Israel's famous crimson dye; harvesters spent long weeks tediously combing oak trunks to gain a few handfuls of the precious globes. At stalls on the opposite side of the square, workers removed a delicate, slimy gland from a rare shellfish collected by Israelite divers from the shoals of the Great Sea. The gland secreted a thick, inky liquid that was carefully blended with other ingredients to yield the purple dye from which the garments of royalty were made.

He was about to settle himself on an earthen bench attached to the city wall when a nearby conversation caught his attention. Three grey-bearded men stopped a few paces from where Rohgah stood. One of them was dressed in robes, *ephod*, and turban that mimicked the garments of the Priests in Shiloh. As he made his way through the crowd, passing townsfolk bowed to him, and it seemed to Rohgah from their cringing postures that they half expected him to strike them as he passed. He did not, acknowledging them instead with an imperious nod.

One of his companions, a short, slight man wrapped in an expensive robe of blue linen, was speaking. "Even if the Axis Lords have not already decided to punish us for his actions, if we let this 'prophet of the hills' continue, he will surely bring their hand against us."

"He is taking in his own hands decisions that should be made by the Elders," the one dressed as a priest responded. "He has not even consulted with the priests of Dan."

"The Axis Lord of Ekron's warning was clear," said the third. "Either we bring this madman to silence or prepare to have the army of Philistia enforce law in Gibbethon."

Rohgah lowered himself onto the bench behind them, hoping that none of these men had ever seen this "prophet of the hills" for themselves. He was not surprised at their anger, or even their willingness to submit themselves to the dictates of the Philistines. It was typical of the people of Israel these days. The three men continued walking, and Rohgah breathed deeply, grateful to have avoided a confrontation for now. He bowed his head a moment, praying that Jehovah would guide him to someone in Gibbethon who would help him to fulfill his commission.

When he looked up again, the three had passed out of sight, and another man was standing in front of him, watching him pray. "May peace be with you, Father," he said kindly.

8

The man held the embroidered hem of his mud-brown cloak in one hand as he bowed; beneath it, a sickle-sword hung easily from his hip, its handle well worn and its scabbard decorated with bright, gold fittings.

A gust of wind stirred the dust in the courtyard and made the draping ribbons of cloth flutter and snap all around them. Rohgah studied the man's face: the smile that glinted mischief from his deep-set, green eyes; the thick, reddish-brown beard that nearly hid his wide mouth. "And peace be with your household, and your children," Rohgah responded with the standard answer.

The man winced at his response, and Rohgah wondered what he had said that caused such a reaction. However, the expression disappeared as quickly as it had come, and the man stepped over to him and gently helped him to his feet. Muscles rippled beneath his tailored, green tunic. "You are a visitor to our city?" he asked.

"I am." Rohgah let the man support him for a moment while he straightened his sore back. He had to look up to meet the man's eyes. "Gibbethon is but my first stop in a lengthy journey."

"I am Manoah, son of Ashnah." He took Rohgah's hands in his own and kissed him on each cheek. "My father's house is not far. You would honor us by staying the night with my family, and refreshing yourself for your journey."

The expected response was for Rohgah to insist that he could not trouble him; then Manoah would say that he would join Rohgah in sleeping in the town square if he would not accept his hospitality, and at last, Rohgah would accept the invitation. But as the years had passed, Rohgah found he had less patience for these empty rituals. "May Jehovah bless you, my son," he said instead. "Your kindness to an old man is an answer to my prayers."

Manoah's smile broadened. "Lean upon my arm, Father," he said, extending his elbow.

He led Rohgah with patient, steady steps down the main road that wound through Gibbethon. Men on the street or on the parapet-railed roofs or walled courtyards of their homes called out greetings to Manoah by name, and he responded to each with a smile and a blessing.

"You are well known and respected in Gibbethon," Rohgah observed.

"My family has been here for many generations," Manoah responded. "I am privileged to serve as an Elder of the city."

"Your family is well?" Rohgah asked.

"They are. You will meet many of them at the evening meal when we arrive home."

"And your crops—has the year been good?"

Manoah frowned. "We will have what we need. But many, I am afraid, will have to rely on the generosity of their brothers to survive this winter."

"You did not mention the blessing of the Priests," Rohgah said.

Manoah thought for several moments before he responded. "The blessing of a priest is nothing if the blessing of Jehovah is not behind it."

"Ha!" Rohgah said, but then thought better of adding any explanation to his outburst.

They reached a tall courtyard wall of stacked stone split by an open gate cunningly forged of bronze bars. The smell of roasting meat greeted Rohgah from within the wall, and his mouth began to water, reminding him of how long it had been since he had eaten a proper meal. He was about to enter when movement from across the street caught his eye. On the rooftop of a nearby house, three men stood, looking down at him. One of them was pointing at Rohgah; even from the distance that separated them, the prophet could tell that their faces were not friendly.

Manoah saw his hesitation and gestured for him to enter, but the prophet stopped first outside the gate. "You should know that you could be exposing yourself or your family to scandal or even to danger by bringing me under your roof."

Manoah looked at him with genuine puzzlement. "Are your hands or your heart stained by some sin?"

"I'm sure you could find many who would say so. Certainly in Gibbethon are men who would turn me over to the Elders without compunction."

"Do they accuse you of turning away from Jehovah?"

Rohgah snorted. "I have served the True God unswervingly for all the days of my life. They cannot say a word against me on that account."

"Then you are always welcome in my home." Manoah beckoned again, and Rohgah, smiling in spite of himself, entered.

Rohgah found himself within a broad, paved courtyard shaded by fluttering date palms that stretched skyward through openings in the pavers. A hush descended as the walls sheltered them from the wind. The aroma of roasting meat rose with a slender plume of smoke from a round, clay oven nestled in one corner of the courtyard. The house itself was constructed of skillfully stacked stone, sealed in white plaster and built right against the city wall, so that that massive bulwark served as the back of the house. Laughter drifted from window openings that glowed with orange lamplight.

As soon as they entered, a tall, slender woman raced from the house to greet Manoah, throwing her long arms around his neck. "The evening meal is ready for you, my husband," she said. She smiled warmly at Rohgah. "And I see we have a guest. May you find peace and rest in our home."

"This is my wife, Naamah," Manoah said.

The woman was beautiful, one of the most beautiful women Rohgah had seen in all the long days of his life. Glossy curls of long, black hair framed an olive-skinned face lit by laughing eyes of piercing blue, blue as the sparkling depths of the Great Sea in summer. Her full, wide lips turned down at either end, as if she were constantly trying to contain a smile. He realized he was staring and bowed, as much to take his eyes from her face as to express his appreciation. "May Jehovah bless you for your hospitality."

When he looked up, he saw Manoah, his eyes hard, pulling himself from his wife's embrace. Sadness crossed her face like cloud shadow, then vanished, though her eyes followed her husband as he strode toward the door. "Come, Father," Manoah beckoned him into the house.

Naamah's shoulders slumped, as if in defeat or resignation, and then she walked across the courtyard toward the oven. Even in her obvious disappointment, she moved like a gazelle, all elegance, grace, and smooth curves beneath her ornamented dress. Rohgah turned at last and followed Manoah up the two stone steps that ascended to a raised porch with a railing of polished oak. On either side of the steps herbs were growing in large, clay pots. As Naamah collected whatever was roasting in the oven, Rohgah and Manoah stepped through the doorway and into the shadowed interior of the house.

Rohgah's eyes adjusted to the orange lamplight that cast a gentle warmth over the long, narrow dining hall. Five adults and five children sat around a U-shaped table in the middle of the room, already set with steaming dishes. He realized with surprise that rather than plaster, lavish panels of wide, cedar boards, stained red with Phoenician vermilion, covered the walls. Egyptian blown-glass bottles rested in niches and alcoves, and a huge, terracotta vase with the distinctive, whirling patterns of Cretan potters stood in one corner.

A young woman came forward from a shadowed corner of the room and helped Rohgah into a chair beside the door as Naamah entered with an oval, wooden platter piled with roasted lamb. The young woman gently removed Rohgah's sandals and, dipping a cloth in a basin of cool water, began washing the road dust from his aching feet. "Ahhhh," he sighed, closing his eyes. "May Jehovah bless you, my child."

She smiled up at him. "He has already done so, by guiding your feet to our table."

She helped him to rise again and find his place at the full table. Manoah introduced him in turn to each of those seated: his father, Ashnah, his two brothers, Heber and Zadok, their wives, Leah and Mirrah, and the children. Manoah stood and raised his arms toward the ceiling, where pools of lamplight quivered above every flame in the room. "O Jehovah, Sovereign Lord, we thank You for this meal, and we pray Your blessing on this food, and this household of Your worshippers. Guide Your people, Israel, in Your righteous ways, and make us truly grateful for Your many blessings."

Naamah and the servant girl poured a cup of golden mead for each person at the table. Leah, sitting next to Rohgah pushed her seat back from the table to accommodate her belly, swollen with pregnancy. She turned to face him, grimacing with the movement. "My gratitude to Jehovah will overflow when this baby is finally born—I'm beginning to feel like I'm carrying a restless calf instead of a child!"

Naamah served rounds of hot, wheat bread, spiced with cumin, along with a bowl of red stew, thick with lentils and leeks. Rohgah dipped his bread in the stew and tried not to eat too quickly. "Will you bring your child to Shiloh when it is born," he asked Leah, "or present the birth-offering to the priests of Dan?"

She tossed her head contemptuously, red curls bouncing. "I would not bring a dog to those false priests—."

Her husband, Heber, towering over her, grumbled from somewhere in his black beard, "You have made it clear how you feel, Leah." He turned to Rohgah. "We sacrifice only at the house of the True God, in Shiloh."

The platter of lamb was set in the middle of the table; the meat had been shredded and mixed with parched grain, chickpeas, and chopped mint. Rohgah popped a piece into his mouth; it was tender, moist, and so hot he had to chew it with his mouth open to let it cool. When he could speak again, he asked, "Who are these 'priests of Dan'? I saw one of them at the city gate."

Rohgah knew the answer to the question already, but he was curious as to how Manoah's family, members of the tribe of Dan, would answer it.

Manoah took the bait. "In the days after Joshua's death, a man named Micah built himself a house of gods in Ephraim, and in it placed an *ephod*, a teraph, and an idol of silver. Turning his back on the Priesthood of Aaron's house in Shiloh, he then paid a young Levite named Jonathan to serve as his own, personal priest.

"Some time later, the tribe of Dan passed by Micah's house on their way to conquer the city of Laish. This young pretender-priest saw an opportunity to expand his influence, and prophesied that they would be successful in battle. Impressed with his charisma, and his favorable prophecy, they stole the *ephod*, the teraph, and the idol and persuaded this Jonathan that he would be better served coming with them and being priest to all the tribe of Dan.

"They conquered the city of Laish and burned it, just as Jonathan had predicted. In its place they built the city of Dan, and set up Jonathan, and later his descendants, as priests for themselves."

"And now these sons of Jonathan have become priests for all the tribe of Dan?" Rohgah asked.

"They have great power among the people of our tribe," Manoah said. "For the Danites who live in the city of Dan, far to the north, they are the only recognized priesthood—those fools have completely rejected Shiloh. For those who live here, in the pasturelands of Sharon and the highlands of the Shephelah..."

"They have most of our people in their hands!" Leah said. "They wander about with a band of armed men, demanding honor and respect in the form of food, wine, and livestock. Their control and influence grow every day."

"They are outspoken in their condemnation of the Priesthood in Shiloh," Manoah said. "Now that so many stories of...of problems in the Tabernacle are circulating, more and more people of Dan believe them, and turn to these false priests to worship."

"I have heard that the sons of Eli have instituted some sort of 'sacred prostitution' in imitation of Baal's priests," Leah said, her nose wrinkling in disgust.

Heber frowned, laying one huge hand on her shoulder. "That is only rumor, Leah."

Manoah swallowed a handful of grain. "In any case, most of the people of Gibbethon have chosen to ally themselves with these priests now—if for no other reason than that they are afraid of the consequences if they do not."

"What happens to someone who refuses to support them?" Rohgah asked.

Manoah shrugged. "They do nothing openly, yet, other than threaten and make a show of force. But the priests serve as judges as well, and if you want a decision to be made in your favor..."

He let the statement go unfinished. "It is only a symptom," said Rohgah. "A symptom of the sickness that is plaguing Israel."

Manoah's brother, Zadok, leaned forward. "The people of Gibbethon may follow these priests in worship, but in all else they follow Manoah."

"If they want to raise an army, it is to Manoah that they come," Heber added.

The children at the end of the table had been whispering among themselves for a few moments. Now one spoke up in his high, musical voice: "Mother, can we have the dates?"

Leah smiled, wrinkling her freckled nose. "Soon—finish what you have set before you."

"Will you have some more wine, Father?" asked Manoah.

Rohgah raised his hand, palm out. "No, no. Your hands have truly opened to me, and I am unsure if I can even join your young ones in dessert."

The children looked at him with wide eyes, as if he were mad. Rohgah chuckled. "Which of these children are yours, Manoah?"

Silence descended, a silence so thick with tension that Rohgah felt the hair stand up on the back of his neck. Naamah froze in the midst of picking up the dishes from the table, and Manoah dropped his eyes to the floor.

Naamah broke the silence with a whispered exhalation of shame. "I am barren," she said, and fled the room.

9

Later that evening, Manoah led Rohgah to the packed-earth rooftop, where in one corner a pair of wool blankets had been stitched together and stuffed with flax stalks to make a mattress. Drying pieces of fruit covered the rest of the rooftop, visible only as rows of unidentifiable lumps sandwiched between layers of linen.

"I hope you will sleep well here tonight, father," Manoah said.

"I have been sleeping among the roots of trees," Rohgah said. "It will be the finest bed I have laid on in…I don't know how long."

"I often come here to watch the sunrise," Manoah said. "Perhaps I will join you here in the morning, if you are awake."

"These old bones rarely let me sleep until the dawn," Rohgah answered. "I will be awake."

Manoah nodded, and did not say anything more, but he did not leave, either. Rohgah watched him a moment, wondering what he was waiting for.

"You have no children," Rohgah said finally, "but you do not keep Ashtoreth images in your home for fertility."

Manoah looked at him as if he had suggested keeping scorpions in their beds. "I, too, am a worshipper of the True God, Rohgah. Besides, I might as well pray to the stones of my house, for all the good an Ashtoreth image would do."

"Many of your fellow citizens would disagree with you," Rohgah said. "I saw idols of pregnant Ashtoreth, and of other gods, in many windows and courtyards we passed on the way here."

Manoah shook his head. "Even if it had any chance of working...I don't have to tell you that to the people of Israel, my wife's barrenness is a curse. They would not say so in so many words, but it is what they believe—a curse that, if it spreads, will lead to our extinction. I have heard my wife ridiculed in the town square—called a reproach!"

"Ignorant old women, nothing more," said Rohgah.

"Even those who love her look upon us with pity. Men and women we call friends cannot forget that barrenness is a punishment listed in the Torah for some disobedience to God. We are spiritually ruined in their eyes, and disgraced among our family and our tribe."

"Jehovah is not the source of your wife's barrenness, Manoah."

"How do you know?" the big Danite snapped. "I have lived with this for years now, and not a day passes that I do not give thought to what could be its cause. We have examined every aspect of our lives together, searching for any sin left unconfessed or atoned for. We have repented of all known sins and offered sacrifices even to cover those unknown.

"We have been subjected to every fabled remedy at the hands of the women of this town: mandrake root, apples, the bladder of certain fish...we have looked for the cause, Rohgah, and found nothing!"

"Then the value of your rejection of appealing to Ashtoreth is even greater in Jehovah's eyes," Roghah said.

Manoah looked westward, at the flamboyant colors the setting sun was splashing across the sky. "It is not what our fathers taught. It is not what Israel practiced in the times when...when we were a great nation."

"Like we were before Judge Jephthah became ill?" Rohgah asked.

"Yes, I suppose. While Jephthah was acting Judge of Israel, we glimpsed for a time the glory that our people once had."

Rohgah smiled. "I remember Jephthah. I met him several times, saw him commissioned as Judge—in fact, brought him counsel from Jehovah once, long ago."

"I fought under him against the Ammonites, and in the civil war against the tribe of Ephraim. He is a good man. A man who understands that Israel is nothing without the Torah and the mighty Arm of Jehovah on our side."

"He is crafty as a fox! Knows what he wants and lets nothing get in the way of his attaining it! Jephthah understands that good men must take action in support of what they believe—even when those actions are unpopular."

Manoah frowned, and open his mouth to speak, but the prophet did not let him. "When I was a child," Rohgah continued, "before you were born, I saw Judge Gideon also. In his day, my family lived through the endless Midianite raids, lived with hunger every day, since the Midianites stole most of what we harvested. I remember hiding in a basket, peering out through the woven grasses as grey-robed riders on camels galloped madly through the city. I saw children I had played with fall into silence under the curved blades of those raiders. Even then I knew that what Israel needed were men who would turn to Jehovah in times of distress—turn to Him with all their hearts, and let Him guide their actions."

"I don't disagree with you…" Manoah said.

"Gideon did all he could to lead the people back to Jehovah," Rohgah continued, as if he had not heard him. "In his day—and in the days of Jephthah's health—Baal worship was all but eradicated from Israel, and the Midianites, and the Ammonites were driven from the Land of Promise."

Manoah was still frowning. "For this, these men will be forever honored in the memory of Israel."

Rohgah turned to look into Manoah's eyes. "And what will you be remembered for?"

Manoah's brow wrinkled in confusion. "I? I am just a shepherd of Dan—."

"Baah!" Rohgah spat back at him, waving one hand dismissively. "You are an Elder of your tribe—a man to whom others look for guidance, for leadership! But I don't mean what will the children of Israel remember you for. How will Jehovah remember you, Manoah, son of Ashnah?"

Manoah shook his head and shrugged. "I can only obey the Torah and do my best to live by the teachings of Moses…"

"And how will you do that when the land of Israel is ground to dust, eh? How will you obey the Torah when the Philistines slaughter you and your wife or you are felled by the plagues that are ravishing this land?"

Manoah straightened, and Rohgah saw the glimmer of pride in his eyes. "The men of Dan have held the Philistines at bay for centuries—."

"All is different now, Manoah. The Hittites have been defeated, and Ugarit reduced to ashes. More Philistines arrive on our shores every day. Do you not see what is happening? Do you not remember what is written in the Torah? 'If you people will not listen to the voice of Jehovah by taking care to do all His commandments and His statutes that I am commanding you today, the Malediction will certainly overtake you. Cursed will you be in the city, and cursed will you be in the field. Cursed will be your basket and your kneading trough. Cursed will be the fruit of your belly—.'"

"Stop!" Manoah held out his hand, and Rohgah could see the muscles of his jaw working beneath his beard. "Stop. I know the words of the Malediction." Anger flashed in his eyes now as he glared back at Rohgah. "I know all too well the curse upon the fruit of the belly."

Rohgah reached up to the taller man and put one hand on each of his cheeks. "But something is about to happen, Manoah—something that will make the ears of those who hear it tingle! A change is sweeping Israel, a spark struck by a child in Shiloh that will become a flame to scour evil from this land! Will it consume you? Or will you help it to spread?"

"What would you have me do?" Manoah asked through gritted teeth. "I cannot take on the evils of the Malediction with these two hands!"

"Jehovah our God is a sun and a shield," Rohgah said, quoting the Torah. "Jehovah himself will not hold back good from those who walk the path of innocence. O Jehovah of armies, happy is the man that trusts in You."

"Will He not hold back good?" Manoah asked, pushing Rohgah's arms away. For a moment, his eyes blazed and his lips parted to reveal his clenched teeth, and Rohgah glimpsed the fear that many men must have felt in the moment before their deaths in battle. But then Manoah turned abruptly away, staring again at the darkening sky, his chest heaving.

"You have sorrow, and you have anger," Rohgah said. "But those are not the path of innocence. Where are you walking, Manoah?"

"What would you have me do, old man?"

"Come with me to Shiloh. Help me to find the child that Jehovah spoke to me of. Help me to reach the doors of the High Priest and deliver the message that Jehovah has sent."

Manoah looked back at him. "What message?"

"Jehovah has given me the spark that will ignite the fire, Manoah. All that we must do is place it in the right hands."

Manoah was motionless in the failing light. "And you think that this...Malediction can be undone, can be defeated?"

"Lend me your strength to reach Shiloh, and we will see what happens when the words of Jehovah are unleashed on the sons of Eli!"

Manoah stared at him for several long moments, and Rohgah held his breath, praying that Jehovah would move the man to aid him.

But he never found out what Manoah was going to say. At that moment, a commotion broke out in the street below them, and a voice called up, "Manoah! Bring out your guest!"

Manoah strode to the parapet and looked down. Rohgah joined him a moment later. Two dozen or more men had come to the gate of Manoah's courtyard—armed men, carrying torches, led by one of the Priests of Dan.

"What business do you have with my guest?" Manoah called down, and two dozen torch-lit faces turned upwards.

"He is a condemned man," the priest said, pointing at Rohgah as if he would skewer him with the tip of his finger. "The Torah demands that you deliver him to the judges of the city!"

Manoah looked over at Rohgah. The prophet smiled. "They will not take no for an answer, I think."

"I cannot just let them have you!" Manoah whispered. "This is a mob, not a delegation from the judges! Perhaps I can reason with them—if they can be convinced that you have done nothing wrong..."

Rohgah leaned over the wall. "I am the Prophet of the Hills! I serve the True God, Jehovah, and I tell you that the priests of Dan are an abomination!"

The group below erupted in howls of rage. Rohgah turned back to Manoah. "I don't think that you will be able to convince them of anything. I think the time for talk is over, Manoah of Dan. It is a time for choosing sides."

He strode to the stairs that led down to the courtyard; he was more than halfway down before Manoah even realized what he was doing and raced to stop him. "Wait—wait, Rohgah!"

Rohgah reached the courtyard and crossed it in seven long strides. Manoah caught up to him just as he reached the gate. Rohgah looked over at him and smiled, then threw the gates open. "What do you want with the Prophet of the Hills?" He demanded.

The crowd surged forward. Three of the armed men grabbed at Rohgah. Manoah pushed them back, placing his body between the prophet and the crowd, his arms spread wide. "This man is under the protection of my roof! Do not do this thing!"

The soldiers lowered their spears until they pointed at Manoah's chest. "Let him go, Manoah," the priest said. "We want no fight with you or your family."

From behind him, Rohgah heard the door of the house open and footsteps rushing across the courtyard toward him. Glancing over his shoulder, he saw Manoah's brothers place themselves on either side of him, their eyes glinting with red torchlight.

"I am an Elder of Dan, and of this city, and you threaten me in my own home when I am unarmed?" Manoah asked.

"Give up the false prophet," the priest said. "We do not want this to end in violence."

One of the soldiers raised his spear, aiming its tip at Manoah's heart. "We can kill them all," he said, addressing the priest of Dan.

The priest held up one hand. "No—I do not want the blood of innocent men on my hands. If judgment is needed, Jehovah will act against them in His due time. Just take the false prophet into custody."

The soldiers lunged forward, using the shafts of their spears to push Manoah aside. He grabbed one of the wooden poles and wrenched it from a soldier's hands, then tried to block their entry through the gate. Manoah's brothers grappled with the guards, jostling Rohgah against the courtyard wall. But they were outnumbered ten to one, and unarmed. In moments,

Rohgah found himself on the street outside the gate, a burly soldier holding each of his arms.

The soldiers' spears hedged Manoah and his brothers, trapping them inside the courtyard. "You overstep your authority!" Manoah yelled. "The judges of Gibbethon will not let this go unpunished!"

"The judges have already approved my decision," said the priest. "All of them but you. You are the only one who refuses to obey the Torah. Do you not remember the words of the True God to Moses: 'The prophet who dares to speak in my name a word that I have not commanded him to speak—that prophet must die!'"

Turning his back on Manoah, the priest gestured to the soldiers holding Rohgah, and the rest of the crowd. "Take him to the house of detention. Tomorrow, he will be stoned for his crimes."

10

    The Axis Lords of Philistia and several dozen guards led Sarnam, Phicol, Sihphil, and a handful of the Gedhudhra across Ashkelon toward the smithies located near the city's southern wall. Sarnam had sent the rest of the Gedhudhra back to the ships to retrieve one of his prisoners and a sample of the cargo they carried.

    His plan had played out perfectly at the temple. Even though Sarnam doubted it every day, Baal was determined to prove to Sarnam that the god was backing him. Sihphil had assured him that the priests of Ashkelon would recognize the signs that Baal had provided, and that they would likely discover that they, too, had seen signs of Baal's desire that they should mount a campaign to conquer the Hebrews and take their land for themselves. And that is exactly what had happened. Of course, the presence of the magical swords he carried had been a powerful incentive for them to believe him. A necessary deception, Sihphil had called it. The swords were magical, but they were certainly not Chaser and Driver, as Sihphil had said to present them as. Nor had Sarnam received them in a dream. He had gotten them from his father, who had stripped them from the still-warm bodies of two wealthy, Hittite chieftains. It did not take a priest to recognize that they were forged by powerful wizard-smiths from the black iron of the sky.

    Sarnam knew that what he was doing was a gamble—he was gambling that the secret he was about to share at the smithies would be enough not only to impress the Axis Lords into letting him live, but that it would convince them to march into battle behind him. They might simply decide to execute him, gather their armies, and do battle with his troops that still remained outside the walls.

He looked over at Phicol, loping along beside him like a hunting dog eager for the kill. Not that they would succeed if they tried to slay him. Phicol, boy though he was, could probably kill a dozen of their best warriors by himself before they brought him down. He had seen the boy continue fighting with two arrows through his gut, laughing and spitting his own blood on his enemies as he slaughtered them. Whatever demon possessed him, it made him more savage than any human being Sarnam had ever encountered. No one knew anything of his background; he claimed to be a son of Baal's sister, Anat, the goddess of savagery. Years ago, not long after Phicol had first come to him, he had asked the boy once how he had lost his nose. Without a word, Phicol had buried a dagger in Sarnam's stomach and ran into the night before anyone even realized what had happened. He did not reappear for several weeks, until after the wound had healed. When he did show his face in the camp again, he acted as if the attack had never transpired. Sarnam had decided to let him live, realizing that a boy who was so careless with his own life, and so quick with a dagger, would be an asset to have at his side in battle—as long as Sarnam kept an eye on him.

He never asked him about his scarred face again.

The Gedhudhra that Sarnam had sent to the ships met up with them as they reached the smithies. They escorted his swarthy prisoner unbound, walking as a man among equals, his long, grey hair swinging like a horses' tail hanging down his back, tied in faded red ribbons. He carried a heavy bundle, swathed in layers of oiled wool, in his scarred, muscular arms.

The smithies' clay-tiled roof shaded a collection of forge-ovens, anvils, molds, clay or stone crucibles, granite mortars, and bronze tools, interspersed with dirty piles of charcoal and raw ore, and oak barrels of rainwater. Heat flowed from the building in shimmering waves, and the pounding of the dozen smiths was deafening. When they saw the Axis Lords, the staccato rhythm of their hammer strokes died until the only sound was the angry roar of the forge fires.

Sarnam pointed to the nearest forge. "Stoke that fire as hot as charcoal can make it."

The smith standing next to it looked in confusion at the Axis Lords. Lord Gath nodded. "Do as he says."

The smith and his assistants loaded charcoal into the mouth of the oven; two of them began to pump the leather bellows, and the flames responded to each exhalation with a draconic roar. When the coals were white hot, Sarnam nodded to his prisoner. "Work the dark magic."

The man stepped forward, his deep-set eyes assessing the flames like a merchant inspecting goods at market. Slowly he unwrapped his bundle, the contents clanking dully in the unwinding oiled wool. From it, he removed one long, black metal rod, roughly hammered into a rectangular bar. He pushed the bar into the coals, shaking it so that glowing embers covered all its surfaces. Then he began to chant, his voice low and guttural against the roaring of the flames:

> "Heeow yewahs wer linnil wer ahmeth il,
> Heeow ya'il yewahs werbreth nelbrin llor fon…"

He continued chanting as Sarnam turned to the watching Axis Lords. "This man is a Wizard Smith of the Hittites. Long ago, in the days of our fathers' fathers, the gods gave the Hittites the secrets of forging, spells they have kept from the rest of the world down to this day. But my forefathers conquered the Hittites and burned Hattusas to the ground. When they left, they took with them more than gold and silver." He gestured toward the Smith. "Their greatest spoil was the Hittite Wizards, who have served us ever since."

The Smith continued chanting for a few more minutes, and then pulled the bar from the charcoal with a pair of blackened tongs. It glowed bright red as he laid it across the anvil. The muscles of his arm rippled as he slammed a hammer down against the blade, and sparks exploded from the metal in all directions. He began to chant again, a different rhythm now:

> "Shir ye'an elber eth lil malneg vililis,
> Mour lil thellis ye methlin, ehneth methlin…"

With each beat of the chant, the hammer fell again on the bar, and molten slag squirted out of it like blood. At first, the Smith seemed to be merely pounding the metal repetitively, folding it over on itself again and again.

"If this man is making iron," Lord Gath said, "you are showing us nothing we don't already know. The copper mines at Timnah occasionally produce iron while smelting."

"And it is useless for weapons," the Axis Lord of Gaza added. "It bends, it won't hold an edge, and if left outside overnight, it begins to rot. Bronze is the only option for a quality blade."

Sarnam did not take his eyes from the Smith, who had now returned the bar to the forge and was chanting his first song again. "This is not the iron you have known. This is the metal from which the gods forge their weapons, the spell for which was passed on to the Hittite Smiths from the craftsman-god Chousor himself."

"Thisss iss much more than sssmithing!" Sihphil hissed. "These ssspellsss will fill the blade with power!"

The Smith removed the bar from the coals; black powder clung to its glowing surface, sparking and flaring. He began hammering furiously. His chant rose to a fever pitch, and Sarnam could feel the power suspended in the shouted words. Beneath the rain of blows, the blade began to take shape.

"It is too long—too thin!" said one of the Axis Lords.

The Smith plunged the blade back into the coals, his head bobbing with the rhythm of his chant. He rolled the metal around in the flames, coating the blade with soot, then pulled it out again and sprinkled it with black powder from a pouch at his waist; as the powder hit the glowing blade, it sizzled and flashed with red sparks. When the powder covered the blade, the Wizard hammered it into its final shape, finely tapering the cutting edges. Then he gestured the assistants working the bellows to pump faster.

From behind him, one of the Gedhudhra rolled forward a clay urn, as tall as the blade was long. He broke the wax seal that held the wooden lid onto its top, and opened it. Lord Gath, standing nearest the urn, dipped his finger into the liquid contents and lifted it for all to see. "It is blood!" he said.

"Human blood," Sarnam confirmed. "Stand back!"

The Hittite Smith was watching the blade roasting in the coals, his eyes glimmering orange reflections of the firelight. He continued his chant, beneath his breath, but the smithy had grown so quiet that all could hear the words of the spell:

"Lissend sigil er ech sahgar,
Tisaer sah ahel narn sarnahsoth,
Heeow il yi'ah sigil wer etherang..."

He lifted the blade from the coals with both hands squeezing the tongs, muscled arms dripping with sweat as he raised them above his head, then plunged the glowing blade into the urn of blood. The thick liquid boiled and hissed, and an acrid smell filled the smithy. When the blood stopped steaming, the Smith removed the blade and laid it yet again amidst the coals, chanting softly.

"This man is but one of more than two dozen Hittite Wizard Smiths that I have aboard my ships," Sarnam said, "ready to forge new weapons for all the armies of Philistia—weapons of this same magical metal."

The Smith lifted the blade from the forge and laid it in a bed of casting sand, where the red glow slowly faded and the metal turned a dull, charcoal grey. Sarnam saw that every eye in the smithy was focused on the cooling blade. "This is iron," he said softly. "But not of the kind that you know. This is red iron of the earth, whose secrets only the Hittites have mastered. For generations they have kept their secret safe and refused to sell or export any of this miraculous metal."

The Hittite Smith brushed the blade with one hand, then turned to Sarnam and bowed. Sarnam nodded and turned toward Lord Gath. "Lord Gath—may I have use of the sword that you carry?"

Lord Gath looked around a moment, but Sarnam knew that even if he were afraid for his safety, he would never show it in front of his fellow Axis Lords. He drew his bronze blade, its wooden grip ornamented with silver spirals, and handed it, hilt first, to Sarnam.

Sarnam took it and stabbed it into the side of the block of wood upon which the anvil sat. The sword stuck out from the block like an outstretched arm. Sarnam then took up the newly finished blade, wrapping a scrap of leather around its rough tang to provide a makeshift grip. He raised it above his head and slashed down at the bronze sword.

With a ring so loud it made everyone gathered jump, the iron blade cut the Axis Lord's sword in half; its hilt fell to the dusty floor of the smithy.

"Ssseee! The power of the sssswordsss of the godsss!" said Sihphil.

The unfinished sword in Sarnam's hand continued to ring, a song of battle and war, a magical paean of death. "With such weapons, we will cut down the Hebrews like wheat," he said.

For several long moments, the only sound was the steady breath of the forge fires and the humming of the blade in Sarnam's hand. Lord Gath was the first to speak. "Do we dare go into battle with blades forged by our enemies?"

"Of course, we test the blades before we take them into combat," Sarnam said. "But the Hittites have never let us down. When my fathers took them captive, they captured also their wives and children. These we keep, contented and safe, well fed and comfortably housed, for as long as the Smiths serve us loyally."

He turned to look at the stoic Smith standing nearby. "They know that on the day that their weapons let us down, they will watch as their wives are raped and their sons are tortured to death before their eyes."

He drew Chaser from its sheath at his belt and handed it, hilt first, to Lord Gath. "Think what our armies could accomplish armed with such weapons as this."

The Axis Lord examined the blade, his tongue running over his lips as he did so. "It is heavy…"

"But no heavier than bronze," Sarnam said. "Lighter, really, since the blade can be made thinner even while its length is increased. Imagine the reach we will have on the Hebrews, wielding such weapons from horseback, or from our chariots, while they try to defend themselves from on foot."

Lord Gath handed him back the sword. "We will need a lot of this raw material to arm even a portion of our army. Do these smiths of yours know how to smelt this red iron from the stones?"

Sarnam shook his head. "It cannot be done. We have brought as much iron as we could carry with us on our ships—even now they wait in the harbor for my command. But you are right—we will need more, much more, to equip our armies."

He paused, looking around him warily. "What I have to tell you next is for the ears of the Axis Lords only."

He walked a few paces from the crowd that had gathered, outside the smithy, to a shadowed cul-de-sac that terminated against the city wall. The four Axis Lords followed him: Lord Gath, Lord Gaza, Lord Ashdod, and Lord Ekron. They waited with blank faces, but he could see the eager hunger hiding behind their eyes.

"What I am about to tell you must remain a carefully guarded secret," he said, his voice hushed. "If this knowledge becomes known to the Hebrews, or to any other nation, all our plans will be for nothing."

They nodded; he was pleased to note that they had let the inclusive phrase "our plans" pass unchallenged. He leaned forward conspiratorially, and they followed his example. "True iron can only be smelted from unique sand found on the shores of the Black Sea. Even now, I have teams of slaves washing that sand to isolate and collect those grains that are required for the smelting. But we must transport that sand to Philistia. It is too heavy a cargo to be borne on Philistine ships, and we cannot trust the Phoenicians with it. Therefore, we must bring it here overland.

"The Great Road runs from the Black Sea through Anatolia and Lebanon—safe enough territory for a well-guarded convoy, since the Hittites were defeated. However, south of Lebanon, it enters the territory of the Hebrews. They allow traffic to flow down the road unhindered, for the most part—because all of it must eventually pass through three of their cities that monitor and control all trade through Canaan. These three Hebrew cities alone have the military strength and the position to stop our convoys: Gibbethon, Lod, and Aphek."

Lord Gaza straightened, surprise registering on his face. "You intend to take control of the entire trade route!"

Sarnam nodded. "We must capture these three cities. We must slaughter their inhabitants without mercy, destroy whatever army is sent to meet us, and fill them with fear. If we do, the Hebrews will draw back, leaving the cities to us. When the trade route is ours, we will be able to arm all of our forces with swords of iron.

"But our Hittite servants bring us more than just magical weapons. They have perfected a chariot with iron scythe-blades attached to its wheels.

It cuts down foot soldiers like ripe wheat. With these advantages, the Hebrews will be unable to stand against us anywhere on the plains."

Lord Ashdod shook his head slowly. "It is an ambitious plan."

"It would be," Sarnam said. "If the gods had not given us so many signs they are with us! Dagon himself is backing us! We cannot fail!"

"We may take the first city without difficulty," Lord Gath said. "But when the Hebrews have a chance to gather their forces—they are many times our number, and they are fierce fighters when roused."

"Yes," said Sarnam. "But our superior weapons and the fighting skills of my Gedhudhra will help offset that advantage. And if that is not enough, an army of allies is marching to meet us right now."

Sarnam saw the shock on the faces of all four Axis Lords. "An alliance?" Lord Ekron snapped. "You have made an alliance in our name without consulting us?"

"I have." Sarnam faced each of them in turn, letting the information sink in. "The time for action is now! The gods have commanded it. And I do not think you will regret having this army fighting at our side."

"What army?" Lord Ashdod asked.

Sarnam smiled. "When we descend on Gibbethon, the Rephaim will battle at our side."

11

Rohgah dreamed that as dawn's light oranged the eastern sky, he and Manoah were leaving Gibbethon. Something was drawing him toward the sound of a child, calling for help, wailing, its plaintive cry carried on the wind that whipped their cloaks out behind them like flags.

"We must go, Manoah, and quickly!" he said, tugging at the big man's arm.

Naamah appeared then, blue eyes glimmering like stars, strands of her dark hair blowing across her face. She grabbed her husband's other arm. "Please, Manoah—stay with me!" she begged.

Manoah hesitated, looking from Rohgah to his wife and back. The child's call swept past them again on the wind, too indistinct to understand its words, but filled with desperation. Rohgah pulled even harder. "We must hurry! The child is waiting!"

Naamah began to weep, pulling the other direction. Her tears streamed down her face and hair and formed a puddle at her feet. "No! No! Stay!"

The tug-of-war continued, and then, to Rohgah's horror, Manoah began to tear in two, like a piece of cloth stretched beyond its strength; a thin seam of blood appeared, running from his chin to his crotch, and he opened his mouth as if in pain, but no sound came out.

Naamah released him with a gasping cry; Rohgah and Manoah tumbled away in the opposite direction, rolling across the countryside like tumbleweeds blown by a windstorm. When they stopped, Rohgah picked himself up and looked around, trying to orient himself to the sound of the child in the direction to Shiloh. But when he heard the wailing cry and turned to locate its source, he found that it was coming not from Shiloh, but from Gibbethon. But the city was no longer there. In its place was a charred ruin of tumbled walls and smoking piles of ash, and the only sound that came from it was the hollow, accusative weeping of the child...

He awoke with a start and at first did not remember where he was. Then he saw the moonlight glimmering through a crack above the door, and the events of the previous day came back to him in a rush.

He was in the House of Detention. Calling it a house of any kind was a bit of an exaggeration, he thought, looking around him. He was lying on a meager pile of moldy straw on the packed-earth floor. That straw was the only piece of "furniture" in the room. The walls had no windows, and only a single, wooden door, latched from the outside and guarded by two armed men.

He struggled to a sitting position, still half-asleep. The cold of the floor had seeped into his bones, and he groaned with the effort to stretch his stiff muscles. He was about to lay back down and try to get more sleep when a sound startled him fully awake.

The door of the room rattled softly. Someone was trying to enter.

He clawed at the wall, pulled himself to his feet, and was rewarded with a wave of dizziness that threatened to lay him back on the floor even more quickly than he had risen. He clutched an alcove in the wall and breathed deeply, waiting for the room to stop whirling and keeping his eyes fixed on the door.

It rattled once more and then slid open, hinges grating softly. A man stepped in, a tall, cloaked shape outlined against the moonlight.

"I have chosen sides."

The voice was Manoah's. Rohgah slumped against the wall, his heart pounding against his ribcage. "If you were trying to pick the side that would frighten me to death, you failed!" he snapped.

He saw the flash of Manoah's teeth as the big man smiled. "Hurry! We do not have much time. And be silent!"

Rohgah followed him out the door. Two men were waiting outside, men that Rohgah did not recognize. Manoah led all three of them noiselessly down the narrow streets of Gibbethon, tiptoeing through alleys, scurrying past courtyards, making so many turns that in no time Rohgah was completely lost. The town around them was silent, and only cold moonlight illuminated their route. Only once did they encounter anyone: a pair of guards armed with spears sauntered past as Rohgah and his three guides plastered themselves against the shadowed wall of some sort of shop, its purpose indistinguishable in the darkness.

After several minutes of soundless travel, Manoah stopped at an earthen wall and knocked on a narrow gate of vertical planks. The gate opened immediately, and they entered into a courtyard. Several people waited there in silence, their faces lit by a single lamp cradled in a cloaked woman's hand. After a moment, Rohgah realized the woman was Naamah, her worried eyes searching Manoah's face, as if he were the one who had been rescued.

"I was able to arrange for two of my relatives to be your guards tonight," Manoah whispered. "Men who recognize the evil of the so-called priests of Dan."

Heber and Leah stood next to Naamah, Leah with one arm cradling her swollen belly. "The men of Gibbethon still respect Manoah as a prince of his tribe," Heber said.

"What will happen to the men who were guarding me?" Rohgah asked. "It will soon become known that they deserted their post."

"They will travel to another town for a while, and stay there with the sons of my father's brother," Manoah said.

Rohgah shook his head. "I do not want their blood on my hands!"

"Don't worry," Leah said, her eyes flashing in the lamplight. "Those two would have paid to get away from their duties here at home! They will consider themselves in your debt, you can be sure!"

Manoah laid a hand on his shoulder. "Come, Father. We must be on our way, and quickly. I want to put many fields between us and this city before the sun rises."

"Where will we go?" Rohgah asked.

"I had hoped you would tell me," Manoah said.

Rohgah thought for a moment. He did not want to endanger Manoah or his household. But he had prayed for an escort to Shiloh, and now this man was offering to provide him with one. He decided that he had better not turn his face away from the True God's answer.

"I must eventually get to Shiloh," he said slowly. "But for now—Gibeon. I know the priests there, and the Elders. I had dealings with them before the war against Ammon. They are good men and will listen to the message that I carry."

"Gibeon is also beyond the reach of the priests of Dan," Manoah said.

One of Manoah's brothers came forward, leading a donkey already loaded with provision baskets. Manoah lifted Rohgah as though he were a child, settling him on the donkey's back. "Are you comfortable?" he asked.

"You have already been more than generous," Rohgah said. "With these provisions and this sturdy animal," he patted the donkey's rump, "I am sure I can make it to Gibeon on my own."

"I am coming with you," Manoah said. "I will hear no argument. I am already packed. You were assaulted while a guest under my roof. I will not leave you until I am sure you are safely to your destination."

He led the donkey to the postern gate and into the street outside, followed by Naamah, Leah, and his brothers. "Watch over my wife. I leave her in your care," Manoah said.

The men nodded; Leah stepped forward and kissed Manoah on each cheek. "Anyone who even dares to cast their eyes in her direction will have to go through me!"

Manoah smiled, a flash of teeth in the moonlight. "Then I pity the man who tries. Be careful, all of you. May Jehovah watch over you."

Manoah kissed his wife, and she threw her arms around his chest and clung to him like a frightened child. After a moment, he gently removed her arms, stepping back from her. Taking up the donkey's rope, he began leading it down the road away from his home.

A moment later, Naamah came running after him. "Manoah!"

He dropped the lead rope and took several steps back toward her. She stopped before she reached him and they stood facing each other, a span between them. They spoke in whispers, but Rohgah could still hear them in the silence of the night.

"Will I see you again?" Naamah asked.

"Of course, Naamah. As soon as may be," said Manoah.

Naamah was silent for a moment. "I...I have to know you are not leaving...that is, not leaving to escape the shame that..."

"I will never leave you, Naamah," said Manoah, his voice cracking with emotion. "But the prophet of God believes that we are suffering the Malediction foretold by Moses. If I can help him to reach Shiloh, perhaps the corruption can be healed. Perhaps...perhaps you, also, can be healed."

She began to cry. "I love you, my husband. You are so good to me; you please me in all things."

"Perhaps ending this Malediction will enable you to be good to me in all things as well," said Manoah, and turning, took up the lead rope and led Rohgah and the donkey out of the city.

12

Manoah and Rohgah traveled east across the coastal plains, moving as swiftly as the moonlit road would permit. A few stars glimmered through breaks in the clouds, and the air was brisk and damp with dew. For a time the only sound was the creak of the provision bags strapped over the donkey's back and the whisk of their footsteps through the dead grasses at the edge of the road that stretched away ahead of them, slashing a narrow swath through the once-fertile farmlands on either side. The Danites had cut the final wheat harvest months before, then plowed and planted, and now awaited the overdue winter rains that would sprout the sown seeds.

They traveled in silence, and although he wondered if that was for fear of being heard or because Manoah was not in the mood for conversation, Rohgah was happy to leave the other man to his thoughts. In the meantime, he found himself reviewing in his own mind just what he was supposed to be doing. He thought about the commission Jehovah had given him, and the results that it must achieve, and had to admit to himself that there was a good deal about the foretold events that he did not know. He had a rough outline of what Jehovah purposed to do, but the details were more than a little fuzzy. It was fine to say that the corruption in Eli's house must be cleansed and the people restored to pure worship, but exactly how would a child accomplish this?

The High Priest was the most powerful man in Israel. In a nation that did not have a king, no authority in Israel could check his hand, and no governmental body could remove him from office. In fact, the Torah did not even address the possibility that a High Priest would have to be rejected.

Then again, he thought, maybe Eli just needed to be convinced to disinherit his two sons, Hophni and Phinehas. It was no secret that they were the real problem in Shiloh—Eli's sin was in doing nothing about it. If the High Priest decided to remove the two Priests from office, and then take a stand for true worship, perhaps the people would follow him.

But where did a child fit in? *The arms of one house I shall cut off, but another I will raise up, a child in Shiloh, and I will fill his hand with power.* Was the child to become a Priest? If so, he could not do so for years, until he became a man. That would not be in time to save Israel, at the rate things were going. So what could a child do to affect the actions of the Priests? And how would the arms of one house—Eli's house?—be cut off?

His musings reminded him of an event from Israel's history, centuries before. Shortly after Moses anointed the first High Priest, Aaron, two of his sons, Nadab and Abihu, had gotten intoxicated and offered an illegitimate offering to Jehovah. The True God had sent fire from heaven and consumed them before the eyes of all Israel. Nadab and Abihu died before they had fathered any sons, and so all the Priests since then were descendants of one of their two brothers, Eleazar and Ithamar.

Was something similar going to happen to Hophni and Phinehas? Fire sent from heaven? If that were so, then why didn't it just happen? Why was Jehovah sending him to Shiloh with a message of doom? And once again he was left with the question: What did the child have to do with it?

He sighed, shifting his weight on the back of the donkey to relieve his cramping muscles. He would have to wait for answers, he knew. In the meantime, he needed to use his time to come up with a sure way to persuade the Elders of Gibeon to help him. He felt confident that he could convince them of the validity of his message—they knew him as a prophet from the days of Judge Jephthah. But he needed them to do more than provide him with safe passage. He needed them to help him begin a campaign to change the hearts of the people of Israel. Only that could overcome the Malediction—to cleanse badness, not just from Shiloh, but also from the entire nation. Would the Priests of Gibeon be willing to take a stand against the High Priest, if it came to that—and against his sons? Would they have the courage to do what was needed?

By the time the dawn began to brighten the horizon above the mountains in front of them, Rohgah and Manoah were nearing the outskirts of Gezer, nestled against a low hill at the foot of the Shephelah. They followed the road as it skirted around the city walls, trying to avoid the first of the day's travelers. Past the city, the road began to rise, ascending the broad Vale of Aijalon into the Shephelah, whose rounded hills rose now on three sides of them. The road hugged one edge of the pass, bordered by scrub and growing rockier as they climbed. As they crested the pass two stags and a group of does bounded away from them, disappearing almost silently under the cover of the trees.

Aijalon was the site of one of the great miracles of Israel's past. In the days of the conquest of Canaan, General Joshua had battled a coalition of five Amorite kings in the valley. On that day, Jehovah had caused giant hailstones to fall among the enemy, decimating their troops. As darkness fell, the Amorites fled, and Joshua knew that if they escaped, he would be forced to fight them again as soon as they regrouped. He prayed to Jehovah, asking for something no one had ever requested of God before: that the setting sun and the rising moon would stand still in the sky, until he had exterminated his enemies.

Jehovah heard his prayer. On that day, unique among all days, the sun and the moon had, indeed, stood still over the battlefield, until the victory was complete. Thinking about the events comforted Rohgah. The God who held in His hand the sun and moon was surely capable of doing whatever He needed to cleanse Israel of corruption.

Manoah spoke, startling Rohgah out of his thoughts. "I am confused about something, Prophet," he said. "What is it you expect the men of Gibeon to do?"

"What do you mean?"

Manoah shrugged. "What influence can Priests in the territory of the tribe of Benjamin have on the priests of Dan, back in Gibbethon?"

Rohgah realized for the first time how little he had actually told Manoah about the situation—about the real purpose of his mission. Manoah still believed that they were traveling in large part to get rid of the apostate priests of Dan and thereby start a process that would hinder the onset of the Malediction. He wondered what the big man would do if he knew that Rohgah bore a message of death to the family of the High Priest himself.

He decided to hold onto that information for a little while longer. "You do not kill a poisonous plant by plucking off its leaves, Manoah. We must find the root of this corruption. We can defeat the Malediction only by reaching the hearts of the people. When the Elders of all the tribes are firmly resolved to clear false worship from their midst, to adhere to the Torah as our people vowed to do, then the Malediction will be defeated, and Jehovah's blessings will again flow through the land."

Manoah shook his head. "That is a tall order. Worship of Baal and Ashtoreth has become so widespread...and all the more so now, when people fear that their crops will fail, and..."

He trailed off, looking again over the hills. Rohgah knew what he had been about to say. "And what, Manoah?"

Manoah hesitated. "And even the seed sown in their wives will not bear fruit."

"Do not blame your wife, Manoah," Rohgah said.

"I don't. It is not her fault. But that does not change the fact of her barrenness. It does not change the fact that I am without sons, that I will grow old and feeble with no one to care for me when I am too weak to walk behind the plow, that the land inheritance that has been in my family for four generations will pass on to other men, and the name of Manoah of Dan will fail."

For a moment, Rohgah almost felt sorry for the man, but his disgust at Manoah's self-pity overcame his sympathy.

"So much has been given you, Manoah," he said slowly. "The privilege of being an Elder of your tribe, a wife who is a shining gem among the women of Israel, wealth and good health, respect and prominence among your tribe, the privilege of worshiping at Jehovah's house in Shiloh…"

"What are you getting at?" Manoah asked.

"Can you not see it for yourself?"

Manoah frowned back at him. "If you are trying to say that my reasons for concern are not valid—."

"I am just amazed that you can carry all these responsibilities when your hands are so full of self-pity!"

The look of stunned pain that passed over Manoah's face was almost enough to make Rohgah regret his words. The big man said nothing in response, just turned and began walking even more quickly up the road, pulling the donkey behind him. *Let him sulk,* thought Rohgah. *Maybe he will find room in his thoughts for someone other than himself.*

They walked on in silence, nearing the end of the pass and the city of Aijalon nestled on the shoulder of a rocky hill on the opposite side, casting its shadow onto the bare fields that spread across the valley. The road climbed sharply, the broad fields giving way to rocky hills and dense patches of forest. They began to pass other travelers descending from the mountains, small groups on foot and strung-out caravans of traders, their wagons loaded with sealed casks of olive oil, bundles of dyed wool, salt from the Salt Sea, casks of tar—all on its way to the Phoenician ports to the north or to Egyptian buyers to the south. Occasionally, a messenger would gallop past on horseback with some urgent dispatch, leaving a cloud of dust in his wake.

The road rose and fell among the rounded hills, forests of sycamore, oak, cedar, and pine growing taller and denser as their elevation increased. By mid-day, they began to catch glimpses of the city of Lower Beth-horon on a hill ahead, visible through gaps in the trees.

Manoah spoke again, and Rohgah was glad to hear no anger in his voice. "People are afraid, Rohgah. They watch their crops failing, year after year, and live with the real worry that famine is about to pounce. They know that the people of Canaan successfully lived in this land for many centuries before Israel conquered it—and they did so without the blessing of Jehovah. So when the Canaanites who still live among us tell them that the way to assure a successful harvest is to make offerings to Baal...some are willing to try anything."

"It doesn't hurt that the worship of Baal calls for unrestrained relations with his temple prostitutes!" Rohgah said. "I have a hard time believing their motives are so pure, Manoah."

Manoah did not respond. After a moment, Rohgah continued, forcing himself to speak more kindly. "Many Israelites keep idols of pregnant Ashtoreth in their homes as well, to protect themselves against barrenness. But you do not. Why?"

"As I have already said—idolatry is condemned by Jehovah."

"And you love Jehovah our God!" Rohgah said. "You love the Laws he gave to Moses! Not even when you are confronted with your greatest fears are you willing to ignore that Law! Do not make excuses for your fellow Israelites, Manoah. There is no justification for worshipping the demon-gods of Canaan—they are the gods that Jehovah defeated before our forefathers when He brought us into this land! He defeated them, all of them, in His love for His people and for the honor of His name. And now we would turn our backs on the True God and worship these idols of wood and stone?"

"I don't disagree," said Manoah. "But I think in some ways it is easier in times of war to see that distinction. Everything seems less ambiguous to people, the enemy clearly delineated. But in times of peace, when men's thoughts turn to their crops, their families..."

"Maybe," Rohgah said. "But if we do not serve Jehovah in times of peace, can we expect His aid when our enemies descend on us? If war came to Israel now, Manoah, would we be ready for it? Could we hope to survive our enemies while we prostrate ourselves before their gods?"

Manoah shook his head slowly, but said nothing. He turned back toward the east and continued leading the donkey up the road. It had grown steeper now, winding into the rounded valley in which Lower Beth-horon stood, a brown lake of farmland shored by forested, green hills. They skirted this city as well and followed the road to the top of a broad, wooded ridge. The valley dropped away sharply on either side, the trees thinning at the bottom of the slopes to give way to rocky pasturelands. The road climbed past Upper Beth-Horon, then began to descend once again into the broad plain that spread below the hill upon which the city of Gibeon stood.

By late afternoon, they could see the city ahead of them, its plastered walls shining in the bright afternoon sunlight. Exhaustion was beginning to take its toll on Rohgah, and he wondered if he would be able to move once they arrived. He tried to force his mind to ignore the growing pain in his back and legs, concentrating instead on the fields they passed through, then on the drooping vines roping their way across terraced hillside vineyards, and the neatly manicured olive groves that huddled against the city walls like chicks hiding under their mother's wings. As they passed through the ancient trees, a half dozen riders burst from the gate and galloped furiously past them, disappearing down the sloping roadway in a cloud of dust.

When they reached the massive double set of gates set in the high walls, the first person to greet them was a child, a son of perhaps ten or eleven years. He marched boldly up to Manoah and bowed. "May peace be with you, my lord."

Manoah and Rohgah both stared. The boy was wearing a knee-length, long-sleeved tunic roughly stitched out of tawny cowhide, with the hair still attached. The tunic had a hood sewn onto it, and thick tufts of brownish hair jutted out like a mane all around its edge. The earnest face that stared seriously out at them from the cowl seemed not to realize how bizarre an appearance he presented. The donkey upon which Rohgah sat shied away, whinnying softly.

"And who might you be?" Manoah asked, smiling.

"I am Kittim, son of Neriah," the boy answered, bowing again. "I am about to go play lion on that hill." He pointed at a terraced hill to the west.

"Indeed?" Manoah's smile broadened.

Kittim nodded. "But I saw that you were strangers in Gibeon, and I did not want to neglect my duties to extend to you a warm greeting. Welcome to our city!"

"Consider your duty fulfilled," Rohgah said. "Where is your father?"

"Right this way," Kittim said, turning and gesturing for them to follow. Rohgah saw that a tufted tail hung from the back of the tunic, and they followed it, bouncing and twitching in the dust, as the boy headed through the crowded city gate.

Just inside the first open gate, a set of benches had been set up, and the Elders of the city, bearing their distinctive vermilion staffs, sat there, hearing legal cases and witnessing contracts. Kittim led them to a man about Manoah's age, extraordinarily tall and strongly built. He stood as he saw the boy approaching. "Kittim! I thought you were playing in the orchard."

"I am, father, and soon—but these men requested that I bring them to you." He gestured towards Rohgah and Manoah with one hand and towards his father with the other. "Traveling men—this is my father, Neriah."

"Thank you, Kittim," his father said. "You may go and play now."

Kittim bowed once more, his tail dragging on the ground. "May peace be with you all," he said, and scurried out through the gate.

"I hope that my son was no trouble to you men," Neriah said.

"Not at all," Manoah answered. He was about to say more, but Rohgah interrupted, his voice urgent.

"We need to speak with the Elders of Gibeon immediately," he said. "I have been sent with a message from Jehovah to the tribes of Israel."

Neriah's eyes widened and he nodded. "It seems it is a day for urgent messages. Follow me, please."

He called to a young man standing nearby and said something too quietly for Rohgah to hear; the young man nodded and left immediately. Neriah led them through the inner gate and into a building that sat just inside it, built onto the wall. When his eyes adjusted to the dim interior, Rohgah saw that it was a meeting hall of sorts, furnished only with a table and benches. A few moments after they entered, men began filing in after them, most of them grey-bearded and wrinkled, taking their places at the benches or standing against the walls. Most of them wore the casual garments of the Priesthood, reminding Rohgah that Gibeon was, after all, a city given to the Priests, and that some of the men from this city could right then be serving their term of duty in Shiloh. Most others carried the vermilion staff of an elder in their left hand.

When all had gathered, Neriah said, "This man brings us a message from Jehovah," then nodded to Rohgah and sat down.

"Are you a prophet?" someone asked incredulously.

"I am," Rohgah said.

"There have been no prophets in Israel for many years," the same voice said.

"I have been in Israel!" Rohgah snapped. "I have been commissioned to speak the words of Jehovah to High Priest Eli in Shiloh!"

The crowd murmured uncomfortably at his reference to Eli. Rohgah pressed forward. "Does a shadow fall over your souls at the mention of his name? What of the names Hophni, and Phinehas? Do you shudder to consider this darkness growing in the heart of Israel? Do you lie awake at night, thinking of failed crops, skies as dry as dust, enemies massing on our borders, weakness and fear spreading through our people like plague? Do you dare to speak the word to yourself in the silence of night, the word that haunts your nightmares: Malediction!"

The men shifted and frowned, and the room darkened as though a cloud had passed over the sun. Rohgah began to pace, feeling the zeal of his commission burning in his veins. "But Jehovah has seen all that is happening to His people, Israel. He has not forgotten us! The word of Jehovah will be heard again in Shiloh!

"A change is coming, my brothers. Jehovah, the God of our forefathers, has promised that a spark struck by a child in Shiloh will become a flame to scour evil from this land."

"A child?" someone asked from the crowd. "What will this child do for us?"

Rohgah rubbed his hands. "He will ignite a fire that will burn with such brilliance it will drive the darkness from our people!"

"Darkness such as the priests of Dan?" Manoah asked.

"Yes!" he said. "Evil such as the apostate priests that usurp your place by setting themselves up over the tribe of Dan in Gibbethon and—."

"Gibbethon?" Neriah asked, brows knitting. "Why do you mention Gibbethon?"

Rohgah was taken aback. "I know that false priests hold it in their claws, leading its people into idolatry and worship of false gods!"

Neriah shook his head. "Do you come from Gibbethon?"

Manoah stepped forward from his place against the wall. "I am an Elder of the city. We have come from there this very day."

The crowd murmured and all turned to look at Manoah, concern etched on their features.

"What is it?" Manoah asked, growing nervous.

"Then you do not know of the threat to your city?" Neriah asked.

"What threat?" Manoah stepped toward him.

"I assumed you knew," Neriah said. "I assumed it was why you had come! Your goal to do something about the…corruption in Shiloh is noble. But if you are from Gibbethon, you have a more urgent problem. Word has just come to us by messenger from the coast. A massive Philistine army is marching from Ashkelon toward your city. They are sweeping everything before them. A campaign against Israel has begun."

13

Manoah galloped furiously westward, driving the horse beneath him with as much speed as he could force from the powerful animal. But no matter how fast he went, he was unable to put any distance between himself and the abject terror that pursued him. Fear nipped at his heels like a predator, always just a step behind, breathing down his neck. The faster he ran, the closer he got to Gibbethon, the more fear closed the distance between them, dragging at him with invisible claws and teeth, threatening to strike him down before he had even seen his real enemy.

He had left Gibeon as soon as he and Rohgah were given news of the attack, purchasing the fastest horse that money could buy in the city. Rohgah had met him at the gate and urged him to be careful, and Manoah had let his fear run off at the old man. "Did you foresee this, Prophet?" he had asked bitterly.

Rohgah had just shaken his head, staring up at him with sympathetic eyes.

"I should have listened to you after all, old man!" Manoah had told him, wheeling the horse about in Gibeon's gateway. "I should have stayed with my family!"

He had galloped off without looking back and still could not bring himself to spare any thoughts for what had happened to the old prophet after he left. He had begged the Elders of Gibeon to send at least a few men back with him—whomever they could spare to help him reach the city safely and do what he could to save his family. They had refused, telling him that they were mustering their own forces, and that all available men had already been sent as messengers to the other regions of Israel, summoning the tribes to war. They had not admitted it in so many words, but the truth was that they had already given up Gibbethon as lost.

The horse was proving itself worth the stack of silver coins Manoah had spent on it, its long legs eating up the miles as they raced by moon and starlight back over the Vale of Aijalon and down to the coastal plain. His mind was numb with fear and worry, haunted by the faces of his wife, his brothers, and his friends in the city. He cursed himself for listening to Rohgah and allowing the prophet's words to overcome his own good sense. He had been so caught up in Rohgah's grand schemes that he had neglected to care for the immediate needs of his own family. It did no good to tell himself that he could have had no way of knowing the Philistines would attack. Whether he had known or not, he had abandoned his family to whatever fate found them, and had put himself too far away to be of any help when that fate descended.

He prayed constantly, his voice shaking with the horse's rhythmic movements. He prayed for his wife and his brothers, for his town, for Jehovah to let him reach the city safely, for the horse's strength not to give out before he could save his family. At times, he could only weep aloud, hoping that the True God heard in his tears a plea beyond all words.

By the time dawn was brightening the distant horizon, the horse had slowed to a trot, its sweating flanks heaving between Manoah's legs. The pace felt absurdly slow, and he pulled at his beard in frustration, fighting the mad inclination to dismount and run the rest of the way to the city. He was still several hours from his destination, and he knew his best chance of getting there quickly was to continue riding, even if the horse slowed to a walk. But the sense of being pursued by some irascible foe grew so great that the hairs on the back of his neck stood up and the muscles of his shoulders and back twisted themselves into rigid knots.

He gripped his worn sword hilt with one hand, his palm itching to take it up and strike a blow in defense of his town, his people, and his family. He knew all too well what an attack by Philistines was like. He had fought them many times in his life—small battles over territory, or in defense of his tribe's lands. There were nations that were crueler, but none more efficient at killing people and desolating a city. He knew that if they had determined to capture Gibbethon, they would not stop until they had brought his hometown to its knees, and they would do whatever was necessary to accomplish their goal.

As he crossed the plains, his eyes began to ache with the strain of searching the horizon for a sight of Gibbethon. The first glimpse he got of his city, though, was a smear of greasy smoke hanging in the pale, morning sky.

He had come too late.

He kicked the horse's flanks furiously, pushing it into a canter and then a faltering gallop. The exhausted beast twisted its muscular neck and fought the reins constantly, whinnying its protest as he tried to push it beyond its capability. It kept up the pace for only a few seconds, then stumbled and slowed to a stubborn trot.

A few minutes later, he could see the walls. The Philistine army spread like a roiling pool of dark water around the city, a black stain that had already spilled through the shattered gates. The desperate sounds of battle reached his ears: the screams of the wounded and dying, the clash of arms. Dancing fingers of flame leapt above the wall in places, tossing smoke into the brightening sky. He began to pass Israelites fleeing eastward toward the hills, their faces haunted. Gore-stained cloths wrapped bodies and heads; children bled tears down dirty cheeks. They looked up at him in confusion, and some yelled at him to turn back. He ignored them, spurring his horse onward.

Finally, the animal simply gave out, coming to a stop in the middle of the road, shifting back and forth in a delicate dance of exhaustion. Manoah slid from its back, patting its sweat-streaked neck and then pulling off the harness and dropping it on the road. "Well done," he whispered. "Go and find rest."

The horse whickered softly, swinging its head upward as if to push Manoah away. He turned and, drawing his sword, began to run through the dry fields toward the walls of the city.

A postern gate opened through the northern wall and he made his way around the bulwark in that direction; since the Philistine attack was focused on the breached gate in the southern wall, no soldiers battled outside the city on the opposite side.

By the time he reached the postern, his heart was pounding so hard against his ribs that he could hear it like drumbeats in his ears. His palm was sweaty against the hilt of his sword, and he gripped it tighter as he reached for the postern gate with his left hand.

It burst open before he touched it, battered down from inside by the flailing hooves of a stallion. He dove to one side, plastering himself against the outside wall next to the opening. The horse must have run off somewhere inside, but a moment later, two Philistine warriors tumbled through the open gateway, their feather-crested helmets and bronze-and-leather body armor making them appear even larger than they were. Their swords were sheathed; between them, they dragged a stunned, young Israelite woman. She was alive, Manoah saw, but barely; her eyes were glassy and blood trickled from a wound in her matted, brown hair. Her clothing hung from her in shreds and fragments, and the olive skin of one gore-smeared shoulder and arm was exposed.

Manoah pounced at the soldiers in fury, all the pent anger of his long night ride exploding from him in the battle cry of his tribe: "Dan and Jehovah!"

He killed the first surprised soldier instantly, running him through before he had even registered Manoah's presence. The other dropped the woman; she fell motionless to the ground at his feet as he tried to draw his sword. Manoah slashed at him savagely, and the man fell, screaming, with his hand still on the hilt of his half-sheathed blade.

The woman looked up at Manoah, then, and dragged herself to her bloodied knees, her eyes glazed with shock. "Flee!" Manoah said, and ducked through the postern.

Inside, all was madness. Smoke rolled from windows and doorways, and people ran in every direction, screaming, clutching children or precious belongings to their chests.

Manoah began making his way across the town, keeping to the alleys as much as possible, trying to reach his home without encountering any of the soldiers hunting in the streets, leaving destruction and death in their wake. His heart continued to pound, and he quickly realized how exhausted he was already from his ride. "Lend me the strength of Your mighty Arms, Jehovah," he prayed in a whisper.

He had nearly reached his home when the sudden approach of a group of soldiers forced him to duck into the doorway of a neighbor's house. His breathing harsh in his own ears, he surveyed the dark room in front of him. Chairs, tables and cushions were strewn across the floor. The family who lived there, a young couple with two children and the wife's aging mother, all lay slaughtered in pools of their own bright blood. He turned away from the grisly sight, peering around the doorframe to see if the road was clear.

Philistine warriors thundered past, a handful of men pacing a chariot carrying three others. He saw with a shock that the wheels of the chariot had scythes attached to its spokes, spraying a fine mist of blood as the vehicle passed. The soldiers had mounted a clay idol of the fish-god Dagon on the harness; it, too, was splashed with crimson.

As soon as they were out of sight, he rushed across the street and sprinted for his own gate. Before he had taken three strides, though, a shout sounded from a house he was passing, and three Philistine soldiers leapt from an open doorway, swords drawn.

He killed the first in the initial rush, but the second hurled a javelin from several paces away, and, though he twisted to avoid it, the bronze head grazed his chest, slashing through his tunic and into the skin below his left collarbone. Howling, the two remaining soldiers rushed at him.

He gritted his teeth against the pain that burned across his chest and battered aside a wild blow from one of the soldier's swords, dancing backwards to avoid a lunge from the second Philistine. *Focus!* He chided himself, swinging his own blade in a wide arc that caught the forearm of the nearest soldier and sent him tumbling to the ground, clutching the wound and screaming.

The other warrior came at him, an oiled-leather shield strapped to his left arm, and rained blows on Manoah so quickly that it was all he could do to defend himself. The Philistine pushed him back, farther and farther, and Manoah was unable to land a blow past the man's shield.

Then Manoah felt the wall of a building against his back and the mindless panic of a trapped animal as he tried desperately to parry his enemy's blows.

The Philistine lunged but slipped in a pool of blood, falling to one knee. Manoah stretched forward, snaking his blade past the shield and into the man's shoulder. The Philistine screamed, and his shield arm went limp. Manoah battered aside his feeble defense and killed him, then turned and quickly finished the other soldier.

Pausing only a second to catch his breath, he raced back up the street toward his home, the wound on his chest aching with every inhalation.

When he reached the gates of his courtyard, his breath caught in a sob of anguish. All three of his brothers had been pinned to the gate with Philistine spears; they hung limply from the shafts that had impaled them, their blood dripping to the flagstones at their feet. Their weight had broken the top hinge of the gate, and it sagged at a rakish angle.

"Naamah!" he screamed, and shouldered his way past his brothers' bodies, feeling hot tears on his cheeks. Crimson splashes streaked the courtyard and spattered the wall of the house next to the entry. He leapt up the steps in a single bound and barreled through the open doorway.

Inside, the house was still and shadowed, like a tomb. There was no sign of his wife.

14

The word of Jehovah had become rare in Shiloh.

That was what people said, and Samuel knew that it was true.

He followed the line of Gibeonites who walked steadily up the streets of Shiloh, their arms cradling bundles of wood like his own, or their shoulders bearing yokes from which hung clay pots of water dipped from the spring outside the wall.

The grey, half-light of failing night still hung over the city. An hour before dawn, Priest Ahitub had sent him to assist the Gibeonites in their traditional duties. It was a privilege, he knew, and he appreciated the break from his normal routine, even if it had required him to wake earlier than usual. But one of the pieces of wood he carried had a jagged knot that was digging into his forearm. He had tried several times to shift the bundle without dropping it, but so far the knot remained tenaciously jabbed into his flesh. He would not complain aloud about it, or ask the whole line to stop for him—after all, it was his own fault for not arranging the wood on his arms more comfortably before he began walking. But his ability to appreciate the privilege and honor of the task was shrinking at precisely the same rate that the pain in his forearm was growing.

They entered the Tabernacle complex through a postern gate in the Curtain Wall and made their way across the dew-damp pavers. When he reached the woodpile next to the Altar, he dumped his bundle of wood atop the stack, brushing dirt and bits of bark from his arms and chest, and rubbing the red indentation the knot had left in his skin. A Priest knelt already before the Altar, feeding wood into the firebox. Samuel watched him a moment in silence, thinking again about the words he had heard repeated in surreptitious whispers by people who had traveled to the Tabernacle.

The word of Jehovah had become rare in Shiloh.

It was as close as faithful Israelites could bring themselves to saying that Jehovah had abandoned them. It was true that the words of the True God had not been heard in Shiloh for some time, since long before Eli's shocking appointment of Phinehas as acting High Priest. No Prophets had come with divine pronouncements, and Eli had not addressed the nation with anything resembling a heavenly revelation for more than a year.

And, of course, other things convinced people that Jehovah had abandoned Shiloh to the corruption growing within its walls.

He realized that he was still staring at the dancing flames and tore his eyes away, feeling a shudder of the morning's cold air run down his spine. To him, the Flame itself was a sign of Jehovah's continued presence with the nation—a living symbol that had been burning since the nation's inception, a link to their hallowed past, like the sacred traditions and the Torah that Jehovah had entrusted to them.

The reddening of the eastern darkness told him that daybreak was nearing and he scurried towards the gate. Eli was already there, still choosing to greet each new dawn with a Benediction upon Jehovah's people, even though he had turned over his official duties to Phinehas. In spite of Eli's failures, Samuel found that he could not help but feel sorry for the old man, divested now of his sacred assignments, imprisoned in the darkness of his blindness, awaiting a death that would leave behind only a legacy of shame, an everlasting stain upon his name.

As Samuel reached the old Priest's side, he saw with surprise that Hophni and Phinehas stood beside him. Phinehas had put on the traditional garments of the High Priest and was talking softly to his brother, his thick arms crossed over his bejeweled breastplate. Samuel slowed and watched them, letting their eyes and gestures lead him to the subject of their conversation.

They were talking about the Women's Corps.

Samuel felt a knot form in his throat as he watched them looking the girls up and down, gesturing provocatively and laughing at the various reactions it elicited from the objects of their attention. Tirzah tried to keep the girls focused on the morning's rituals, ignoring the winks and pursed lips cast in their direction. She was more or less successful—Samuel saw some of the girls stealing glances at the Priests, or struggling not to do so.

Passing Levites and supplicants flowed around Hophni and Phinehas, keeping space between them, like flies swarmed away when someone approached a pile of offal. He saw how Hophni looked down his bulbous nose at them, his stance a challenge and a threat.

Samuel walked forward slowly until he was within earshot of the Priest's conversation; they were certainly not making any effort to conceal what they were saying.

"They are a herd of does waiting for a good hunter," Hophni said, and licked his lower lip slowly. "A herd of ripe does."

Phinehas laughed, a curt, mirthless sound. "It is the herder that has my eye lately, brother." He raised his eyebrows. "Tirzah has been developing curves like the art of a potter's hands!"

"Oho! No mud-palmed potter should be allowed to touch such yielding curves!" Hophni said. "Let them be saved for the gentle hands of a High Priest!"

They both broke into raucous laughter, even as Samuel heard from behind him the Levite who was attending the Altar sing:

> "Out of the depths I call to you, O Jehovah.
> O Jehovah, do hear my voice!
> My soul has waited for Jehovah
> More than watchmen for the dawn!"

The trumpet blast shattered the silence, signaling the sunrise, and at that moment, Samuel could hear the echoes of the sound reverberating all the way into the past, to trumpets blown at the gates of Shiloh centuries before, in Joshua's day. Where was a Joshua when you needed one, a fearless general who would stand up even to the Priesthood? He squeezed the handles of the gate in sweating fists and paused a moment, bowing his head in prayer. *Please, O Jehovah. For the sake of Your great name, and for the sake of Your people—let this gate open upon a day of change in Israel, a new dawn that brings the light of Your favor back to Your house in Shiloh.*

He took a deep breath and pulled the gates open, stepping to Eli's side as the mass of penitents surged into the opening to watch the morning service. Samuel scanned the crowd, not really knowing what he was looking for. The face of someone who could bring change? The face of a Prophet? Of a Judge?

What he saw were anxious Israelites, the same sorts of faces he saw there every morning. *Eyes wet with worry. Skin drawn with hunger, or pocked by sores. Uplifted faces. Hands raised, palms up. Lips whispering unheard prayers. Hope without any expectation of hope's fulfillment.*

He felt something deep inside him harden, a place in his heart that could not bear to ache any longer with yearning for deliverance from fear and doubt. He wondered briefly if what he felt was just a part of growing up, of becoming an adult in a world that gave men like Phinehas and Hophni the highest offices in the nation chosen by God.

Israel was the same today as yesterday, he decided as he examined the crowd. For four centuries they had struggled to hold onto their past, to live in the strict traditions of their forefathers. Perhaps that decision had forced them into this destiny, when their resistance to change was what needed to change the most. Since the time of Moses, every day had begun with the opening of the gates of the Tabernacle, an endless succession of repeated patterns, connecting one day to the next, Sabbath to Sabbath, new moon to new moon. He felt a strange sense of guilt that he had become responsible for a tradition that, by its repetition, locked the nation into a pattern that was now destroying them. Not that the traditions themselves were bad—they were the Torah, given by the True God to guide His people. They were true and unchanging, but by their nature, they created opportunities for corruption. He did not know how to explain it clearly, but the traditions reminded him of the columns of blank vellum left between the text on scrolls—an emptiness that gave the words definition, but also left room for someone to scribble additions. An emptiness had been left where the Torah failed to provide for an instance in which the leaders of Israel had rejected the True God in their hearts, and now Phinehas had annotated those columns with his own unspoken amendments to the Law.

Behind him, a Priest laid the sacrifice on the grating, and the Levites led the gathered crowd in the daily Psalm. Samuel heard the airy voices of the Women's Corps rising, light and elegant, above the voices of the supplicants.

> O God of vengeance, shine forth!
> Raise Yourself, O Judge of the earth.
> Return retribution to the haughty.
> How long will the wicked, O Jehovah,
> How long will the wicked themselves exult?"

How long, indeed! He thought bitterly. Israel was the same today as it was yesterday. Even the air had stopped moving, as if the clouds themselves were refusing to change.

The word of Jehovah has become rare in Shiloh.

He forced himself to mouth the words of the song, but that morning he could not actually sing them, finding that he was not sure if he believed them. It was wrong of him, he knew—a lack of faith. But to sing of Jehovah taking action against wickedness while standing within arms-length of two of the most wicked men in Israel who now held the nation in their filthy palms...

> "Your people, O Jehovah, they keep crushing.
> And Your inheritance they keep wearing down.

The widow and the immigrant they kill,
And the orphans they murder.
And they keep saying: 'Jehovah does not see us;
The God of Jacob does not comprehend what we do.'"

The silvery tones of a trumpet sounded a break between verses, and like the susurrations of a summer breeze, the whispered prayers of the gathered supplicants wended their way heavenward with the smoke of the incense and the morning sacrifice.

He met Ahitub's deep-set eyes. The Priest was watching him with knitted brows, and Samuel felt the blood rush to his face, sure that his mentor had somehow seen that Samuel was not singing aloud as he should have been. Turning toward the ascending smoke, he forced himself to join loudly in the next verse of the song, more afraid at that moment of losing Ahitub's approval than of any discomfort he might feel at participating in a ritual that felt so empty.

But as he began to sing again, he heard the lyrics anew, as though in all the hundreds of times he had sung them before this, he had failed to listen with some vital part of his mind that had only now begun to function.

"Understand, you blind fools;
You stupid ones without insight:
The One planting the ear, can He not hear?
Or the One shaping the eye, can He not look?
The Instructor of nations, can He not reprove?"

He glanced over at Hophni and Phinehas. They were supposed to be leading the song, but it looked as if they, too, realized the way the words from their own mouths were condemning them: *Shifting feet. Eyes constantly moving. Biting lips. Trying to appear unconcerned.* Samuel turned to face them, staring his anger at Phinehas' fleshy face as he sang even louder than normal.

"For Jehovah will not forsake His people,
Nor abandon His inheritance.
For judgment will return even to righteousness,
And the honest-hearted will follow it.

"But Jehovah will become a secure height for me,
And my God the rock of my refuge.
And He will turn back upon the wicked their villainy,
And will bring them to silence with their own wickedness.
Jehovah our God will bring them to silence."

As the song concluded, he saw that Hophni was glaring at him with his jaw knotted and eyes narrowed. Samuel felt a current of fear run though his body, but he forced himself to turn away from the Priest's scowl as though he had not noticed it, and instead raced to Tirzah's side.

She saw his approach and smiled. "Samuel! May this morning bring you peace!"

He took her hands in his own. "Tirzah—you must leave here at once!"

15

Tirzah cocked her head, still smiling. "Whatever do you mean?"

"Please, Tirzah—go and conceal yourself somewhere, at least for the rest of the day. Now that Phinehas is High Priest, anything could happen…"

She stopped smiling and shook her head. "I cannot abandon my responsibilities." She gestured at the gate, and the Corps gathered behind her. "This is my assignment at Jehovah's House, a sacred duty given me by High Priest Eli himself."

"Phinehas is High Priest now! Today, they will try to…take you—I just know it. They will force you to…"

He could not say the words, but he saw that he did not have to. Her face changed: *Lips tightening. Shoulders tensing. Breathing faster and shallower. Corners of the mouth hardening. Fear and determination mixing, trying to hide the former.* "No one will force me to do anything, Samuel," she said quietly. "I will not be defiled. Jehovah will not let it happen. Did you not listen to the words of the Psalm this morning? Jehovah will not leave His loyal ones."

"Some say that Jehovah has already—that Jehovah has left the land."

She frowned. "You know that is not true. Jehovah will act in His due time."

"Jehovah has not acted in time for the women Hophni and Phinehas have taken to their beds already!" he blurted out, surprising himself with his own anger.

Tirzah glanced around, as if to make sure no one had heard his outburst. "Shame on you! Do not dare to ascribe bad to Jehovah! Those women you refer to have made a choice, Samuel. You know the words of the Torah. It states clearly that if a man tries to force a woman, she must fight, she must scream. Jehovah expects us to fight to remain clean in His eyes. They did not. They gave themselves over to badness."

Samuel remembered the way some of the women who had been led to the homes of Phinehas or Hophni had looked as they went: *Haunted eyes. Tightening of the muscles around their lips. Shoulders drawn forward. Hands grasping hands or forearms. The ticking of their pulse in the veins of their necks. Quick, shallow breaths when the Priests were near.* He was not sure he could call it choice. Tirzah had been kept safe so far because the Priests feared her ailing father, Jephthah ben Gilead, the Judge of Israel and commander of the nation's armies.

But Samuel did not want to argue with her. Tirzah squeezed his hands in her own, and then let go. "I must attend to my duties," she said, and walked back to join the girls standing at the gate.

Samuel remained where he was, watching and waiting. *Waiting*, he thought bitterly. *It is all I ever do. Watch and wait. Watch and wait.* He saw Hophni leave Eli's side and swagger over to Tirzah, saying something to her that Samuel could not hear. Tirzah nodded in response, just a slight dipping of her chin, and walked slowly to her girls, gesturing for them to gather. *Shoulders slumped; steps short and shuffling; head bowed: sadness and resignation.* She glanced over at him once, then quickly turned away when she saw that he was watching.

The girls formed a line against the Curtain Wall, and Hophni and Phinehas paced back and forth in front of them like caged wolves. Samuel knew the ritual. Ostensibly, the girls gathered this way each morning to be chosen for a day of special service in the Tabernacle. But everyone knew that in reality, this was when the two Priests decided whom they would take to their beds that night.

He studied the women's different reactions to the Priests. A tall, slender girl with large blue eyes and a dress that appeared to have been made for a smaller girl: *batting lashes; lips pouting; shoulders pushed back: wanting to be chosen.* Another girl, short and petite, face half-hidden under her indigo head covering: *swallowing, hard; a knot of jaw muscles working below her ear; eyes held steady, straight ahead; hands clenched into fists at her sides: scared, but trying not to show it.* A third girl, wrapped in a brightly patterned dress with a long, blue fringe that dragged about her constantly shuffling feet: *mouth never stops moving; finger twisting her clothing, her hair; resting weight on one foot, then the other: Nervous.*

Tirzah stood to one side, scowling at the Priests as if she could destroy them by her force of will alone. They ignored her, knowing she could do nothing to stop them. Samuel watched Phinehas halt his pacing directly in front of Tirzah, looking her up and down unashamedly. She said something Samuel could not hear, and Phinehas guffawed, but he moved on and pointed to another girl, then turned and sauntered toward his home.

This is not why these girls had come to Shiloh, Samuel thought. It summoned his memory of his own childhood, of the great sacrifice that his parents made in bringing their child to serve in this place.

It had begun when he was a son of three years. Those memories had stayed with him, like shadows haunting the dark recesses of his mind. They crept out only in the nameless hour between waking and sleeping, a kind of hazy dream in which he once again remembered walking with his mother, Hannah, through the gates, past the guards standing quietly at their posts. He remembered her weeping.

It was only years later that he had learned from one of his uncles how difficult things had been for his mother before his birth. She would not complain to him, of course, even as he got older. Hannah was less likely to complain than a stone was. She felt unworthy to be dissatisfied with her lot in life when she knew so many people had even less than she did. The two things Samuel had never seen his mother do were complain or accept a compliment. To her, there were no greater sins.

Perhaps that was one of the reasons her situation put such a strain on her. His father's brother died years before in a hunting accident. According to the Torah, under those circumstances Elkanah was expected to take his brother's widow for his own wife and to raise up sons in his brother's name so that his brother's inheritance would not fail, would remain in his family for eternity.

Elkanah had done so, but the widow, Peninnah, was so jealous of the love he had for Hannah that she did all she could to make Hannah's life miserable.

As the years passed, tensions in the household only grew worse. Peninnah began having children, two sons and a daughter in the first five years. Hannah was barren. Peninnah used every opportunity to try to win over her husband's affections by pointing out Hannah's failure to give him an heir. Even at the thrice-annual conventions in Shiloh, she would mock Hannah's barrenness before the entire family.

His mother had told him repeatedly the story of how things had changed, of how he had come into her life. One day, during the Festival of Unfermented Cakes, she had knelt before the doors of the Tabernacle itself and begged Jehovah for a son. She had promised that if He answered her prayer, she would give the son to Jehovah, to serve Him in the Tabernacle all the days of his life as a Nazirite. So intently had she prayed that High Priest Eli had mistaken her for drunk.

But Jehovah had heard her prayer. Within the month, she was pregnant. That was why Samuel was so much more than just a son to his parents, and especially to his mother. He was the miraculous answer to a desperate mother's prayer, the heir to his father's name and property, living evidence of Jehovah's concern and His power to provide whatever his people needed.

They had explained the Nazirite vow to Samuel when he was still young and had continued explaining it to him until he could repeat the passages from the Torah in his sleep: "If a man or a woman vows to live as a Nazirite before Jehovah, he must abstain from all alcohol. For all the days of his vow, he must not eat anything made from the grapevine, from the unripe grapes to the skins. And no razor should pass over his head; until the full measure of the days of his dedication to Jehovah come to the full, he must be separated to Jehovah and prove himself holy by letting the locks of the hair of his head grow. And he must not draw near to any dead soul. Not even for his father, his mother, his brother, or his sister may he defile himself when they die, because the sign of his Naziriteship is upon his head."

For most Nazirites, 'all the days of their vow' were a year, or even less, after which time they returned to their normal lives. But his mother had dedicated Samuel as a Nazirite before he was even conceived. Her vow was binding on him all his life.

His early years at the Tabernacle were gone, swallowed by the passing of time, except for a few glimpses still lingering in his memory: High Priest Eli, before his blindness, honoring his mother's sacrifice by giving Samuel the job of opening the gate each morning; Judge Jephthah's daughter, Tirzah, coming and befriending him at a time when he felt so alone he could not seem to stop weeping. He could even remember the wonder he had felt as he gradually realized what it really meant to be a Nazirite, the sacred privilege endowed by his parents: to serve in the most holy location in the holy city of Shiloh, at the heart of the holy land of Israel. Every male in Israel was required to come to Shiloh three times in the year for the annual festivals, and every woman had to come to honor Tirzah four days in the month of Shebat, so that in his gate-keeping duties, Samuel ended up seeing the faces of almost everyone in the nation. And they did not fail to notice him—his waist-length hair identified him to everyone as a Nazirite for life, the famous young gatekeeper of Shiloh. He saw the distance in their eyes when they looked at him.

Now, the word of Jehovah had become rare in Shiloh.

Worshippers continued entering the gate, and he looked over the offerings they brought with them. Elders in different regions had sent representatives with large, clay vessels of olive oil, the firstfruits of the season. But it was less than in previous years. The animals were often smaller and thinner than they should have been. And the people showed signs of hunger and weakness as well. He saw eyes haunted by desperation.

Something was happening to Israel, to the land, but Samuel did not know what it was. He had tried to talk to Ahitub about it, but the Priest would not tell him anything. At least, he would not *say* anything—the look in his eyes when Samuel had asked the question told Samuel a great deal. Whatever was happening, Ahitub was afraid of it.

He began making his way toward the Altar where he could glimpse Ahitub working alongside other Priests. Perhaps his mentor could find the time to talk to Samuel about it this morning. As he walked, he passed a woman hurrying by, head bowed and face hidden in her head covering. He did not need to see her face to recognize her. She was Mara, Phinehas' wife and Ahitub's mother, and she was seven months pregnant. Her pregnancy had come as a shock to everyone at Shiloh, as much because of her advanced age as because of the public infidelity of her husband. She rarely showed her face in the Tabernacle these days, driven into seclusion by the shame Phinehas heaped upon her. The last time Samuel had seen her, two Sabbaths before, he had been shocked by how much she had aged, her dark hair shot through with streaks of grey, the skin around her wide, brown eyes wrinkled and dark.

Samuel reached the Altar and stood to one side, waiting while Ahitub finished assisting an elderly couple who were sacrificing a male goat as a sin offering. Another Priest had already slit the animal's throat and caught the steaming blood in a copper bowl. Ahitub dipped his fingers into the crimson liquid and walked slowly around the Altar, smearing a portion of the blood on each of the Altar's four horns. The Priest assisting him poured the rest of the blood down the drain at the base of the Altar.

The Priest then cut the fat from the flesh and handed it to Ahitub, who flopped it onto the copper grating; it hissed for a moment and the two elderly supplicants raised their arms toward the ascending smoke and prayed silently for acceptance of their offering. The Priest cut the remaining flesh into various pieces: a portion for the Priests to eat was dropped into an earthenware pot of water sitting on braziers filled with glowing coals from the Altar's firebox. The water boiled until the meat was sufficiently cooked, and then Levites lifted the pot from the coals and removed the meat with long, copper forks. Then they poured out the water into the drain at the base of the Altar, and lifting the pot above their heads, smashed it against the Courtyard flagstones. The sound of it shattering punctuated the constant murmur of voices, the bleating and lowing of animals, and roar of the Altar fire. The offering that had been boiled in it symbolically bore the sins, and even the tiniest fragment of sacrificial flesh that remained in the pot would render it ceremonially unclean. It had to be destroyed so that it could never be used for any sacred purpose again.

Samuel looked down at the shards of pottery, scattered among hundreds of similar fragments and piles of foot-printed clay powder from offering pots broken earlier in the day. Moses had written so many safeguards into the Torah to keep Israel spiritually clean, to maintain the level of holiness required for them to commune with Jehovah in worship. And in spite of it all, corruption had found its way into Shiloh.

He raised his eyes to the shrouded walls of the Tabernacle, thinking about the Ark of the Covenant within the Holy of Holies and the miraculous *Shekinah* still burning above the outstretched wings of the cherubs on the Ark's lid. Only Jehovah could extinguish that flame; its continued presence was a constant assurance to Israel that Jehovah was watching over them.

He was about to pray when a grating voice from behind him interrupted his thoughts. "So the little gatekeeper prays before the Tabernacle—just like his mother!"

He turned to find Hophni standing and watching him. A sardonic smile twisted the Priest's wide, thin-lipped mouth, and his neck was so short that the jowls of his bulging cheeks hung almost to his narrow shoulders. Samuel remembered that the Priest had seen him singing that morning, directing the condemnation in the song's words at Hophni and his brother. He scanned his face anxiously: *Flared nostrils. Pupils dilated. Hints of tensed muscles beneath the layers of fat: Fear or anger.*

"You are so loyal, Samuel, so faithful in carrying out your little task," Hophni said, his voice heavy with sarcasm.

He leaned in closer, and the mocking smile disappeared. "I know what you are," he whispered. "Others may believe your act, but you cannot fool the Priests of the Most High. You look at me in judgment, but it is your sins that stand out clearly in the sight of God! You pretend to be righteous, but inside you crave badness. Can you honestly deny it?"

Samuel said nothing. He realized that he was playing with the end of his braid, and forced his hands to be still.

Hophni shook his head. "You will never be the great person you desire to be—no matter how long or hard you try, you will always be nothing."

Samuel looked at the ground, wishing he knew what to say, wishing he had the authority or the courage to lash back at the Priest with cold power. But there was too much truth in Hophni's words. He knew that he did not deserve the reputation he had. People came to Shiloh and praised him, never realizing that their faith was greater than his own was. He thought of a clever retort, but swallowed it, and was silent.

"Your family arrives tomorrow," Hophni said. "It is your father's shift of duty, is it not? I recommend that you learn to show proper respect for the High Priest and his brother, or we may be forced to discipline you before the eyes of your parents, and your siblings. Or, something very…unpleasant could happen to your mother or your sisters while they are here."

Samuel looked up then, rage and fear burning through him. Hophni smiled at his reaction, the cold smile of a serpent. "Oh! The child is angry!"

The Priest turned on his heel and sauntered away, chuckling to himself. Samuel remained still a few moments, trying to wrestle his anger into submission. When he was calm again, he scurried to his room, his questions for Ahitub forgotten, and tears burning the corners of his eyes.

The next morning, when Samuel opened the gate, an old man was standing in the crowd, leaning upon a staff, cackling softly to himself, a wrinkled, stooped old man with eyes as bright as a bird's. At the moment Samuel swung the doors wide, a wind burst in through the opening, a warm summer's-breath of a wind that leapt eagerly between the gateposts and into the Tabernacle enclosure, brushing Samuel's skin with ethereal fingers. He turned and watched the wind make its way across the Courtyard, whipping the cloaks of the guards, scattering ashes from the Altar, painting rows of marching lines across the water of the copper Laver, and billowing the heavy layers of fabric shrouding the Tabernacle itself.

He turned back toward the crowd and saw the old man staring at him, smiling glee and expectation. "The arms of one house I shall cut off," the old man said, rubbing his palms together as if he were about to dig into a long-anticipated meal. "But another I will raise up, a child in Shiloh, and I will fill his hand with power!"

Samuel let himself smile back, not knowing why, confused by the old man's words, not sure how to feel, except that somehow the man's presence, the wind, and the spiders-legs of chill running up and down his spine spoke to him.

They told him that, at last, change had come to Shiloh.

16

At that moment, Samuel's mother rushed to him and threw her arms around him. He could feel her body shake with her weeping as she clung to him. He glanced over her shoulder, through the strands of dark brown hair that had pulled free of her head covering and tickled his ears, but the strange old man had disappeared somewhere into the crowd.

"Samuel! Oh, my Samuel," Hannah whispered over and over again into his ear. "Oh, how you have grown!"

She released him from her embrace, only to hold him at arm's length, one tepid palm pressed to each of his cheeks. "You look more like your father every time I see you!"

Her wide, brown eyes, as gentle and warm as a young doe's, were shining and wet with emotion. His mother's mouth had always seemed to him unsuited for anything but laughing or weeping, and he watched both expressions dance across it like the play of sunlight though rustling leaves. *Full lips open slightly, and then shut. Corners of mouth turn up; bites bottom lip, then corners of mouth turn down. Eyes blink repeatedly.* Samuel felt the flush of embarrassment warming the skin of his face. He looked past his mother to where the rest of his family stood.

His family. It felt wrong to call them that, these half-strangers that he saw only three or four times a year. His father, Elkanah, beamed at him from a few feet away; gathered around him were Samuel's two half-brothers, his half-sister, and his two younger whole brothers. Peninnah, Elkanah's second wife, was not with them; she did not travel to Shiloh anymore with the family. One of his brothers held a woven rope whose other end looped the neck of a yearling lamb. "Ah, my son!" Elkanah said. "My firstborn!"

His siblings smiled at him, too, but it was not the smile they reserved for each other. It was the deliberate smile that a person put on for someone they wanted to feel comfortable, to feel accepted—a smile that was the child of kindness and courtesy. It was not the smile he saw pass between other brothers and sisters who visited Shiloh. It was not the unguarded, unrehearsed smile that took control of a person's face when they encountered those things in their life that sparked emotion unasked-for in the heart, the flash of childish ecstasy that stretched your visage whether you wanted it to or not.

He smiled back. The deliberate smile. It wasn't that he didn't love his family—he did, a love that went beyond what he could express but that lay quietly in some forgotten corner of his heart. He knew there was nothing they could ask from him that he would not willingly give. And he knew, with equal certainty, that they would never ask anything of him. They had each other. They had their mother and father. He was alone in a way that they could never understand, and his solitude was one they could not breach, even if they had wanted to.

Elkanah came forward and hugged him, and he embraced his brothers and sister as well. When his half-sister, a year older than him, put her arms around him, he felt her hands touch his braid, hanging down the center of his back. For the briefest instant, her hands jerked from the touch in surprise. When she pulled away and looked him in the face, he read her thoughts in the distant set of her eyes: *Nazirite from birth. Brother I do not know.*

They prayed together in silence as the incense rose, and then his mother was in front of him again, smile firmly in place now. She handed him a familiar bundle of folded linen. "Here is your gift," she said.

He took it from her and unfolded it, although he knew already what it was. A moment later, he held a new *me'il* in his hands, similar to the one that the Priests wore. "Thank you, Mother," he said, glancing down at the coat he wore, the one that she had made him the previous year. It was threadbare and clearly too small for him. "I'm afraid this coat has seen better days."

"I didn't get to finish it the way I wanted to," she said. Her smile was stiff—not due to any lack of love or kindness, but because her mind was too busy squelching the pride she might otherwise have felt at making a beautiful garment for her son. "But at least I finished it."

He looked back up at her, trying to read her expression. *Eyebrows slightly raised. Eyes opened wider than normal. Glancing from him to the new coat. Shoulders tight.* He knew she wanted to watch him put the new garment on, but today he could not bring himself to change clothes in front of his siblings and all the people who flowed past them in and out of the

Courtyard. "I will join Father at the spring for the morning ablutions," he told her. "Then I won't be putting a clean coat on over a dirty body."

She nodded, but said nothing. He could see in her eyes that she was disappointed, and he hugged her again. "Thank you so much. It's beautiful."

She smiled back at him briefly, and then looked away, less comfortable with his compliments than if he had begun shouting obscenities in front of her.

They left the lamb to his mother's care. Samuel followed his father and brothers out the gate and down Shiloh's main avenue as the daily Psalm echoed from the Courtyard wall. The city was waking around them, merchants and hawkers setting up their booths and stalls, pilgrims and petitioners wending their way through the maze of buildings toward the Tabernacle, leading sheep, goats, and cattle or carrying baskets and bundles of various offerings. The street was alive with smells as the humid air blended the pungent odor of livestock with the perfume of ointment makers and the startling scents of spice merchants.

Outside the city gate, a broad trail paralleled the wall, following it south, then west. Hills rose above the city in every direction but southwest, where a broad valley of sunburnt grass awaited festival crowds to fill it with tents and makeshift shelters. On the terraced hillsides below them, sunrise oranged the gnarled trunks of the olive groves and the roping vineyards. Shepherds and their flocks wandered slowly among the rocky valleys and pasturelands, and old, stacked-stone watchtowers squatted atop a few distant hilltops. Sometimes, when Ahitub gave him leave to wander outside the city, he would make his way to one of those watchtowers to sit and just watch the scenery below him. On a couple of occasions he had seen shaggy, brown Aramaic bears wander out from the scattered trees, meandering across the hillsides with their funny, swinging gait.

In the shadow of the southern wall, the trail widened and led to a yawning cave mouth that opened amidst a tumble of mossy boulders. A spring bubbled out through cracks in the rock a short distance into the grotto, and flowed to a stone-lined, circular pool the city's earliest inhabitants had built in front of the cave. As Samuel and his father and brothers approached, Samuel could see a dozen other men already standing in the water to their knees, stripped to their undergarments and splashing their faces and arms.

Elkanah and his sons pulled off their own clothing and waded in. In the chill morning air, the water was frigid; they entered with indrawn gasps of breath. Samuel saw his father watching him, his broad smile showing a flash of white teeth amidst his dripping beard. "It is good to be here with you, my son," Elkanah said. He looked around at Samuel's brothers. "With all of my sons."

An old man leaned against the edge of the pool nearby, rubbing a wet cloth over his wrinkled skin. "You have been given a full quiver," he said to Elkanah.

Samuel's father nodded. "I am most blessed among men." He pointed at Samuel. "Among my arrows is Samuel, gatekeeper of the House of the True God."

"Ahhh," said the old man, nodding and peering at Samuel with watery eyes. "I thought I recognized him. A Nazirite from birth, eh? Then you are twice blessed."

Elkanah beamed at Samuel, and he pretended not to notice, busying himself with washing. His father's commendation only furthered the immeasurable distance that already separated him from his siblings. He watched them out of the corner of his eye, noting their easy conversation with his father and with each other and the ready understanding they shared that comes only from endless days and nights spent together.

When they emerged together from the pool, Samuel pulled on his mother's coat. As always, it was too big. He knew that she made it too big on purpose, so that it would continue to fit him while he grew. But putting on oversized clothing always made him feel smaller than he was, reminding him that he was only a child serving among men. Trying to ignore the way it dragged about his ankles, he followed his father and brothers back into the city.

They met up with his mother and sisters in the Courtyard and together went to the Altar to offer their sacrifice. Ahitub greeted Samuel's family warmly and accepted the lamb while another Priest raked the coals with a shard of earthenware.

Samuel's little brother leaned down and caressed the lamb they had brought. Samuel could not hear his words, but he saw the expression on his face and read what must have been going on in his brother's mind. He had watched this lamb be born, had fed it from his hand, had spent days and weeks watching over it as it grew. Samuel wished he had the words to tell his little brother how much the sacrifice meant to Jehovah and that he, Samuel, appreciated what his brother was giving up as well. But to do so felt like it added to the distance between them, as if Samuel were trying to set himself up as more lofty than his siblings.

Hannah chattered excitedly, explaining the Tabernacle furnishings and rites to the youngest children, her soft hands reaching out to stroke Samuel's shoulder or head whenever he was near. Samuel had to smile watching her—his mother had always loved the ancient traditions, the formality and ritual of it. He knew that she had passed that love on to him, and at that moment, he felt that this love was perhaps the thing that let him remain in Shiloh without going mad. When so much in the Tabernacle had been corrupted, the rites of the Torah remained as they always had been, a link to Israel's hallowed past. No matter how complicated his relationship with his mother was, he was grateful beyond words that she had given him her adoration of Israel's heritage. Israelite blood in one's veins was an accident of birth; being a true Son of the Torah in one's heart was a gift—and one that grew rarer with every passing year.

The Priests had just finished separating the fat and were getting ready to place it upon the Altar when Hophni appeared near the Tabernacle entrance with three of his Attendants, men who followed and obeyed him in an attempt to share in whatever power he wielded over others. Samuel glanced over at Ahitub, who had seen his uncle as well. *Breath coming faster, more shallow. Movements hurried. Shoulders tensed. Muscle in jaw working as teeth clenched.*

He turned back toward Hophni, who was speaking to the Attendants. The men nodded, and all three Attendants approached the Altar. Samuel prayed silently, desperately: *Please! Not now! Not my family!*

Ahitub looked at Elkanah and Hannah from under lowered brows. "Elkanah. Perhaps you should take your family over to the booths, and wait there for the offering to be finished."

Elkanah looked puzzled but put an arm around Hannah and would have led her away. But Samuel's mother shook her head vehemently. "No! I do not...I want to stay! Why must we leave, my lord?"

Samuel ground his teeth, seeing Hophni's Attendants drawing closer. "Please, Mother," he whispered. "Go with Father."

She looked from Ahitub to Samuel to Elkanah, then reached out and took her two youngest children's hands in her own. "I don't understand! This offering is made in our behalf. Why should we not stay and watch it?"

There was no time for an answer. The Attendants arrived, and stopped a few paces from the Altar. Samuel's parents looked at them in confusion, unsure what they were doing there, and his little brother hid behind his mother's skirts. Ahitub pretended to ignore them and began to place the fat upon the grating; the flames sizzled and rose in eager tongues to meet the dripping grease.

"Wait, Priest!" one of the Attendants, a man named Mallothi, called out. He sauntered closer to Ahitub, a thin, hawk-nosed man with a protruding Adam's apple: *Eyes narrowed. Walks too close to people, expecting them to make way. Sneering.*

Mallothi reached the Altar and lifted one of the copper, three-pronged forks that hung there, tapping the prongs against his palm. "Give us some meat from that lamb for Chief Priest Hophni."

Ahitub raised his eyes from his task and met the arrogant gaze of the Attendant. "The fat has not yet been offered to Jehovah. When the Torah has been satisfied, Hophni's portion will be sent to him."

Mallothi swaggered closer to Ahitub, pointing at the Priest's chest with the fork. "Hophni doesn't want boiled meat," he said. "He wants it raw. And make sure that some of the fat is left on his pieces." He reached past Ahitub and poked at the meat sizzling on the altar with the fork, inspecting it.

Ahitub batted his arm aside. "Do not dare to touch what is holy!" he said, his voice low and venomous.

Mallothi's face darkened, and he was about to respond, but suddenly Elkanah stepped forward, palms raised. "Please! Please, my lord," he addressed the Attendant. "Let the offering take place as prescribed by the Torah. I myself will see to it that one of the legs is brought to Hophni—"

Samuel felt a scream seeking a way to his mouth. Mallothi turned on Elkanah in a rage, the copper fork brandished before him like a weapon. "Don't presume to talk to me, Levite!" he shouted. "You would do well to remember your place! Chief Priest Hophni will take whatever portion he desires!"

He turned and stabbed the fork into the boiling pot next to the Altar until he brought up a gobbet of flesh, splashing hot water and grease across Elkanah's face; Samuel's father stumbled backwards, wiping at his eyes with the back of his hands.

"This he will take, if he wants it!" Mallothi growled. He skewered a piece of fat from off of the Altar grate. "And this!" He reached out and tore an uncooked piece of flesh from the hands of the Priest assisting Ahitub. "And this!"

"What are you doing?" Hannah said, her voice shrill, one palm pressed to each cheek. Samuel's little brother began to cry, clinging to Hannah's skirts.

Samuel felt his hands balling into fists of their own accord, and a bitter ache opened in his stomach. He saw the looks of horror on the faces of his family, the anger in his father's eyes. *Lips drawn tight. A knot appearing and disappearing on his jaw, beneath his ear.*

Do not speak, Father, he pleaded silently.

"Do not dishonor Jehovah in this way, please," Elkanah said. "You will bring ostracism upon Israel."

Mallothi pushed forward until his nose was a hand's-breadth from Elkanah's nose. "And who are you to dictate to the Chief Priest of the Tabernacle?"

"I *am* a Priest!" Ahitub stepped forward as well, lifting the rest of the fat and throwing it onto the altar grating. "A Priest and a grandson of High Priest Eli! And I say that Hophni dishonors his office!"

Mallothi glared at Ahitub, and Samuel held his breath in fear. Then like a snake, Mallothi lashed out with one hand and struck Elkanah viciously across the cheek. The force of the blow battered Samuel's father sideways, and Hannah cried out and stumbled toward him. "Maybe that will teach you not to disrespect the Attendants of Priest Hophni!" Mallothi growled, then turned and strode off towards his master.

Elkanah's cheek was already turning red. Ahitub finished offering what was left of the sacrifice mechanically. "I am sorry, Elkanah," he said in a whisper. "I am so sorry."

Tirzah suddenly appeared at Hannah's side, grasping her elbow. "Come, Hannah. Bring the children."

Samuel gave a silent prayer of thanks to Jehovah for the quick thinking of Jephthah's daughter. Herding Samuel and his siblings, Tirzah led them away from the Altar and across the Courtyard. Elkanah followed a short distance behind. Samuel saw his father watching as Hophni's Attendants delivered the stolen meat to their master, then turning away in anger. They were nearing the dining booths built along the Curtain wall when Phinehas strode toward them. He glanced back at his brother, then smirked at the angry faces of Samuel's family. "Tirzah!"

She stopped, and Samuel's family stopped with her. "I have need of you," Phinehas said. "Send these people away and follow me."

Something in Phinehas' look caught Samuel's eyes: *Pupils dilated. Cheeks flushed. Nostrils flared. A subtle—and futile--tightening of the muscles of his stomach and chest.*

Tirzah hesitated, turning to Hannah and Elkanah. "We are alright," Elkanah said to her. "I will take my family to their quarters in the city and return for my duties tomorrow."

"Tirzah!" Phinehas said again, more loudly. Elkanah led his family away toward the gate while Tirzah turned to follow the big Priest the other direction across the Courtyard. After only a moment's hesitation, Samuel turned and followed Tirzah. He kept his distance, trying to avoid Phinehas' notice.

It quickly became apparent that the Priest was leading Tirzah toward his home. After a few moments, she stopped walking. Samuel ducked behind one of the pillars at the corner of the Priest's quarters. Phinehas must have heard her footsteps cease—he stopped as well, turning toward her inquisitively. "Well?"

"What is it you would have me do, my lord?" she asked. Even from a distance, Samuel could hear the quaver in her voice.

"I will tell you when we get there." He smiled at her, but it was a serpent's smile, a mask to hide a forked tongue.

Tirzah was still not moving. "Please, my lord, do not be angry with your maidservant. I wish to know where we are going."

Phinehas put his hands on his enormous hips and took three slow steps toward her until he was standing only a hand's breadth away. Then he reached out and felt her hair between his thick, blunt fingers, as if he was testing the quality of a piece of fabric. "You have become a very beautiful woman, Tirzah." He exhaled the last syllable of her name slowly.

Samuel swallowed hard, watching. Tirzah said nothing, but he could tell that every muscle in her body was poised to flee.

"They say that to bear the child of a Priest is to be forever blessed," Phinehas continued, still fingering her hair. The red tip of his tongue played against one corner of his mouth. "Do you not wish for blessings, Tirzah?"

Samuel saw the abrupt movements of her shoulders as her breathing quickened. "Please, my lord. Do not do this."

"Do what?" He smiled benignly. "Bring pleasure to a beautiful woman? It was Jehovah who put these…desires within us." His eyes studied her body, and his hand fell from her hair to her shoulder and slid along it. "It was Jehovah who made us capable of—."

"No!" She pulled away, her hands balled into fists at her sides, her teeth clenched. "Do not do this!"

His smile disappeared, replaced by the snarl of a predator. "I can take you by force, woman! I am High Priest! Do you think I cannot do with you whatever I wish?"

"You cannot, Priest Phinehas." She kept her eyes lowered respectfully, but no uncertainty weakened her voice.

"Cannot?" He laughed derisively. "I could have you brought to silence!" he threatened. "I could drag you to my home right now, and no man here would dare stop me! What makes you think I cannot?"

She looked up at him then, and Samuel recognized the fierce look of her father in her cold eyes, and the rage that blazed suddenly in her made her voice hard and chill. "Because I am the daughter of Jephthah ben Gilead, Judge of Israel! If you touch me, my father and his armies will descend on you with the wrath of God in their hands, and he will raze this place to the ground, and after your execution he will make the name of Phinehas, son of Eli, a curse to time indefinite!"

Her words and her intensity set him back, and for a moment Samuel saw the fear that her father's name had kindled in his eyes. "So be it," he finally answered, his words slow and deliberate. Glancing around, he saw a Levite passing some distance off and called him to him. "Take this woman to the Altar," he told him. "Tell the Priests on duty that she is to spend the rest of the day carrying the offal out of the city. Phinehas commands it!"

The Levite hesitated, but then nodded. Tirzah strode to his side and then followed him toward the Altar. Samuel felt his heartbeat pounding in his throat and the taste of metal filled his mouth.

"Perhaps your father and I will meet, one day," Phinehas called after her. "I am not afraid of that meeting!" But his words sounded hollow even from a distance, and she did not turn.

Phinehas slammed the door of his home open and disappeared inside. Samuel waited for just a moment, then ran around the Tabernacle to his own room and, ducking within, threw himself onto the bed, trying to stop his racing thoughts. The events of the morning played repeatedly in his mind, and he imagined himself doing everything differently. He thought of kinder words for his mother, words to make his father proud, clever retorts to Hophni's Attendant, cutting rebukes for Phinehas. He cursed his inability to do anything right and his lack of courage when evil reared its head. He felt at times as if he were nothing but a shadow, able to see every symptom of the sickness that plagued Shiloh, but without the power or substance to do anything about it. *No*, he corrected himself. *You have power enough. You just choose to do nothing.*

All his life he had been told stories of the heroes of Israel, men and women who took action when they saw corruption or wickedness around them. He wanted to be like them, like the Joshuas and Gideons of Israel's gloried past. Since Judge Jephthah had become ill, even he was taking no action to lead the nation into following Jehovah's standards. But action was what Israel needed—now, perhaps, more than ever before. Something terrible was happening to their people. Samuel saw it. He saw it every day, but he was doing nothing but watching.

He tried to sit up, but his new *me'il* caught under him and he angrily pulled it free. He felt like he had spent his whole life trying—and failing—to fulfill someone's hopes. He saw the expectation in his mother's eyes every time she came to visit him, her undying belief that he would somehow become more than he was. He thought of the way that his brothers and sister had looked at him, as if he was a different creature than they were. It made him angry, this separateness that had been forced upon him. He knew he was not the same as other children—the miraculous circumstances of his birth, the Nazirite vow he lived under, his parent-less childhood in Shiloh all set him apart from every other child he knew. He could not hide it—the long braid hanging down his back proclaimed his separateness to everyone who saw him. But his loneliness went beyond the requirements of his circumstances. It felt like the people around him, even his own family, did not want him to belong to the same world they lived in. Like his mother, they looked at him and expected more than they even asked of themselves. In one way or another, he had spent all of his life striving and failing to fill the coat that someone else had made for him.

He heard a rustling sound at his doorway and turned just in time to see the heavy cloth that hung there pushed aside. A man stepped into his room, a wrinkled, stooped old man who looked at him with piercing blue eyes, as bright as a bird's, nodding gently to himself as if Samuel were the answer to a question he had been pondering.

"May you have peace, Samuel," the old man said with a cackling laugh. "I am the prophet Rohgah."

17

Samuel stared, unsure whether he should be frightened or not by this strange, old man who had suddenly appeared in his room. It took him a moment to realize that this was the same man he had seen when he had opened the gates that morning.

"You are a prophet?" he asked, immediately realizing how silly the question was.

"You don't listen very well, do you?" Rohgah asked, shaking his wrinkled head. Only then did Samuel remember his manners and stand awkwardly, gesturing toward his low bed, the only piece of furniture in his room. "Please, grandfather—have a seat here. Please…let me get you something to eat or drink."

Rohgah shuffled over and slowly lowered himself onto the bed next to Samuel, groaning with the effort. He sighed deeply and patted the blankets next to him. "Sit, little Samuel."

Samuel obeyed, smelling travel-stained clothing, the scent of earth and leaves mingled with the pungent odor of some animal's sweat. "You have traveled far?" he asked.

A crooked smile twisted the old man's face, and he cackled softly. "Do you know what it is to be a Prophet for the True God?"

The question took Samuel by surprise, and he struggled to come up with an answer. Was the man asking if he knew how far he had come with his message? Or about the nature of a Prophet's assignment: to have God speak to you, to know the future, to be commissioned by the Sovereign Lord of all Creation? He realized that he had never really thought about it before.

"To be a messenger sent by Jehovah?" he answered.

Rohgah's blue eyes were fiercely bright; he waved his hand dismissively. "Yes, yes. That is the standard answer. But Prophets are also called Seers. Why?"

Samuel turned from the old man's intense gaze, staring instead at the floor. "Because they see things that are hidden from other men?"

Rohgah reached over and gently turned Samuel's chin until he was looking at the Prophet again, and Samuel felt a thrill prickling his scalp and the back of his neck. "What do *you* see, Samuel?"

Samuel shook his head. "I don't know what you mean…"

Rohgah reached out with his other hand and grabbed Samuel's arm in a grip like iron. "Think, boy! What are the ideas that go through your mind when you open the gates each morning, the thoughts you do not dare to tell to anyone else? What do you *see?*"

Samuel swallowed, feeling more uncomfortable by the minute. He examined the old man's face and saw no signs there of anger, or deception—only a burning intensity that glowed from within. "I see people struggling to keep hope alive in their hearts," he answered in a rush. "I see failing crops and herds. I see a sickness ravaging the land that infects more than the body. I see…I see a corruption that eats at the heart of Israel and threatens our very existence."

Rohgah released his arm and leaned back, nodding slowly. "Failed crops. Hunger. Disease. Barrenness. Threats and dangers, ready to pounce and devour us. Do you know the name the Torah gives to this beast that even now crouches at our door?"

Samuel shook his head.

"Malediction." Rohgah's eyes flashed. "It is called the Malediction.

"And it must occur," he intoned, "that if you will not listen to the voice of Jehovah your God by doing all that He commands and obeying all of His laws, then this Malediction will certainly overtake you: Cursed will you be in the city, and cursed will you be in the field. Cursed will be your gathering basket and your kneading trough. Cursed will be the fruit of your belly and the fruitage of your soil, the young of your cattle, and the offspring of your flock. Cursed will you be when you come in, and cursed will you be when you go out.

"Jehovah will send upon you the curse, confusion, and rebuke in every undertaking of yours, until you have been annihilated, because of the badness of your practices in that you have forsaken your God."

Rohgah's eyes bored into Samuel. "Do you not see it, little Samuel? Do you not see it happening all around us?"

Samuel nodded. He remembered other aspects of the Malediction, then, images that had filled his mind when Ahitub, or someone else, had read to him from the Torah years before: people ravaged by terrible sickness, flocks and herds lying dead in parched, yellow fields, wild animals roaming the streets of empty cities, and an enemy nation slaughtering and besieging until Israel's desperation drove them to unthinkable acts of self-preservation.

He pictured his family at their home in Ramathaim-zophim, their skin drawn and pale from hunger, their eyes wide with fear. He thought of his father trying desperately to protect his mother and sister from the spears of cruel warriors who descended on their village. He found that he could not force his mind to dwell on the thoughts.

"Can it be stopped? Can it be overcome?" he asked.

Rohgah leaned back and slowly rubbed his hands together. "Just before the Torah warns of the Malediction, it describes blessings that may also be experienced by the nation that is obedient. 'And it must occur that if you unfailingly listen to the voice of Jehovah your God by carefully doing all of His commandments, Jehovah your God will certainly raise you above all other nations of the earth. And all these blessings must come upon you and overtake you because you keep listening to the voice of Jehovah your God.

"'Jehovah will cause your enemies who rise against you to be defeated by you. By one way they will come against you, but by seven ways they will flee before you. Jehovah will bless your stores of supply and every undertaking of yours, and He will certainly bless you in the land that He is giving to you. Jehovah will establish you as a holy people to Himself, just as He swore to you, because you continue to keep the commandments of Jehovah your God, and you have walked in His ways. And all the people of the earth will have to see that Jehovah has put His name upon you, and they will indeed be afraid.

"'Jehovah will also make you overflow indeed with prosperity in the fruit of your belly and the fruit of your domestic animals and the fruitage of your ground. Jehovah will open to you his good storehouse, the heavens, to give the rain on your land in its season and bless every deed of your hand; and you will certainly lend to many nations while you yourself will not borrow.'"

Rohgah clasped his hands and nodded. "So it is written in the Torah."

Samuel's mind raced. He was still trying to figure out what this strange old man was doing in his room at all and why he was speaking to Samuel about these things. But the Prophet's words had woven their spell about Samuel's mind and pushed all other thoughts aside. All of the terrible things that were happening in the land around them, all of the trials that the nation was experiencing since Israel's defection from true worship—they were not an indication that Jehovah had left them. They proved the opposite—that His promises were trustworthy. Things were happening exactly as the True God had said that they would.

"What must be done, then, to overcome this Malediction, Samuel?" Rohgah asked.

"The nation must be cleansed," Samuel answered. "They must return to true worship, to all the teachings of the Torah. The festivals must be celebrated by all the people, and the Torah must be once again taught in every corner of the land."

"You are correct. But we must do more. We cannot kill this poisonous vine by plucking off its leaves."

Samuel looked at the Prophet, emboldened but unsure how to say what he was thinking. "The...the Tabernacle must also be cleansed."

"The corruption of Eli's sons is a plague that is strangling Israel!" Rohgah's eyes were bright and cold. "We will not be healed until this corruption is torn from the heart of Shiloh!"

Samuel glanced at his door, his heart racing with fear, wishing the Prophet would lower his voice. He did not dare chide this old man, but he knew what would happen if Hophni or Phinehas heard him speaking this way.

But Rohgah was not done. "There is no greater, no more dangerous evil, than the man who believes his own opinions constitute truth!" In a softer tone, he asked, "Now, what will you do, Samuel?"

Samuel shrugged. "Me? I am only a child. I—."

Rohgah cut him off, waving his hand dismissively as though batting at a fly. "You are more than a child, Samuel. You are a Nazirite from birth, promised to Jehovah for sacred service in His house since before your mother conceived you. Do you think Jehovah's hand is cut short because you are young? The True God can use you for His purposes, no matter what your age. Youth does not relieve you of your obligation to do all that you can to obey Him."

He paused, looking into Samuel's eyes, and Samuel felt once again as if those eyes were piercing his thoughts and taking the measure of his soul. "When the time comes to act, Samuel, you will know."

The Prophet held his gaze a moment longer, and then stood abruptly, pulling himself up with his staff, one hand pressing against the small of his back. "I will leave you now. I must fulfill one more assignment before my time in Shiloh is ended." His eyes went distant, focused on something far beyond the walls of Samuel's room. "It will not be an easy task. I must prepare myself to carry out the will of Jehovah."

The Prophet turned without another word or a backward glance and strode through Samuel's door; the wool cloth hanging over the doorway flapped once, and was still.

Samuel was left sitting on the edge of his bed, his mind racing with unasked questions. But through it all, one thought stood out triumphantly, like a ringing trumpet call in the orchestra of his mind: Israel could be saved! The Tabernacle could be saved! Jehovah had not forgotten them. Samuel just needed to look for whatever role he could serve in accomplishing this purpose, what he could do to cleanse the Tabernacle and impel the people toward true worship. He knew that Ahitub and Tirzah would have ideas for him about how to do this...

Tirzah! He had completely forgotten about her and the punishment that Phinehas had given her. He jumped up and raced out into the Courtyard.

It took him some time to find her, but when he did he cursed himself for not guessing sooner where she would be. She was washing in the pool before the mouth of the cave outside the city walls. When he got close enough to see her clearly, his heart sank and tears sprang into his eyes. She was pouring pitchers of water over her bowed head, trying to rinse the blood and bits of flesh from her hair. She must not have been there for long--her dress was still sticky with blood and covered in matted animal hair. He watched for a moment as she scooped dampened ashes from a shallow bowl and scrubbed her skin with them.

She must have seen him from the corner of her eye because she turned abruptly toward him and, to his surprise, smiled broadly. She tossed back her long, wet hair, wringing it dry. "Samuel!"

Red water dripped from her dress into the pool. "I am so sorry, Tirzah," he whispered.

She laughed. "It is all right with me, Samuel. The work today was hard, but still honorable. Every task in the House of God is an assignment of honor. But don't come any closer!" She laughed again. "I don't want to get your beautiful new *me'il* dirty!"

"It is not a job for women!" Samuel protested, ignoring her teasing. "Phinehas had no right to...you should never have had to do it!"

She cocked her head sideways, rubbing water from her right eye. "Ahitub sent someone to relieve me after only two trips to the refuse dump. Have you ever had to lift a wet bull's skin onto a cart? I think it weighed twice as much as me!"

"Are you not angry?"

"I am happy to serve in whatever way I can. It is a rare privilege even to be here."

Samuel shook his head. "It is hard for me to see it that way sometimes."

"No it isn't. You treasure this assignment more than anyone I know. That is why the...the bad things that happen here affect you so much."

She looked out across the undulating hills and softly sang:

"How beautiful Your grand Tabernacle is,

O Jehovah of Armies!
My soul has yearned and pined away
    For the Courtyards of Jehovah
My heart and my flesh cry out joyfully
    To the Living God:
Happy are those dwelling in Your house!
    They still keep on praising You.
For a day in Your courtyards is better
    Than a thousand spent anywhere else."

She cupped water in her hands and washed her long, thin arms. "Jehovah will not leave his loyal ones, Samuel."

Samuel thought about what Rohgah had said, and for the first time in weeks he felt hope blossom in his heart. "And I will not leave Him," he whispered. He turned toward the city wall, picturing the gleaming copper pillars of the Tabernacle's entrance. "I will not let the Malediction consume us while there is breath in my body to fight it."

Somewhere in the distance, across the mountains of Judah and the hills of the Shephelah, thunder rumbled ominously in response.

18

When Samuel woke the next morning, he pulled his new *me'il* on over his head and hastened to the gate. It was not yet dawn, but he was eager to begin the new day, energized by Rohgah's words and imbued with a fresh sense of purpose. He was at the gate even before Eli arrived, and stood hugging his arms to his chest and hopping from one bare foot to another to keep warm in the chill morning air. He saw his father and his half-brothers enter the Courtyard through one of the side doors and take their positions, inspecting animals and assisting the Priests. He waved to them and Elkanah rewarded him with a wide smile.

Eli arrived, led by Ahimelech, the firstborn son of Ahitub, a child several years Samuel's junior. Shortly afterward, the morning rites commenced, and when the trumpet was blown, Samuel threw the doors open. He joined in the morning song with real zeal and felt the power of his singing lift away the last remnants of shadow that had been hanging over him for the past several Sabbaths.

When the song concluded and the people began filing into the Courtyard, Samuel stayed at the gate, watching and greeting them. A middle-aged man limped past, carrying a wicker cage in which a pair of turtledoves fluttered, wings spread to keep their balance on their perch. Samuel examined the man quickly: *Coat and cloak threadbare. Eyes downcast, but glancing at the more valuable offerings others were bringing. Ashamed at his poverty. Worried for his future.*

"May you find peace in Shiloh!" Samuel called out brightly, and the man turned, startled, confusion wrinkling his brow.

"Whatever your ills, whatever your fears, there is hope and joy to be found in the Tabernacle of Jehovah," Samuel said. "Leave your burdens here, with the Priests of the True God, and let His boundless mercy bear you swiftly back to your family."

The man smiled—the risible smile of a long-tethered joy unleashed. "May Jehovah bless you, Samuel ben Elkanah. Bless you, and your righteous heart."

Samuel glanced around again; a young couple approached the gate, leading a yearling lamb, small but healthy and white as new snow. The man stared at the road in front of him, but his wife raised her eyes to the column of smoke spiraling up from the Altar: *hands balled into fists at her sides; lips gently mouthing unheard words; eyes wet with yearning.*

"Jehovah is the Hearer of Prayers!" Samuel called to them, so loudly everyone nearby turned toward him. Some of them grinned at him like shepherds watching the antics of a newborn lamb, but he forced himself to ignore them. He saw that the young woman was staring at him in surprise, and he tried to look into her eyes as Rohgah had looked into his own the day before. "Do not be afraid," he said to her. "He reads even the desire of your heart. Come into His house of prayer with your sacrifice, and see if He does not return it to you tenfold!"

He saw tears glitter in the woman's eyes as she turned toward her husband who was now staring at Samuel as well, puzzlement and joy struggling for control of his features. They said nothing, but both quickened their pace and hurried through the gates toward the Altar.

An old man hobbled up the road, leaning on a gnarled staff with one hand and carrying a basket of figs and bread in the other. Samuel leapt to his side and took the basket from him. "Let me carry this for you, grandfather," he said, then put the man's free arm over his own shoulders and supported him as he shuffled toward the gate.

"Thank you, my child," the man said, wheezing. "May Jehovah see your kindness to an old man, and remember you for good."

"He already has," Samuel answered. "He has given me faithful examples like you, to teach me the true meaning of sacrifice and devotion."

The man chuckled softly. "You are Samuel, the gatekeeper of the House of God?"

Samuel nodded. "I am Samuel, and High Priest Eli gave me the assignment of opening the gates each morning when I was a son of five years—the kindness of an old man to an eager child."

"It is a privilege," the man said.

"It is. But the true blessing of this task is that it allows me to see the generosity and appreciation of our people."

They reached the line of penitents waiting to approach the Altar and stopped. Samuel handed the basket back to the man, who leaned down and kissed the top of his head. "Bless you, my child. Happy are the father and mother who gave you birth."

"And happy the grandchildren who play in the shadow of your home!" Samuel called back to him as he strode away toward the gate.

The next people who caught his eye were led by a heavy, middle-aged man wearing a pale linen robe trimmed in yellow and blue, with a necklace of rubies set in hammered gold hanging from his neck. He wore a tall, white turban on his head, wrapped by a slender golden chain, and swung a vermilion staff before him as he walked. Two women followed him. The first was tall, long-legged, and beautiful, but she walked with the same arrogant bearing as the man, her pale blue eyes finding only dissatisfaction in everything that met her gaze. Golden hoops glimmered in her nose and both ears, and a dozen or more gold and silver bracelets tinkled gently at her wrists with each delicate movement.

A black veil hid the other woman's face. She stumbled as she walked, led forward by a rough, palm-bark rope that had been looped around her neck over the veil; the rich man's fat hand gripped the other end. Her simple, wool dress was torn and threadbare, and her bare feet dark with blood and dust. When they were closer, Samuel saw that bruises purpled the woman's arms, and a filament of dried blood ran from under her veil down her neck.

The man saw Samuel staring. "You-boy! Bring me Phinehas! Tell him Argob, son of Enlil has arrived."

Samuel nodded and started to leave, then thought better of it. "Shall I send someone to tend to…to this woman's wounds?"

The man rolled his eyes and laughed, a short bark of sound. "No, little fool!" He turned toward the woman and spat at her feet. "Why heal she who is condemned to death?"

Samuel could not think of any appropriate response. He nodded again and bolted off to find Phinehas. It did not take him long—the Priest was standing near the Altar, looking over the offerings the people were bringing as if he were disappointed in all of them. When he saw Samuel approach, his face darkened with anger. "I am busy, Samuel! Go and…do whatever you do here."

Samuel bowed and swallowed his fear. "Forgive me, my lord Phinehas. I was sent by Argob, son of Enlil."

"Argob?" Phinehas eyebrows shot up. "Where is he?"

"At the gate—he just arrived."

"I hope you hurried, boy. Argob is one of the richest men in Judah. You don't keep a man like that waiting."

Phinehas gestured to a couple of Priests to accompany him and strode toward the gate. Samuel followed, weaving through the crowds of people and animals. When they reached the gate again, Argob bowed deeply. He did not seem to realize that as he did so he yanked on the rope in his hand and pulled the woman behind him to her knees. "High Priest Phinehas! May you have peace!"

"And peace to you, Argob. Have you a place to stay while you are here?"

"I am not staying—I don't dare leave my household for more than a few days. Even that may be enough time for that idiot son of mine to sink us all into poverty."

Phinehas nodded sympathetically. "Then let us help you get quickly on your way. What is your business in Shiloh?"

The man jerked his head back toward the veiled woman, still on her knees in the dirt behind him. "I caught another concubine lying down with another man," he said, as if he were discussing the weather. "I would have handled it myself, back in Anathoth, but you may remember the last time this happened…"

Phinehas continued nodding. "Some of the Elders there insisted that you bring these cases to Shiloh."

"I don't know why. Whether in Anathoth or Shiloh, adultery is adultery, and a stoning is a stoning."

Samuel went cold. The only reason the Elders would insist on such a thing was that they did not believe the man's testimony but were afraid for some reason to pronounce his concubine innocent. He looked at the veiled woman on her knees in the dirt. She raised her head at last, and in a voice that sounded as though she had been forced to eat dust, she said, "Please, my lords. My hands are clean in this. I have done nothing—."

Argob yanked at the rope around her neck again, and she fell onto her forearms on the gravel of the road. "Do not dare to speak to the High Priest, you filthy harlot!"

Phinehas looked around and saw that a crowd was gathering, watching with consternation. "You do have the two witnesses required by the Torah?"

The man looked at him in surprise. "Two witness…Well, yes, I suppose I do, if you insist on it! I am one witness, and…and…" He turned toward the tall woman who stood on the other side of him. "And Noalah, my new concubine, is the other. She saw it too—did you not, Noalah, my dove?"

Noalah bowed gracefully. "It is even as my lord says."

"Satisfied?" Argob asked. "I have business to attend to before I leave the city."

"Where is the man?" someone from the crowd yelled out.

Phinehas looked futilely for the speaker and cleared his throat. "Hmm. Yes, Argob—where is the man? The Torah says specifically: 'In case a man is found lying down with a woman already owned by a husband, then both of them must die together, the man and the woman.'"

Argob threw up his hands. "My lord High Priest—is it really necessary we drag this out? When I have put these problems in your hands before, you never hesitated to uphold the Torah. The woman is an adulteress! She is condemned to death by stoning, even as you have just quoted."

Phinehas said nothing in response, glancing at the angry faces of the growing crowd. Samuel realized he was holding his breath and released it slowly. He could not see Phinehas' face clearly, and he wondered what was going through the big man's mind. Perhaps he was thinking of Mara, his pregnant wife, abandoned to shame while he lay down with every woman he could drag into his bedchamber. Perhaps he was having a difficult time ordering someone's execution for adultery.

"So be it!" Argob said after a moment. "The man is dead. I would have brought him as well, but the night before we left, he was found dead in his bed. He must have killed himself in shame."

"He killed him!" the veiled woman cried, pointing at Argob. "Argob owed him money—."

Argob whirled and struck the woman brutally in the side of the head. She collapsed in a heap on the road, her shoulders shaking with weeping. The crowd murmured angrily. Argob looked up at Phinehas, snarling like an animal. "Am I speaking to the High Priest? Or did I travel all the way to Shiloh to have my case heard in the court of public opinion?"

"We don't stone adulterers in Shiloh!" the voice from the crowd called out again. "We make them High Priest!"

Blood flooded Phinehas' face and he whirled toward the sound of the voice. But the speaker did not identify himself, and no one in the crowd gave any indication as to who it was. Phinehas scowled at them all, then straightened and pushed back his shoulders. "It is written in the Torah: 'In case there should be found in your midst a woman who should practice what is bad in the eyes of Jehovah your God, you must bring that woman to your gates, and you must stone her with stones, and she must die. At the mouth of two or three witnesses she will die. The hand of the witnesses first of all should come upon her to put her to death, and the hand of all the people afterward; and you must clear out what is bad from your midst.'"

He looked around him at the angry crowd. "So Jehovah your God spoke to Moses. So it shall be done."

He turned to one of the Priests who had followed him, a short, stocky man with a thin, black beard. He whispered in the man's ear, but Samuel was close enough to hear his words. "Gather a crowd and bring them to the city gate. You know the type of people we need. And bring my sandals."

The Priest nodded and strode back into the Courtyard. Samuel began to shake. *This cannot be happening*, he thought. *He cannot really be going through with this.*

The condemned woman pulled the veil from her head and Samuel winced at what he saw there. Her whole face was a mass of bruises. Her top lip bulged, split in two places, and blood oozed from a gaping wound above her left eye. "Please!" she begged, her voice ragged and gasping. "Don't let him do this! I am innocent…"

Someone had apparently sent for Hophni, because the fat Priest shuffled out through the gates, panting, his jowls shaking with every heavy step. A dozen of his loyal minions followed him. He nodded at the rich Judean. "Argob." He turned toward his brother. "What's going on?"

"A stoning," said Phinehas.

Hophni looked back at the mob of his followers. "Get your sandals. Take her to the city gate," he instructed them.

The sycophants donned the footwear stored in the guardhouse. One grabbed each of the woman's arms and began to drag her backwards down the street. Hophni pointed at her with one thick finger and scowled at the crowd. "Look! Look and see, you sinners, what happens to the woman who fails to respect the Torah, and the power of the Priests!"

"I am innocent!" the woman cried again. "He is angry with me, and has found younger concubines…he accused his last concubine of this crime, and she, too, was stoned outside these walls…"

Her voice faded as the men dragged her farther down the street. Samuel felt a hand clamp down on his shoulder and looked up to see Hophni grinning down at him, his broad face split by his wide, thick-lipped smile. "You, too, Samuel. You are zealous to uphold the Torah, are you not? Then come and demonstrate that zeal!"

He began walking, his hand still fastened on Samuel's shoulder, pushing him down the street ahead of him. As they made their way through the city, Samuel saw people emerging from houses and shops to follow the crowd. Some of them jeered at the woman or spat at her feet, not realizing the speciousness of her conviction. But most just stood and stared, or walked slowly behind her, their faces grim and set.

The procession eventually made its way to the gates of the city and pushed outside. The Elders who sat to one side of the gate stood and joined the crowd, approaching Phinehas with confusion etched on their features.

"Today we uphold the Law in Israel," the Priest said to them. "This woman is an adulteress, and she must be stoned."

Samuel saw one of the Elders place himself in Phinehas' path.: *Hands shaking. Breathing shallow and quick. Legs spread wide in forced determination. Knuckles white where he clutched his vermilion staff.* "Did the woman confess her sin?"

Phinehas crossed his arms over his chest and answered loudly, playing to the crowd. "Sadly, she has added lying and false accusation to her sin of adultery. Clearly a woman without remorse."

The Elder still stood in Phinehas' way. "Are there three trustworthy witnesses to the crime?" he asked.

Phinehas looked down his nose at the Elder. "The Torah requires only two witnesses. Her owner, an Elder of Anathoth, and his concubine have come themselves with the charge."

"It is our tradition to have at least three witnesses to a capital offense," the Elder said.

"The word of the High Priest has strength beyond any tradition," said Phinehas. "I tell you she is guilty."

The Elder looked into Phinehas eyes. "And you have seen fit to condemn this woman to death for…adultery?"

Phinehas bared his teeth and his nostrils flared. "Get out of my way!" He took a broad step, closing the distance between them. In a hissing whisper, he added, "Or you may find yourself *shammata*, expelled from the congregation of Israel."

The Elder hesitated only a moment, and then stepped aside to let Phinehas pass. Phinehas raised his arms above his head and looked around at the crowd. "You people of the land are ignorant of the Torah, and so I may let your sins pass by. But the Torah is clear—hear this, and remember it well: 'If a judicial case is brought before the Priests, they must hand down to you their decision. Then you must do in accordance with the word that they will hand down to you.'" He turned toward the Elder who had questioned him. "'And the man who dares to behave presumptuously in not listening to the judgment of the Priest—that man must die, and you must clear out what is bad from Israel.' So it is written in the Law of Moses."

He beckoned to Argob and began walking again. The rest of the mob straggled forward as well, and Hophni, chuckling, followed them, pushing Samuel ahead of him.

Not far outside the gates, the main road passed a rocky abutment that jutted through a pile of tumbled stones. On the other side of it, the land dropped away sharply for about twice the height of a man, and at the bottom was a rock-strewn hollow, as big around as the city gate. Argob led the woman to the edge of the precipice, and Phinehas took his place beside them. He waited until the crowd had gathered in a rough half-circle. Samuel saw among the watching faces many of the Priests and Levites who had taken up with Hophni and Phinehas. He also saw the young couple he had greeted that morning at the Tabernacle gates. The man was staring at Phinehas with a look of horror, but the woman was looking at Samuel. He saw accusation and the bitter pain of betrayal in her eyes.

"This woman has rejected the seventh of the sacred commandments that bind our people," Phinehas announced. "In accord with what is written in the Torah, she must die as an adulteress." He bent and picked up two fist-sized stones and handed them to Argob and the concubine Noalah. "'The hand of the witnesses first of all should come upon her to put her to death, and the hand of the people afterward, and you must clear out what is bad from your midst.'"

Samuel felt Hophni's grip tighten on his shoulder. "Pay close attention, boy," the big man whispered in his ear.

Phinehas placed himself directly in front of the woman. He dwarfed her, his hulking form casting a shadow across her battered face. But she looked up at his eyes boldly, poised on the edge of the precipice. "Jehovah is my Judge," she said.

Phinehas arms shot out and he pushed her from the embankment. Without a sound, she tumbled over the rocky edge and disappeared from view.

The crowd pressed forward, and Hophni stiff-armed Samuel along with them, until they stood at the edge of the abutment. In the hollow below them, the woman lay in a heap. After a moment, she began to rise slowly.

With a gentle sound, like a breath of wind through leaves, a stone whizzed past Samuel and hit the woman in the chest. She lurched backward, and her eyes went wide, but still she did not cry out. Samuel had never witnessed a stoning before, but he knew that the witnesses who threw the first stones were supposed to strike the criminal in the head, to render her unconscious and immune to the pain that would otherwise follow. But the second stone also missed her head, striking her instead in the groin, and the woman doubled over with a low moan.

After that, things happened quickly. The Priests and Levites brought by Phinehas and Hophni rained rocks onto the woman. Samuel tried to turn away, but Hophni grabbed his head and forced him to face the scene. He closed his eyes, but before he did so, he saw a jagged stone collide with the side of her head, and the woman collapsed into an unmoving heap.

A moment later, Hophni's grip relaxed. Samuel twisted free immediately and ducked through the crowd, pushing his way past the throng of people and then racing for the city gate. He heard Hophni call out his name, but ignored it. He tasted bile in his throat and his stomach churned as if he were sick.

Rohgah had been wrong about him. He did not know what to do. When the time had come to act, once again, he had only stood and watched. Adulterous Priests stoning innocent women—this is what had become of the Torah, of the ancient traditions of Israel.

He reached the Courtyard gates and entered, averting his eyes from the Altar and the gleaming Tabernacle. Everything here was a lie! There was no justice, no healing to be found in the House of God.

The word of Jehovah has become rare in Shiloh.

He ran to his room and ducked inside, throwing himself down on his bed and letting the tears flow. For several moments he just lay there, face pressed against his blankets, weeping silently and waiting for his stomach to stop churning. He thought back bitterly to the joy he had felt that morning, to the empty hope he had let himself entertain that he could do something to counter the evil that was strangling the city of Shiloh and the nation that looked to it for direction. *Malediction!* his mind whispered, and images of horror flooded his thoughts like a nightmare. He could no more stop it than he could stop the sun from setting each night. Darkness was coming to Israel, swift and certain, and it would swallow all that the nation aspired to with the ease of an inhalation.

He cursed himself for his futile efforts at the gate and wondered what people would think of him now. The foolish little gatekeeper of the Tabernacle, who had urged them to come to Shiloh to have their burdens lifted! Instead, they found here only an evil that grew in power each passing day. And whether he liked it or not, he was a part of this evil, with a role in this corrupt system. He opened the gate every morning and released this darkness on the nation. The Tabernacle belonged to Phinehas now, since it had become nothing more than any other pagan temple, a haven for criminals and adulterers. And if the Tabernacle belonged to Phinehas, then its gatekeeper was, willing or unwilling, Phinehas' minion.

For too long he had hid behind his youth, telling himself that he was not responsible, that what was happening in Shiloh was somehow separate from him and his actions. But Rohgah had stripped him of that self-deception, and he felt himself drowning now under a wave of guilt and regret. For thousands of days he had opened the gates of the Tabernacle and stood blithely aside while evil flowed in and out past him. He had seen it, even as a child, and it had sickened him. But he had done nothing, and now the opportunity had passed. Thousands of times it had passed, until now he was forced to confront the fact that he had allowed wickedness to settle into Shiloh and put down thick roots, so entrenched that Hophni and Phinehas could even publicly execute an innocent woman with impunity.

He heard footsteps outside his door and sat up just as a hulking figure pushed his way through the curtain and into his room.

It was Phinehas.

"It is time that you and I had a talk, Samuel," the Priest said darkly.

19

Phinehas filled the room, towering over Samuel. "I was under the impression that you were a Levite dedicated to the service of the Priests, Samuel."

Samuel was silent, his mind wound in too many knots to come up with a suitable response.

"Is it not your obligation to set a pattern for the people in obedience to the Torah?" Phinehas asked. "These people of the land expect to find at Shiloh examples they can look up to—not cowards who run from their duty."

Samuel played with the end of his braid, trying to fight back the fear that had settled in his neck and shoulders. "I did not know my duties included execution."

Phinehas smiled. *Lips thin. Eyes flat and hard.* "Do you know what people in Israel think of you, Samuel? Do you know what they are saying about you? That you are a hypocrite. They cannot believe that my father has let you continue even in your childish job as gate opener. Do you know why?"

Samuel shook his head.

"Because you have no zeal for the Torah! The people come to Shiloh to see the Torah in action, law upheld, justice executed. They rely on we who serve here to make the hard choices they are unwilling or unable to make. But even when the opportunity is placed in your hand, you fail to act! Hophni saw that you lacked the strength to do what must be done, and so he led you where your feet were too afraid to go. He did everything but put the stone in your hand. And still, you refused to do what Jehovah requires."

PROPHET OF ISRAEL

Samuel's mind whirled. Could Phinehas be right? Was he somehow failing to take a clear stand for upholding the Torah, even when he did not understand the reasons for the judgment?

Phinehas knelt so that he was looking Samuel in the eye. "Do you not feel turmoil within yourself, Samuel? Did fleeing the stoning bring you peace? Or did you find that you could not extinguish the conflict that rages in your heart? I know how to end that conflict. I am High Priest of the Tabernacle, the spiritual leader of the holy nation of Israel. Will you not listen to my advice, and find the peace you seek?"

Samuel felt a terrible pressure in his chest. The Priest's words made so much sense, but he could not quiet the voice in the back of his mind that screamed revulsion at what Phinehas was saying. How could it be right to execute an innocent woman? How could it be right to allow Hophni and Phinehas to take the women of the Corps to their beds?

Phinehas stared into his eyes a moment longer, then sighed, and Samuel saw genuine pity soften his features. "I feel sorry for you, Samuel-- so young, and forced to confront such complex questions as the ones that must be racing through your mind right now. Believe me—the first time I had to order an execution, I was every bit as conflicted as you are now. You probably believed the woman's claims that she was innocent—in a sense, I hope you did! A man as young as you should not yet be as jaded as I have become. But a healthy measure of cynicism is needed for this assignment, Samuel. You cannot simply believe everyone who claims to be innocent— anymore than you can hastily proclaim anyone guilty.

"Take Hophni and I. I know that you believe us to be wicked men who ignore the Torah. But why do you believe that? Is it not it because of what my son, Ahitub has told you? Have you ever thought to question his motives, Samuel, the way you question mine? Is there not an obvious reason why he might want to see me removed from the Priesthood?"

Samuel shook his head in confusion. "Ahitub only wants to assure Jehovah's blessing on Israel..."

Phinehas smiled at him sadly. "As do I—whether you believe it or not. But think about it Samuel—think, not about what you have been told, but about what the evidence supports! If Hophni and I are removed from the Priesthood, then what will happen to Ahitub?"

Samuel could not bring himself to meet Phinehas' eyes. "He will become High Priest," he whispered.

"Exactly." Phinehas paused to let the thought sink in. "A powerful motive, would you not agree? I am not saying that my son is a bad man," he added hurriedly. "Only that he believes that what Israel needs is a High Priest like himself. And to accomplish that goal, he is willing to do what needs to be done—to get rid of his own father and uncle, by whatever means necessary. And he has recruited a number of the people here at Shiloh to his cause."

"I don't believe you," Samuel said.

"But a part of your mind recognizes there is truth in my words, if you are willing to admit it." Phinehas put one hand on Samuel's shoulder. Samuel felt his insides recoiling from the touch, but he forced his body to remain still. "The choices before you are simpler than you think, Samuel. Will you obey the High Priest that Eli has chosen to succeed him, or will you oppose Jehovah's representative here on earth? Will you uphold the Torah even when doing so is difficult, or will you allow yourself to be ruled by your emotions and what you wish to be true?"

Samuel looked up, thinking about Mara. "Is it obedience to the Torah that moves you to be unfaithful to your wife?"

As soon as the words left his mouth, he regretted it. Something akin to rage flashed across Phinehas' cold eyes, but then it was gone, replaced by the same flat, dull look. "Ah, Samuel. If only we had spent more time together as you grew up. But Ahitub has always kept you away from me, wanting to assure himself that you would grow up as a supporter of his claims.

"I will not try to explain to you here all the complexities of the Torah that a High Priest must consider. I am certainly not obligated to justify my actions to you. But I will give you one thing to think about. Do you remember the account regarding a man named Zelophehad, in the days when Moses was acting as Judge over Israel?"

Samuel shook his head. "I'm not sure…"

Phinehas waved his hand dismissively. "It is an obscure account. But you do realize that the Torah commands that a father's inheritance is to be divided among his sons, not his daughters?"

Samuel nodded. "The daughters share in the inheritance of the men that they marry."

Phinehas smiled. "Very good. Then you would also agree that anyone who refused to obey this direction—who decided instead to divide his inheritance among his daughters—you would agree that such a person would merit Jehovah's judgment?"

Samuel shifted uncomfortably. "Anyone who refuses to obey the clear direction of the Torah is a criminal."

Phinehas leaned closer. "And yet, even though the Torah makes this clear, when the rich man Zelophahad died, it was his daughters who divided his inheritance among themselves. That was Moses' decision, and Jehovah approved of it—even though it went against the words of the Torah."

Samuel examined Phinehas' face. He did not remember the account, but he could see no signs of deception in the Priest's features.

"I tell you this," Phinehas continued, "so that you can understand that there are times when the leaders of Israel must make adjustments in how the Torah is followed. Times change. We must change with them. Among the changes that my father Eli instituted in his days as High Priest were having Hophni and I take sacred concubines from among the ceremonially clean women who serve in Shiloh. The reasons for this are complex, but I assure you—it is necessary for our survival as a nation. And while I deeply appreciate your concern for my wife, Mara, I would have you remember that she is pregnant with my child—I have not neglected her as a husband." For a moment, he turned away, and a look of sadness crossed his fleshy face. "She is not a healthy woman anymore. A sickness has taken hold of her that even the physicians of Egypt can do nothing about—a sickness of the mind. You do not know how I have struggled to find a cure that would allow her to be happy once again, as she was in the days of her youth…"

He shook his head and smiled sadly at Samuel. "Do you understand what I am telling you?"

"Eli commanded you to…?"

"Of course," Phinehas said. "Do you think he would have appointed me as High Priest if he did not approve of what I was doing? If Ahitub is as righteous as he claims he is, then why didn't the High Priest, on whom the spirit of Jehovah resides, appoint him as his successor?"

Samuel looked at the floor, trying to think through what the Priest was saying. He knew that Phinehas was manipulating him, but he could not see how. Everything he said seemed to make so much sense. Samuel felt even more like a child than usual, whining and protesting things he did not fully understand.

"Do not be too quick to condemn me—or Hophni," Phinehas continued, "although my brother can be coarse in his manners from time to time. You may not understand it now, but our uniting with the women of the Corps brings them many blessings, if they willingly submit to it. And there is a law that has ruled this land for much longer than the Torah of Moses—an ancient code that the people of Canaan have obeyed since the days of Abraham to assure good harvests and abundant flocks and herds. What kind of High Priest would I be if I ignored the dictates of a law that could save our people from famine and death?"

"Jehovah is the one we must look to for salvation," Samuel whispered. "His ways are higher than any other nations'—."

"Do not lecture me, child," Phinehas interrupted, his face darkening. "I have been a student of the Torah since before your parents were born, and there are men who are as old as my father and who will tell you that a hundred years spent studying the holy words are barely enough to scratch the surface of understanding. Do you really think that you, a son of twelve years, have a better grasp on its principles than the three highest religious leaders of the children of Israel?"

Samuel shook his head. "I...I know I still have much to learn."

"Remember that the next time you decide to condemn the High Priest of Israel—even in your mind!" Phinehas rose abruptly. "I have given you a great deal to think about. I will take my leave of you. But Hophni is waiting just outside your door."

Samuel looked up in surprise. "Waiting for what?"

"To take you to do your duty as a Levite," Phinehas said. "If you wish to shake off the reputation you have gained for yourself, then you must be seen to take action in support of the Torah. Are you willing to do what the Law of Moses requires?"

Samuel stood as well. "I am always willing to obey the Torah."

Phinehas smiled and again rested one huge hand on Samuel's shoulder. "Good. Then listen to what my brother tells you, and free yourself of the conflict that is raging within your soul."

The big Priest ducked out the door, leaving Samuel standing in the middle of his room, his mind awash in a sea of doubt and confusion. A moment later, Hophni shuffled in, wheezing as if he had hurried to get there. The Priest's wide face split into a cold, reptilian grin. "Are you prepared now to support the justice dispensed in Shiloh?"

"What would you have me do?"

Hophni gestured toward the door with one hand. "Follow me."

The Priest led Samuel out his door, back across the Courtyard to the gate and then down the main road through Shiloh. It was only a few minutes before Samuel realized Hophni was leading him to the site of the stoning. His stomach began churning as he followed the Priest's broad back past Shiloh's shops and homes, and even above the sounds of the busy city streets, he could hear Hophni's labored, wheezing breaths.

When they arrived, Hophni led him down the steep path that descended to the grotto where the woman had fallen. Samuel followed slowly, his heart in his throat. A mound of stones was piled there now, and through gaps in the rocks he could just glimpse the color of the woman's dress. Ravens and vultures hopped on the stones, their beaks probing down into the cracks in an attempt to reach the body. Two Levites waited near the stones; Samuel did not recognize them, but from the easy way they greeted Hophni, he could tell they were supporters of the sons of Eli.

Hophni stopped next to the mound and turned toward Samuel. "It is not enough that justice has been executed upon this sinner," he said, still panting heavily. "For our nation to benefit, they must *see* that justice has been done. For that reason, we do not leave an adulterer buried beneath the stones of her judgment. Let your hands be with the hands of these two men in uncovering her body, and hanging it upon a stake next to the gate of the city. Everyone who enters or leaves Shiloh will see how Jehovah deals with an adulteress—and they will see that Samuel, son of Elkanah, is truly zealous for the Torah."

"I am a Nazirite!" Samuel said. "By the force of my mother's vows, I am forbidden to touch a dead body!"

"Calm yourself!" Hophni said. "No one is asking you to disobey your vows. These men will handle the body itself. You are to assist them in whatever other ways they may need."

Hophni leaned down and picked up a stone with one thick hand; he shoved it into Samuel's arms. "There are, you may notice, a lot of stones to be moved."

The big priest began climbing slowly up the trail out of the grotto. Samuel stood for several moments watching him, the stone still held against his chest. "Well, boy," one of the Levites said. "You had best get to work."

Samuel labored with the two men until the sun began sinking toward the hills to the west. The time passed like a nightmare. Each stone Samuel tossed aside revealed some further gruesome detail of the woman's shattered body. Some of the stones were still wet with blood. When the body was sufficiently uncovered, the two Levites dragged it free. One of the legs twisted backward unnaturally, and white bone jutted from gaping wounds on the woman's head and hip.

Throughout the day, a continual stream of people flowed in and out of the city, and not one soul passed without stopping to look down on their work. Samuel forced himself not to meet their gaze, but he could feel their eyes boring into the back of his head. Were they thinking that he was now a follower of Phinehas? Did it appear that he approved of what the Priests had done? Did any of the passersby pity him, or guess at the turmoil that raged in his heart?

Samuel chased away the carrion birds as the two men carried the body up the trail to the city gate. He stood and watched them tie it, wrist and ankle, to a shaved log, which he then helped them raise and drop into a shallow hole. The corpse hung there limply, her head fallen forward and her long hair, matted with blood and dirt, covering her face.

Samuel fled back to his room. Running up the crowded streets of Shiloh, he heard the words of Phinehas playing over and over in his mind. *People see you as a hypocrite.* Was it true, or was it just another of Phinehas' falsehoods designed to make him excuse the Priest's actions?

When he reached the Courtyard, people were gathering near the entrance of the Tabernacle, and a hush had fallen over the crowd. Samuel wormed his way through the people until he was near the front of the throng and could see what they were all looking at. Tirzah was there also, and she smiled warmly when she saw him. But something else was trying to hide in her face: *tension around the eyes; shoulders raised; head bowed slightly.*

Phinehas was standing in front of the gleaming, golden pillars at the front of the Tabernacle, dressed in the ceremonial garments of the High Priest. Hophni, of course, stood next to him. Phinehas raised his arms and quieted the crowd. "People of Israel: In my new role as High Priest, I seek always to build up and encourage, to strengthen you, my people, against the trials that you face in your lives. But at times, I am required to deliver news of the most sorrowful nature.

"Such it is my duty to report to you now--news that has just reached Shiloh."

He paused for effect, and Samuel saw with surprise that the High Priest's eyes had found Tirzah's eyes. "We have looked to him for guidance. We have praised him for deliverance from the sons of Ammon. We have relied on him for leadership. But now, he is lost to us.

"Jephthah ben Gilead, Judge of Israel for these past six years, has died."

A cry, like that of a small bird, escaped Tirzah's lips, and she would have fallen if the people around had not reached to catch her. The sounds of weeping and groaning swept through the crowd. Samuel stood in stunned disbelief, unable even to form a coherent thought.

"With the passing of this great man," Phinehas continued, "Israel is left without a Judge until Jehovah appoints a new one. Until that happens, I ask that you pray for me and for my father, on whom I rely so much for guidance. Your High Priest is now the only ruler in Israel."

Tirzah began to weep loudly next to Samuel, her shoulders shaking as she slumped against the people around her. Slowly, they led her away, the crowd keening and wailing. Samuel wanted to follow, but he did not know what he could say to her, and such a press of people surrounded her that he did not think he could reach her. Instead, he walked slowly toward his rooms, letting the tears run down his face. Tirzah had been there for him—had supported him when things looked bleakest during Samuel's childhood. Now, he wanted to support her in the same way. But she was surrounded by dozens of people more qualified for the task than he was.

He looked up and realized that he was following Hophni and Phinehas at a distance. When he saw both of them enter Eli's home, he ducked into the narrow space between the home of the High Priest and the storage building next to it. The wall was linen stretched over wood panel frames, and through it he could hear the conversation taking place inside.

"No, my sons," Eli was saying. "People see it, and they know…You have become notorious, and the name of our house is a stench in Israel."

"A stronger hand is all that is needed," Phinehas answered. "When the people see what happens to anyone who dares to disrespect the Priesthood, they will learn again to honor us with their lips."

"Even you must be accountable to the words of Moses," Eli said. "Men come to Shiloh and their ears hear the Levites instructing them in the Torah, but their eyes see you men violating it."

"We are the Torah!" Hophni snarled. "It is we whom Jehovah chose to act as Priests in His house! We cannot expect the common men to comprehend the complexities of the Torah and its application. Let them look at us and take our actions as the measure of what a Priest should do."

"But the Torah!" Eli repeated.

"The Torah was for another time," Phinehas said. "We must change, and adapt the teachings of Moses for the days in which we live. And if our judgment is not perfect—then that is what the sacrifices are for. I have just sent *Azazel* into the wilderness. Whatever sins we may have committed have gone away with it."

"*Azazel* is a symbol of what Jehovah can choose to do for you, not a goat-god with the power to carry away sin!" Eli said. "If the Judge of all the earth condemns you, how much good do you think a goat rotting in the hills will do?"

"You must let us do as we see fit, Father," Hophni said. "Leave these worries to younger men."

"Speak to Jehovah in our behalf," Phinehas soothed. "Make offerings for us, if you feel it necessary."

"I may be able to smooth things over between you and the people," Eli said. "They still honor me for my service as High Priest and accept my apologies and excuses offered in your behalf. But I am only a man. Who will intercede for you before Jehovah? You must stand before Him on your own!"

"Please, Father!" Hophni's voice was scornful. "For decades we have served as Priests. Do you think to frighten us with such threats now? We have been standing before Jehovah, and He has done nothing. If what we were doing were so wrong, He would have removed us from office. He has not. Would you try to take the place of God?"

A long silence hung in the air before Eli spoke again. When he did, it was in a weak voice that Samuel knew, words uttered that he would not back with action. "Please, my sons. It is not good what you are doing."

"We are the Priests!" Phinehas said sharply. "We will decide what is good!"

They must have left then, for the argument ended and Samuel went to his bed. *Word from Jehovah has become rare in Shiloh*, he thought again as he lay there, eyes closed, trying to sleep, and then he thought of Tirzah's words: *Jehovah will not leave his loyal ones.* But what will He do? he wondered silently. And when?

What am I to do, Jehovah? he prayed silently. *What is your will for me? Ask of me, and I will do it! I will hold nothing back!*

He drifted off, but a nightmare of *Azazel* denied him real rest. The goat wandered back from the wilderness, bleating pitifully, its throat cut and dripping blood on the dusty streets as it returned to Shiloh and entered through the Tabernacle gates. Priests tried to stop it, tried to herd it back outside, but it lashed out with its sharp hooves at any who came near, and the Priests stumbled away, torn and bloodied. Eli came forward then, spreading his arms before it as if to command it to halt, but the goat reared up on its hind legs and savagely bit the old man in the face. Eli collapsed, and *Azazel* lurched forward, climbed onto the Altar and, standing in the midst of the flames, bleated accusation at Samuel and all Israel behind him.

The next day, beneath heavy, ashen skies, the Prophet Rohgah came to confront High Priest Eli.

20

Manoah stared in horror at his empty house. The remains of a meal still lay on the table; flies buzzed around hemispheres of half-eaten pomegranate and fragments of bread. There was no blood, and no signs of a struggle—everything indicated that the house had been hurriedly abandoned before any violence had taken place. He ran through each of the rooms of the house, upstairs and down, but all were equally empty and silent. Once, as he crossed the courtyard, a group of soldiers galloped past, and he crouched behind the clay oven until they were gone. Panic threatened to overwhelm him, and he forced himself to breathe more deliberately, trying to slow his pounding heart. An image of the injured woman he had encountered on entering the city flashed through his mind and he forced it away. Naamah must be alive! Somehow, she must have found a way to escape the soldiers, or to hide from them...

Abruptly, he remembered somewhere in the house that he had neglected to look. He got to his feet and raced back inside. Near the dining table, a braided rug covered part of the tiled floor. He dragged it aside, revealing a small, wooden hatchway set in the tiles. It was a tiny storage space for valuables, and so small that he had not at first thought of it as a hiding place.

He dropped to his knees and slid his fingertips into the crack between the hatchway and the tiles. As he lifted it, he was rewarded with a muffled squeal of terror from beneath. He released his breath in a rush and pulled the hatch the rest of the way open.

Knees tucked against their chests, Naamah and her sister-in-law Leah were wedged into the tiny space. When they saw Manoah, both began to weep openly. He helped them climb out of the tiny hole, marveling that Leah had managed to squeeze herself, pregnant belly and all, into the opening with his wife.

He clutched them to him. "Are you hurt? Is either of you hurt?"

Naamah just shook her head as she wept into his shoulder. Leah stepped away and took a deep breath. "We are all right. The city has fallen?"

Manoah nodded. "Keep away from the doorway. The streets are crawling with Philistine dogs."

He glanced over at Leah and saw cold resignation settle onto her features. With typical candor, she asked, "Your brothers…the men are dead?"

Manoah hesitated, fresh grief welling up in his throat as he thought of her husband. "They died defending our home, placing you on high…"

Leah nodded, and Manoah was amazed to see just a single tear trickle down one cheek. Her hands cradled her swollen belly instinctively. "We need to leave here quickly," she said, her voice breaking.

Manoah nodded, and putting one hand on each of Naamah's shoulders, gently pushed her away. "Bring only what is absolutely necessary. We need to travel far, and quickly."

Leah reached down into the storage pit and lifted out a small, oilskin bag. "We have already gathered money and a few provisions."

A crash and a scream rang out from the street, and all three of them flinched. Poised to run, they stood for a few moments in silence, but heard nothing more than the distant crackling of flames. Manoah was about to lead them out when he remembered something. "Stay here!" he ordered, and ran into the courtyard.

He went immediately to the gate, peering out to make sure that no soldiers were nearby. The street was empty of anyone living; the air had grown thick and hot with smoke, and ashes fluttered down around him like dirty snow. Hardening himself against the rage and sorrow that threatened to consume him, he dragged his brothers from the gates to the corner of the Courtyard, laying them carefully on the flagstones, composing their stiffening bodies as well as he was able. Casting about, he spotted the potted palms near the house doorway, and he tore the plants from their clay vessels and laid them over the corpses to hide them from view. He hated that he could not give the men a proper burial, and he could not bear to think about what might happen to the bodies after he left. But at least now Naamah and Leah would not see the corpses of their loved ones.

He ducked back inside. The women had wrapped traveling cloaks over their shoulders, and they followed him across the courtyard and into the still-empty street. After passing just a few homes, Manoah led them into a narrow alley that cut across to a less-traveled avenue.

They had just emerged when a chariot burst into view behind them in a clatter of hooves and iron-rimmed wheels. "Run!" Manoah yelled, but it was too late. The chariot was on them in seconds. Manoah grabbed Naamah's hand and dove into the nearest doorway as the whirling scythe-blades slashed past them. He caught just a glimpse of the three men in the chariot: two massive, armored Philistines and the driver—a young man with an unruly mop of sandy hair and a mass of red scar tissue where his nose should have been.

Inside the house, Manoah got to his feet, keeping himself between Naamah and the road. Suddenly, he realized that Leah was nowhere to be seen. He glanced quickly out the door and saw with horror that the young Philistine driver had gotten off his chariot and was facing his pregnant sister-in-law who leaned against a wall on the opposite side of the road, her face white with terror. The Philistine held a throwing axe loosely in one hand, and half a dozen freshly severed hands hung from the young warrior's blood-soaked belt.

Manoah drew his sword and was about to rush to Leah's aid when he heard a choking sound behind him and turned to find his wife bent over, vomiting. He wrapped his arms around her and realized that she was about to start sobbing. He clapped his left hand over her wet lips, barely containing her choking gasps of grief, wondering if the soldiers outside had already heard her.

He gently eased his wife to the floor, keeping his hand over her mouth. "Naamah!" he whispered. "Sshh! Stay here, and be silent. I will be right—."

A shriek of pain interrupted him from the street and he leapt to the doorway. Across the street, Leah still faced the scarred soldier, but his axe was now buried in her shoulder; a bloodstain on her dress was spreading rapidly outward from the wound. The soldier stood several paces away from the cringing woman, pointing his long, black-bladed sword at her belly. "How long until the baby is due?" he asked casually, his voice a strange, nasally rasp.

One of the huge warriors still on the chariot glanced in Manoah's direction, and he ducked back behind the wall of the house, his mind racing. They were three trained warriors, two of them bigger than he was, and all of them armored in breastplates and mail. If he went out now and failed to kill all three of them, he was sentencing his wife and Leah to certain, tortuous death.

He peered around the doorway again. The scarred warrior had stepped closer to Leah and placed the tip of his blade against her stomach. "I was just curious—I wondered what the child would look like when I tore it from your split belly."

Leah's face twisted in terror. Behind him, Manoah heard Naamah choking again and whirled to help her. At the same moment, Leah's scream echoed off the city walls. Manoah ground his teeth and, clutching his skull, tore fistfuls of hair from his scalp. From outside, he heard the scarred warrior yelling. "I am Phicol, son of Anat, goddess of savagery! I am Phicol! Hear my name and know—the sword reveals the heart!"

The chariot raced away in a clatter of hooves. Manoah fought to keep his emotions in check, burying his grief beneath his rage. He pulled Naamah to her feet. "Quickly—Naamah, I know this is hard, but we must go quickly!"

She looked up at him, her face white. "The baby is dead."

He nodded. "But if we wish to live, we must flee now—quickly and quietly."

She nodded. He took her hand and led her back out the door and onto the street again. Manoah pulled his wife in the opposite direction that the chariot had gone, not wanting her to see Leah's mutilated corpse. They raced down the smoke-shrouded streets, Manoah's eyes and ears straining to discern any approaching soldiers in time to hide. The wound on his chest burned, and the muscles around it had begun to throb with every hurried step. Several times, he pulled Naamah into some shadowed alcove or doorway just in time to avoid passing warriors. The bodies of slaughtered Israelites were everywhere, some of them savaged by war hounds, others charred into anonymity.

They were nearing the wall at last when a Philistine warrior stepped from a doorway into the street in front of them, his dripping sword held out before him. He saw them instantly, and Manoah pushed Naamah behind him and raised his own blade, studying the man. He was unlike any Philistine Manoah had ever seen before. He was clad in black clothing and armor, and the sword he carried was long and black-bladed as well. Even his crown-like helmet was black. He smiled coldly at Manoah, and then leapt toward him, sword raised.

Manoah battered the attack aside, but the man riposted so quickly Manoah barely ducked clear of the blow. An angry ringing echoed in the alleyway, like the peal of a poorly made bell, and Manoah realized with a shock that it was the warrior's sword making the noise. He lunged again, but the Philistine danced easily aside and slashed toward him. This time, the black blade slit the sleeve of Manoah's tunic just below the shoulder, and he felt the warmth of blood trickling down his left arm.

The Philistine smiled again, and Manoah realized that the man was toying with him. He attacked furiously, raining blows toward the man's face and neck, but the warrior blocked them easily, his movements so swift Manoah could barely follow them. Manoah knew that the long, night ride had weakened him, but he was certain that this man was quicker and stronger than he was even at his peak. They battled back and forth in the street while Naamah cowered against a wall. Manoah tried to stave off the fear and desperation that were growing in his heart, but he was tiring, and he knew that he was not a match for the black-clad warrior in front of him.

He had nearly made up his mind to try to flee when the Philistine warrior abruptly stiffened, grimacing. It was only after a rough circle of blood blossomed on the man's chest that Manoah saw the arrowhead protruding through his bronze breastplate.

The Philistine toppled forward, toward Manoah, onto the street. Twenty paces away, an elderly Israelite man stood atop his roof, a bow in his hands. Manoah met his eyes, and the man nodded once, then ducked behind the cover of his parapet and disappeared. Manoah grabbed Naamah's hand and raced further down the street.

They were almost to the city wall when they came upon a cloth storehouse engulfed in flame. Thick clouds of black smoke rolled out of the windows, shrouding the street in darkness, and charred wisps of fabric whirled into the air on the waves of heat and flame. Manoah and Naamah covered their mouths with one corner of their cloaks and ducked through the smoke. They emerged into a broad courtyard, disoriented, coughing, and rubbing their stinging eyes. A wagon had been abandoned in the courtyard, and they leaned against it for a moment, trying to clear their lungs of smoke.

When Manoah looked up, nine black-clad warriors stood amidst the smoke in the courtyard gateway, swords gripped in their gloved hands.

Manoah glanced around him in a panic. The only exit besides the gate was through the building behind them that was erupting with smoke and flame. He turned back toward the group of warriors advancing toward them, seeing the poise with which they held themselves, their relaxed movements, the easy way in which they handled their weapons.

He had fought in dozens of battles in Israel, against enemies from many nations. He had defended cities and fought in open plains. He had defeated foes in single combat and stood alongside a wall of his fellow Israelites, stopping the mindless cavalry charge of the enemy on the ends of their spears. He was a warrior born of warriors, and he knew with all the cold awareness of his experience that he could not defeat the nine men who approached. He knew that even if all of his brothers had stood beside him, they would not have been able to overpower the black-clad Philistines who closed on him within that courtyard.

Out of the corner of his eye, he saw Naamah cowering against the wagon, her mouth open in a silent scream. In that moment something died within him, as if all the failures of his life raged through his mind and body, leaving him as hollow and fragile as the fragments of burnt cloth that drifted to the ground all around him.

He heard himself praying, but it was as if he were listening to someone else's voice. Waves of heat washed against his back, stirring his hair like the gentlest wind. His mouth went dry, and it seemed for an instant that time had slowed to a crawl. In that moment, he realized that he had come at last to the day of his death, and the death of the woman he had sworn to protect.

Then a shadow detached itself from the smoke swirling against the courtyard wall.

It was a man, dressed all in ash-grey but without armor, an Israelite man. The handle of a sword jutted from behind each shoulder—Manoah had never before seen anyone carry their blades in such a way. The Philistines turned toward the newcomer, startled, but he did not approach any closer. He stood with his head tilted down, like a man ashamed but angry about being so, looking up at them fiercely from beneath lowered brows. Manoah did not recognize him—he was sure that the man did not live in Gibbethon. Something in his features and style of dress made Manoah think he was perhaps a Zebulunite, a smaller tribe from the north of Israel. His clothing looked newly made, tailored meticulously to his slender frame, and his straight, black hair and beard were oiled and neatly trimmed.

"If it is a battle you seek," he said, so quietly that his voice was almost indiscernible above the crackling of the flames, "then attack me."

One of the black-clad Philistines chuckled, and three of them stepped toward him.

Manoah's mouth fell open in disbelief when he saw what happened next. The Zebulunite launched himself across the square and into the Philistines like a snake striking, covering four paces in a single, effortless leap. His long, slender sword flashed twice, and three Philistines fell, clutching at wounds in their stomachs or necks. They had not even had the time to strike a blow.

Before the other six could fully comprehend what had just happened, the Zebulunite was in their midst, whirling like a dancer. The slender sword swept up, then down, snaking past every effort the Philistines made to defend themselves. Watching in stunned disbelief, Manoah was sure that any one of the nine Philistines would have been a match for him in single combat, but they could not touch the grey-clad warrior. His every movement was flawless, no effort wasted, and with each fluid motion, a Philistine crumpled, dying. There was something impossible about the way the Zebulunite moved, a lightness, as if he were not held to the ground as other men.

It was over in seconds. The Zebulunite stood, head still bowed, in the middle of nine bodies sprawled in a rough circle on the courtyard flagstones around him. He was still for a moment, a grey statue of a man; then he sheathed his sword silently over his shoulder.

None of his enemies had touched him.

He had not even wrinkled his clothing.

"We must get you out of the city," he said, glancing over at Manoah and Naamah from beneath his still-lowered brows. His voice was soft and quiet, giving no indication that he had just battled nine warriors.

Manoah realized the man was waiting for a response. "Yes—I...we must...my wife and I must get out."

"Follow me. Stay close." The Zebulunite turned on his heel and strode back out into the street, gliding over the ground like a cat on the hunt. Manoah grabbed Naamah's hand and they followed.

The grey-clad warrior led them along alleys and side streets toward the city wall, toward the postern gate that Manoah had been seeking earlier. They did not encounter anyone else along the way, finding no signs of life except for carrion birds hopping among the broken bodies of men and animals. They saw that the gate lay, split and shattered, on the ground; blood dripped down the wall on either side.

The Zebulunite ducked through the opening and disappeared. He returned a moment later, swords still sheathed. "The way is clear. Where will you go?"

"To the shepherds' caves under the hills to the northeast," Manoah said. "From there, we will flee to Aijalon."

The man nodded once, a curt bob of his head. "Get your wife to safety. May Jehovah be with you," he said, and loped back toward the middle of the city.

Manoah led Naamah through the postern and into the fields outside the walls. As they made their way through the dry grass toward the distant hills, they could see dozens of their fellow citizens streaming across the lowlands as well, trying to get as much distance as possible between themselves and the ruined city that had been their home. Surreally, soldiers of Philistia prowled among some of them, killing men, women and children while their neighbors or family raced past, just paces away.

Smoke rose in an inky cloud, and the sound of slaughter and destruction continued to echo from the walls. Manoah thought about his dead brothers left in a heap outside his house, about Leah lying slaughtered on the street, about the friends he had grown up with in the city that his family had called their home for six generations. His palm itched for the hilt of his sword, and he longed to race back and make someone pay for what had been done to him and the people he loved. But Naamah was walking only because he had hold of her hand, her eyes glassy and her movements wooden. He must care for her first, and that meant getting her to whatever safety they could find.

He headed for a grove of bushy sycamores and broom trees that concealed the mouth of one of the deeper caves that dotted the hills. Glancing back at Naamah, he could see that she would need to stop soon. The past few hours had stretched her nerves to the breaking point. If she were to make it to Aijalon in one piece, they would need to find somewhere where they could rest and recover.

"We will make our way to Aijalon," he said to her. "We will be safe there."

She did not even acknowledge his words, just kept walking forward with her eyes fixed on the brittle, yellow grass that she crushed underfoot with each step.

Reaching the mouth of the cave, Manoah heard a sound behind them and spun, drawing his sword. Startled by his sudden movement, Naamah collapsed to the ground, covering her face with her hands. Manoah placed himself between her and whoever was approaching through the brush.

The grey-clad Zebulunite emerged from the trees and glided toward them. "A raiding party is coming," he said softly.

Manoah raised Naamah to her feet and supported her with one arm around her waist. "Quickly, Naamah. Quickly."

She continued sobbing softly, but he could do nothing about it. They hobbled forward into the cave, not stopping until they were deep enough that the darkness and shadow concealed them. Manoah turned to the warrior. "You saved our lives. We will be forever in your debt."

The man shook his head, the merest hint of movement. "Not so."

"Well, I consider the debt owed, whether or not you acknowledge it. I would like to know to whom I am indebted."

The man looked at him from under lowered brows. "I am a Zebulunite, from Shimron."

"Your name, man! Who are you?"

The man's eyes bored into Manoah and through him, eyes filled with an unspoken hunger and an anguish beyond all words. "I am Elon-tohr."

21

Every man of war in Israel knew the name of Elon-tohr.

The nation celebrated the battle skills of the tribe of Zebulun. Unlike the other tribes, Zebulun did not specialize in a particular aspect of warfare but instead prided themselves on their skill with every type of weapon, in any military situation. Their territory was constantly under attack by the Philistines from the south, the Phoenicians from the north and west, and the Ammonites and Moabites from the east. They maintained the best-trained and most celebrated army in the entire nation, the greatest warriors in Israel.

And Elon-tohr was the most celebrated of the Zebulunites.

His name had been a legend from the time of his youth, and his deeds were recounted by old men gathered on rooftops at sunset or whispered by boys huddled under tented blankets in the darkness trying to stave off sleep. Manoah knew the stories. He had told them himself, to his nephews, or to frightened young men who came to him seeking courage on the night before a battle.

When Elon-tohr was still a youth, a mob of Geshurite raiders rode into his territory on camels and attacked his home. They killed his father with an arrow while he was working in the fields. His brothers and his mother fell beneath the Geshurites' wicked, curved blades. Elon-tohr had escaped with his younger sister into their vineyard. After placing her atop an old stone watchtower among the vines, he had met the raiders at the tower's base. They were twelve men, hardened cavalrymen all, with heavy scimitars and copper spears. Elon-tohr had only a worn bronze sickle.

He had killed all of them. He was not even injured.

He began to wander the length and breadth of Israel then and, some said, to travel to other lands as well. Rumors told him settling briefly in Beersheba, and marrying a woman there. If that story were true, Manoah did not know what had become of her. Some reports had him battling the Libyans in Egypt, the Hittites in Anatolia, or pirates on the ships of Phoenicia. It was hard to know anymore which stories were true, since so many circulated. But those that Manoah had heard from reliable eyewitnesses were no less astonishing than the ones that were probably fictitious. Everywhere that he went, new legends were born, stories of a skill in battle that bordered on the supernatural. He had never been defeated in single combat.

Elon-tohr had spent some time in Bethlehem when the Jebusites that held the city of Jerusalem had tried to expand their territory to the south. When the Jebusites besieged the city, they were unable to penetrate Bethlehem's walls. But during a massive attack launched on the city gate, a spy within Bethlehem had secretly opened a postern in the rear wall to admit a highly trained strike force of the enemy.

Somehow, Elon-tohr had discovered what was happening just as the Jebusite strike force was penetrating the wall. He had stood in the narrow gateway and battled the entire force by himself. When he was discovered by his countrymen, he was moving bodies out of the opening so that he could close and bar the gate. None of the two-dozen men sent by the Jebusites had survived the assault.

But other stories circulated also, less flattering rumors regarding Elon-tohr's beliefs and worship. It was well known that he failed sometimes to come to Shiloh for the annual festivals. No one accused him of worshipping false gods—just of failing to demonstrate any real zeal for the worship of Jehovah…

Manoah realized he was still staring at the grey-clad warrior in awe. He flushed. "I am Manoah of Dan. Can you help us get to safety in Aijalon?" he asked before he even knew what he was saying.

"I am not sure that there is any safety to be found in Israel," Elon-tohr whispered. He glanced back over his shoulder at the scene behind them, framed by the cave's mouth. Smoke was rising from the city in thick, black clouds. "Gibbethon had a mighty wall and strong gates, and it fell in a day."

Manoah wracked his brain for something to say to the hero to convince him to accompany them, but nothing suitable came to his mind. But Elon-tohr was not waiting for him.

"I assume there is another way out of this cave?" he said, walking past Manoah and Naamah and peering into the darkness beyond them.

Manoah nodded. "A tunnel branches off to the south a short distance further in, and comes out in a tumble of boulders beyond sight of the city. We must wade a small pool, but it is not dangerous."

Elon stood silently a moment, staring into the blackness of the cave. "It is not far to the Forest of Hereth," he said, almost to himself. "We will try to reach its borders by nightfall."

"We?" Manoah asked. But Elon-tohr just started moving farther into the darkness, and Manoah clutched Naamah's hand and followed him.

For a short distance, the light from the cave's mouth was enough to see vague forms and outlines around them, but soon they reached the branching tunnel to their right and, when they turned down it, even that weak light was lost to them. Manoah could not see Elon-tohr ahead of them anymore, but he could hear the man's gentle footsteps in the sandy soil. The Danite used his free hand to feel his way along the rough stone of the cave wall.

It had been several years since Manoah had come to this cave himself although he knew some of his shepherds brought their flocks here to winter. He did not remember how long the tunnel continued and so was relieved to see the gleam of light ahead of them after just a few minutes. When they emerged into the daylight again, blinking and shading their eyes, Elon-tohr stopped for a few moments, looking back at Manoah from beneath still-lowered brows. "How will you avoid the Philistines?" he asked quietly.

Naamah sat on one of the stones, her eyes still wild and her breathing shallow. Manoah shook his head. "I don't know. I do not think I really believed that we would even escape Gibbethon alive. I hadn't planned beyond that."

The grey-clad warrior blinked. "You cannot travel by road. The Philistines will be raiding deep into the countryside in every direction, and you will not be able to outrun their chariots."

"We will keep to the hills," Manoah said.

"The hills will lead you quickly into the Forest of Hereth. Have you ever walked beneath those trees before?" Elon-tohr paused, but not long enough for Manoah to answer. "I have," he continued. "There are things living in those shadows that are many times more dangerous than the warriors who burned Gibbethon."

Manoah wanted to reach out and grab the man's arm and plead for his help, but something stopped him, an unidentifiable sense that even that plaintive touch would be unwelcome by the man in grey. "There is greater safety in numbers," he said instead. "If you would come with us, we would stand a better chance of surviving whatever the Forest might deliver to us."

Elon looked back at the sky, where an inky shroud of smoke hung against the graying clouds. "They will hunt for us with war hounds," he said, as if he had not heard Manoah's plea. "To be torn by the dogs—that is a death I would wish on no man."

"They will call off the hunt by nightfall," Manoah answered. "They have captured the city—they will want to enjoy their spoils."

Elon shook his head slowly. "No. These are not the Philistines we have known. These black-clad warriors are…There are men among them who will not rest until all of us are destroyed."

He turned to face them. "I will take you to Aijalon. The armies of Israel will likely be gathering there to respond to this attack. I should join them—and so should you."

"We would welcome your help," Manoah said. "For myself, I am determined to unite with our brothers to meet this threat."

Elon-tohr nodded once and apparently considered the matter settled because he began walking quickly south and east, across the rolling grasslands and towards the distant, tree-covered hills.

Manoah and Naamah followed him in silence. For the better part of an hour they walked without a pause through the dry grasses, keeping their thoughts to themselves. Manoah glanced worriedly at Naamah, plodding along a short distance behind him. He could see that the horrors of the attack and Leah's death had taken their toll on her—she did not speak and paid no attention to anything around her, moving constantly forward with short, steady steps, her eyes fixed on the ground at her feet. He took her hand at times or put his arm around her shoulders, but she did not respond, her mind still struggling to come to grips with the fact that she had lost both home and family. He could think of nothing to say that would help, and so he remained silent as well, frustrated by his inability to comfort her, angered by the guilt that his powerlessness wakened within his heart.

"Manoah." Elon had stopped and was staring back across the grasslands. Manoah turned and, following his gaze, saw what had given the Zebulunite pause.

A group of chariots was racing toward them over the plains, leaving a whirling cloud of dust in their wake.

They began to run. Manoah found himself hunching as he loped forward, pulling Naamah behind him, as if by ducking a few inches he could prevent the approaching warriors from seeing him. He ran without looking behind him, keeping his eyes focused on the ground ahead, not even sparing a glance for his wife, just keeping her hand gripped tightly in his own. He could not outrun the chariots. Their only hope was to reach the cover of the trees before the riders caught up to them. The Forest of Hereth was dense and tangled; the horses and chariots would never be able to enter. If the Philistines were so determined to catch their quarry that they dismounted and pursued them on foot—well, then, they would have to face Elon-tohr.

A few moments later, even those thoughts were driven from his mind, replaced with the solitary determination to keep running, to keep his heavy legs moving and his burning lungs breathing. Once, briefly, it crossed his mind to be amazed that Naamah was still running behind him, but he allowed himself to be grateful without analyzing how it was possible.

The tree line was clearly in view before them when the thundering of hooves reached their ears as well. Manoah risked a glance over his shoulder and immediately regretted it. Three chariots were bearing down on them. In that one glance, he clearly saw the merciless faces of the nine riders, their weapons already raised as they closed on their quarry. The logical part of his warrior's mind told him that their blades would probably never reach him—he and Naamah, and Elon-tohr as well, would be trampled beneath the sharp hooves of the massive, war stallions and cut to ribbons by the scythe-wheels of the chariots before they could defend themselves.

Fear pulsed through his veins and he tried to put on a final burst of speed, but his body was exhausted by more than a full day without sleep and the rigors of his ordeal. He saw Elon-tohr glance behind as well, but the warrior's face was an expressionless mask, and he turned immediately back toward the forest and continued running.

They passed the first few trees; Manoah heard Naamah make a sound like a choking cough, but she continued gripping his hand tightly and maintaining their maddened pace. A horse whinnied angrily, and the sound of the hooves changed; Manoah did not turn, but he imagined that the scattered sycamores were forcing the chariots to slow.

Then Naamah's foot caught in a clump of dried grass, and she tumbled to her knees. Manoah drew his sword as he turned and grabbed her arm, trying to pull her to her feet and keep moving forward. The pounding of the horse's hooves shook the ground, and he looked up to see one of the chariots, near enough that he found himself staring into the hard eyes of its helmeted driver. Behind him, a spearman had his weapon in hand, poised to throw at them. Naamah kept trying to rise, crawling forward on her knees as Manoah pulled on her hand to try to help her. She grabbed at his tunic with her other hand and pulled herself up just as one of the chariot horses screamed, and it seemed as though its hot breath blasted the back of Manoah's neck.

Ahead of them, Elon-tohr reached the dense wall of scrub and saplings that marked the forest's edge. Moments later, Manoah and Naamah reached it as well, and as they did so, Elon leapt behind them, drawing his sword. As soon as Manoah passed the line of brush, he risked another look behind him. At the moment of his glance, he saw two javelins hurtling directly toward him and his wife. He shoved her to one side, and both of them tumbled to the ground among the rotting leaves and gnarled roots of the sycamores. Rolling onto his back, he watched in amazement as Elon-tohr's slender blade flashed in a wide arc over his head, slashing the shafts of both javelins and sweeping them away to plunge harmlessly in the brush.

The grey-clad warrior sheathed his blade as he leapt to Naamah's side and helped her to her feet. Arrows whistled through the trees as the three of them clambered up a low rise, pulling themselves along by the slender tree trunks.

When they reached the top of the hill, they crouched a moment behind the cover of some rough, moss-covered boulders, trying to catch their breath. Elon risked a look over the rocks and back down the hill. "They are not yet following," he said.

"Perhaps they have decided to pursue larger quarry," Manoah said.

"Or they are waiting for the dogs to arrive." Elon continued scanning the forest below them for a few moments, then turned and looked down at Manoah and Naamah. "We must keep moving either way."

22

Manoah helped his wife to rise and they continued through the forest, following the Zebulunite. He maintained a steady pace, its speed determined by the uneven terrain. At one point, Manoah tried to engage him in conversation, but the grey-clad warrior gave him only one-word replies, or less, and after a few moments, Manoah abandoned the attempt and continued in silence.

He did what he could to aid Naamah, but he knew the only thing that could truly help her now was reaching a place of safety and comfort. Until then, the best thing he could do for her was to keep her moving toward that goal. He felt strangely alone as they walked, distanced from Elon-tohr by the invisible wall of mystery and seclusion that the warrior had constructed around himself and separated from Naamah by his inability to penetrate the mental cave into which she had retreated. His feelings of loneliness made him extraordinarily aware of any signs of life in the forest around them. There were few. Birds occasionally flitted through the high branches of the sycamores and oaks, and once something larger scurried off noisily through the underbrush and leaves, but it vanished in the scrub before he could see what it was.

Perhaps it was this awareness that caused him to glance over his shoulder at a rocky ridge that jutted through the trees several hundred paces to the north of them. He stopped abruptly. A man was standing on the ridge top, silhouetted clearly against the afternoon sky, watching them make their way through the forest.

"Elon!" He pointed surreptitiously, although the man was likely too far away to see the gesture.

Elon-tohr just nodded. "Rephaim."

The grey-clad warrior started walking again, and Manoah followed him because he had no other choice. But terror had lodged in his heart. He looked back at the ridge top again, but the figure had disappeared.

Rephaim was the Hebrew name for a race of men who inhabited a corner of Israel far to the north, near the Sea of Galilee. No army had ever been able to drive them from their ancestral lands—not even the divinely backed armies of Joshua and Caleb had succeeded in doing so, although Joshua had defeated their mightiest king, Og of Bashan, in a fierce and bloody battle at the Amorite city of Edrei. They were a race whose entire way of life was war—as soon as their children could walk, they began to train them in battle. But it was not only their military skills that caused others to fear them.

The Rephaim were no ordinary men. They were giants.

To this day, the Ammonites preserved Og's great sarcophagus of black basalt in a shrine within their capital city, Rabbah. It was more than twice the height and width of a normal man.

Manoah had once provided lodging to a woodcutter from Bashan who was delivering a cartload of oak staves to Phoenicia for the shipwrights there to fashion into oars. After they had eaten, the weather-beaten man had sat on the rooftop with Manoah, sipping slowly on a cup of wine. "Have you ever seen one of the Rephaim?" he had asked, with the glint in his eye of a man with a story to tell.

"No," Manoah had answered. "I know them only by reputation."

The man shook his head slowly. "Then you don't know them at all!" He glanced to the right and to the left, as if he were about to tell a great secret and wanted to make sure no one else heard it. "I met one once, back in Bashan. Hadn't much of a beard—couldn't have been a son of more'n sixteen or seventeen years. But you wouldn't have guessed it by his size!"

The woodcutter leaned closer, deep-set eyes widening. "Standing on my toes, I couldn't have touched the boy's forehead! His thighs were as thick as my waist! And the strength in those tree-trunk arms! I saw him with my own eyes tear apart the links of a heavy chain!"

Manoah knew, as did all Israelites, that a few tribes of the giants still lived among the mighty oak trees of Bashan and the dense woodlands of northern Gilead. But they kept to themselves, hiding out in the forests and leaving Israel and all other people alone. It was rare for anyone to even see one of the Rephaim anymore, let alone face them in battle.

Manoah noticed that Elon-tohr had come to a stop ahead of them, and he paused as well, leaning heavily against the trunk of a nearby tree, pulling Naamah against his chest and putting his arms around her. Elon gestured toward the sandy soil with his chin. Manoah released his wife and stepped closer.

A swath of sandal tracks crossed the forest duff, clear and unmistakable even in the dry earth. They were enormous, easily as long as Manoah's arm from elbow to fingertip. Manoah looked up to ask Elon-tohr what he knew about this strange development, but the warrior was already walking again, continuing his southeasterly path through the trees. Manoah took Naamah's hand again and started after him.

By the time they emerged from the cover of the forest, the sun was already sinking over the hills to the west, splashing the sky with brilliant oranges and reds that filtered down through the leaves and gave everything around them a rosy glow. Naamah was stumbling with exhaustion by now, leaning heavily on Manoah for support. He knew that he could not go on much longer, either. When he suggested to Elon-tohr that they take a brief rest, the enigmatic warrior shook his head. "When we reach Timnah."

"Timnah?" Manoah asked, struggling to keep up with the tireless pace their guide was setting. "Is that where you are taking us?"

Elon-tohr did not answer, but Manoah was not going to let this newest revelation go unchallenged. "Timnah is in the hands of the Philistines! Why not just turn around and go back to Gibbethon?"

"We will not enter the city of Timnah," Elon-tohr answered, nonplussed. "We are going to the mining camp in the hills outside the city."

"Oh, wonderful!" Manoah said, practically shouting now. "A mining camp controlled by Midianites on the outskirts of a Philistine-occupied city! What makes you think the Midianites won't just turn us over to the Philistines—or take us as their own captives?"

"Because there are no Midianites at Timnah this time of year," the warrior answered without turning. "The Midianites let their Kenite workers manage the mines with little supervision—as long as they keep sending copper and bronze to their masters."

"This is ridiculous!" Manoah shouted back. He stopped walking and waited for Elon-tohr to notice. "I'm not going to let you lead us into the hands of the Midianites—or their allies! Do you think they have forgotten that Judge Gideon slaughtered their kings and princes and devastated their army less than a hundred years ago? Or perhaps you feel they have forgiven Israel for that defeat?"

Elon-tohr stopped walking and turned to face him, his handsome face still expressionless. "Have you ever had dealings with the Kenites?"

"What difference does that make?"

"If you had, you would realize that they will do anything for money—even help out the enemies of their overlords."

Manoah threw up his hands in disgust. "Why do we need their help? Why not just keep heading east until we reach the main road, and head to Aijalon as quickly as possible?" He took two steps closer to the Zebulunite, exhaustion causing his anger to bubble up more than he intended. "For that matter, why have you been taking us southeast at all? Aijalon is northeast of us—and there are a lot more direct routes to choose for an exhausted woman and an injured man!"

The grey-clad warrior frowned, head bowing so that he was looking at Manoah from beneath his lowered brows. "We do not need a direct route. We need a safe route."

"Safe? Are you mad? How safe do you really think a Midianite mining camp is going to be?"

"Safer than this forest, or any road within a day's journey, when the Philistines catch up to us."

"I won't do it!" Manoah shouted back, crossing his arms over his chest. "If you insist on walking into—."

"Lower your voice!" Elon-tohr's voice was still soft, but it had an edge to it that even Manoah could not ignore. "Do you really think I would lead you into danger or certain death? Do I have a reputation for being a fool, Manoah of Dan?"

Manoah gritted his teeth, but did not answer, realizing that he had probably said too much already.

"We need to go somewhere where it will be difficult for the Philistines to follow us—and for their hounds to track us. We cannot outdistance them—not, as you say, with an exhausted woman and an injured man. If we pay the Kenites to lower us into their mine, we can follow it and emerge far to the north—and neither the Philistines nor their hounds will be able to trace our passing easily. Even if they do pursue us into the mines, they will be forced to abandon both horses and chariots to do so."

It was by far the longest speech Elon-tohr had made since Manoah had encountered him in Gibbethon, and Manoah admitted to himself that the warrior was making a great deal of sense. He nodded, feeling foolish, and Elon-tohr turned without another word and began walking once again.

The forest started to thin shortly thereafter, and they descended into a broad valley dotted with scattered oaks. Across the valley, they could just see the walls of Timnah, a dark line behind dusty fields and roping chains of grapevines. Nearer to them, at the valley's floor, the mouth of a mine gaped, surrounded by a flurry of activity. Not far from the mine, Manoah could see a Kenite temple tucked beneath a rocky overhang on one of the hills. A base of cut stone supported two rows of elegantly sculpted stone pillars, over which draped a tent-like linen roof.

As they drew closer, the air filled with the pungent smell of charcoal fires and molten metal. Sweat-streaked Kenites emerged from the mine carrying baskets of ore over their shoulders, the skin of their faces, arms, and chests blackened with grime. They dumped their burdens into piles on the dusty ground, from which other workers took handfuls of stone and arduously crushed it into powder in granite mortars. Separating the copper ore from whatever other impurities broke free, they weighed it and carefully combined it with beaten fragments of tin, purchased from the Phoenicians who imported it from lands so far away they had no names in the languages of Canaan. The smelters poured this mixture into basalt crucibles resting atop clay furnaces, fired by seasoned acacia wood. Teams of Kenites took turns pumping endlessly at the wood-and-leather bellows that kept the coals nearly white-hot. In some crucibles Manoah could see that the ore had already melted into shining pools of molten bronze; workers skimmed off the dull, grey dross that floated atop the pure metal. When the metal was pure enough, they poured it into waiting wooden, clay, or stone molds to form rough swords, plow blades, jewelry, or ingots.

Elon-tohr led Manoah and Naamah to the mouth of the mine. Several of the workers glanced their way as they went by, but with no more than passing curiosity in their eyes. Just inside the mine's black maw, the shaft plunged straight down, disappearing into shadow. A burly Kenite with a shaved head was manning a thick rope that wound several times around a polished log suspended over the vertical shaft, then attached to a huge rope basket framed in wooden slats. The log had been fitted with large spokes that the Kenite could grasp to control the lift's ascent or descent. As Manoah, Naamah, and Elon-tohr approached, he lowered four miners who stood in the basket slowly down the shaft.

He did not look at them as he worked, slowly releasing rope to let the basket descend. "Hebrews?" he asked, his accent thick.

"We are," Elon-tohr answered. "We wish to buy passage down into the mines."

The Kenite paused for the briefest of moments, knotted cords of muscle in his arms and back straining. Then he continued lowering the basket, still without turning to look at them. "You running from something?"

"Yes." Elon-tohr shifted so that he could better see the Kenite's face. "We will pay you well for your trouble."

The basket must have reached the bottom of the shaft—the rope went slack and the Kenite stood, grimacing and pushing his shoulders back to stretch his muscles. He turned at last to face them. "Have you ever been in a mine before?"

Manoah was about to shake his head no, but Elon-tohr nodded curtly. "I have." He dropped a handful of coins into the Kenite's gloved hand. The bald miner glanced at the coins, and his eyebrows rose appreciatively.

"You will find no one down below who will help with your woman if she gives out in the darkness," the Kenite said. "These are miners, not soft-hearted farmers."

Manoah put one arm around Naamah's shoulders. "I will care for my wife, as long as someone will help us find the other exit."

The Kenite studied them a moment longer, as if weighing the idea in his mind, then shook his head and slipped the coins into a pouch at his waist. "You are all mad, but I will gladly take your money."

He hauled the basket back up again, and Manoah helped Naamah into it, then clambered in himself. Elon-tohr vaulted in smoothly, landing half-crouched, like a cat. As the Kenite began lowering them, Elon looked up at him one last time. "Philistine soldiers may be following us. You should warn your men to be ready to defend themselves."

The big Kenite just shook his head, as if this confirmed his assessment of their mental state, and continued slowly releasing the rope.

They descended in fits and jerks, clinging to the sides of the basket to keep from falling. Torches had been ensconced on all four corners of the basket, and the air in the shaft was thick with smoke and dust. The reddish torchlight glimmered against sheer walls of rock on all four sides, sometimes glittering off veins, pockets of crystals, or metallic flecks.

Naamah crouched in the bottom of the basket, her arms around her knees. Manoah knelt next to her, trying to see her face in the darkness. "Is it alright with you?" he asked softly.

She nodded but did not speak, her eyes fixed on her sandals. The basket lurched sharply, swinging and bouncing off the wall of the shaft. Manoah clutched one side, trying with his other arm to support his wife. He glanced upward where the square of light above them was steadily shrinking. "I will get you to safety, Naamah," he said.

She did not respond, and Manoah stood, sorrow, fear, exhaustion, and frustration threatening to tear him apart.

At that moment, shouting echoed down to them from above, followed by a sharp clatter, as of a clash of arms. The basket lurched again, dropping dramatically, and stopped so quickly that Manoah found himself sprawled atop Naamah on its wooden floor. He pulled himself back to his feet.

A shout sounded above them, and a moment later a body came hurtling down the shaft and crashed into them. Naamah screamed as one of the ropes supporting the basket snapped, and one woven side tore apart; the basket careened sideways and all of them clutched desperately at whatever they could reach to keep from tumbling over the side into the blackness below.

All but one of the torches had fallen or been extinguished, and the shaft was plunged into near-darkness. Manoah grabbed the body, and heaved it over the side of the lift, recognizing as he did so the face of the burly Kenite who had taken Elon-tohr's money.

More shouting echoed from above them, and Elon reached out and grabbed Manoah's shoulder. "Hold onto something!" he hissed.

The basket suddenly began to ascend, and Manoah realized with a shock that whoever had killed the Kenite was now pulling them back up to kill them as well. He had no doubt as to who would be waiting for them at the top of the shaft.

Then Elon-tohr's slender blade was in his hand, red, as though bloodied, in the torchlight. Before Manoah could even think to protest, the blade hacked twice at the thick rope that supported the lift. The strands of hemp fiber separated with a snap, the basket lurched once more, extinguishing the last torch, and they plummeted through the blackness.

23

The fall lasted only a moment before they crashed to the bottom of the shaft, all three of them tumbling into a heap amidst the wreckage of the lift. It took a panicked moment to extricate themselves. Manoah pulled his wife to him in the darkness. "Naamah! Is it all right with you?"

He felt her arms go around him, holding him tightly for a moment. "I am not injured," she whispered into his ear, and he hugged her even more tightly, scowling up at Elon-tohr, who was vaguely silhouetted against flickering lamplight from somewhere down the tunnel before them. The grey-clad warrior ignored him.

Manoah helped his wife to her feet. They were following Elon-tohr down the mineshaft before he realized that Naamah had spoken, the first words she had uttered since Gibbethon.

A tunnel leading away from the lift shaft gradually descended through the rock, and torches burned in brackets every few dozen paces along its length. Removing two of them and handing one to Manoah, Elon-tohr led them swiftly down the mine. Over the crunch of their sandals on the rocky soil beneath their feet, they could hear the sound of hammering and loud conversation echoing from somewhere ahead of them.

After only a few minutes of walking, the shaft emptied them into a large, high-ceilinged room, not chipped out by the hands of miners, but molded and shaped by the slow efforts of natural forces. Clusters of smooth, twisting clumps of stone and conical stalagmites jutted from the floor. Several dozen miners were scattered through the cavern, chipping away at the walls by torch and lamplight. Six shafts exited from the chamber, some of them lit by torchlight as well; others were impenetrable, black maws gaping in the stone walls. Manoah glanced upward at the massive, multi-colored stalactites suspended overhead. The room echoed loudly with the sounds of the miners' work, and Manoah saw that many of them had tied bands of cloth around their ears to block out the incessant cacophony.

One of the miners finally noticed them and, turning toward them in surprise, shouted something to the men working nearby. They others put down their hammers and stared as well until the chamber had fallen into a hollow silence. Manoah held Naamah close to him, noticing how her voluptuous figure drew the miners' black-rimmed eyes.

"Your mine has been attacked by the Philistines," Elon announced, his voice echoing eerily. "The lift is destroyed. You must leave here before the soldiers discover a way to descend."

The miners talked among themselves in low voices for a moment. "Who are you?" one of them asked at last. Apparently, he was one of the Kenite overseers, for he carried no tools.

"I am an Israelite from the north," Elon-tohr answered. "The Philistines who attacked you were pursuing my companions and me from the sack of the city of Gibbethon."

The overseer dispatched one of his workers with a gesture, and the man ran back down the tunnel toward the lift. A moment later he returned, nodding solemnly. "The lift is shattered, and I could hear sounds of battle from above."

"Fools!" The overseer snapped. "The Philistines should know better than to anger the princes of Midian!" He turned back to Elon-tohr. "Follow us, and quickly."

The miners abandoned their tools and began streaming into two of the tunnels that exited the chamber. The three Israelites followed the overseer into one of them, pausing a moment while he removed a torch for himself from one of the brackets. Behind them, other miners were extinguishing every light in the cavern. Manoah smiled grimly. If the Philistines did find a way down, they would have a difficult time discovering which tunnel their quarry had used to exit the mines.

The shaft they were following wound through the darkness. The walls were sometimes smooth, the stone bearing the marks of hammer and chisel where the miners had dug their way through solid rock. In other places, they were clearly following some naturally formed passage, the walls and ceiling rough with glittering crystals and crumbling stone.

Manoah walked with one arm around Naamah's shoulders. "We are going to a place of safety, my love," he whispered. "Elon-tohr and I will keep you on high. When we are clear of these mines, we will go to Aijalon. You always liked that city when we visited it before—its walls are high and strong. We will be safe there, among friends."

A couple of times, Manoah thought he felt her nodding against his shoulder, but she did not speak. For the first time since he had ridden out of Gibeon, he felt his body beginning to relax. He realized that he had not slept for more than a full day and night, and exhaustion was rapidly catching up to him. Perhaps when they were clear of the mines, they would find a safe place to stop and rest.

A sound echoed from the tunnel behind them, and the miners turned and glanced worriedly over their shoulders. "They are in the chamber," the overseer whispered, and they quickened their pace. Behind them, someone was yelling, not in anger, but as though they were trying to convey some important information to the fleeing miners. But the words were lost in the endless echoes of the caves, and the Kenites did not slow.

The tunnel they were traveling through began to narrow, until they reached a spot wide enough for only one man at a time to squeeze through sideways. On the other side, the tunnel made a sharp corner, and then continued into blackness. When they had pressed through the narrow opening, Elon-tohr touched Manoah's shoulder.

"Follow these men to the exit." The black-clad warrior's eyes bored into Manoah's; the torch's orange flame glimmered in each dark socket. "I will wait here and make sure you have time enough to get clear of the mines."

Manoah hesitated. "The Philistines may never find us in this maze. Come with us, Elon—I would not have your life on my conscience."

The Zebulunite smiled—the first time Manoah had seen him do so. "Do you have no faith? We are fighting for the Almighty. We will not lose."

"That doesn't mean that you will not die," Manoah said.

Elon-tohr looked away, back down the blackness of the tunnel. "If I die to accomplish the unalterable will of God, then what does it matter? I will wake in Paradise."

He turned back to meet Manoah's eyes. "But I will not die. Go. Get your wife to safety."

He drew his sword and placed himself next to the narrow opening. Manoah waited a moment longer, and then loped down the tunnel after the Kenites, pulling Naamah along behind him.

By the time he caught up to the miners, the sounds of pursuit from behind them had become clearer. A man was yelling after them, his voice high-pitched and strange in the cacophony of echoes. But before they turned down yet another tunnel and the sounds were lost, Manoah made out what the man was saying: "I will cut, sow, and winnow you like grain! The sword reveals the heart!"

Manoah did not have time to wonder at the strangeness of the words. Hurrying forward, they followed the Kenite overseer through the endless darkness. Manoah's feet and legs had gone numb, and he was moving through willpower alone when they reached the exit. They emerged in a dense forest of oaks, with moonlight shining down through the broad leaves and intertwined branches above them. The mining overseer bid Manoah and Naamah a safe journey, then led his men back toward Timnah, no doubt to try to recapture their mine and its valuable yield.

Manoah gripped his wife's hand tightly and, wondering what had become of the enigmatic Elon-tohr, led her slowly into the cover of the forest of Hereth.

24

    The day's activities were ending in the Tabernacle when Rohgah strode boldly through the gates and into the bustling Courtyard. Ahitub was officiating at the Altar, and Samuel was nearby, holding animals while the Priests inspected them for defects. Neither Hophni nor Phinehas had appeared that morning, but Eli was sitting on his carved, wooden chair in front of the golden pillars that bracketed the entrance of the Tabernacle, his sightless eyes staring out over the throng of people and animals filling the Courtyard, his worn staff resting across his knees.

    Rohgah's voice rang out over the clamor. "Eli!" he screamed, and in the silence that followed that call, it was as if all of Shiloh paused and turned.

    The Prophet stood in front of the gateway, both arms raised high; in his right hand he grasped his own gnarled staff. Even from a distance, Samuel could see the fire that burned behind his bright eyes, the hidden energy that pulsed within his bent frame. "High Priest Eli! Will you hear the word of Jehovah?"

    He did not wait for an answer. Instead, he strode forward toward the Tabernacle, staff swinging, and the crowd of people, hushed and staring, parted before him. It was so quiet that Samuel could hear the sizzling of the fat upon the distant Altar. The fire popped, and everyone nearby jumped at the sound.

    Eli leaned forward and tried to heave himself up out of his chair. His first attempt failed, his bulk overcoming his weakening arms, and he sank down again heavily, his staff clattering onto the flagstones at his feet.

Samuel raced across the Courtyard without thinking, grasping the old Priest's thick arm and helping him to rise.

Rohgah stood in front of Eli now, only two or three paces away, the staff planted firmly in front of him. "Will you hear the word of Jehovah?" he asked again, loud enough that his voice carried across the still Courtyard.

Eli turned his milky eyes on Samuel. "Who is it that speaks, my child?"

"It is a Prophet of God, my lord," Samuel answered, and Rohgah nodded to him in pleased confirmation. Something in the look the Prophet gave him made Samuel vaguely uncomfortable, as if somehow Rohgah felt that he and Samuel were partners in what was about to happen.

Eli turned again to face the Prophet, rising stiffly to his full height. "I will hear your words, man of the True God." Then, to Samuel: "Lead us to my room, my son."

Samuel picked up Eli's staff and gave it to the old man, and they began to walk. As they made their way toward the door of the High Priest's home, nestled against the south wall of the Tabernacle, Samuel could feel the eyes of everyone in the Courtyard upon him, and he suddenly regretted his spontaneous decision to go to Eli's assistance. But in a few moments, they passed through Eli's door, and Samuel helped the High Priest to a seat on a wide, U-shaped divan nestled against one wall.

Samuel saw Rohgah's deep-set eyes sweep the room once, taking in the spare furnishings: a writing desk, the divan, a cushioned chair, an empty scroll box. The remnants of Eli's breakfast still lay on the writing desk. The Prophet finished studying the surroundings and his eyes fixed again on the High Priest, now seated, breathing heavily. Eli still clutched the staff in one hand. Samuel stepped backward and stood silently in a corner of the room, trying to melt into the shadows.

They did not exchange pleasantries. "This is what Jehovah has said," Rohgah began, his voice somber and heavy with accusation. "'Did I not make Myself known to the household of your forefather, Aaron, when they were still slaves to Pharaoh of Egypt? I chose him out of all the tribes of Israel, to act as Priest for Me, to go up to My Altar and make the smoke of sacrifices ascend—to bear the *ephod* before Me, and to receive the Priest's portion from all the offerings.'"

Rohgah paused, but Eli did not respond. He bowed his turbaned head, his thick shoulders hunched as if a great weight rested upon them. The Prophet continued: "'These were the privileges that you and your sons inherited! So why do you men keep kicking at My sacrifice, and at the offerings I have commanded to be made in My house? And you, Eli, keep honoring your sons more than you honor Me, by fattening yourselves from the best of every offering—My offerings, from My people!'

"That is why Jehovah the God of Israel says to you: 'Although I did, indeed, say that your house and the house of your forefather would serve before Me to time indefinite, now I say that it is unthinkable on My part to let you continue to act as My Priests, because those honoring Me, I shall honor; but those despising Me will be worth little in My eyes.

"'Look! The day is coming when I will cut off the arm of your forefather's house, so that no man of your house will live to see old age. An enemy of yours will serve in My dwelling. There is one man of yours that I shall not cut off from being at My Altar, but most of your house will all die by the sword, so as to cause your soul to pine away in grief.

"'By this sign I demonstrate My judgment against your sons, Hophni and Phinehas: On one day both of them will be brought to silence.'"

Eli's head had continued to sink as the Prophet spoke until now his white beard was splayed across his chest, and he was looking down at his lap. At the Prophet's last words, a choked sob escaped Eli, and Samuel saw tears dripping from his long nose onto his robe. Rohgah must have seen them as well, but he continued to speak. "'And I shall certainly raise up for Myself a faithful Priest, a Priest who will do what is in My heart and in My soul. For him I will build a lasting house. And it must occur that anyone remaining of your house will come and bow down to him, begging to serve him for the payment of a piece of bread.'"

Rohgah thumped his staff twice on the floor of the room. "So Jehovah has spoken. I have delivered the words of Jehovah."

"Wait!" Eli said, his voice cracking. He struggled to rise, pulling himself up with his staff. To Samuel's horror, the staff bowed and then shattered with a great crack under the High Priest's weight, and the old man fell heavily to his knees.

Rohgah said nothing, just looked down a moment at the hunched form of the man crumpled on the floor in front of him among the shattered pieces of the staff. Then he turned and found Samuel in his shadowed corner. A strange sadness swept across the Prophet's features, like the shadow of a cloud passing over the sun. "Farewell, little one. I am sorry we did not have more time together. May Jehovah be with you."

Rohgah pulled his mantle tighter around his shoulders and strode purposefully out of the house. The oak door banged closed behind him, and he was gone.

For a few moments, the room was silent but for the quiet sobbing of Eli. Samuel felt lightheaded, as if he was falling endlessly or the earth was rolling by underneath his feet. Jehovah had seen what was happening in Shiloh. He had delivered His judgment, and it could not be thwarted.

Hophni and Phinehas had been sentenced to death.

Samuel was trying to decide what to do next—whether he should try and comfort or aid Eli or simply sneak out the door as if he had not seen what had transpired. But before he made up his mind, the door slammed open again, and Hophni and Phinehas strode into the room.

Phinehas took in the scene at a glance—all of it except Samuel, who stood behind the two Priests, hidden in shadow. He went to his father and raised the old man back onto the divan. "Father? What has happened?"

Eli looked up at his son's face, tears running down the creases in his aged skin. "The word of Jehovah has been heard again in Shiloh," he whispered.

"The old man?" Hophni asked, glancing back over his shoulder.

"That *young* man was a Prophet!" Eli said. "Jehovah has delivered a message of doom to the house of Eli."

Hophni smirked. "Pay him no heed, Father..."

"Close your mouth, Hophni!" Phinehas snapped. He knelt beside Eli. "What did the man say?"

"He has prophesied the end of our house!" Eli said. "He has uttered a curse upon us and foretold that the Priesthood will be ripped from our hands."

Phinehas was still for a long while, studying his father's face. "Perhaps he spoke of a time still many years away—."

"He has prophesied your deaths!" Eli snapped. "Both of you have received the unalterable judgment of God! Both of you will die in one day!"

Hophni's mouth opened, but no sound came out, and his face turned white. Phinehas was silent also, but tight-lipped and grim as he studied his father's tear-streaked face. Both brothers stood frozen for several moments, and Samuel was suddenly aware that he could once again hear footsteps, voices, and animals in the Courtyard outside.

Phinehas broke the silence in the room. "You are High Priest, Father. Make supplication for us, and offer the sacrifices of cleansing that this judgment might pass us by..."

"You are High Priest!" Eli roared, his face red. "The time for sacrifices is past! The two of you have brought this down upon your own heads—and I doubt very much if many of the children of Israel will be found weeping at your burial! Your arrogance and selfish disregard for the Torah have summoned the Malediction that Moses foretold, and from Dan to Beersheba, the people you are supposed to serve are suffering under its smothering darkness! You have ignored my warnings and the protests of the Elders of the twelve tribes for too long! And now it is too late for you."

Phinehas stood, teeth clenched and eyes narrowed. "We have lived this long. We will live longer, I think. Jehovah is not the only god with the power of life and death!"

"You dare to say those words within these sacred grounds!" Eli raged, his hands white-knuckled as they clutched the front edge of the divan. "Get out of here! Get out of my home!"

Hophni took a step forward, fist raised, and Samuel cowered, afraid that the big Priest was going to strike down his own father. But Phinehas held his brother back.

"No half-mad dreamer is going to sit in judgment of the Priests of Israel and leave here unharmed!" Hophni snarled. "He has violated the Torah, and he will pay for his crimes! We will see who lives and who dies."

"Get out!" Eli yelled again, and the two brothers strode from the room, slamming the door behind them.

Samuel waited several moments in the shadows, trying to quiet the sound of his breathing as Eli continued to weep. Then he crept on tiptoe to the door and slipped into the twilit Courtyard.

He had taken only a half dozen steps across the flagstones when a voice stopped him. "Samuel!"

He froze and turned slowly to find Hophni standing beside the door of Eli's house, staring down at him, his wide face split by its cold, reptilian smile. "Did you think you had escaped my notice, eavesdropping in the corner?"

Samuel was about to defend himself when he realized it would make no difference. He instead stood in silence, looking at the ground.

Hophni took three slow, measured steps toward him. "So! Our little gatekeeper thinks his unspoken judgment against the Priests is justified now! You feel that you are somehow above us, lofty Levite that you are!"

He leaned down and grabbed Samuel's chin with a grip that made his jaw ache, and raised Samuel's face until their eyes met. "No one is above the Priests, Samuel. A son of Aaron has filled my hand with power. I hold your life in my palm." He smiled sardonically and let go of Samuel. "But that doesn't frighten you, does it? You think, perhaps, that you will be protected from harm. But Jephthah was the Judge of Israel, a great warrior who also dared to speak out against us. And he is now dead."

The sun must have sunk below the hills at that moment, for the silver trumpet rang out, signaling the end of the day. The sound traveled down Samuel's spine like a chill, and he heard Rohgah's words in his mind: *When the time comes to act, Samuel, you will know.*

An emotion that he could not identify filled him, something that stirred and leapt within his chest, like flames erupting from a disturbed bed of smoldering coals. He pointed toward the trumpeter. "Do you hear that, Hophni? The day ends. Your day ends! A darkness is descending on Israel, a night whose dawn you will not live to see! And on the day that Jehovah cleanses this holy place of the sickness with which you have infected it and those who dare to defy the True God are brought to silence, then all Israel will rejoice at the brightness of that sunrise!"

Hophni released him and took a step backward, licking his lips and glancing around as if concerned that someone had heard Samuel's words. "Perhaps you have forgotten the dead woman who hangs now at the gates of Shiloh," he said, trying to force bravery into his voice. "Do you think this could not happen to your mother, or your sister? Do not dare to repeat what you heard tonight, or I will take payment for your error out of the skin of those you love."

Samuel stared at the big Priest: *Eyes wet and wide; pupils dilated. Shoulders moving with quick, shallow breaths. Thumbs sliding back and forth across clenched fingers.* Recognizing fear in every sign, Samuel dared a smile, Without a word, he turned his back on Hophni and walked, without hurrying, to his own room.

Inside he collapsed on his bed, so awash in emotions he felt as if his head would burst. Change had come at last to Shiloh. The only questions that remained were whether or not it had come in time and whether the children of Israel would accept it. For so many centuries they had lived and died on the strength of their traditions, relying on the Priesthood and the Levites to keep them in check, failing even to learn the true meaning of the Torah and how they should apply it in their lives. They would have to learn new ways now, and that would not be easy—especially for those who had adopted false worship and superstition as a part of their daily lives. They would have to learn to swim in the flood of change that Rohgah's prophecy had unleashed or be swept away by its unstoppable force.

He did not realize that he had fallen asleep until he started awake. His room was black, but out his narrow window he could see the deep blue color of a clear sky that was nearing dawn; a single, bright star glimmered like a beacon against the darkness. He sat up, pulling his blanket around his shoulders, wondering what had woken him. He had been dreaming, he remembered, a dream that was more feelings than images, a dream of being caught up in something grand and wondrous, of being summoned toward some lofty task...

A Voice cut through his sleep-fogged thoughts, and Samuel felt fear and awe sweep through him with the shocking suddenness of plunging into a pool of cold water on a hot day.

—*Samuel*—

25

Samuel sat bolt upright in bed, his heart pounding against his ribs. By some trick of the still night air, the Voice sounded as if it were coming from all around him, or resonating in his mind as though it were part of his own thoughts.

"Here I am!" he answered, sliding from his bed to the cold floor. No one responded; he padded silently out of his room and scanned the moonlit Courtyard. The flagstones were damp with dew and chilled his bare feet. All was silent and empty.

It must have been Eli, he thought to himself. The Voice had not really sounded like Eli, but perhaps that had been a trick of his somnambulant mind. Who else would be summoning him in the middle of the night?

Confused, he scurried across the Courtyard the short distance that separated their rooms, slipping through Eli's front door and across the room where he had hidden the day before. He poked his head into the High Priest's sleeping chamber.

"Here I am!" he announced, surprised to find the room dark and silent.

Eli sat up in bed, rubbing his sightless eyes and casting about for the source of the voice. "Eh? Samuel? Is that you?"

"Yes, my lord." Samuel's confusion deepened. Eli looked as if Samuel had woken him. "You called for me, and…and here I am."

Eli coughed once, and then cleared his throat. "I did not call for you. Go and lie down again, my son."

The High Priest lay back on his bed, pulling the blankets up to cover his massive bulk. Samuel waited a moment, and then walked slowly back to his own room. Someone had called him! It had been the voice of a man, strong and kind. It had not been Phinehas, or Hophni, or Ahitub—of that he was sure.

He got back into his bed but did not lie down, sitting instead with his knees pulled to his chest, his wool blanket wrapped around him. An owl hooted softly in the distance, and the sound made Samuel feel suddenly alone. The events of the day swept through his mind: Rohgah's condemnation, Hophni's threats...

—Samuel—

A chill prickled his scalp and raced down his spine to his toes. He slid out of bed again, terrified, until he convinced himself that Eli must have thought of something he wanted to tell Samuel now that he had been wakened.

He padded swiftly across to the High Priest's home again and walked once more into his bedchamber. "Here I am...," he announced, his voice trailing off as he realized that Eli was not waiting for him. The High Priest was still in bed; he sat up when Samuel entered, and the bed frame creaked warningly.

Samuel's fear and confusion deepened. "Here I am, for you did call me, my lord!"

Eli sighed. "Samuel...I did not call, my son. Go lie down!"

Samuel hesitated, wondering if he should say anything more. Then he thought better of it and backed slowly out of the room. "Yes, my lord."

He scanned the Courtyard carefully as he returned to his room, his mind racing and his nerves on edge. He half expected the unknown speaker to leap out at him from every shadow. Someone was calling him! If not Eli, then who?

He sat on the edge of his bed this time, his heart pounding. Every night sound startled him; every flicker of a shadow caught his eye. He crossed his arms and tried to slow his breathing.

—Samuel—

He leapt to his feet and began to cry in spite of his determination to be brave. Running across the Courtyard, he forced himself not to look constantly over his shoulder, haunted by the sensation that someone was following him. Again, he burst into Eli's sleeping chamber, and the High Priest sat up abruptly at the sound of his entrance.

"Here I am, my lord, for you must have called me!" Samuel said through his tears.

Eli sat silently for a few moments. The room was black—Samuel could not make out the old man's expression.

"Samuel," he said gently. "Go back to your bed."

"But, my lord—."

"Go back to your bed," Eli repeated firmly. "Lie down, and if you hear the voice call to you again, you must answer: 'Speak, Jehovah, for your servant is listening.'"

Samuel felt a lump in his throat that he could not make disappear, and his mouth went dry. "My lord? I don't understand…"

"Do as I say, Samuel," Eli said, his voice warm in the darkness.

Samuel walked woodenly back toward his room. As he crossed the Courtyard this time, he looked over at the shadowy form of the Tabernacle itself. Changing direction, he headed to the entrance of the great building, wanting for the moment to be anywhere but back in his room. The moon was bright over the western horizon, shining from between fluffy clouds to cast its cold glow over everything inside the Curtain wall. Through small gaps between and beneath the curtains that served as the door of the Tabernacle, he could see the glow of the menorah still burning inside. It would have nearly run out of oil by now, he knew—within an hour or two, a Priest would enter and refill it and re-ignite any of the seven flames that had gone out. Standing close to the entrance of the Tabernacle, he could smell the unique aroma of the smoke-laden cloth, infused with the incense, the formula for which was a sacred recipe used only at the Tabernacle for holy purposes. The sweet smell was so familiar to him, and he realized with surprise that to many people it was foreign. So much of his everyday life was comprised of things unknown outside the walls of the Tabernacle Courtyard. So much that was sacred he too often took for granted.

He raised his eyes to the roof of the Tabernacle, towering above him. Beneath the shroud of those dark, sealskin coverings, hidden within a paneled room, the Ark of the Covenant sat. Above it burned the *Shekinah*, a miraculous sign of Jehovah's Presence. He had lived within a few feet of that Presence since he was a small child, and had felt no fear. But tonight, at the thought of speaking with the One the *Shekinah* represented, he was nearly overwhelmed with terror.

He forced himself to cross the Courtyard once more and entered his room, curling up on one corner of his bed, arms hugging his knees, waiting in silent fear for what he knew was about to happen.

Almost immediately, the Voice came.

—*Samuel*—

He tried to swallow and failed; his mouth felt as though it were caked with dust. "Speak, Jehovah," he croaked, "for your servant is listening."

The Voice answered instantly, kind, loving, and immeasurably powerful. It swept through Samuel like a warm breeze rippling the grass on a hilltop, resonating in him the way that thunder shakes one from within when it rumbles close by.

—*You are ready, Samuel, to tell to My people the miseries that are coming upon them. I am doing something in Israel that will cause the ears of all who hear what I have done to tingle. On the day that I choose, I will certainly do just as I have spoken respecting Eli and his house, from beginning to end. The sons of Eli will die in one day—*

—And you must tell him that I am judging his house forever for his error, because his sons are calling down evil upon God, and he has not stopped them. For he has loved his sons more than he loves Me and the high office I have entrusted to him. And that is why I have sworn that no sacrifice or offering will exempt the error of the house of Eli from punishment, even for eternity. You must tell him, Samuel—

—Speak My words to Eli, even as I have said them to you—

The Voice faded, and an unnatural stillness settled over Samuel's room. He sat motionless on the edge of his bed, the words echoing in the recesses of his mind. He felt as if he had stepped abruptly into cool shadow from the heat of the summer sun and he shivered, feeling goose bumps prickling his arms and neck.

He remembered his anxiety earlier in the day, recalling the phrase repeated by so many pilgrims to the Tabernacle: *The word of Jehovah has become rare in Shiloh.* He himself had wished that the True God would once more make Himself known in the city, would take action against the corruption in Shiloh and once again appoint a spokesman for Himself within the boundaries of His holy house.

But not me! he thought, his eyes tearing with anxiety. *It cannot be me!*

He wanted the Voice to return, frightening though the experience was, and give him the opportunity to refuse the assignment, to tell Jehovah that he was only a child and unready for such a duty. But even as the desire crossed his mind, he remembered the words of Rohgah: *You are more than a child, Samuel…Do you think Jehovah's hand is cut short because you are young? When the time comes to act, you will know.*

But if Hophni and Phinehas were angry with him already for not supporting their judgments or submitting to their authority, imagine how they would react when he proclaimed their imminent deaths! He remembered Hophni's threat. The Priest's words had sounded hollow and empty that evening, but he knew all too well what the sons of Eli were capable of if someone aroused their anger.

He could not be a Prophet! So much within him was sinful and weak! Phinehas and Hophni had seen it, and although their condemnation had been harsh, it also carried a healthy serving of truth. He wanted to be a good person, but found himself far too often contemplating what was bad in Jehovah's eyes. He had neither wisdom nor courage. If people in Israel admired him as the Gatekeeper of the House of God, it was because they did not truly know him, did not see into the hidden darkness in his soul. What would happen now, if he were thrust into the light, if by speaking the pronouncements of Jehovah he brought the eyes of all Israel on himself?

He would not withstand that scrutiny. They would see quickly what he really was, just as Hophni had said. He did desire to be a great person. He desired to have praise from his fellow men. But inside, he knew, in spite of how others looked at him, that he was the same as they were. He was not the special child they wished him to be. He was only Samuel, and that was not enough.

The sky outside his room shifted from black to deep blue to light blue, streaked with the reds of dawn. The transformation seemed to happen more quickly than ever before. Soon, the Priests and Levites would begin tending to their duties in the Courtyard. He would have to go out and open the gate, and when he did, Eli would be waiting for him. He did not rise though, sitting on his bed with his arms wrapped tightly around his knees. For a few more moments, he pretended that if he simply stayed here on his bed, he could imagine that none of this had happened. He could pretend that he did not have to look into the blind eyes of an old, old man and tell him that his only children would be ripped from him without redemption at a time when all that remained to Eli was the legacy of his offspring, and his failing hope that they would repent of their sins.

Quiet voices sounded outside his door, and soft footsteps passed by. He heard Ahitub's voice announcing something to the Priests and realized that sunrise was near.

He forced himself to his feet, binding his hair with a ribbon of cloth. Sliding his new *me'il* over his head, he thought suddenly of his father and mother. It would not be long before they heard that he had spoken condemnation against the sons of Eli. Would they even believe what he said? Would anyone believe that Jehovah had spoken to him, a child without any great lineage, without any qualification other than that he was a Nazirite in Shiloh?

But he thought about Eli's reaction during the night, and he knew that people would believe it. Eli already knew what had happened. Samuel was a Prophet in Israel, and he did not think that the High Priest would hide that fact, even though Samuel's prophecy was one of judgment against Eli's sons. And the people would want to believe it as well—they were desperate for some indication that Jehovah had not left them.

He rose and went to the gate. He was surprised to find that Eli was not there. The horn blew, and he performed his office, perfunctorily greeting the people who entered. A part of him felt strangely alienated from them, from everything that had been a normal part of his life before that night. They smiled and thanked him as they did every day, and he wanted to grab their shoulders and shake them, yelling: *All is different! Can you not see that nothing is the same?*

When he turned to go to his breakfast, Eli was waiting for him.

The High Priest stood alone near the Curtain wall, leaning heavily upon a new staff, his sightless eyes looking toward the open gate. Samuel froze, thinking for a moment of sneaking past the blind man and hiding for a day in his room.

"Samuel, my son." Eli raised one arm and beckoned him near.

Samuel immediately heard Jehovah's words in his head, boiling within him like steam seeking escape from a lidded pot. Only his fear and anguish kept him from screaming them out immediately. He walked toward Eli, but not within reach of his outstretched arm. He could not bear to be that close. "Here I am, my lord."

Eli's voice was gentle. "What has Jehovah spoken to you, Samuel? Please—do not hide it from me."

Samuel hesitated, battling the insistence of the words roiling in his mind, trying to ignore their scream for release. A memory suddenly came to him from many years before, a memory of sitting with other children at the feet of Eli somewhere in the Courtyard. The High Priest was telling them the story of the crossing of the Red Sea, holding out his staff before him like Moses, marching along with broad, confident steps. Samuel remembered himself and the other children laughing, and the twinkle in Eli's bright eyes.

Eli noticed his hesitation, and his voice grew stern. "May God do so to you and so may He add to it if you should hide from me one word of all that He has spoken to you!"

The rosy light of dawn glowed on the High Priest's face and robes. Samuel felt tears in his eyes and brushed them away. His inner defenses crumbled, and in a rush, the words poured out of him; he repeated them just as Jehovah had spoken them, as the Voice had branded them into his memory the night before. When he finished speaking, he stumbled forward into Eli's arms, and the High Priest held him close. Samuel pressed his cheek against the old man's woolen robes, breathing in the grandfatherly smell that had become so familiar to him.

"It is Jehovah that has spoken." Eli's voice was heavy with resignation. "What is good in His eyes, let Him do."

26

Within a few moments of exiting the Midianite mines, Manoah had found a small clearing amidst the dense sycamores and oaks of the Forest of Hereth. He and Naamah collapsed onto a thick bed of dry leaves amidst the sprawling roots of an ancient oak, huddling together under their cloaks for warmth. Manoah did not have any way to light a fire; even if he had brought flint and tinder, he would not have dared to reveal their presence to any who might find their way out of the mines in pursuit of them.

Naamah fell into a deep sleep as soon as they lay down, and Manoah dozed fitfully beside her. His exhaustion allowed him to ignore the cold and discomfort of their makeshift bed, but he still started awake every time some noise pierced the nighttime silence of the forest. Once, he woke to a lion roaring in the distance, but after listening for a moment, he realized how far away it was and went back to sleep. In the blue-black hours of early morning, a terrible bellowing waked him, a sound he did not recognize. It reminded him of the angry warning of a bull in breeding season when it felt something was threatening its cows. The noise continued for only a few moments, but its proximity and foreignness put his nerves on edge again, and he was unable to go back to sleep.

Instead, he lay against the roots of the tree, cradling his sleeping wife in his arms. He was far more anxious for her than for himself—had he been alone, he knew that by now he would have been up and hurrying toward his destination. But her presence, her fragility, his own obligation to protect and help her, was a burden that he could not—would not—escape.

He looked down at her beautiful face, still and serene in repose, her full lips parted and a hint of a smile curling the corners of her mouth. He loved her desperately, and at the same time, felt a terrible sense of frustration whenever he allowed himself to think about their situation. He would do everything in his power to get her safely to Aijalon, but what then? If they managed to survive the dangers of the forest and the pursuing Philistines, even if they regained their home once again, would it not be only to find themselves back in the same situation as before: shamed before all Israel, the Prince of Dan who could not bring forth an heir? What future did life hold for them? He tried to imagine all the years ahead, watching the children of his brothers growing into men while he and Naamah descended into the weakness of old age. And one day, he would be unable to work anymore, and he and Naamah would have no sons to plow their fields for them, to tread their grapes in the heat of the summer sun. He tried to picture himself, stooped over in a neighbor's field, attempting to glean enough spilled and overlooked grain to provide a meal for himself and his aging wife, and the thought filled him with bitterness.

Naamah stirred against his chest and made a soft, contented sound, no doubt lost in some dream of happier times. Moonlight filtered down through the leaves and glowed gently on her flawless skin. He could see each of her long, thick lashes distinctly against her cheeks, even in the half-light. He remembered the awe in his brothers' faces when he had brought Naamah home to be his wife. They had never seen a woman so beautiful. No one was surprised at their match—Manoah had been a leader among his people since his young manhood, his fields, flocks, and vineyards blessed by Jehovah, his hand mighty in battle against their enemies. The tribe of Dan expected that his parents would negotiate a wife for him from among the most beautiful women in all Israel.

His brothers did not look that way at him or Naamah anymore. The sight of their own sons and daughters had filled the hunger he used to see in their eyes. Now men of Gibbethon who had once respected him looked on him with eyes softened by pity. It angered him, and yet he could not blame them for their concern. Families were the way of life for the people of Israel. Children to carry on one's name, children to live and work in the ancestral lands of their family. Sons, heirs, were the greatest wealth a man could have. And rich as he might be in other ways, in this most important way Manoah was a pauper. Whatever he might do in his years as a man would be lost on the day of his death. His name would die out in Israel.

The strange bellowing echoed through the forest again—closer this time than before. Remembering Elon-tohr's warnings about the Forest of Hereth, he wondered if something were pursuing them that was even more dangerous than the Philistines were. Glancing at the color of the starlit sky, he guessed that it was still an hour or two until dawn.

Sighing, he wrapped his arms tighter around his wife and wondered if he really wanted the day to come.

As soon as Naamah woke they began traveling again. Their muscles ached, and they started moving to the sound of their stomachs growling. For over an hour, they clambered through the dense brush of the tangled Forest of Hereth, weary in spite of their night's sleep. At times, Manoah had to draw his sword and hack a path for them in the dry, intertwining branches. They spoke little, but Manoah was relieved to hear his wife speaking at all, and he let the occasional sound of her voice and the bright warmth of the sun above them cheer him.

He was even more relieved when they stumbled from the trees onto a road, winding its way east. Few roads transversed the Forest of Hereth, and, based on what he knew of their location, Manoah was confident that this one would eventually take them to Aijalon. They quickened their pace and followed the rutted thoroughfare through the trees.

Not long after they reached the road, Manoah spotted some berries growing, vine-like, up a tree. He collected them, only partly successful in avoiding the long thorns that grew from the vine. He did not know their name but remembered eating them when he was a child. The berries were hard and sour, but palatable, although Manoah's stomach growled even more loudly after he ate them. A little later on, they came upon a fig sycamore leaning over one side of the road with a few figs still on it—the birds had not yet managed to eat them all. Manoah had to climb the tree to reach them, and when he had tossed Naamah about ten of the ripe fruits, the branch he was clinging to snapped and dumped him unceremoniously onto the road. He was not seriously hurt, and he was rewarded for his discomfort with a mischievous smile that flashed across his wife's face. The smile did more for his hunger than the figs.

When they had eaten their fill, they continued down the road, their mouths and fingers sticky with fig honey. The sun had begun to sink toward the hills to the west when Manoah heard the baying of hounds and the thunder of approaching horse's hooves. They dove back into the cover of the forest and began to travel as swiftly as possible across country once again.

Unfortunately, Manoah was in such a hurry to get off the road and distance them from any pursuit that it was not long before he realized that he had become hopelessly turned around in the gulleys and folds of Hereth. At times, even the sun was not visible through the dense treetops, and he had to keep re-orienting himself to maintain a roughly southeasterly direction, at the same time ensuring that they did not end up too close to the road where the hounds would certainly get their scent. But the forest grew so densely in places that it chose their path for them, and forced them to travel long distances in the wrong direction before they found a break in the tangled brush that would allow them to return to the proper course.

He stopped finally, with the shadows lengthening all around them, unsure of where to turn. At that moment, the strange bellowing from the night before echoed again off the hills, closer now than before. Naamah grabbed his arm, looking around in fear. Manoah gripped his sheathed sword's hilt with his left hand, trying to determine from which direction the sound was coming. He did not have to wait long to find out. To the west of them, they heard something big moving through the brush, snapping limbs and saplings as it came.

Manoah grabbed his wife's hand and they clambered east through the trees and underbrush. Even as they ran, he could tell that whatever was pursuing them was gaining—the sound of its violent passage grew louder and louder. He drew his sword and began looking for a place to make a stand against it.

They burst into a copse of trees, a nearly circular hollow surrounded by thick oaks on all but one side. He helped his wife scramble up one of the trees; she clung to a thick branch several spans above his head, her hands white-knuckled where they clutched the rough, mossy bark. Turning, he gripped his sword tightly and waited for the thing to appear.

Time congealed. Leaves drifted down to the forest floor all around him, swirling and skating on a breeze wafting through the branches. Each breath filling his lungs, each beat of his heart kept time with the thundering approach. The ridges of leather tooled into the grip of his sword pressed against his sweaty palm. He wished vainly that he had some idea of what he was about to face. Above him, he heard Naamah trying to stifle her weeping and he gritted his teeth, vowing that he would not sell his life cheaply.

Unbidden, the thought passed through his mind that if only he had sons, they would be standing beside him. He cursed himself for the thought and felt tears burning the corners of his eyes. This was not how he had pictured his life ending: hunted like an animal, caring for a woman turned helpless by circumstances, knowing that when he was gone, his name would disappear with him.

The creature bellowed again, and this time the force of its cry shook the ground. Trees snapped as if flattened by an avalanche, and leaves and branches rained down through the forest canopy onto the path of the thing's approach.

Something huge and black hurtled toward him from under the shadow of the trees, plowing into the circle of oaks. It tore a gnarled trunk, thicker than Manoah's waist, from the ground as it burst into the clearing. Branches shattered, sending splinters of wood flying in every direction.

Before Manoah's unbelieving eyes stood an aurochs, the largest and most savage creature in all of Canaan. It was a type of bull, its shoulders, knotted and ridged with muscle, higher than Manoah's head, its powerful, black body as long as two horses placed end to end. It paused for just a moment when it saw him, tossing its massive head and snorting steam from its scarred, black nostrils. Knife-sharp, curling horns arched forward from behind its angry eyes, wider than Manoah could span with both outstretched arms. One hoofed foot, as big around as a buckler, pawed the ground in challenge.

It roared again and charged toward him. The sickle-sword in Manoah's hand felt absurdly small, and he dove out of its path at the last moment, rolling to his feet with his back to the oaks. The aurochs continued past him, but then turned like a cat, a snap of movement, fluid and graceful, and faced him again.

Manoah knew the creatures by reputation only. Fierce, intractable, they killed anything that moved in mindless defense of their territory and for the simple joy of killing. No one had ever captured an aurochs, and even the teams of hunters who occasionally went in pursuit of one had killed few. They inhabited only the wildest reaches of Canaan, and they had no natural predators.

The brute studied Manoah, its head lowered, baleful eyes glaring. Manoah heard it breathe out a great rush of air, and its muscles rolled and tightened beneath its armor-tough skin.

Without warning it shot forward, spraying leaves and detritus out behind it. Manoah spun away as it closed on him, slashing out wildly toward the creature's legs. He felt his blade connect for a moment, but then the beast was past, turning again with fluid grace, the only sign of Manoah's success the thin line of scarlet along the edge of his sword.

This time, the aurochs did not even pause before spinning back on its own tracks and lunging for Manoah. The Danite felt its breath, hot against his face, before his mind even registered that he was too slow to avoid its charge. Instinct born of dozens of battles spun him clear of the knifing horns, and the beast's forehead slammed into Manoah's chest with explosive force.

He heard Naamah's scream as he was lifted from the ground and launched across the clearing. He hurtled into one of the oak trunks, felt something crack in his back as he bounced off, and landed on his face in the dead leaves and moss carpeting the forest floor.

He rolled over, his mind screaming for him to get to his feet, but he could not get any air into his lungs. He fought desperately for breath until the muscles of his abdomen relaxed and he gasped a chestful of air.

He sat up just in time to see the aurochs closing on him again, its churning hooves carving a path through the duff that led directly to the spot where he lay.

Manoah grabbed his sword with both hands and swung furiously upward toward the creature's throat, simultaneously rolling to one side and praying that the massive hooves missed him.

Again, his blade slashed into the animal and came away bloodied. And again, the aurochs did not even seem to notice.

Manoah could see a trickle of blood on one of its legs, but the cuts he had made were barely scratches to the monster that loomed over him.

He scrambled to his feet, vaguely aware of Naamah weeping somewhere above him. He knew that his only hope was somehow to escape its attention. He could not kill it. Even if he could get close enough, he doubted he would have the strength to push the blade of his sword through the creature's hide.

He was about to look for a tree to climb when the aurochs charged again, hurtling toward him, head lowered, kicking up a flurry of twigs and leaves beneath its churning hooves. From the limbs above his head, Naamah screamed. An instant too late, Manoah realized that he had again waited too long to escape the reach of the wide horns and he dove once more to the side, praying that by some miracle the beast would miss him.

And a miracle happened.

From out of the trees another shape leapt, a towering giant of a man, roaring an answer to the aurochs' bellow. The giant leapt toward the mighty bull and tackled it, throwing his arms around its thick neck. So huge was Manoah's rescuer that the force of his attack tumbled both man and bull to the leaf-strewn ground in a flurry of hooves and limbs.

An instant later both were on their feet again, and in the giant's hands was an enormous, double-bladed battle-axe. He leaned forward, facing the aurochs, and still he stood half again as tall as Manoah. The aurochs launched itself at the giant without a moment's hesitation, but the huge man twisted to one side with unexpected agility, just dodging the swipe of a razor horn, and brought the blade of the axe down on the back of the bull's skull. With a crack like the sound of a woodcutter chopping into an oak tree, the axe blade buried itself in the creature's neck. It fell forward onto its face, its legs crumpling under it until it lay, a black hillock of sweaty flesh, atop the leaf-strewn forest floor.

The giant man straightened and turned to face Manoah, who was standing with his mouth open, still clutching his sword.

Seconds later, Elon-tohr bounded into the clearing like a black panther, skidding to a crouch, a slender sword held in each hand. The giant jerked his axe free of the aurochs' spine and cradled it in his hands. He and the grey-clad Zebulunite faced each other for several moments, each sizing the other up. Then Elon nodded as if he had made a decision, sheathed his swords fluidly over his shoulders and turned to Manoah.

"I can see you have been busy while I was gone," he said.

27

The Rephaim giant slid his battleaxe into a sheath on his back and, drawing a long, bronze knife, began to bleed and skin the aurochs as if it were the most normal thing in the world. Manoah watched a moment in stunned silence, then looked over at Elon-tohr for some explanation. The grey-clad warrior just glanced once at the giant and shrugged. "I will gather wood for a fire."

Manoah helped Naamah clamber down. He held her tightly when her feet were once more on the ground; across the clearing, Elon-tohr had gathered a pile of deadwood and was crouched next to it, striking sparks from a flint. Naamah looked at Manoah, and he studied her face, trying to determine how much the stress of the last few minutes had affected her. "Is it all right with you, my love?" he asked.

She nodded.

He glanced over at the hulking form of the Rephaim, cutting away strips of bright red meat from the corpse of the aurochs. "Are you hungry?" he asked Naamah.

"Starving!" she said, smiling, and Manoah let himself smile as well.

He walked over to where Elon-tohr was slowly adding wood to the small fire he had started. He crouched down beside the warrior, glancing over his shoulder at the giant, still butchering the aurochs. "Who is he?" he asked.

Elon-tohr shrugged. "I've never seen him before."

Manoah almost fell over in shock. "But I thought...I assumed he came with you!"

Elon-tohr shook his head and began trimming branches with a long knife to form a spit.

Manoah leaned closer. "Then why...then can we trust him? How do we know which side he is on?"

Elon-tohr stopped what he was doing and turned to look at the Rephaim for several moments. The giant stood, his hands clutching strips of meat, then draped them over a nearby branch. "It appears, for the moment, that he is on our side," the enigmatic warrior said softly.

Naamah had seated herself on a rounded stone near the fire and was holding her hands out to its flickering warmth. The Rephaim brought some of the strips of meat over and handed them to Elon-tohr, who skewered them and placed them on his spit over the flames.

"I am Elon-tohr, of Zebulun. What is your name?"

The giant squatted next to the flames. In the failing light, the fire cast blue-black shadows over his deep-set eyes. His nose was wide and flat, crooked as though it had been broken years before, and lines of dots had been tattooed across his pocked cheeks. "I am Saphold of the Rephaim," he answered with a rumble, his accent thick.

"What is a Rephaim doing so far from Bashan?" Manoah asked.

Saphold leaned forward to turn the spit on the fire; grease dripped from the meat into the coals with a hiss. "Sarnam, Axis Lord of Ashkelon, has made a treaty with my people. An army of our warriors has joined Sarnam's Philistines to do battle with the Hebrews."

Manoah tensed, glancing over at Elon-tohr. Did the giant not know that they were Israelites?

Elon-tohr, too, seemed to be considering the Rephaim's response. "What, then, brought you to our aid this evening?"

Saphold sat back on his heels and scratched his curly, black beard. "I had a...disagreement with the leader of my *Metteh*—my tribe. I have been banished from the company of the Rephaim until I am prepared to defend myself in trial by combat."

Manoah shook his head in confusion. "I'm not sure I understand."

Saphold studied him for a moment. "Whenever there is a disagreement between the leaders of the Rephaim, our gods demand that the matter be settled by combat. The gods will favor the one that is in the right, and grant him victory." He paused a moment, looking into the fire and stirring the coals with a stick. "It is what our people believe."

Elon-tohr shifted. "But not what you believe?"

Saphold shrugged. "If I come face-to-face with any Rephaim from today onward, and he challenges me, we must immediately battle to the death, no matter what else may be happening around us. If I am killed, the baru-priests say this is proof that the gods have judged me in the wrong.

But if I win, then the next Rephaim that I meet must again challenge me. This will continue until I am killed."

Elon-tohr nodded. "So your innocence would be proved only if you killed off every Rephaim in Israel."

Saphold grunted. "Every Rephaim in Canaan. Only your people call the land Israel."

Elon-tohr was silent for a moment, staring into the flames. Saphold lifted the spit and examined the meat. "What do you know about this Lord Ashkelon?" Elon-tohr asked him.

"Very little," the giant rumbled. "But he has offered the Rephaim magical weapons in exchange for our services, as well as gold in abundance. And he does not fear us."

"Why not?" Manoah asked.

"Because of his own warriors, death-troops that have come with him from the wars in Egypt," Saphold answered.

Elon-tohr nodded and glanced at Manoah. "Lord Ashkelon calls them his Gedhudhra. I fought some of them in the mines at Timnah. They are good fighters. I was slightly injured by one of them."

The grey-clad Zebulunite turned toward Saphold. "What will you do now?"

The giant shrugged again, pulling a strip of meat off the spit and blowing on it. "I do not yet know. I was passing through the forest when I saw a woman in a tree threatened by an aurochs. My plans did not extend beyond saving her."

Naamah looked over at the giant and smiled, her skin made even more beautiful by the firelight. He handed her the roasted meat, nodding in a subtle bow, but Manoah could not tell if he hid a smile beneath his thick, black beard.

"Why not join us for a while?" Elon-tohr said after a moment. "We travel to the city of Aijalon to muster Israel's forces against the Philistines. We could use your arms in battle."

Saphold stared at him a long time, so long that Manoah began to wonder if he had gone into a daze. At last, the Rephaim stood and walked over to a nearby tree. Sitting down among the roots, he wrapped his cloak around his massive form and leaned his thick mass of black curls back against the gnarled bark. "I will sleep on it."

He closed his eyes and was still. Manoah watched him for a few moments, glancing over at Elon-tohr to gauge the warrior's reaction. But the Zebulunite was busy removing another strip of meat from the spit. At last, he saw Manoah looking at him. "I will take first watch," he said softly. "Get some sleep—and your wife as well."

Manoah looked over at the giant. "I'm not sure any of us should sleep tonight."

Elon-tohr bit a piece off the meat in his hand. He ate delicately, as if he were afraid of getting dirty, holding the roasted flesh daintily between the thumb and forefinger of his left hand. "If he wanted to harm you, Manoah, do you think he would have to wait until you were asleep to do so?"

Nervous as the idea made him, Manoah knew the Zebulunite was right. He helped Naamah find a flat spot under the outstretched oak branches. Together, they picked out as many rocks and twigs as they could find, then mounded leaves on the spot. They finished eating the roasted flesh of the aurochs, feeling drowsiness steal over them after their first real meal in days. After wrapping Naamah in her cloak, Manoah lay down next to her, determined to stay awake and keep one eye on the Rephaim on the other side of the fire.

Within moments, he was fast asleep.

It was after midnight when Manoah awoke. The moonlight shone brightly through the branches overhead, dappling everything in the glade with shadows. He sat up quickly, embarrassed that he had failed so miserably despite his determination to stay awake. The fire was out, but not far from it, he could see the silhouette of Elon-tohr sitting silent and still, his cowl pulled over his head. Nearby, a shadowed mound against the roots of another oak was all he could see of the sleeping Saphold.

Manoah stood and went to Elon-tohr's side. Sitting in the leaves and grass beside him, he touched the enigmatic warrior's shoulder. "Thank you for letting me sleep. Please—I will watch for a while. Get some rest yourself."

Elon-tohr nodded but made no effort to stand. "Will your wife be all right?" he whispered.

Manoah shrugged and smiled. "I wish I knew."

"You must see that she is kept safe, Manoah. That, above all else, is your responsibility."

"Your words only echo the thoughts that chide me endlessly," Manoah said.

"I had a wife once," Elon-tohr said. "Many years ago."

"I had heard...I did not know," Manoah stammered.

"To be loved by a woman, to represent her to Jehovah," Elon-tohr breathed, shaking his head. "It is the greatest thing we can hope to accomplish in life, is it not?"

Manoah struggled to find an answer. "It is a two-edged blessing, I think—sharp enough to cut the hand that wields it."

Elon-tohr raised one eyebrow. "You speak like a man with too many concubines."

Manoah felt his face flush with embarrassment. "I had not heard that you were skilled also in the complexities of love."

He regretted the words as soon as he said them, but the grey-clad warrior did not seem angered, just turned away to stare out into the darkness of the forest around them. "What have you heard about me, Manoah?" he asked after a moment's pause.

Manoah looked over at him, but could see nothing of his expression in the shadows of the man's cowl. "That you are the greatest warrior in Israel—some say the greatest there has ever been."

Elon-tohr nodded slowly. "Some men have a gift for shaping clay into pots. Others for raising sheep—or fashioning a crown from an ingot of bronze." He turned toward Manoah, and the moonlight glowed on his shadowed face. "I have a gift for taking life from other men."

Manoah did not know what to say; instead, he waited in silence.

"I am a warrior," Elon-tohr continued after a moment. "Killing is what I do best. From the first time I held a weapon in my hands, I knew it. Ever since that day, I have tested myself against every possible martial situation, and I have learned that my first impression was not wrong. This is who I am."

He turned to face Manoah, and now the Gadite could see the anguish on the man's face. "But Jehovah is a God of peace! Peace is what He wants for His people! Our promise from Him is a land without war—without even the threat of war! Where will Elon-tohr fit into such a land, Manoah?"

"You may have other gifts," Manoah said. "Gifts for times of peace."

The dark-clad warrior's eyebrows arched. "Ah, yes, I may." He leaned closer to Manoah. "But I have no desire for peace. I want to want it—but I do not. My gift is in death, in handling a blade. Without war, I am a man without a place."

Manoah shook his head. "You do not love war."

A sardonic smile flashed across Elon-tohr's face. "Do I not? Do you know what it is to have mastery of something, Manoah of Dan? Do you know the feeling of being so good at a single discipline that it shapes your every footstep, your every word—that it even haunts your dreams? Have you ever felt the yearning for something so intensely that to go without it is like going without water, or light?"

He held his slender hands out in front of him, palms upward, studying them as though they belonged to someone else. "Like those of a Priest, these hands have been filled with power," he whispered. "A power to save my people by killing those who would see them destroyed. It is a worthy cause, is it not? To execute judgment against those who refuse to live by the law of the Great Lawgiver?"

He closed his hands and let them fall into his lap. Turning again, he looked intensely into Manoah's eyes. "But I must wonder—am I also, perhaps, marked by Jehovah for judgment? If I am sent by God to execute wrongdoers, then whom will He send to execute me?"

Before Manoah could say anything, the Zebulunite stood and strode silently into the shadows of the trees, disappearing into the blackness beneath their sprawling limbs.

Manoah did not imagine for one moment that the enigmatic warrior was sleeping.

28

The next morning, Elon-tohr led Manoah and Naamah from the cover of the forest once again and followed the winding road through the Vale of Aijalon. Saphold joined them, rising at daybreak and strapping his axe across his broad back. He offered no explanation for his decision, just followed the group as they left the forest glade and made their way through the dense forest of Hereth.

Sullen clouds hovered on the western horizon, but the morning sun was bright and clear, and cheerful birdsong accompanied them as they traveled. Manoah could not stop looking over his shoulder for the Philistines, but Elon-tohr seemed unconcerned, setting a swift pace as he led them along the rutted road.

They reached the city in mid-afternoon without incident. As they approached its massive walls, they merged with hundreds of other travelers, primarily men of war, streaming into the city from east and west. The Elders had sent a summons to the four corners of Israel, and the warriors of the land were responding.

A sprawling village of tents filled the valley plain outside Aijalon's wall, divided into sections for each tribe and identified by tribal flags that fluttered lazily in the warm northeasterly breeze. The camp was a flurry of activity—men loading supply wagons, smiths repairing and sharpening weapons, soldiers rubbing leather shields with animal fat or olive oil. A stream trickled from the city wall into a small pool in the valley, and Levites and Priests there sanctified men for battle, washing them ceremonially in the muddy water.

In spite of the steady stream of travelers, the company from Gibbethon did not blend into the crowd. Men stared in unabashed awe at the giant Saphold, unspoken questions or outright fear in their eyes. Manoah almost laughed aloud at some of the expressions, but he knew what a spectacle they must present: a battered Danite warrior, a shockingly beautiful woman, a hulking Rephaim giant, and Elon-tohr, his grey clothing still meticulously clean and neat. It was likely the oddest group of travelers that had ever walked in the shadow of Aijalon's walls.

The Elders of Aijalon met them at the city gate, two dozen awed men clutching their vermilion staffs. Staring up at Saphold in obvious fear, they sent the group to a command tent set up nearby. Manoah noticed immediately that the banner fluttering above the tent was emblazoned with the cluster of grapes of the tribe of Ephraim.

At the door of the tent stood a gruff, stocky, middle-aged man with a huge, bristly black beard. He introduced himself to them as Deker of Ephraim, commander of the forces mustering at Aijalon.

Manoah gripped Deker's knotted forearm firmly. "I am Manoah of Dan—formerly of Gibbethon."

Deker's eyes narrowed, and he shook his head sympathetically. "I am glad that you escaped that heartless attack. Too few did. May Jehovah see it, and remember!"

He looked curiously at Naamah. "Your wife traveled here with you?"

Manoah nodded. "This is Naamah. I am hoping that she can find a safe place here and be cared for until this…this conflict is past. She has endured much in the past few days."

"Wait one moment," Deker said, and disappeared into the tent. Seconds later, he emerged with a woman about his own age. "This is my wife, Ileah."

Ileah went immediately to Naamah's side and put her arms around her. "My poor dear—you must be exhausted." She turned to Manoah, leaving one arm around Naamah's shoulders. "If my lord wishes it, I will take her to our home in the city."

"I am already in your debt," Manoah said. "May Jehovah bless your hospitality."

He hugged his wife and kissed her. "I will come to find you as soon as I can." He brushed her soft hair with his hand. "You are safe now, my love."

She nodded, but he could see the tears starting in the corners of her eyes. "Do not be gone from me for too long."

"I won't," he promised.

Ileah led Naamah through the gates and into the city, talking softly to her as they went. Manoah watched them for a few moments, thinking that his wife was now in better hands than his.

Deker was greeting the Zebulunite. "It has been a long time, Elon-tohr. I cannot say how glad we are to have you here. Do any others of your tribe accompany you?"

Elon-tohr shook his head. "No. But they will not ignore the summons. No doubt they will meet us soon."

"Well, we are grateful for your help, in any case," answered Deker. He pointed across the field at a sprawling tent surrounded by men eating on the grass. "Please get yourselves a meal, and join me back here at the trumpet blast for a meeting of commanders."

He looked up at Saphold. "And what are we supposed to do with this one?" he asked Elon-tohr.

"I will vouch for him," the warrior replied.

Deker shrugged. "The word of Elon-tohr is good enough for me. I will see you back here soon."

They went to the tent where groups of women ladled roasted beef and lentils spiced with garlic and cumin over hot rounds of wheat bread. While they ate on the grass outside, a continuous stream of people passed them on their way into the city—many more soldiers, but hundreds of refugees as well, coming in from the coastal plain. The refugees were immediately identifiable—they traveled as families, carrying few belongings with them, and fear and anguish clouded their faces.

A few Danites came to find Manoah as well. Some of them were men he knew from the area around Gibbethon, and he stood and embraced them in greeting. They stared at Saphold in wonder, and Manoah explained over and over that the giant had decided to join them in their struggle against the Philistines. Some of the men expressed their gratitude, but he could see in their eyes that most of them did not like the idea of having a Rephaim in their midst.

By the time Manoah had finished eating, several dozen Danites had gathered nearby, and Manoah realized abruptly that Deker must have been sending them to him, expecting that Manoah, as an Elder of his tribe, would take responsibility for them and lead them in the battle. He was glad to find that one of them bore the tribe's banner stitched around the shaft of his spear: the coiled snake of Dan. He planted it at the border of the encampment set aside for them, and told the men to go to the Priests and sanctify themselves.

The horn was blown, and the commanders of Israel gathered at Deker's tent, staring at Saphold as he settled in, nonplussed, at the edge of the ring of men.

"May Jehovah bless all of you for coming," Deker said. "And may His hand be strong against our enemies."

The men murmured and nodded in response.

"Contingents have arrived from most of the tribes," Deker continued. "I will be in command of three thousand men of Ephraim—it is all that could be gathered from my tribe. Perhaps more will join us on the battlefield. I hope so.

"We have learned that the Philistine force that conquered Gibbethon has marched north, toward Lod. It is unlikely that we will reach them before they destroy that city as well. Our best hope is to beat them to what appears, from the information our spies could gather, to be their final goal: the city of Aphek. I have already sent word to Aphek warning them to ready the city for an attack. Our plan is to join the forces already there as quickly as possible and stop the Philistines in the fields outside the city."

He turned to a lanky man with fair skin and sparkling, green eyes seated to his left. "This is Basar, who will lead the men of Benjamin. Four hundred slingers have left their flocks to come with him."

Manoah studied the Benjaminite, thinking about the scandalous history of the tribe. They were shepherds, highly skilled with their short bows and their slings. Benjaminite children would have their dominant hand bound behind them by their parents, in order to teach them to be ambidextrous. Added to that, as shepherds they spent countless hours shooting crows from off the backs of their sheep. They were the best marksmen in Israel—it was said that the Benjaminite slingers simply did not miss.

But they were few in number, and many men of the other tribes still scorned them for a dark chapter in their history. The tribe of Benjamin had fought a civil war against all the other tribes many years before. The war was initiated by a horrific crime committed by a group of Benjaminite travelers—they had gang-raped the concubine of a man in Gibeah, raped her until the woman had died. Unbelievably, the rest of the tribe had condoned their actions and refused to execute the men as the Torah required. The other eleven tribes gathered against them at Mizpah. In the first two battles, the tribe of Benjamin had defeated the combined forces of the other tribes—both because Benjamin's army was extraordinarily large, and because of their exceptional skill with bow and sling. But in the third battle, an ambush by the other tribes had all but exterminated the Benjaminites. Only six hundred of their soldiers survived the slaughter that followed. Although many decades had passed since the war, soldiers of the other tribes still viewed the men of Benjamin with distrust.

Deker was speaking again, pointing to a man seated in the shadows to his right. "This is Arod of Gad, who brings a thousand of his tribesmen to our ranks."

Arod stood, a tall, well-built man with a great mane of reddish-blonde hair and beard. He smiled broadly at the gathered leaders. "May Jehovah give strength to our arms, and wisdom to our minds."

Manoah had fought alongside the Gadites before, in the war against Ammon. They were from the rough hill country east of the Jordan and had traveled far already to get to Aijalon. They fought with lance and shield and were well known for their swiftness, agility, and fierceness in battle. Arod had gained himself a reputation as a fearless fighter.

The introductions continued: Lodan, an Issacharian who specialized in military intelligence, had brought with him a few dozen spies and runners from his territory, many miles to the north. He expressed hope that a few more of his people would join them, but did not expect many. He was a cautious, quiet man, methodical and careful.

A wealthy and experienced war-leader, Azor, brought the largest single force—three thousand Judean spear and shield men. Azor was a stocky, red-bearded man with eyebrows that jutted out wildly in every direction. He scanned the gathered commanders with penetrating, deep-set eyes, as if he were testing the mettle of them all.

Five hundred men had come from Reuben, and a handful of scattered soldiers from other tribes. The muster had produced fewer men than any of them hoped for—less than nine thousand, all told. Everyone hoped that more men from the tribes of Naphtali, Zebulun, Manasseh, and Asher would join them at Aphek.

"What do we know of the Philistine army?" someone asked.

"My spies estimate their number at nearly fifteen thousand men," Lodan answered quietly.

Deker smiled. "And Lodan's spies are well known for overestimating the enemy," he said bluntly. "Lodan is the most cautious man I know!"

A few men chuckled, but most of them were still contemplating the slaughter that would soon happen at Lod. Elon-tohr stood smoothly. "As you have seen, this Rephaim, Saphold, has chosen to join with us in this battle. He comes to us with news of our enemy that all of you should hear. A new Axis Lord of Ashkelon is behind this attack, a general named Sarnam. He comes from the wars in Egypt, and he brings with him seasoned death-troops that he calls his Gedhudhra. They are armed with iron weapons, and ride swift Hittite chariots into battle with iron scythes affixed to their wheels."

"No army can be armed entirely with iron!" someone protested.

"I have seen them," Elon stated simply. "I have fought against them at Gibbethon. They are the most deadly warriors I have ever encountered. But I am afraid there is more bad news."

He paused; every eye was on him. "Sarnam has made an alliance with the Rephaim of Bashan. That is what brought Saphold to this country. When we encounter the Philistines at Aphek, we will be battling Rephaim giants as well."

A hush fell over the room. Few in the tent had even seen a Rephaim before Saphold arrived at Aijalon, but all of them understood what this latest development meant.

"So be it." Deker clapped his hands once, rubbing them briskly, palm to palm. "The Philistines are marching toward Aphek. We must not allow them to take the city and gain control over our trade routes. It would mean defeat for Israel by trade, as sure and deadly as a defeat in war."

Deker scanned the room slowly, his black beard bristling. "We march at dawn."

29

Eli did not hide Samuel's words. News of the child-prophet spread through the Tabernacle and swept through the streets of Shiloh like a fire blown by an autumn wind. By mid-morning everywhere Samuel went he found crowds pointing and staring or approaching him with words of praise or honor. He went about his duties numbly, trying futilely to sort out his feelings about himself and embarrassed that he expected to. He was the same person as the day before—or was he?

He began to try to avoid the crowds, seeking tasks that took him into the more private places in the Tabernacle complex. But that effort, too, failed. Even the Priests and Levites on duty looked at him strangely as he walked by; men who would never have given him a second glance now stood still while he passed, nodding or bowing respectfully toward him.

Things got worse when his family arrived from the city. A Levite found him at work in the wood storage room, stacking the dry pieces of Altar firewood gathered by the Gibeonites from the hills beyond the city. "You are needed at the gate, my…Samuel," the man said nervously. Samuel glanced at him. *Head slightly bowed. Shoulders raised. Hands clasped in front of him. Eyebrows arched.* The man was fifteen years his senior, and still he was acting nervous and subservient, as if he were afraid Samuel was about to condemn him, as well.

Samuel brushed the woodchips off his arms and chest. "Is it Ahitub who sent you?"

The man shook his head and smiled. "No—it is your father. Your family is asking for you."

Samuel found his parents and siblings anxiously awaiting his appearance when he arrived at the gate. His father hugged him and told him how proud he was, but Samuel could see the discomfort trying to conceal itself in his face, a sense of confusion as to how he was supposed to feel about this stranger in front of him. *I left a son at Shiloh*, his eyes said. *I return to find a Prophet and a child I do not know.*

It was worse with his siblings. They stared at him as if he had grown a third arm he was hiding behind his back, and they were waiting for him to pull it out with a flourish. He had already felt like a stranger to them—now the gulf between them had widened into a chasm that neither he nor they were big enough to reach across. He was amused to find himself pitying them as he realized how strange their predicament must be. They had been asked to come to terms with a brother they did not know who was honored as Hannah's firstborn and as a Nazirite—now they were required to add Prophet to the list of strangenesses that defined this foreign sibling. He was pleasantly surprised that he did not find anger or jealousy in any of their eyes.

His mother hugged him tightly. "We are proud of you," she whispered into his ear, as if afraid that his brothers and sisters might hear her.

He pulled away a moment, his emotions coalescing into unreasonable irritation. "Why, Mother? I have done nothing to deserve this honor."

She smiled down at him, but he could see in her eyes a shadow of something that might have been wariness. "Jehovah has chosen you for His spokesman!" she said, as if that were an answer to his question.

"It is a great honor," his father added belatedly.

"But do not let it raise the height of your nose," Hannah said.

"I have nothing to be proud of," Samuel said, looking at the ground, knowing it was what his mother wanted to hear.

"Be grateful to be a servant of Jehovah," Hannah answered. "You simply have a new assignment now."

Samuel heard the words she did not speak: *and that is no reason to think more of yourself.*

Samuel looked up from the ground. "Thank you for coming, but I must tend to my duties—and I am sure that you have things to do as well."

"Get back to work," Elkanah said, nodding endlessly. He seemed relieved that the conversation was at an end. "We will talk later."

Samuel turned and walked swiftly across the Courtyard, feeling his face burning with embarrassment. He thought about his mother's words and remembered the day that she brought him to Shiloh. People told him he could not possibly remember events that happened to him when he was a son of three years, but he did. He remembered everything.

He remembered his mother holding him tightly in her arms as they climbed the road through the city. It had been a quiet morning, bitterly cold, and a light drizzle misted down all around them. Samuel remembered seeing droplets clinging to the looping threads of his mother's head covering. The hawkers and shopkeepers paid no attention to them as they passed—the greyness and chill dampened even their commercial enthusiasms.

His mother held him so tightly, and he liked the way the warmth from her body seeped into him. It was the first time he had come to Shiloh. His parents had talked to him about his destiny ever since he was old enough to understand, but Hannah could not bring herself to take him there, even for a visit, until the time had come to give him up. Even then, he could tell that his parents sometimes had to force themselves to sound happy about fulfilling their vow, and he wondered in his naiveté what bad thing would happen to him in Shiloh that they were so afraid of his going there.

His father led a bull behind them on a lead rope, a bull that had been born the same day as Samuel and that Elkanah had dedicated as the gift offering they would make. Samuel could see the bull over his mother's shoulder and how the burden of damp wineskins and baskets of grain slung across its spine jostled back and forth with each step the animal made.

Samuel remembered his excitement when they entered the Courtyard and his first glimpses of the smoking Altar, the copper Laver, the sacrificial animals everywhere, and the great, sealskin-tented box of the Tabernacle itself. Smells and sounds overwhelmed his senses, and he stared and pointed in unabashed enthusiasm, not understanding why his parents did not share his joy.

Ahitub was the young Priest who had met them that bitter morning. He spoke with Elkanah for a moment; Samuel could not hear their words. Then Ahitub padded toward Hannah and Samuel. When Samuel saw him approaching, he had asked excitedly, "Are you the High Priest?"

Ahitub had smiled warmly. "No—but my hands are with the High Priest in offering sacrifices to Jehovah. Will you join your hands to ours, Samuel?"

A group of Levites were slaughtering a goat; the animal had collapsed soundlessly onto the flagstones, and Samuel watched as they hoisted it on a hook to be bled and dressed. Hannah set him down, and as he separated from her warm body, he felt the cold of the morning stabbing through his clothes like daggers. His mother crossed her arms and hugged herself tightly, as if trying to hold onto some part of him still.

"You must remove your shoes, Samuel," Ahitub told him. "We serve barefoot in the Courtyard of the House."

Samuel took off his sandals; the stones were frigid against the soles of his feet. "It's cold!"

Ahitub led him across the Courtyard to the Altar, and opening the firebox, allowed him to push two pieces of wood into the bed of coals. He noticed the dryness of the acacia and the way that the fire swirled around it, then leapt swiftly away as if the flames were alive and eternal and the fuel only a dead, fading thing.

Elkanah had led the bull forward and placed Samuel's palm on its forehead where the stiff, dark hairs splayed out from one spot like the petals of a flower.

"Accept this offering, O Jehovah, in behalf of my son," Elkanah said, his voice cracking.

A Priest slaughtered the beast with a long, bronze knife, and when it collapsed in a heap on the stones, another Priest captured the blood in a copper bowl. Samuel remembered looking back and forth from the streaming blood—it flowed endlessly—to his mother; in his child's mind, it was as if the blood was somehow draining also from her cheeks as she stood mutely, tears trickling down her paling face.

The bull was butchered and sacrificed, and the grain and drink offerings followed it onto the grate. Samuel stood near the flames, palms outstretched toward the Altar, innocently warming his hands at the sacred fire and watching the smoke writhe upwards into the drizzle. Ahitub leaned down next to him. "Jehovah is pleased with your sacrifice, Samuel. At this moment, our God is thinking about you and your family. He is thinking of how He will bless you for what you have done here today."

Samuel looked back at his mother, excited to share the moment with her. She was still weeping, and so he turned instead to his father. "How will He bless us, Father?"

Elkanah's mouth opened as if to respond, then closed again and he swallowed.

Hannah took a gasping breath, and her chin shook as she kneeled next to him. "You did well in helping the Priest, Samuel."

He nodded, confused at her emotion. "That's my job now."

She nodded back, trying to force her unwilling mouth to smile, then reached out and pulled him close. "It is time for you…it is time for you to stay…here at the Tabernacle, where the Ark of Jehovah is." She glanced at Ahitub. "It is time for you to keep on helping…"

It was what they had been telling him would happen for as long as he could remember, and her words held no surprise for him. He did not truly comprehend yet what the words meant, the separation that was about to take place—to his child's mind, an inexplicable banishment. His entire experience was the passing of twelve seasons. He could not understand that one life was ending, and another was beginning.

His father had offered a prayer then, a prayer whose exact words Samuel would not remember in the years to come. But the memory of the prayer's sentiments stuck with him, like an echo in the back of his mind that never died. He talked of how grateful he was to Jehovah for this son, and for the three years they had spent together. He petitioned Jehovah to accept the bull they had sacrificed, and with it to accept the child as one set apart for special service. He renewed the vow that Hannah had made, promising that Samuel would serve as a Nazirite to Jehovah all his days. He pleaded with God to be with Samuel, to give him wisdom and a righteous heart, to guide his path as he grew that he might bring honor and glory to the God of Israel by all that he said and did. And he begged the Most High for the strength and wisdom to continue living without his son.

By the time the prayer was over, both his mother and his father were weeping openly, and Samuel found himself crying as well, not understanding why, only knowing that his parents were more upset than he had ever seen them before. Ahitub spoke to Elkanah briefly while the offering continued to burn behind them, and then his parents led Samuel toward the door of the Tabernacle.

High Priest Eli was sitting in his throne-like chair in front of the Tabernacle entrance, between two of the pillars. His head was bowed over his chest, and his huge stomach sagged across his thighs beneath the folds of his robes. Hannah approached him, holding Samuel's hand in her own. "Excuse me, my lord!"

Eli looked up with a start and saw them approaching. Leaning forward, he heaved his great bulk out of the creaking chair and stood waiting for them, leaning on his staff.

"Excuse me, my lord," Hannah repeated when they got closer. "Do you remember me?"

Eli looked from her to Elkanah, then to the child, and paused, confusion etched on his features.

"I am the woman that stood with you in this place four years ago," Hannah continued. "You spoke to me as I was praying to Jehovah."

Eli looked puzzled for a moment. Then he nodded slowly. "Yes...I do remember. One evening as the sun set. You were praying...very intently."

Hannah nodded. "That day, I prayed to Jehovah for a child. I made a vow that if He heard my request, I would give the child to serve here, at His House." She laid her hands on Samuel's shoulders. "And Jehovah has answered my prayer." Her voice cracked, and she bowed her head and wept for a moment, then composed herself and continued. "So I have come back, to loan him to Jehovah. As long as he lives, he will belong to Jehovah as a Nazirite."

Eli looked again at Samuel, then back at his parents. "This is your only child, my daughter?"

Hannah nodded.

"What you have done is of great value in Jehovah's eyes," Eli said. "May He give to you many more children in the place of this one you have lent to Him."

Samuel remembered how Hannah had blushed at the High Priest's compliment and begun fussing with Samuel's hair.

Eli raised his arms heavenward, staff still clutched in one hand. His deep voice boomed out ceremoniously. "May Jehovah bless you and keep you. May Jehovah make His face shine toward you, and may He favor you. May Jehovah lift up His face toward you and assign peace to you."

Hannah had knelt next to Samuel again and whispered, "You will make your father very proud."

She had then said her own prayer, the one that haunted Samuel's dreams. "You cause my heart to exult, O Jehovah. By Your power, the barren woman has given birth. Jehovah summons death and quickens to life; He brings down to the grave and He resurrects. Jehovah impoverishes and enriches; He abases and He exalts. He raises the poor from the dust, and lifts the needy from the ash heap to seat them with nobles, and to bestow on them a throne of glory. You are the Judge of all the earth. Guide, please, we Your people. For it is not by his own power that a man will gain the victory—it is by Your strength. Against the enemies of those who serve You, You will thunder! Give strength to Your chosen king, that he may lead us to exaltation. Strengthen the one whom You anoint, that he, in turn, may exalt You."

Samuel's parents had left Shiloh then, left him standing next to Eli. He remembered the High Priest wheezing softly in the silence that filled the space his parents had occupied. Samuel would not see them again for many months—an eternity to a son of three years.

Samuel shook off the memories and forced himself back to the concerns of the present. His mother's greatest fear was still that pride would sprout in his heart and produce a deadly fruit that would turn him into a person she could not abide. She would deny that, of course. She was a mother—to her, her love for her children was a constant that neither time nor distance could alter. And the pride that Elkanah expressed toward Samuel was not a father's pride in his son. It was an Israelite's pride in his nation's Prophet. Samuel did not think his father would ever be able to unify those two people in his own mind: son and Prophet.

He made his way back to the wood-storage room and was glad to find it empty—he would be able to work alone for a while. He needed time to think, to escape the stares and deferential postures of people who sought him out. He found comfort in stacking the mound of fuel into neat rows, the rhythmic, musical echo of wood knocking wood, the satisfaction of watching the rows grow, a mindless task that allowed him to mull over his situation without distraction.

He wondered what he was supposed to do now. The True God had given him a Prophecy and commanded him to speak it to the High Priest. He was a Prophet now—there was no denying it. But what did that mean for his everyday life? He had, of course, never thought about it before, but what was the role of a Prophet when he was not prophesying? He wished once again that Rohgah was here to talk to, but the wizened old man had disappeared after his condemnation of Eli's sons, and no one had seen him since. Samuel knew he was not supposed to spend his life repeating his one prophecy, and he could not just sit in his rooms waiting for another one.

He remembered abruptly something that Rohgah had said to him when the old man had come to visit Samuel in his rooms. He had referred to another name for Prophets who were given visions of what was to come: Seers. He had asked what Samuel saw. Samuel had not had the time to think about it since, but it was as if Rohgah knew that Samuel saw things other people did not. He wondered if that was some clue as to what he was supposed to do now—to keep on seeing what others missed, and recognize the significance of what he saw.

He finished stacking the wood and stretched, critiquing his work. He wanted to go to Ahitub with his questions, but he felt that his Prophecy had put a distance between them that was not there before, an awkward discomfort. Samuel had become instantly famous for predicting the death of Ahitub's father and uncle. No matter how much Ahitub disagreed with what Phinehas and Hophni did, it had to be difficult for him to come to grips with how to feel about the child who had pronounced their condemnation and execution.

Samuel made his way back out to the Courtyard. As soon as he left the wood-storage room, he saw Ahitub leading a travel-worn man toward the gate, his right arm over the man's shoulder, talking softly to him as they walked. They embraced at the gate, and the man left. Samuel took a deep breath and, in spite of his misgivings, hurried up to his mentor.

The Priest saw him coming and smiled wearily. "Samuel! This day has brought new challenges to both of us."

Samuel nodded, grateful for the Priest's tact. "That man—where was he from?"

"He is a messenger from the coast. The Philistines have begun a major campaign against Israel. Already they have destroyed the city of Gibbethon. The men of Israel are gathering at Aphek to try to stop them."

Rohgah's words and the images they conjured flashed in Samuel's mind. *Malediction!* "But Jehovah will give them the victory, won't He?"

Ahitub looked at him a long time, and then sighed. "I wish that I could say yes with confidence. But so many of our people have turned to the worship of false gods, and so much of what should be holy in Israel has been polluted…"

He drifted off and stood in silence for a moment, then smiled again. *Lips tight. Head slightly bowed. Eyes still frowning.* "We must pray for Jehovah's mercy and forgiveness, and wait to see what He will do."

Ahitub patted him on the head and left before Samuel could say anything more. Instead, Samuel crossed the Courtyard to where a group of Levites were inspecting and preparing animals for sacrifice, intending to join them. As he got closer, he became aware that people were staring at him, pointing and whispering to each other as he passed. A woman whose black hair was shot through with streaks of grey came up to him and bowed. "Jehovah has blessed us through you, child of the True God!"

Emboldened by her, another woman, about the age of Samuel's mother, stepped forward. "Happy is the mother at whose breast you suckled! Praise be to Jehovah, for He has raised up for us a Prophet again in Shiloh!"

Samuel felt his face flush with embarrassment, and he forced himself to nod and smile, not knowing what to do with the women's words. He did not like the feeling of having everyone's eyes on him, eyes that were filled with such longing and expectation, such a hunger for him to do something wonderful to lift them from their fear and despair.

He kept walking, but now the crowd ebbed forward with him. A man came alongside him, holding out a round loaf of bread. "A gift for the Prophet of God!"

Samuel shook his head. "Please—give it to the Priests, that it may be used for sacred service."

The man continued pacing him. "The winter rains have not come—can you tell us when our grains will sprout?"

"I do not know…" Samuel began.

"Will we be delivered from the Philistines?" someone else called out.

"But we must have rain," the man who was following him continued. "Could you not inquire of Jehovah for us—?"

Samuel began to run, passing the Levites at their work and ducking into the nearest door he could find in the Curtain Wall. He slammed it behind him and pressed his back against it, closing his eyes and letting his heartbeat slow.

Through the door, he could still hear the louder of the voices: "May Jehovah protect you from the wrath of Hophni and Phinehas!"

He opened his eyes and looked around, finding himself in the storage room for the instruments of the Tabernacle musicians. Just a few paces away, Tirzah and another, younger woman were sitting in chairs that had been set to face each other. Both women were staring at Samuel—he had obviously interrupted them in the middle of a conversation.

Tirzah turned to the other woman with an easy smile. "That is all for now. But do not forget what I have told you."

The young woman nodded and stood. She walked past Samuel with a quick bow and exited out the door he had just entered.

Tirzah smiled up at him, her unique, laughing smile. "And how is the Prophet today?"

He rolled his eyes at her teasing. "Not you, too, Tirzah."

She laughed. "Prophet or not, you are still my friend, Samuel. You are the same person you were yesterday."

"Am I?" He took a few steps closer to her and leaned on the chair opposite hers. "Can I be?"

He saw the pity awaken in her, like a mist that softened her smile and her eyes. "It is Samuel who was chosen by Jehovah as a Prophet," she said, "not some person Samuel wishes he were, or whom he may someday become. Jehovah, who can read the heart, knows you are capable of fulfilling this assignment."

Samuel stared at her a moment, then let his gaze drop to the floor, unprepared to handle her kindness or her confidence in him. "Or perhaps He has some other purpose in mind, a purpose that no one sees." *To show everyone what I truly am: weak, sinful, and afraid.*

Tirzah waited a long time before speaking again, and Samuel looked up from the floor to see tears shining in the corners of her eyes. "What will you do now, Samuel?" she asked.

He shrugged. "I wish I knew."

"You have become the hope of Israel. The eyes of all the people are upon you, whether you wish it were so or not. You must do whatever you can to guide them."

"I am a child, Tirzah!" he shouted. "I don't know what they should do! I don't even know what I should do most of the time!"

She frowned at him and cocked her head to one side. "That's not true, Samuel. You have always been more than just a child—even from before your conception you were marked as one set apart for special service. The High Priest and his family, a handful of Gibeonites and Levites, you, and I—we make up the only permanent residents of the Tabernacle. Everyone else comes, serves for a time, and then returns to another life. But we stay, and by our continued presence here we become, willing or not, the example to all Israelites of what sacred service should be."

She gestured toward the empty chair, and Samuel sat down heavily, fighting the anger he felt because she was not pitying him.

She reached out and took one of his hands in her own; her skin was soft and warm, her touch as subtle as the heat of a distant fire. "Samuel—you are a Levite, like your father before you. And now, you are a Prophet, the latest in a long line of men and women whose history and deeds you have known since your childhood. What is the obligation of all Levites and Prophets?"

He frowned. "For Levites—to assist the Priests. For Prophets—to proclaim the words of Jehovah."

"What words?"

"Whatever Jehovah tells them," he answered, still confused.

"And other than what the True God spoke to you last night, what other words has He given you to speak?"

"None!" Samuel threw up his hands. "That is all He said!"

"Not so—He gave you words to speak centuries ago, words that those who take the lead in sacred service must continue to speak, and to exemplify if we are to have our God's favor."

Samuel sighed. "The Torah."

She nodded. "The Torah."

They were both silent for a few moments as Samuel thought about what she had said. A part of him immediately recognized it as truth. This was his role in Israel—no different than it had been before Jehovah spoke to him. A Prophet was a spokesman of Jehovah's words, and Jehovah's words were the Torah. Prophets lived and spoke divine instruction to the children of Israel, whether those words were read from a scroll or recited from a memory blazoned into their minds in the silent dark of night. His job was, and always had been, to teach by example the value and meaning of the Torah. It was the obligation he must continue to fulfill—but more than that, it would downplay that which was making him stand out from others. Teaching the Torah would put him on equal footing with all other Levites, and still allow him to fulfill his role as Prophet.

He thought about what Ahitub had told him earlier—that the Philistines had attacked and that the armies of Israel were gathering at Aphek to try to stop their advance. He could not go to battle at Aphek, but he could fight a battle of his own, here in Shiloh. He could find ways to teach and promote the Torah in Israel, even if Hophni and Phinehas killed him for it. The greatest good he could do for the people who came to Shiloh full of hope, or for the men who were marching into battle, full of fear, was to turn the hearts of the people back to Jehovah, to lift the curse of the Malediction and to invite Jehovah's blessing on the nation.

Tirzah was still watching him, waiting for his response. He let himself smile at her. "You are right, of course," he said. "I will do my best."

She smiled broadly, that mocking, laughing smile that was uniquely hers. "Jehovah could not have chosen a better person with whom to entrust this assignment. You may save us all, Samuel."

Her praise, and the feelings of pride it evoked, shamed him. But he only shrugged, and turned to go back out into the Courtyard and face the waiting crowds.

30

As the rising sun reddened and purpled the billowy clouds that massed over the mountains east of Aijalon, the army of Israel prepared to march to war, and Manoah said goodbye to Naamah.

They stood together in the soft light of morning amidst the mass of men, wagons, and animals assembling behind tribal flags that drooped in the still morning air. Naamah clung to him, her arms wrapped tightly around his ribs, her eyes closed and her cheek pressed against his chest as if to listen to every beat of his heart. He held her close, rubbing her back with one hand, and trying to know what to say.

They had not spoken of his parting at all—not the night before, and not since rising that morning before dawn to prepare his belongings for travel. Their only words had been practical ones, quiet discussions of what Naamah would do in the days to come at Aijalon and of what Manoah might need for the journey north.

But holding her that morning, Manoah could not escape the guilt and self-reproach brought on by his true feelings, the feelings he tried to keep buried deep inside himself: he was relieved to be leaving his wife at Aijalon.

He would miss her, of course; he did not *desire* to be parted from her. But at the same time, being with Naamah just reminded him of how powerless he was to do anything to help her. Being near her filled him with an anxiety that he could do nothing to alleviate. Witnessing how she had been devastated emotionally by their experiences of the past few days had torn him apart—an anguish intensified by the fact that he did not know how to heal her pain. He knew that, staying at Aijalon, she would be in better hands than his own. A sense of failure came with admitting that to himself, and perhaps, he reflected, it was that sense of failure more than anything else that made him wish to distance himself from this woman he loved so much. He was her husband—he was responsible for her, obligated to provide for her whatever she needed. But the battle at Gibbethon had placed their relationship, already strained by their childlessness, into the crucible. Manoah was afraid that he himself was one of the impurities that testing had revealed.

Naamah stirred against his chest. "Stay with me, my husband," she whispered.

He fought back the anger that arose in him at her words. She knew that he must go. Could she not say something to make the parting easier, instead of filling him with guilt over what he had to do?

"I cannot stay," he said, trying to keep the hard edge from his voice.

She looked up at him, her eyes searching his. "Are you angry at me?"

He sighed. "No, Naamah. But I have to go."

Trumpets sounded, two short blasts followed by a long blast. It was the signal to depart, and all around them the army began to ease forward.

She was still studying his face. "I could not bear it if something were to happen to you."

He could not smile at her. He did not need to be reminded of what she could not bear—he needed her support, her assurance to him that she would be all right while he was gone. "If Jehovah wills it, I will soon return."

Her arms were still around his ribs; he gently extricated himself, glancing east to where the Danite contingent was already marching toward the road. When he looked back at his wife, she was standing, still and silent, amidst the flattened grasses of the field. A gentle breeze wafted past them: banners unfolded themselves, and Naamah's hair blew across her face like a black veil. Her hands gripped each other, white-knuckled, and he could see the tears welling in the corners of her eyes. In spite of the masses of people moving all around her, she looked immeasurably alone.

"I will return," he said again.

"I love you, Manoah," she said, her voice hardly above a whisper.

He nodded, and turning on his heel, strode swiftly through the mass of moving soldiers toward his place among the Danites.

The Israelite army marched out of Aijalon to the beating of drums, strung out behind their standard bearers: the heirs of the highest ranking Elder of the tribe. Manoah, awaiting his place in the rearguard, watched the proud banners pass: the donkey of Issachar, the grape cluster of Ephraim, the open tent of Gad, the blazing sun of Reuben, the lion of Judah, and the poised wolf of Benjamin. Some of the men sang as they descended through the Vale of Aijalon, gradually leaving the mountains by late morning, bypassing the city of Gezer and descending to the broad, coastal plain, where groves of olive trees still bore the last remnants of the year's harvest. A short distance past Gezer, Deker led them northwest by a less-traveled road. It was a slower, more difficult route, and it took Manoah a few minutes before he realized what the grizzled veteran's motivation was for choosing such a path: he wanted to avoid coming in sight of the destroyed city of Gibbethon. Manoah knew it was likely that a strong Philistine force now held what was left of the city, but perhaps even more importantly, Deker would not want to damage the morale of his soldiers by allowing them to see what had been done to the people of Manoah's hometown.

It was only an hour and a half from Gezer to the great north-south road, the main trade artery running through the Promised Land from Egypt to Lebanon and beyond. They followed the road northward, and in less than an hour began to see evidence of the destruction that the Philistine army had left in its wake. Some fields and orchards had been put to the torch, leaving great swaths of barren, scorched earth as the only indication of groves of trees that had been standing for centuries. Greasy, black smoke still hung in the air over villages that they passed, and at one of them, they could just glimpse the distant forms of people moving amongst the wreckage, survivors forced to the grisly task of trying to discover what remained of their lives beneath the cinders and ash.

They passed few travelers on the road, all of them traders from south of Gibbethon. No traffic came from the north, an ominous sign of what awaited the army. The merchant's caravans pulled off the road to let the troops pass, calling out encouragement and greeting to them as they went by. Some plied their trade, loudly extolling the virtues of whatever products they had that they imagined soldiers might want. They had no takers. Manoah glanced over their wares as the army passed them by, seeing coccus scarlet cloth, ingots of copper, salt from the Salt Sea, honey, great vats of olive oil, grain, wine, and spices. One merchant carried black-stained urns of bitumen from the tar pits near the Salt Sea, used by shipbuilders for waterproofing their craft. All of the merchants were nervous and visibly relieved to see the army marching ahead of them. Word traveled quickly, and the countryside was held captive to the fear that the invading Philistines had spread with their passing.

The army approached the city of Lod by mid-day. It was a small but prosperous city that marked the southern end of the fertile Plain of Sharon, and the last city that guarded the great north-south road before Aphek.

Lod was destroyed. Smoke still wafted from the walls and draped like a shroud in the still air above the city. As they drew closer, they saw that stakes lined the roadway leading to the city, dropped in shallow holes on either side of the road. On each stake, the Philistines had impaled a body, most of them hacked beyond all recognition. The army was forced to walk between the grisly rows of corpses, sickened to see that among them were the bodies of women and children.

They continued north, some of them eating bread as the sun peaked and then began its slow descent into the west. Most of them had no appetite after seeing what their enemy had done at Lod.

By mid-afternoon, they neared Aphek. Deker called a halt and summoned his commanders. The heat was stifling; they gathered in the shade of a grove of gnarled oaks not far from the road. The brittle, yellow grass crunched beneath their sandals, and grasshoppers and cicadas chirruped around them. As he joined the group, Manoah studied their faces. These were veterans of many battles, and they knew how to read the signs they had seen on their trip north. Manoah could see the fear and anger in their eyes.

"Most of my scouts have returned," Lodan reported quietly. "The city of Aphek is already in the hands of the Philistines."

The commanders were silent as they allowed the news to set in. "And the inhabitants?" Deker asked.

"The majority fled into the hills to the east. The Philistines did not hinder them, except..." Lodan paused, his features tightening with anger. "They tore children from their mother's arms and then let the women go free. If the mothers resisted, they simply killed them and took the children anyway."

Manoah's stomach churned. All of them knew the meaning of this particular piece of butchery—the Philistine demon-gods demanded child sacrifice as the payment for their support in times of war. The capture of the children was brutal but effective, demoralizing in ways nothing else would be.

"The Israelite forces that have assembled here are encamped at Evenezer," Lodan continued. "It is only a short distance inland. The encampment is nestled against the foothills, which provide some protection for their flanks in case of a surprise attack."

"Do we expect a surprise attack?" Deker asked, his voice harsh and abrupt.

"No, my lord," Lodan responded. He paused, looking at the men assembled around him. "The Philistines will wait for us to come to them. They are the stronger force, and they have already achieved their objective. They are not even manning the fortifications of the city. It appears they will meet us in the open field."

"Of course," Deker said bitterly. "Their chariots will do them no good inside the walls." He glanced at the commanders around him. "Send word among your men. We have nearly reached our destination. The armies of Israel will encamp tonight at Evenezer."

The commanders returned to their tribal contingents. The army left the highway and headed east, towards the highlands of the Shephelah, their countless footsteps widening the straight roadway. The sun was beginning its descent in earnest, now, and the sky to the west had started to darken with the first hints of the sunset's colors. The air began to cool, and a refreshing breeze swept down from the hillsides toward the sea.

In a little more than an hour, they reached the encampment at Evenezer. Manoah scanned it bitterly, unable to hide his disappointment. Four banners sagged above a meager gathering of tents and men, fewer than two thousand in total. Within a few moments of their arrival, a messenger from Deker brought Manoah the details of the forces: six hundred spear and shield men from the tribe of Naphtali, under the sign of the leaping hind, five hundred skilled warriors from the tribe of Zebulun, under the banner of a sailing ship, come to serve under Elon-tohr, five hundred farmers, shepherds, and fishermen from the tribe of Manasseh bearing a flag with an embroidered palm tree, and a few dozen men from Asher's territory, far to the north, under the sign of a blooming sycamore. Their total forces now stood at fewer than eleven thousand, all told. Eleven thousand men, Manoah thought, shaking his head in frustration, about to face a trained army of over fifteen thousand who had a better defensive position and fought from iron-wheeled chariots!

Manoah guided his men to a small grove of willows, and there they set up a makeshift camp. They had brought tents with them on wagons and the backs of their donkeys, and for several minutes all that could be heard was the sound of tent-pins being driven into the soil and the calls of men working together to stretch the cords tight. Manoah was busy setting up his own accommodations with Saphold's help when another Danite approached him, a scowl on his narrow face.

"May Jehovah give us victory," the man greeted him.

"May His Arm be mighty against our enemies," Manoah responded.

The man paused a moment, then took a step closer. "I am afraid the danger for you, my lord Manoah, may begin before the battle."

"What do you mean?"

The man gestured over his shoulder. "The priests of Dan are here—including some from Gibbethon. If rumors can be believed, they are still determined to see you pay for the escape of the man of God."

31

Manoah looked in the direction the man indicated. Four Danite priests were walking through the encampment. By their gestures it appeared that they were blessing the gathered forces. Manoah dropped what he was doing and, ignoring Saphold's puzzled glance, strode furiously across the encampment to Deker's tent.

When he pushed his way through the tent flap, the grizzled general was seated inside, poring over brown, vellum maps of the region while a plate of lentils cooled sat on the table next to him. He looked up in surprise at Manoah's entrance.

Manoah could barely contain his anger. "You have allowed the priests of Dan to join with our forces!?"

Deker frowned. "We have need of Jehovah's help if we are to win this battle, Manoah."

"And you think we will get it by having apostate priests in our midst?"

The general leaned back in his chair. "They are still priests of Jehovah, not some false god. Just because they do not serve at Shiloh—."

"They are an abomination!" Manoah snapped. "They are not of the family of Aaron! I lived with these men, Deker. They are not concerned with bringing us Jehovah's blessing. They crave power, and they will bring the wrath of God down on us!"

Deker stood abruptly, his face darkening. "You forget your place, Manoah!" The two men faced each other for a moment, both of them fuming. Then Deker sat back down, leaning forward and lowering his voice. "Have you looked around? Have you noticed, perhaps, that we are outnumbered by a better-trained force with better weapons who already occupy a strong defensive position? We need every man we can muster. I did not request the presence of these priests—they volunteered. Many of the soldiers of your own tribe are glad to have them here—they improve morale among the men. If the priests of Dan want to stay and give us their support, then I will take it! When you command an army, you can decide differently—but today, you will leave this decision in my hands!"

The two men glared at each other a moment longer, then Manoah turned and stormed out of the tent.

Deker summoned the commanders for a final meeting later that night, after the sun had set. The tent was quiet as the men assembled, their faces grim. The older Chieftains sat in a circle in the middle of the floor, while younger men like Manoah stood behind them, in the shadows against the walls. He had left Saphold back at his tent in the middle of the Danite camp. Elon-tohr was out scouting somewhere in the night, and another man, a slender, old soldier, took his place in the circle.

Lodan the Issacharian spoke first. "Most of you have some sense of the enemy we face, and of the advantages they bring to this battle. As you have heard, they are equipped with Hittite chariots with iron-bound wheels, fitted with scythes. The soldiers are well armed and armored—many of them carry weapons of iron. But perhaps the greatest surprise is the fact that the Philistine army has an entire contingent of Rephaim mercenaries."

All eyes turned toward Manoah, and he thought for a moment that they would ask him to say something. But Lodan continued talking. "My spies have learned that this Sarnam, who proclaims himself Axis Lord of Ashkelon, is determined to capture Aphek to control the trade route, just as we suspected. Whether he has some purpose beyond this, we do not know. But he is determined, and an experienced warrior. He brings with him his own jihad troops from the war in Egypt. They are called the Gedhudhra. They are highly trained and well-equipped fighters, to a man. But even more worrisome is the fact that they appear to be willing to unhesitatingly give their lives for their cause." He paused, looking around at the gathered commanders. "Beware of these Gedhudhra."

Deker stood abruptly. "Many thanks for your tireless efforts, Lodan. I know you are anxious to get back to your men."

Lodan hesitated a moment, as if he would say more, then nodded and exited the tent. Deker smiled at the remaining commanders. "Lodan is a useful man—no one can keep a secret from him. But if you listened too long to his perspective, you would never go to war!"

The men responded with a quiet chuckle, but no one was ready to discount the warnings of Lodan yet. Deker clapped his hands together. "Very well, then. Tomorrow, Azor and I will lead the Judeans and Ephraimites as the core of our forces. Arod will flank us on either side with his Gadites."

"My men are making new shafts for their spears as we speak," Arod inserted, a broad smile splitting his face beneath his wild, red-blonde hair.

Deker nodded. "The Benjaminites will position themselves on whatever high ground is available and fire with bow and sling down on the enemy." He looked over at Basar, the lanky, young leader of Benjamin. "You must target the chariot troops, these Gedhudhra, and the Rephaim."

Basar nodded. "Our missiles will fall upon them like rain. Will we have protection from the Philistine archers?"

"The Danites, under Manoah, will be divided into two groups—one to guard our Benjaminite slingers and archers, and the rest to provide a rearguard in case the enemy tries to slip behind us.

"The Zebulunites under Elon-tohr will be our vanguard. Elon is out...scouting right now, but I have already spoken to him. His tribe is charged with overcoming the chariots as swiftly as possible."

Deker glanced around the group once more. "The members of the other tribes will fill in wherever they are most needed."

"We must neutralize their chariots!" Azor growled, as if he did not think the point had been emphasized enough. "They will mow us down like wheat on the open plain!"

Arod smiled brightly. "My men will do all that they can. It is not the first time we have faced chariots. And we can rely on Elon-tohr."

"Most of you have probably taken a look at the land around us," Deker said. "The swamp and the lake that feed the Yarkon River will provide us with some protection—if we stay near them, they will block the chariots more effectively than a wall. Our foot soldiers will be more mobile on the soft ground all along the swamp—if we must retreat, we should try and use that to our advantage. The Philistines are likely to concentrate their forces to the west of us—the farther east they go, the more hills and ridges they will find that will hinder their chariots. By the same token, we must not be drawn too close to the walls of Aphek until we are prepared for a siege. We do not know how many men they will leave inside the city, and we will be vulnerable to any archers or spearmen atop the fortifications."

The grizzled general looked around at them one final time, as if taking the measure of his forces. "Very well," he said at last. "Purify your hearts, and spend the night in prayer. May Jehovah be with us all."

Darkness settled over the plain of Evenezer, a moonless, black night in which dense clouds shrouded even the brightest stars. All was still, the air oppressive and thick with the smell of men, of horses, of wood smoke, and of fear. As Manoah paced slowly between the dark rows of pavilions, cautiously weaving through the web of taut guy lines, he let the sounds and movements of the encampment envelop him. Men sat in groups around small fires, smearing olive oil or animal fat over the stretched leather hides that covered their wooden shields, or sharpening their sickle-swords and spears against whetstones in rhythmic, rasping sounds that punctuated the night. The glittering firelight painted the camp in dancing strokes of orange and black, so that even in the darkest shadows there was movement.

The big Danite breathed the muggy night air as he walked, letting his legs guide him on a path that wandered as aimlessly as his thoughts. Passing the moonlit banner embroidered with an open tent, he saw Arod seated in a ring of men around one of the fires, his countenance even ruddier than usual in the flame's vibrant light, his hair and beard forming a mane around his grinning face. The smiling Gadite held a buckler in one hand, and beat time on it's stretched, leather surface with the other as he sang:

> "If I sharpen my gleaming sword,
> And put judgment in my hand,
> I will bring down vengeance on my foes
> And retribution on my enemies.
>
> My arrows will be drunk with blood,
> My sword will gorge itself on flesh,
> And feast upon the blood of the slain,
> On the heads of my enemy's chieftains."

Manoah could not help but smile at the wild soldier's fierce song. Theirs was a people that had carved out their place in the world with swords and spears, a people that Jehovah had commissioned to exercise His judgment against demon-worshipping encroachers who refused to accept the sovereignty of Almighty God. Violence and warfare had followed them since they had become a nation at the foot of Mount Sinai four and a half centuries before.

Thinking of their military history made him remember Elon-tohr's words to him a few days earlier. In the wild rush of the past days and nights he had not given much thought to the cryptic speech the Zebulunite warrior had made to him that night in the Forest of Hereth. He had not seen Elon-tohr since they had arrived at Evenezer—the grey-clad warrior had disappeared into the surrounding countryside, perhaps scouting to learn the lay of the land or spying on the enemy camp. He seemed to spend as much time alone as possible, and Manoah wondered if the tendency had something to do with how Elon had lost his wife. The Danite felt like there was a good deal more to be known about the enigmatic warrior—secrets that might clarify his personality, if not his uncanny skills. Manoah shook his head ruefully. He was glad that the Zebulunite had chosen to confide in him, but he did not understand the man. Perhaps no one really did.

He realized that his feet had carried him back to his own tent. As he approached, he saw the hulking form of Saphold seated near the entrance flap, as still and silent as a boulder. Shadows hid the giant's face.

"May Jehovah bless us on the sun's rising," Manoah greeted him.

Saphold was silent for a moment. "My people make many sacrifices to our gods to assure their help in times of war. Animals, plants, men, women, children—all are given to the fires." He turned toward Manoah, his eyes black pits of darkness. "What is done to gain the help of your god?"

Manoah sat down on the ground next to the Rephaim. "The children of Israel live in a covenant relationship with Jehovah, the Creator, the Ruler of all other gods. He promised His servant Abraham that He would give his descendants this land. He gave to us the Torah, a book of laws that set us apart from all other peoples and that guide us in our ways of life and worship. It is by the strength of Jehovah's mighty Arm that we were able to come into this land and drive out the inhabitants. Our poets from long ago, the sons of a chieftain named Korah, sang:

> 'It was not by their own sword that they took
>   possession of the land,
> And their own arm was not what brought them
>   victory.
> But it was Your right Hand and Your Arm and the
>   light of Your Face,
> Because You took pleasure in them.'"

Saphold looked at him in silence for a moment. "If this is so, and your god is, as you say, the Ruler of all other gods, then why did your people ever lose a battle?"

Manoah realized abruptly that he was talking to a Canaanite whose people Israel had failed to conquer and drive out of their ancestral homes in Bashan. "When our nation is loyal and obedient to Jehovah, He aids us, and we are invincible in war. But if the nation turns from His lofty worship to lesser gods, if we disobey the words of the Torah, then Jehovah takes His spirit from us, and we are as all other peoples."

Saphold nodded slowly. "Is this Jehovah a god of war, that he rewards only with victory in battle?"

"Jehovah is a God of love. It is His desire that we live in peace. We can achieve this peace only when the people who have vowed to destroy us are themselves destroyed. But days are coming, Saphold, when Israel shall be blessed as no other place on earth is blessed. The Torah promises us: 'Jehovah will decree a blessing on your storehouses and every task that you undertake, and He will certainly bless the land that He has given to you. He will make you overflow with prosperity in the fruit of your belly and the fruit of your domestic animals and the fruitage of your soil. Jehovah will open to you His storehouse, the heavens, to give the rain on your land in its season and bless every deed of your hand; and you will certainly lend to many nations, while you yourself will not borrow.'"

The Rephaim giant turned so that he was facing Manoah. "Because of this promise, you are willing to die for this god?"

"He does not want us to die, but to live," Manoah answered. "But for the sake of His great name, and for the sake of His purpose I will give my life, yes. His purpose is served by our living, but if it is necessary for me to die to secure that purpose for others, then I will gladly do so."

"This is what makes you strong," Saphold said softly, his voice a rumble in the darkness. "I have heard of these things. The Rephaim will not soon forget the defeat of our mightiest king, Og of Bashan, and all who inhabit this land felt the ground shake beneath them when they heard about the destruction of Egypt's army in the Red Sea. The story of your coming to this land has become a legend among your enemies: the crossing of the Jordan in flood, the crumbling of the mighty walls of Jericho, the defeat of the combined armies of five Canaanite kings at Makkedah. In six years, the children of Israel flooded this land, sweeping all before their swords."

The giant went silent, and Manoah waited a moment for him to say something more. When it became apparent that he would not, Manoah said, "Why is it you ask about these things, Saphold? Do you seek the God of our forefathers, the god of Abraham, Isaac, and Jacob? Are you ready to reject the gods of Canaan?"

"The gods of Canaan have rejected me," the giant rumbled. "But I am Rephaim. I have been a killer of men from my youth. I am trained in war alone—I know no other life. I do not know if this god of love you speak of could accept me."

"It is written in our law," Manoah said softly, "'The alien resident who resides with you should become to you like a native, and you must love him as yourself, for you also became alien residents in the land of Egypt.'"

Saphold nodded slowly, then stood, towering suddenly over Manoah like some great tree trunk. "I will think on what you have said," he answered, and turning, disappeared into the darkness.

Manoah stared after him for a few moments, then pushed aside his tent flap and lay down inside, pulling his cloak around him. He thought of Naamah, and let himself enjoy for a moment a sense of relief that she was safe at Aijalon, far away from the danger that he would face tomorrow. He was just beginning to doze off when the door of his tent was pushed aside, startling him awake.

A figure entered and crouched beside him, and he jerked upright, reaching for his dagger. The figure put an arm on his shoulder and whispered, "Peace, Manoah!"

Manoah recognized Elon-tohr's voice "What is it?"

"I have seen the enemy," Elon-tohr whispered, calm and emotionless. "We will not win the battle tomorrow. When the time comes, you must flee the field and stay close to me."

Manoah was still searching for words to say in response when the dark soldier stood gracefully and disappeared back into the night.

32

In the sight of the city of Aphek's walls, a ring of torches and the flames of an altar fire glowed from within a grove of oaks. Lord Sarnam Ashkelon approached the grove with the dark-robed priest, Sihphil, and the scarred, young warrior Phicol, as if drawn forward by the eerie music that floated from the copse. On entering the ring of firelit trees, they were greeted by the upraised faces of two dozen or more worshippers, nubile young priests and priestesses of Philistia clothed in shifts of sheer linen. Sihphil had gathered them earlier for the sacred rite they were about to perform,. In the middle of the grove a small clearing opened, and it was in this clearing that an altar of cut stones, pulled from the homes of Israelite chieftains in the city of Aphek, had been hastily constructed. On one side of the altar, Sihphil had erected two stubby, sacred pillars of black basalt, fertility symbols in honor of the goddess Asherah. Across from them, a single, phallic shaft of peeled wood jutted up from the earth, a sacred pole representing the virility of Baal.

The music rose in pitch and tempo when Sihphil lurched into the center of the ring, tambourines and drums pounding a licentious rhythm against the melodies of harp and pipe. Figures from the edges of the clearing slithered into the firelight to join his dance, writhing to the music, running their hands over each other's oiled bodies. *Assinu* priests, dressed in women's clothing and long wigs, their eyes outlined with black Egyptian kohl, danced against *sinnishat-zikrum* priestesses, dressed in the clothing and armor of men.

Near the altar, a *baru* priest stepped forward and poured melted fat from a pitcher into a bowl of spring water, leaning over the swirling mixture and studying the whirls and bubbles that formed. A moment later, he stood, arms raised triumphantly. "The gods look upon us with favor!"

The same priest shuffled to the altar, using a copper shovel to remove a handful of coals from the fire's base. Dumping them into a censer, he reached into a pouch at his belt and sifted incense onto the coals. Tendrils of smoke writhed upward, and he studied their sinuous shapes, his eyes wide and glittering in the firelight. "They promise devastation upon our enemies!"

The gathered priests howled in response, tearing off their robes to dance naked around the flames, the orange light gleaming on their oiled bodies. Some slashed their chests with obsidian-bladed daggers, and blood flowed in jagged, crimson ribbons down their torsos to drip into the leaf-littered ground at their feet.

Sihphil raised his arms, his draping sleeves widening his robe so that he appeared suddenly larger and more imposing, casting a huge, black shadow across the sacred pole and pillars. "The godss demand a ssacrifice," he hissed. "Let uss sshow them our devotion by an offering of flessh!"

From the dark fringes of the grove, priests carried forward bundles of cloth, kneeling and unrolling them next to the altar. A few of the bundles began to whimper or cry, but most were silent, even when they were raised in the priest's arms to reveal that they were the infants of Aphek, torn from their mothers the day before.

"Accept our offeringss, Baal, Rider of the Cloudss; Asherah, Lady of the Ssea; and mighty Dagon, Father of Mankind! Accept our giftsss, O Anat, Mistress of the Godsss!"

One by one, priests laid the children on the altar fire, and the smell of burning flesh filled the clearing. Sihphil watched the small forms go from still to silent, then turned and nodded toward a priest who stood nearby, a Chanter who leapt onto a nearby stone and, spreading his arms over his head, began to sing:

> "Mot, the Lord of Death,
> Has opened his mouth toward us!
> His hunger for flesh must be sated!"

Sihphil slid into the light again, pulling back his cowl to reveal his shaved head. Another priest handed him a headpiece, which he put on: a skullcap of bone to which had been affixed the arching bull's horns of Baal.

> "Mot, the Lord of Death,
> Sought to murder Baal and to steal his throne,
> "In his insatiable hunger,
> Mot would consume all that lives and grows.

But Baal was wiser than Mot—
He sought out a cow from among Dagon's herds."

Attendant priests led a heifer, garlanded with herbs, forward into the firelight, her stomach swollen with pregnancy. The music built again, to a fever pitch, and the dancers whirled and chanted wildly. The priestesses dropped their robes onto the ground, their writhing bodies streaked with sweat, rubbing against the nude priests licentiously.

"Baal found a way to defeat
Even the boundless hunger of Mot!"

The priests tied the heifer to nearby trees with four ropes, one attached to each of her legs. She lowed mournfully, swaying but unable to move. Sihphil slowly approached the beast from behind, his mouth open in a soundless scream, his eyes rolling back beneath his horned headdress. The dancers screamed and sparks whirled up through the trees.

Sihphil advanced and slashed open the belly of the cow with a long, hooked knife. She collapsed against the supporting ropes, blood spurting from the wound across the priest's naked skin. The embryonic calf slid out onto the forest floor in a puddle of blood, placenta, and milky fluid. Immediately, a *baru* priest and his assistants hunched over the calf, muttering and cutting with flint knives.

Sihphil stepped up to join them, his bare feet squashing through the gelatinous mass; he bent and plunged his hand into the vivisectioned body. When he stood, he held the calf's liver in his upraised fist, blood running down his arm in dark rivulets. For a moment, the music stopped, and all eyes fixed on his firelit form in the sudden stillness. "Praisse be to Dagon, the Father of Mankind! Praisse be to Baal, Prince of the Earth! Praisse be to Anat, Misstresss of all the godss! It iss written in the liver! It iss sspoken in the ssmoke! It iss foressseen in the sswirl of oil! Tomorrow, the godss will grant uss victory over our enemiessss!"

The crowd erupted in a wild cheer, and the music burst forth in an explosive cacophony of sound. As the gathered people began to dance again, Sihphil leapt atop the rock that stood near the altar, his own gore-spattered form gyrating with the rhythm of the music. "O Priestessess of this temple! Baal waitss for Anat hiss ssisster to unite with him! Work the deep magic, that by our unionss Baal'ss lusst can be ssatissfied and he may go into battle for uss fulfilled in all but hiss thirst for blood; that Anat may wake tomorrow hungry for the flesh of our enemiesss!"

The priests and priestesses threw themselves at each other, tumbling to the forest floor and copulating with the abandon of animals, a mass of naked flesh that roiled among the leaves and duff in the throes of religious and carnal ecstasy.

From the edge of the trees, Phicol watched them, firelight glimmering in his wet, black eyes.

33

In the cold, still hour before dawn, the commanders of Israel's army gathered into a huddled group near Deker's tent, standing silently before one of the Priests that had traveled with them from Aijalon. He was an old, hunched man robed in white linen, his face a mass of seams and wrinkles, darkened by eight decades spent under the glaring Canaanite sun. When all had assembled, he turned to the east, toward the distant Tabernacle in Shiloh with his arms spread, palms upward, in a plea to heaven. "O Jehovah the God of our forefathers, You are the Almighty, Ruler over all nations; mighty is Your hand and powerful Your arm. In Your undying love of our forefather Abraham, into his children's hand You gave this land, and drove out of it those nations who would not recognize You as God. And now, these sons of a foreign people from across the sea, these Philistines have come against us in war, to drive us out of this land that You gave as our possession. O God, will You not execute judgment upon them? For in Your hand is the battle—we ourselves are without power, unless it be granted us by Your loving-kindness. Be with us, O Jehovah, that we may proclaim the greatness of Your name in this land You promised to Abraham, Isaac, and Jacob for all eternity."

When the prayer was concluded, Deker stepped forward to the Priest's side and studied the faces of the tribal commanders. For several long moments he watched them, and Manoah wondered what speech the general might be preparing to give. But in the end, he simply nodded at them and smiled a grim, tight-lipped smile. "We march with the rising sun," he said. "May Jehovah be with us."

"May Jehovah be with us," the commanders echoed, and strode quickly to their contingents. Manoah found the men he had appointed as chiefs over hundreds ready and waiting for him. He gave the order, and the men dispersed among the Danite soldiers to make sure all were prepared to march at Manoah's signal. Saphold appeared a moment later, his massive, double-bladed battle-axe held loosely in his gnarled fists. He looked over at Manoah with a hint of a smile on his lips, and nodded once. Manoah nodded in response, and tried to smile as well.

The sun crested the hills to the east, drums thundered, and a trumpet call rang out, fierce and proud, shattering the murmurings and rustlings of the army. Manoah felt his heart quicken, and he gestured to the young soldier who carried the standard of the tribe of Dan; the man raised the pole high above his head, and the emblazoned serpent flopped loosely in the breeze that blew down on them from the direction of the sea. Behind Manoah, the unmistakable sounds of an army in motion filled the rolling fields: bronze scale-mail rattling, horses and donkeys whickering their quiet protests, sickle-swords whispering dangerously out of oiled sheaths. Like wax melting, the army slowly eased forward, Manoah leading his men to their place at the rear of the main force.

The sun rose, shreds of golden light stabbing through the lowering clouds that hung across the sky. They marched across the matted, dry grasslands with its rays behind them, heading west, toward the city of Aphek, toward the destiny that awaited. In the distance, the first fingers of red sunrise began to play across the endless expanse of the Great Sea, darkening the wave tops like a spray of blood. The army picked up speed, falling into a steady rhythm of movement as each man found his place, and the thrum of sandaled feet across the earth blended into a steady rumble of momentum and power.

At Deker's command, the host began to sing as they marched, the centuries-old song of their God's great triumph over Egypt: The Victory Song of Moses. Clear and strong their voices echoed from the hills, and the sound of their own singing filled them with joy and power.

> "My Strength and my Song is Jah
> He has become my salvation.
> This is my God—I will praise him;
> My father's God, and I shall raise Him on high.

Their route took them quickly westward, their breath steaming in the brisk morning air. Leaving the hills behind, they descended toward the basin in which sat the swamp and shallow lake from which the river Yarkon flowed. The land around them grew greener as they neared the swamp—ahead, they could see an impenetrable jungle of reeds, bushes, and clustered trees. A great swath of emerald cut through the dry, yellowed fields of the pastureland of Sharon, following the meandering Yarkon toward the city of Aphek and from there, down to the Great Sea. Skirting around the marsh, they passed over neglected barley fields and descended toward the snaking river—a dark, sullen stream that crept sluggishly through the dense brush. As they drew closer to its tree-lined banks, Manoah could see shapes stirring in its waters—black water buffaloes buried to their eyes. The creatures stayed hidden as the army passed, watching them with brooding, angry expressions.

Blaring and bold in the stillness of the morning the words of the Israelite's song rang out in time with the rhythm of their march.

> "Jehovah is a Mighty Warrior
> Your right hand, O Jehovah, is majestic in Power;
> Your right hand, O Jehovah, shatters your enemy."

Less than an hour from when they began their march, they climbed a low rise and abruptly came in sight of the walls of Aphek, and their enemy.

The sight was overwhelming. For a moment, their singing faltered, drowned out in the deafening roar of fury and defiance that burst from their foe.

Sprawled out before them, covering the plains and low hills surrounding Aphek, was the great army of the sons of Philistia. They filled every inch of ground like a dark flood, roiling among the clusters of trees and the massive walls of the fortress. Thousands upon thousands of men surged toward the Israelites, their mad calls filling the air with a roar like the crash of the tide upon a rocky shore.

Manoah saw the fear on the faces of his soldiers as they realized the huge disparity between their own numbers and those of the enemy. He glanced over his shoulder to where, atop a nearby rise, a cluster of the apostate Danite priests gathered, their arms raised toward the heavens. The sight filled him with a hollow, inexplicable fear.

On a distant ridge a gathering of men waited at the rear of the Philistine force. A massive, armored figure rode in a gleaming chariot pulled by a pair of huge black stallions, his driver sawing on the reins as the horses reared and lunged in their eagerness to charge the approaching army. Manoah realized the armored man must be Sarnam, the new Axis Lord of Ashkelon. Next to him was a small figure shrouded in black robes, his cowl pulled over his head, surrounded by a group of scantily-clad Canaanite priests.

Manoah slid his sword from its sheath, and its rasp whispered to him of the eternal silence it granted. He took a deep breath and rested the flat of the blade against his forehead a moment—the blade was cold as death, slender as a starving man in its insatiable hunger for the flesh of his enemies.

Ahead of Manoah, someone picked up the Victory Song again, and the men joined their voices, screaming it out as they charged, like a weapon hurled against the faces of their enemy.

"In the greatness of Your power,
You throw down all who oppose You
You unleash Your burning anger
And it eats them up like stubble!"

The armies closed on one another. Even from the rearguard, Manoah began to glimpse the faces of the Philistine warriors, battle-madness in their eyes. He raised his sword high above his head and sang as he charged, and the sons of Israel sang with him as they descended on their enemies like the waves of a storm-tossed sea.

"Who among the gods is like You, O Jehovah?
Who is like You, majestic in holiness?
The One to be feared with songs of praise,
The One working wonders."

At the forefront of the Philistine horde, several hundred men on horseback galloped wildly toward them, whipping their mounts forward with the reins until pink froth fell from their bridles. Behind them, the black-clad Gedhudhra ran like leopards across the plain, leading a wave of scythe-wheeled chariots. *Let them come,* Manoah thought darkly, gripping his sword tighter as he ran. *Today, we are the mighty arm of Jehovah of Armies. Today, we are undefeatable.*

With a crash that shook the ground, the armies collided. Iron swords slashed through bronze armor and shields of wood and hide; scythe-wheeled chariots mowed through rows of men in a spray of blood. Dogs were unleashed and raged into the Israelite ranks, tearing out the throats of any they could reach. A rain of arrows and sling stones fell upon the Philistines, and dozens of men crumpled to the ground. The Philistines ran and rode over their own dead, fierce battle cries filling the air.

In moments, they began to drive Israel backwards. Their ranks thinned slowly across the hills, breaking into knots of embattled soldiers locked in desperate struggles for their lives. Elon-tohr's Zebulunites slipped among the horsemen and chariots, their blades flicking out to hamstring horses on either side of them. Behind the vanguard, the Judean force ground into the enemy rush.

Then, horribly, Azor of Judah disappeared beneath a charge of chariots. The Judean ranks faltered; a few tried to rescue their commander, but it became quickly apparent that he would not rise again, and the dispirited Judeans fell further back.

The whole of the Israelite army began to lose ground. "Stand firm!" Manoah screamed to the Danite rearguard. "Brace yourselves, men! Stand firm!"

Then Arod led his Gadites in from the flanks to the center of the fighting, his mane of reddish-blonde hair flying wildly, a wide smile on his face, calling Israel to rally to him. A swarm of leaping forms followed him: the Danite hill-men, their spears raised over their heads as they charged, the open-tent banner flapping from one of their shafts.

Moments later, stolid Deker stood beside Arod, at the forefront of the Ephraimite ranks, their lances braced between their shields in a long, unbroken line. A fresh wave of Benjaminite arrows and sling stones rained down on the Philistines, and their charge faltered as they collided against the Ephraimite line with a muffled crunch.

The line held. Horses and men impaled themselves on the Ephraimite spears, and the air filled with the cries of the dying. For several moments, both forces were locked in a desperate battle, but slowly, the greater numbers of the Philistine force overwhelmed the Israelites, and their flanks began to crumble under the relentless assault.

Manoah screamed out his battle cry and led the Danites into the fray, rushing forward to strengthen the embattled Ephraimites and Judeans. He was aware of Saphold beside him, his massive axe swinging, smashing soldier's bodies like wasp's nests.

Then a ram's-horn signal echoed out over the field, and from the hill near where Sarnam watched the battle, dozens of Rephaim giants stumped onto the field through their own ranks and toward the front lines, their massive battle-axes cradled in their long arms. Towering over their Philistine comrades and bellowing like angered bulls, they hurled themselves against Israel's front lines with the force of a storm-swept wave.

The line shattered, Judeans, Ephraimites, and Gadites swept aside by the great, arcing blows of the Rephaim axes. Arrows, sling stones, and javelins glanced off the giant's heavy armor or struck grazing blows that the huge warriors shrugged off.

Then Saphold rushed past Manoah, his axe clutched in one hand raised above his head. With his other hand, he beat his chest, and bellowed out a challenge in the Rephaim tongue. Instantly, the giant mercenaries saw him, stopped their attack, and rushed to meet him. They formed a circle in the midst of the battling armies, facing outward, fighting only to defend themselves if any dared attack them. Saphold was in the middle of the ring, and another Rephaim joined him there, where the two of them circled each other, roaring and bellowing.

Manoah pushed toward the ring, struggling to reach Saphold's side but did not dare come within reach of the Rephaim defense—their axes swept aside anyone who came near enough.

Inside the circle, Saphold and his opponent began to duel, their teeth bared as they chopped and slashed at each other with their heavy weapons. For several moments they dodged and parried, and then through a narrow gap in the Rephaim defensive line, Manoah saw Saphold land a solid blow on his opponent's shoulder, splitting him nearly to the navel.

The Rephaim circle let out a booming chant: "Doom-aah! Doom-aah!" They turned toward Saphold, who stood, shoulders heaving, over his fallen opponent. Saphold flipped his axe upside-down, placing the blade against the ground, and said a single word that Manoah could not understand. With that word, the other Rephaim turned and threw themselves back into the fray around them as if nothing had happened.

To Manoah's astonishment, Saphold lumbered from the field of battle. "Saphold!" he screamed, his voice lost amidst the clamor of the fighting all around him. Then a knot of Philistine warriors crashed into him, and for several moments Manoah could think of nothing but trying to stay alive, instinct taking over as he parried and ducked, then struck out viciously against his enemies.

When he had a moment's pause to look again, Saphold had disappeared.

All around him, the Israelite defense was collapsing, the flanks curling back upon themselves, the middle of the line penetrated in half a dozen places. Groups of Philistines had made their way around the main force on either side, and the Benjaminite slingers under Basar were now locked in hand-to-hand combat, their Danite defenders trying desperately to give them sufficient protection to rain more missiles down on the enemy.

Manoah felt desperation creeping through him, a cold fear that overwhelmed even the madness of battle, and he knew in his heart that the Israelite line would not hold.

Then fresh horror galloped down upon them in the form of a line of scythe-wheeled chariots, each of them bearing a driver and two heavily armored Gedhudhra. The Philistine ranks thinned to allow them through, and the chariots collided with what remained of the Israelite ranks with a horrible crunch. The huge stallions and the massive vehicles they pulled thundered over men as if they were nothing more than stalks of wheat, leaving in their wake great swaths of crippled and dying soldiers. Elontohr's Zebulunites, their numbers decimated by the initial attack, tried desperately to stop the horses, but there were simply too many of them.

They would all have been lost if not for Arod. The lion-haired Gadite led a counter-charge against the chariots, his fearless hill-men racing in and jamming multiple spear-shafts through the spokes of the chariot wheels, halting their progress so abruptly that many of the riders tumbled over the front of the vehicles and into the harnesses of their horses. The Zebulunites fought beside the Gadites, hamstringing the flailing horses. For a few moments, the entire Philistine charge ground to a halt.

Then Manoah saw Elon-tohr. He came through the enemy like a dark whirlwind, moving toward Manoah, and wherever he went, death followed. He left a swath of bodies behind him, spinning and whirling, a slender sword held in each hand. In moments, he was at Manoah's side.

"Quickly!" he yelled. "We must flee!"

At that moment, a trumpet rang out from the rear of the Israelite army, sounding the signal for retreat. Manoah hesitated, and three Philistine warriors broke from a group nearby and hurled themselves toward him, weapons raised, screaming madly. Elon-tohr spun like a dancer, swords flashing in a wide arch, and all three men fell dying.

"Quickly, Manoah!" he said again. "We cannot stand against them on the plains!"

All around them, the Israelite army was fleeing eastward, the Philistines in pursuit. Manoah called to his trumpeter waiting nearby; the young man was still standing, but one arm dangled uselessly at his side, streaked with blood. He nodded wearily at Manoah's signal and raised his trumpet to repeat the call of retreat for the rearguard.

But the signal meant something different for the Danites than for the rest of the army—it meant that they would now become the focus of the Philistine attack, charged with hampering their enemies' pursuit so that their brethren could escape to the cover of the hills. The Danite rearguard would now become Israel's first—and last—line of defense.

As their standard-bearer raised the coiled-serpent banner, Manoah's men formed a wall of spears and shields; turning to face the approaching enemy, they moved slowly backwards as well. The rest of the Israelite forces slipped past them, racing across the barren grasslands toward the distant hills.

Not far behind, the Philistines pursued them, their battle cries turning to howls of glee as they saw their enemy retreat. Crawling across the motionless forms of the slain, the Philistine warriors raged toward Manoah and the Danites.

The last of the Israelites passed the rearguard, and Manoah signaled the Danites to close ranks and regress even more quickly to the east, maintaining a swift but steady pace in pursuit of their countrymen. Elon-tohr and a handful of his Zebulunites had remained back as well, strengthening the Danite ranks. They kept just ahead of the Philistines at first, their enemy's advance hampered by the bodies of men and horses strewn across the blood-soaked battlefield.

Manoah signaled the Danites to increase their pace and they broke into a loping run. His head whirled as he ran, struggling to grasp what had happened. They were the chosen nation, the inheritors of the Land of Promise. But Jehovah had not given them victory. He remembered his feelings before the battle at seeing the priests of Dan among the army, and rage filled him at the realization that their presence could have been responsible for Jehovah's abandoning of the army.

The sound of approaching horse-hooves distracted him and he looked over his shoulder to see that one of the pursuing chariots was closing on him quickly, having found a route through the refuse of battle. For a moment, he caught a glimpse of its driver: a young man with a shock of blonde hair and a mass of reddened scar tissue where his nose should have been.

Memories of Gibbethon and the slaughter of his brothers raged through him as he realized that he was fleeing from Leah's killer. Tightening his grip on his sword, he broke from his position in the rearguard line and turned abruptly to face the approaching chariot. Elon-tohr saw him and turned as well.

"What are you doing?" he yelled.

Manoah did not answer, just studied the footfalls of the horses across the dark red ground as they approached, trying to determine the best way to dodge the hooves that trampled bodies, lying heavy and loose as sacrificial carcasses, and reach the fierce warrior who drove them forward with merciless strokes of his whip.

Then Elon-tohr launched himself past Manoah and toward the chariot, landing on one knee directly in front of the pounding hooves. The horses reared and swung away from him, and the grey-clad warrior's sword snaked out to the side, once, twice, slashing among the stallions' legs. The horses collapsed in a tangled heap, squealing, legs flailing and spattering crimson. The chariot crashed on its side, spilling the driver to the blood-soaked ground—Manoah heard him yelling in pain and anger.

Elon-tohr rolled clear of the screaming horses and came to his feet in one smooth movement. He grabbed Manoah, who stood staring in awe at the tangled pile of animals and chariot harness--and at the driver struggling to extricate himself from the leather straps and ropes. For a moment Manoah resisted Elon-tohr, desperate to reach Leah's killer and execute him while he had the chance. But Israelites were fleeing all around them, and hordes of Philistine soldiers were loping across the plains towards them, interspersed with chariots and hulking Rephaim. Manoah let the Zebulunite lead him forward, and they ran once again toward the east, toward the cover of the trees.

34

Lungs burning, muscles aching, Manoah and Elon-tohr entered the forested foothills of the Shephelah just behind Arod and the Gadites and several dozen Benjaminites under the long-limbed commander, Basar. They did not pause but fled through the trees and sparse underbrush, fighting the constant urge to look over their shoulders to see how close their pursuers were.

The wounded stumbled among them, bent double as though their agony was a burden unbearable. Not far ahead of Manoah a burly Judean carried a young man over his shoulder like a sack of grain. At every jolting step, the young man coughed wetly, gargling, and his eyes writhed as though trying to escape some vision of horror.

Gradually their pace slowed, hampered by the thickening forest and by the wounded they supported or carried. They divided quickly into small groups, clambering through the uneven, choked countryside in an effort to make it more difficult for their pursuers to follow. The land began to change as they traveled eastward, broken by steep-sided ravines, dry wadis and rocky inclines. They scrambled forward, constantly hearing behind them the sounds of pursuit and, at times, the clash of battle.

They entered a long, narrow valley, its steep walls strewn with loose shale interspersed with clusters of short, stunted scrub, its bottom sandy and smooth from countless flash floods that had raged down its length during winter rains. By the time they were a quarter of the way down the valley's length, a group of Philistine raiders burst out behind them, weapons raised, screaming. Manoah might have kept on running, hoping against hope to outdistance their attackers, but Arod turned instantly and led the Gadites back into the fray, his wild hair flying. Elon-tohr and Basar spun and joined them, and for several minutes they battled furiously near the mouth of the valley. Manoah's fear vanished when he threw himself into the struggle, his bronze sickle-sword so blunted by now that he used it more as a club than a blade. On one side of him, Elon-tohr whirled and danced, a grim shadow of death; on the other side, Arod stood at the forefront of the Gadites, grinning from ear to ear as he raged into his enemies like a cornered lion. So furious was their defense that within a few moments, the Philistines withdrew to regroup, leaving dozens of their dead lying on the sandy canyon floor.

Immediately, the Israelites turned and fled back down the valley. As they neared its far end, Manoah could see beyond it tangled slopes of twisting, broken country, full of easy cover and myriad hiding places. The group quickened their pace and had nearly broken out of the valley when several dozen horsemen burst from the trees to the south. All of them were clad in the black armor of the Gedhudhra, and at their forefront rode a young man with a shock of blonde hair and a mass of red scar tissue where his nose should have been.

They heard the remains of the Philistine force behind them screaming their battle cries, and Manoah's heart sank as he realized that they were now pinned in the valley between two superior forces.

Arod and Elon-tohr did not hesitate. They leapt toward the mounted Gedhudhra, weapons raised. The scarred warrior who led them raised his long, black-bladed sword. "I am Phicol, son of Anat, goddess of savagery! Hear my name and know—the sword reveals the heart!"

The Gadites collided with the mounted Philistines with a muffled crunch, and the air filled with the screams of horses and men impaled on their spears. But many of the Gedhudhra dodged the thrusts that sought them, wheeling their mounts and holding their shields out before them, and then spurring their huge black stallions forward into the Israelites, sharp hooves churning. Dozens of Gadites died in the first charge. Phicol pointed his sword at Arod and then drove his mount savagely toward the lion-haired warrior, screaming. Arod, still smiling—still smiling!—ran toward the horse, at the last minute leaping toward it like some wild creature, grabbing its mane and wrapping both legs around its neck as if to ride it upside-down; then using both hands to bury his sword in the beast's throat, roaring all the while. The horse crashed to the ground, pinning Phicol beneath it, and Arod rolled to his feet several paces away.

The charge of the Gedhudhra ground to a halt against the furious battling of the Gadites, and Manoah and Elon-tohr raged into their lines along one flank. Elon-tohr wove and danced among his opponents like a shadow, as untouchable as smoke. No matter how many of the deadly Gedhudhra surrounded him, his slender swords blocked every cut and thrust and found openings in the warrior's defenses no one else could have seen.

Manoah glanced over at him once to see him fighting with his eyes half-closed, a rapturous look on his face.

The Benjaminites under Basar were scrambling up the steep canyon walls, trying to find positions from which to use their slings and bows; the first few missiles hissed down into the Gedhudhra, thinning their ranks further. Phicol remained pinned beneath his mount, screaming in rage and pain, slashing at the dead horse with his sword, trying to cut himself free of its crushing weight.

But these were not normal Philistine warriors—they were Gedhudhra, and in spite of being outnumbered, even the deadly skill of the Gadites and Elon-tohr were hardly a match for dozens of the mounted death-troops. Their iron blades slashed through the Gadites' leather shields and notched or shattered their bronze swords. The Gedhudhra threw themselves at their opponents with reckless disregard for their own lives, fighting on despite wounds that would have killed other men.

Then Manoah glanced over his shoulder and saw that the other Philistine force had nearly reached them. Screaming out a warning to the men around him, he and roughly half of the Israelites turned to face this new threat, leaving Elon-tohr and Arod to lead the fight against the remaining Gedhudhra. Manoah tried to catch his breath and braced himself for the charge that was closing quickly toward them. Beside him, he heard one of the Gadites praying aloud: "O Jehovah, You are a sun and a shield…"

The Philistines were only a hundred paces away when a roar erupted from the top of the steep, shale walls of the valley. All eyes looked upward.

Poised like a great tree at the top of the rise, Saphold stood, arms raised, his mighty bellow echoing from the hills around them. Then he threw his shoulder against a boulder the size of a vineyard hut poised in the shale atop the canyon wall. Unbelievably, the enormous stone lurched forward, tipping slowly, and then tumbling over the edge, crashing through scrub and rock, building momentum. All around it, the shale and stones of the valley wall began tumbling as well, and the dust rose in a thick cloud from the landslide.

The Philistines saw what was happening and tried to turn back, racing away from the Israelites up the valley. But it was too late. With a thunderous rumble, the avalanche smashed into the fleeing Philistines, burying a third of their force and leaving a wall of boulders and rubble that spanned the floor of the canyon.

The Benjaminites under Basar had not squandered the opportunity this distraction gave them: they had found their positions on the canyon walls and now began to rake the remaining Gedhudhra and the rest of the Philistines with arrows and stones. The Philistine force fell back, knowing they had to find another way past the obstruction, unable to climb over it when the deadly accuracy of the Benjaminite missile warriors guarded it.

PROPHET OF ISRAEL

The archers and Elon-tohr dispatched the last few Gedhudhra, and the Israelites raced once more for the cover of the trees, leaving the wounded and dying behind them.

As they left the valley, Saphold loped out of the cover of the trees and joined them, his broad face unreadable. Together, they wound through the dense trees and brush, up and down ravines, scrambling until their throats burned and their muscles ached with exhaustion. Men had lost their sandals in the flight, and their limping footprints were flagged with smears of blood.

Elon-tohr finally called a halt in a sheltered grove of sycamores. They had heard no sounds of pursuit behind them for some time, and all of the men were near to collapse. A tiny spring seeped from beneath a cluster of stones in the grove, and the soldiers scooped the muddy water to their parched lips. Wounds were bound or packed with poultices of herbs, oil, and dried figs.

Only then did they see the true cost of the battle. Young men leaned against the trunks of trees, shaking as though they were freezing, eyes wide and fixed on images burned into their memories. Some wept aloud and unashamed, bulging eyes staring in disbelief at the red-bandaged stump of a severed limb. Fathers held the forms of sons, and sons of fathers, clutching them and rocking as though to coax life back into cooling flesh.

Manoah turned to Saphold. "You deserted us at Aphek! I spoke up for you, gave assurances to my people, and you abandoned us!"

Saphold looked at him for a long time, brown eyes dark and unfathomable. "You told me that Jehovah fought for you in your battles. What I witnessed today, on the field of Aphek—was that the work of your god?"

Manoah felt his anger drain away, replaced by shame and bitterness. He shook his head.

"That is why I left," Saphold said.

"Then…why are you here now?" Manoah asked.

"I did not see evidence of this god, Jehovah, at Aphek," Saphold said. "But I do see him in you, Manoah—in your faith and zeal. If I am to learn of this new god, I know you will be the one to teach me."

Elon-tohr called out then, and they wearily stood and began making their way east once more. They wandered through the broken wilderness with no set direction, only needing to put as much distance as possible between themselves and their pursuers.

Manoah wondered at Saphold's words, feeling privileged to have had such an effect on the giant warrior, uncertain as to what he had done that had so impressed him.

After a few moments, though, his thoughts turned to Naamah. Some part of him awakened only when they were apart, a hunger and an appreciation that only her presence quelled— so much so that, when they were together, he forgot that the hunger ever existed. Now, fleeing through the forests of the Shephelah, he felt alone in a way that only she could alleviate.

It was mid-afternoon before they broke free of the trees. They had been climbing a steadily rising ridge for some time, ascending through thinning underbrush, when abruptly the forest ended and they emerged onto a barren crest of rock that jutted out of the surrounding forest like a gnarled spine. A few more minutes' clambering brought them to the top of the ridge, and they were granted a view of the land around them for several miles. They kept low against the rocks at first, worried that they might be making themselves easily visible to any Philistines who still pursued them. But they had neither seen nor heard any signs of pursuit for several hours now, and Manoah felt reasonably certain that the Philistines had abandoned their chase and returned to Aphek to enjoy the fruits of their victory.

From the ridge top they could scan the land around them in all directions, and within moments the Benjaminite Basar spotted a large force of men traveling west on a road to the south of them—the remnants of the Israelite army. Shaking off their weariness, the band descended to catch their companions. It took them another hour before they reached the rearguard of the army and sent messengers to the commanders that they had arrived.

Eventually, Manoah, Arod, Basar, and Elon-tohr met up with Azor's son, the new commander of the forces of Judah, a tall, charismatic man named Imri, his black hair sprinkled with grey, his eyes hard. He welcomed them bluntly.

"Reinforcements are coming from nearly all the tribes," he told them. "Tens of thousands of men, if initial reports can be believed, moving to join us again at Evenezer. The anger of Israel has been roused, and we will drive those dogs out of Aphek and back to Philistia."

Manoah shook his head. "It will need to be many tens of thousands if we are to defeat them this time. We have not yet seen their full strength, I think."

Imri smiled coldly. "Things will be different this time. Deker has gone to retrieve a weapon the Philistines will not be able to stand against—a weapon that has never seen defeat in war."

The eyes of everyone in the group fixed on the warrior. "Deker has gone to Shiloh, to bring the Ark of the Covenant into battle."

35

A wind from the east was sweeping across the rooftops of Shiloh, a rare thing at that time of year. The breeze was hot and dry, carrying with it the perfumed scents of sand and dust from the great desert beyond Gilead. Samuel stood in the Tabernacle Courtyard as the wind swept over him, lifting his nose and sniffing like a wolf on the hunt. He set the vessel of water he was carrying down, stretching his aching muscles and glancing at the gate.

It was an unconscious movement that he repeated endlessly during the course of the day—as did many other people in Shiloh. They looked to the gate for the arrival of some messenger, some indication of what was happening far away in Aphek. This time, as always, Samuel's look was rewarded with nothing more than the normal comings and goings of penitents and petitioners, the same endless patterns that had been repeating themselves for centuries.

He knelt again on the flagstones and dipped his brush into the mixture of water and lye in the clay vessel. His knees were wet, but the cool water felt good against his skin as he scrubbed the section of stonework he had been assigned. Sweat tickled his brow and he brushed it away with the back of his hand.

Hophni had given him the job of cleaning the flagstones this morning—not Hophni himself, of course. Neither of Eli's sons had so much as spoken to him since Eli had made it known that Samuel was now a Prophet in Israel. But they sent messages to him regularly—orders delivered by the Levites and Priests who remained loyal to them, in spite of Jehovah's condemnation. They kept him busy with an endless list of menial tasks—

tasks for the most part designed to keep him out of the public eye and away from whatever attention his newfound notoriety brought him. Samuel did not mind the work—in some ways, it was a relief to be able to concentrate on simple, mindless jobs and give his thoughts time to settle and sort themselves out.

Besides, he reflected, every moment spent in the sight of those people who now looked to him as the savior of Israel brought closer the inevitable day when they would discover that he was not the paragon they thought him to be. He knew the truth about himself—all of his own flaws, weaknesses, and his own endless string of sins, and such a vast chasm lay between his self-knowledge and the image projected on him by the people that he felt himself a hypocrite every time they looked at him. He wanted to do what he could to help them, to fulfill his determination to teach and exemplify the Torah and battle the lawlessness that was leading to the Malediction. Instead, he found day after day going by without any real alteration in the rhythm of his life. It was all well and good to decide to change the nation, but it remained nothing more than a fancy while the passing hours were filled with the duties and patterns that had comprised his life in Shiloh since childhood. It made him feel like a child again, his mind wandering through visions of his own greatness while his hands were immersed in water dirtied by the feet of the men he obeyed.

His family had left a few days earlier to return home to Ramathaim, his father's course of duty at Shiloh completed. But Samuel still felt his mother's eyes on him everywhere he went—eyes that chided him for his ambition and yet saw him as an answer to her most fervent prayer—eyes that called him Prophet, but did so with such softness that the sharp edges of the title were stripped away.

He dipped his brush in the vessel again and looked over at the Altar's gleaming surface. Copper plates covered it entirely, forged centuries before by a Priest named Eleazar. Israelites remembered the source of the copper as a shameful chapter in their history. A Levite named Korah had fomented a rebellion against Moses and High Priest Aaron, asserting that Korah and a group of his followers were more qualified to lead the nation and serve as Priests. Korah, Aaron, and two hundred and fifty of Korah's followers assembled in front of the Tabernacle with copper censers in their hands, awaiting a sign from Jehovah as to which of them was His choice for Priestly service. Jehovah's answer was swift and definitive. He had sent a whirling torrent of fire from heaven, burning Korah and all his followers instantly to ash. The heat of the flame melted their censers into puddles, scattered like manure piles across the Courtyard. Jehovah had commanded Aaron's son Eleazar to gather them and forge them into plating for the Altar, as a reminder to Israel that no man who was not a descendant of Aaron should ever attempt to usurp the position of the Priests.

A sound from somewhere in the city below reached Samuel's ears and he paused in his scrubbing to hear it more clearly. It had sounded for a moment like the commotion of a crowd, as if some event had elicited a cheer, or a cry of grief. The breeze blew across his face and he closed his eyes, enjoying the way that, in spite of its warmth, it cooled his sweaty forehead.

The thought that Jehovah had again pronounced a death sentence against someone serving in the Tabernacle and that he, Samuel, might possibly witness something like the fire that had come from heaven in Korah's day made his heart beat faster with an anxious fear. He wondered if one day people would speak about Hophni and Phinehas the way they now spoke about Korah and his followers. Samuel realized abruptly that his own name might be a part of that story and he a character in a chronicle that parents taught to their sons and daughters in Israel for centuries to come. The realization awakened in him the familiar ache that was both a hunger and a humiliation—a desire for such recognition, and the self-loathing that filled him for having such a desire.

Then a keening and a wailing erupted from the city, this time unmistakable. Samuel dropped his brush in the water vessel and jumped to his feet, racing across the Courtyard toward the gate. All around him, people paused in their activities, then joined him as they, too, responded to the commotion.

In a few minutes, a crowd from the city emerged into view, climbing the road that led to the Tabernacle. Hophni, Phinehas, and Ahitub met Samuel and the Levites gathered at the gate, waiting for the crowd to reach them. The people who approached were wailing their grief, tearing their garments and throwing the dust of the road over their heads—it hung like a dirty cloud around them as they swayed forward.

When they reached the gate, Samuel saw the reason for the commotion. From the keening crowd a handful of men pushed forward, dressed for battle, their clothing and hair streaked brown with dried blood and matted with sweat and dust. Samuel recognized one of them immediately, a thick, grizzled old warrior with a bushy beard: Deker, an Elder of Ephraim.

Deker bowed curtly to the Priests. "I must speak with the High Priest," he said, his voice hoarse.

Behind him, Samuel heard Ahitub calling for water and food to be brought. "What has happened?" Phinehas asked.

Deker spat on the dusty ground, then wiped his mouth with the back of his hand. "Israel has been defeated."

Phinehas blanched, and he and Hophni led Deker and the men with him toward Eli's home. Ahitub followed as well, and after a moment, he turned back and saw Samuel standing at the gate. "Join us, please, Samuel," he said. "As Prophet of Jehovah in Shiloh, this concerns you as well."

A thrill prickled Samuel's spine, and he hurried to catch up to the group. They entered Eli's home and settled into places on the woven rug. Samuel slipped behind the old High Priest, who sat in a chair looking as if their entry had wakened him from a nap. Levites brought water and food, and Deker and the men with him drank deeply, but did not eat.

"Israel has been defeated," the general repeated after a moment. "We were overwhelmed by the forces of Philistia at Aphek. The cursed dogs have hired Rephaim mercenaries!"

"Rephaim?" Hophni asked, his fleshy face slack with fear.

Deker nodded. "They were led by a death-squad that the new Axis Lord of Ashkelon has brought from Egypt. His Gedhudhra, he calls them. They are suicidal warriors, armed with swords of iron. We were overwhelmed by their numbers, driven from the field like sheep!"

He looked slowly around at the faces in the room. "Four thousand Israelites lie silent on the field of Aphek."

A hush fell over the already still room. An image of the Prophet Rohgah flashed into Samuel's mind, and a single word screamed through his thoughts: *Malediction!*

"What is the situation of our army now?" Phinehas asked.

"The commanders are re-assembling the men as we speak," Deker said. "Gibbethon, Lod, and Aphek now lie in Philistine hands—and with them, control of all trade along the Great Road. Our brothers are gathering from across the land to strengthen our hands, but numbers alone will not be enough. We have come for the aid that only Shiloh can provide. We must have Jehovah's help if we are to retake our fallen cities."

"We will offer prayers and sacrifices for the success of our warriors," Ahitub said. "The best of what we have in Shiloh—."

"I did not come for prayers," Deker interrupted. "I have come to take the Ark of the Covenant to Aphek."

A stunned silence settled over the room. Samuel, scanning the faces in the room around him, saw shock even in the eyes of Hophni and Phinehas.

"The Ark is not a weapon!" Ahitub objected. "It has not been removed from Shiloh since…for centuries!"

"The Ark used to often be carried by Israel in times of war," Deker growled. "It was there when the walls of Jericho were felled—it was at Aijalon when Joshua commanded the sun to stand still over the field of Gibeon."

"But it is not a talisman whose presence alone will assure victory!" Ahitub said. "We must soften Jehovah's face if we are to—."

"Silence!" Hophni barked. "You forget your place, Ahitub! As usual, you fail to show respect for your elders and take it upon yourself to speak before your father the High Priest!"

The room fell into stillness again. After a long pause, Phinehas shifted and let out a rush of breath. "This is not a matter to be decided lightly. Moving the Ark is one of the most solemn duties of a High Priest, and taking it into battle—well, that is something no High Priest has done since before the days of my grandfather's grandfather. My over-eager son is correct—it is not a weapon, and it alone will not assure us of victory."

"Has Israel ever lost a battle when the Ark was present?" Deker asked to no one in particular.

"We fled from the men of Ai!" Ahitub said.

"History is unclear as to whether the Ark was with them in that battle," Deker said.

"But it was not with the rebels who attacked the Amalekites and Canaanites after the ten spies returned to Moses," said one of the men with Deker. "And without the Ark, they, too, lost the battle."

Samuel felt the tension in the room building. "There is," Phinehas continued slowly, "one vital fact about the Ark that must influence my decision in this. It has never been captured by an enemy. The True God would not allow it, for it is the most sacred of all the holy contents of the Tabernacle. It is the sign of His continued presence with His people.

"We know that the army of Israel must face the Philistines—we cannot allow them to gain control of trade in the land that Jehovah promised to our forefathers. Reason tells us that since we must face our foes on the battlefield again, it is logical to obtain every advantage possible in order to offset their greater numbers and superior weaponry. The Ark *may* give us such an advantage—it is, in fact, likely to, for it has proven to be a harbinger of victory for our people in the past."

Ahitub started to interrupt again, but Hophni held out a hand and glared him into silence.

Phinehas continued. "If by taking the Ark into battle we were, in fact, exposing it to danger or threat, then it would be difficult to justify such a course. But to even suggest that the True God would allow uncircumcised dogs to harm or capture his Holy Ark reveals a sad lack of faith."

He turned slowly, looking at the faces gathered around him—but, Samuel noticed, avoiding Samuel's eyes and even the blind eyes of his own father, Eli. "To acquiesce to the request of the Elders of Israel might give us the advantage we need to conquer our foes. Doing so poses no threat either to the Ark itself or to our army. Therefore, as acting High Priest I command that the Ark of the Covenant be carried this day from Shiloh, to join the army of Israel at Aphek."

"No," whispered Ahitub, and Samuel felt a sickening knot tighten in his stomach.

"So be it," said Deker, nodding.

"What is more," Phinehas continued, "I myself, Phinehas, son of Eli, High Priest of Israel, and my brother, Hophni, Chief Priest, will accompany the Ark into battle! Let the sons of Philistia hear it and shake with fear!"

"Your courage and decisiveness will be our salvation," Deker said, but Samuel barely heard him. He was looking at Eli's wrinkled face, seeing the tears that trickled down the deep creases in the dark, blotchy skin.

"My sons," Eli said, and the room quieted. "If you do this thing—if you remove the Ark from Shiloh, you do so without my blessing."

"Father—." Phinehas began, but Eli interrupted him.

"If you do this thing," he repeated, "then you should come no more into my presence."

The silence deepened, and Samuel could hear Eli's labored breathing. For several long moments no one moved, and Phinehas' face reddened; Samuel could see the muscles of his jaw working as the Priest ground his teeth in anger, staring down at the wrinkled, fleshy face of his father. When Phinehas spoke, he had barely mastered his emotions, and Samuel could tell he was making a concerted effort to keep from spewing his rage out against his father in a torrent of words.

"You have yielded the High Priesthood to me, father," he said slowly. "For many years you served our people faithfully, but those years have at last caught up to you. You are too old to take on this responsibility."

Phinehas lifted his eyes to look once again at the group around him. "We will leave Shiloh at daybreak tomorrow. We will carry the Ark of the Covenant to Aphek and return with victory firmly grasped in our palms! So I have spoken."

36

The sun's last glow faded from the western horizon, and a grave darkness settled over Shiloh as a Levite blew the horn that marked the close of day. Heavy clouds had drifted in from the west, and both moon and stars were shrouded behind their grey mass so that the empty Courtyard was lit only by the flickering flames of the oil lamps that burned at its perimeter, and by the sullen glow of the coals beneath the Altar. From the distant hills, the haunting cries of nightjars and owls were too feeble to pierce the darkness, muffled by cloud and fog, like sounds in a half-remembered dream.

Samuel sat on the flagstones near the Altar, staring into the coals, dreaming the fire. Atop the grating, the evening offering smoked and smoldered, but the Priests had banked the firebox for the night, and only a few flames slipped from the glowering coals to lick at the gobbets of charred flesh that remained. Near where Samuel sat, the shattered fragments of an earthenware pot lay scattered across the stones—in the chaos of the day, some Levite had forgotten to clean them up.

Samuel watched the play of light and darkness amidst the coals and tried to sort out his feelings from the events of the past few hours. He had prayed a dozen times since coming here at the end of the day, begging Jehovah for guidance, help—or some indication as to what he, or Ahitub, or anyone should do. But no answer had been forthcoming. Samuel wondered what it meant—of all the times when Israel needed guidance, surely now was such a time! Jehovah had seen fit to give Samuel a message of condemnation that basically repeated what the Prophet Rohgah had already said, but the True God chose not to speak to him now, when Phinehas was about to do the unthinkable and take the Ark into battle.

He knew that Jehovah was certainly capable of giving them the guidance they sought, but for some reason He had chosen not to in this case. Why? Did the True God's silence mean that He wanted the Ark carried into this battle? Was there some as yet unseen purpose that He was fulfilling, a purpose that lay beneath the surface, invisible under the chaos that Israel was experiencing?

The coals popped loudly, and a handful of sparks leapt out into the darkness, landing on the flagstones and glowing there a moment before fading into the blackness of the night. Samuel shifted his weight and sighed. He knew that Jehovah had a purpose, and that He was neither ignorant nor unconcerned with what was happening in Shiloh. But Samuel could not see what that purpose was. It was like a bank of sleeping embers under a bed of ashes, waiting for the right wind to fan them into a flame. Who would be caught in the light of that flame? he queried silently. Who would be warmed by it, and whom would it consume?

Jehovah's words haunted him: *The sons of Eli will die in one day.* He wondered abruptly if the Prophecy he had uttered had influenced Phinehas' decision to leave Shiloh with the Ark. The Priest could not fail to notice that the people of Israel had welcomed his condemnation to death, although the anger and disdain they directed at the Priest did not affect Phinehas' attitude in any way. But Samuel knew that, like himself, Phinehas cared about how others saw him. The big Priest knew that he could not maintain his hold over the people, the power that he so enjoyed wielding, if the entire nation turned against him. Samuel wondered if his surprising decision to bear the Ark to Aphek and lend his personal support to the army was some effort to redeem himself in the eyes of the people. Although the inhabitants of Shiloh would likely hate him even more for taking the sacred chest out of the city, Samuel knew how quickly their hatred could turn into admiration if Phinehas returned triumphantly. Moreover, many of the other tribes would see the actions of the new High Priest as brave and unselfish, and as evidence of a type of leadership that had been lacking in Israel since Eli had grown too old to leave the Tabernacle.

The fire hissed and the coals shifted and settled, sending another handful of sparks whirling skyward. Samuel let his eyes follow them and slowly raised his open palms toward the heavens. *What am I to do?* he pleaded silently. *What are your people to do?*

His only answer was the now-familiar rumbling of distant thunder over the far off hills of the Shephelah.

The next morning, following the rituals of sunrise and the morning sacrifice, Phinehas and Hophni appeared in the Courtyard with a group of Priests and Levites who were loyal to them, all of them dressed in simple Priestly linens. Phinehas had put aside the garments of the High Priest—they were not practical for traveling. He disappeared into the Tabernacle, entering the Holy of Holies backwards to drape sanctified cloths of blue and purple over the Ark, and then pull aside the thick, woven curtain that separated the Holy of Holies from the rest of the Tabernacle and hid the Ark from view. The Priests entered then, and carried the covered Ark into the Courtyard on a pair of long, gold-plated poles threaded through rings fastened to its base.

A Priest on duty blew a single, sustained blast on his trumpet, and Phinehas raised his arms before the watching crowds and recited the verses that Moses had repeated each time the Ark had been transported, centuries before, in the days of Israel's wandering through the wilderness: "Do arise, O Jehovah, and let Your enemies be scattered! Let those who intensely hate You flee from before You!"

The Priests bore the shrouded Ark out of the gates of the Courtyard and down the road that wound through the city of Shiloh. People lined the road on either side, many of them weeping; some begging Hophni and Phinehas not to take the Ark from the city. Samuel stood next to the gate and watched helplessly; tear-streaked faces turned toward him, their eyes insisting that he do something to stop the Priests.

He could do nothing. The sons of Eli had determined that they would take the Ark into battle and so guarantee Jehovah's protective presence with the army. But if Jehovah, in the form of the Ark, was to be taken to Aphek, that meant He must be removed from Shiloh, from the House he had chosen for Himself. Samuel knew that it was more complicated than that—that Jehovah could not be confined or limited by geography or physically bound to an object like the Ark But the Ark, with the *Shekinah* burning above it, had been given by the True God as a sign of His presence. If that sign were taken away, especially under such circumstances, would the Presence remain behind? Samuel did not think so. No pillar of cloud or fire hovered over the shrouded Ark. The *Shekinah* had been extinguished. Jehovah was no longer in the Tabernacle of Shiloh.

One of the Levites was leading Eli forward to the gate. The old man was dressed once again in the garments of the High Priest, and Samuel wondered what that might mean. Was Eli regretting his decision to turn the office over to his son? Was he trying to reassume responsibility for the Tabernacle now that Phinehas was leaving for a time?

Samuel was surprised when the Levite leading Eli brought the Priest directly to Samuel, whispering in the old man's ear, "Here is the Prophet Samuel, my lord."

"Samuel," Eli said, his voice strained by the exertion of walking so far. "Take me outside the Curtain Wall, my son. I wish to sit outside the wall, to face the west, where all our hopes have gone."

Samuel took the wrinkled hands in his own and slowly guided Eli through the gates. A pair of Levites fetched the High Priest's chair from in front of the Tabernacle entrance and placed it just outside the gates, along one side of the well-traveled roadway. Samuel eased Eli into his seat, and the old Priest immediately raised his blind eyes and stared westward. Samuel could still hear the wailing that accompanied the departing Ark, fading as the company that bore it left the city. Shiloh grew still in the wake of its passing—like an animal being bled, it sank slowly into stunned unconsciousness, unable to comprehend what was happening to it.

Samuel stood next to Eli in that silence. The old man's blind gaze never wavered. Tears occasionally streaked his wrinkled cheeks, but he did not break his sightless stare to the west. Samuel, too, felt anxiety drawing his eyes westward, and a great hollowness emptied in him, a feeling that something had been irreplaceably lost. The sounds from the city were subdued, and no worshippers climbed to enter the Tabernacle—why would they, when that which sanctified the Tabernacle was gone? Phinehas had torn the heart from Shiloh, from Israel, and the emptiness that remained behind was a sort of death for which no one was truly prepared.

When the day had passed, and the sun sank redly through the somber clouds on the western horizon, Eli still sat next to the Courtyard gate, silent and unmoving, his milky eyes reflecting the colors of the sunset. Samuel waited with him, unsure of what he could do to comfort the Priest, only feeling the need to stay nearby, watching over him. Far in the distance, clouds were massing in great, black pillars over the Judean mountains, but they did not look to Samuel like the rain clouds that the land so desperately needed.

Phinehas' wife, Mara, appeared, her eyes reddened from weeping, one hand cradling her swollen belly. Samuel smiled, glad to see her—she had remained secluded in shame for so long. "Is it all right with you?"

She returned his smile, but weakly, as though in her pregnancy she was too exhausted even to do that with vigor. She nodded toward Eli. "We must get him to his bed."

Samuel grasped the old man's hand—it was clammy, and shook. "Let me guide you to your room, my lord," he said softly.

Eli blinked, but did not move. "Has the sun gone down, Samuel? I cannot feel it anymore—no warmth reaches my bones."

"It has nearly set," Samuel said.

Eli waited a long time before speaking again. "Let us, then, wait here a little longer."

"The evening sacrifice is about to be lit," Samuel said. "You must get some sleep."

"I sleep already," Eli said. "All Israel sleeps, and this is the nightmare that visits us, to waken us from our slumber. But we do not wake. We do not wake, for the darkness has not yet lightened, and we cannot feel the dawn."

"The sun will rise again," Samuel said. "A new day will break."

"Will we recognize it when it comes?" Eli said softly. "Is a day without light or warmth truly day? Or has a night finally come that will endlessly seek for the morning, but never find it?"

Samuel gripped the High Priest's hand tightly, but said nothing, feeling his own sadness overwhelming him. He remembered his conversation in this same spot with the High Priest weeks before when the old man had confidently assured him: *No man can hide the sunrise.* Samuel's anger flared, thinking bitterly that Hophni and Phinehas had stolen something from their father, too, an unspoken seed of joy that all fathers entrusted to their sons, hoping that they would prove worthy of that trust and return the gift with a tenfold harvest.

"I cannot feel the sun," Eli whispered, and Samuel watched the last light fade in the west and wondered if any of them would ever sense the warmth of day again.

37

By the time that Manoah and his traveling companions had made their way back to Evenezer, the sun was beginning to set over the wave-wrinkled expanse of the Great Sea. Under the gentle, evening light, the camp of Israel roiled like a single, huge organism, grown to a massive sprawl of tents, wagons, animals, and men, spreading out across the trampled grasslands from horizon to horizon. Strings of soldiers had marched in from three directions all day long, coming by the thousands, coming to bolster the defeated army and recapture the city of Aphek. Manoah was amazed at their numbers—it was without a doubt the greatest military force he had ever seen assembled in his lifetime, a sea of moving figures filling the plain, men from every corner of the Promised Land. The atmosphere grew strangely festive as the sun went down, reports were made to the commanders, and the Israelites realized just how many had responded to the summons to battle—and they realized how much stronger their position was now than when they had been defeated days before. Men embraced and called out greetings to each other, shouts and laughter echoing among the sounds of smiths sharpening and repairing weapons and armor, the creak and rumble of wagons, and the snapping flags and standards in the western wind. The sheer mass of their own forces made the children of Israel confident; it made them feel invincible.

As he wandered through the maze of men and animals to the Danite encampment, all around him Manoah heard people talking about the Ark. News of Deker's mission to Shiloh had spread rapidly, and a sense of eager expectation gripped the camp. Most saw the Ark's coming as a sure guarantee of victory, even if they would not admit it in so many words.

Within the hour, Imri of Judah summoned the tribal leaders who remained to the command tent. "Four thousand spear and shield men from Naphtali, four thousand Zebulunites under Elon-tohr, two thousand archers and slingers from Benjamin—Basar has them making arrows as we speak," he began. "Arod has gathered four thousand eight hundred Gadite hill-men, and Issachar's force has grown to five thousand five hundred under Lodan. Ten thousand Ephraimites will fight under Deker's banner; four thousand Reubinites and five thousand Danites will serve at Manoah's command. Add to that about two thousand fishermen from Asher who arrived this evening and the nineteen thousand Judeans and two thousand Simeonites that I will lead, and Israel finds its forces nearing seventy thousand men."

He smiled grimly. "With this and the imminent arrival of the Ark, we are in a considerably better position than last time. Messengers have just brought word that the two sons of Eli are themselves bringing the Ark to Evenezer."

Their growing numbers lightened Manoah's heart, but he wondered what it meant for them that two corrupt Priests delivered their hope of salvation. Rumors had flown through the camp that the Nazirite boy Samuel had become a Prophet in Shiloh and that he had spoken condemnation and a sentence of death against the Priests.

Lodan stepped forward, bowing to Imri. "Our forces are not the only ones that have seen a surge in numbers. Philistine troops have been arriving throughout the day, traveling up the road in chariots, on horseback, and on foot, swelling the ranks of those encamped at Aphek."

Imri nodded. "But by your best estimates, our numbers are greater than theirs, are they not?"

"My estimates are truly estimates," Lodan replied. "But yes—I believe our numbers are more than those of our foes. However, my men have not yet returned from the lip of the sea. I feel we must hear from them before determining when we will attack."

"Do you have some reason to believe there is a threat from the west?" Imri asked.

"The Philistines could be bringing more troops north by boat," said Lodan. "I am just—."

"Being cautious?" Imri interrupted, and a few men laughed.

Lodan bowed again in confirmation. "Caution is not undue here, my lord."

"Deker will make the final decision," Imri said dismissively. "He has already sent word that he is planning to attack tomorrow morning. I am sure he will consider your input when he comes at dawn."

Deker arrived at Evenezer in the cold, quiet hour before daybreak, shattering the stillness of the sleeping encampment with the growling blat of ram's horns and the pounding of drums and tambourines. Manoah stumbled from his tent, rubbing his bleary eyes and casting about for the source of the commotion. All around him half-asleep soldiers appeared, ghostlike as they emerged into the moonless night. Someone a dozen paces from Manoah's tent lit a lamp, and he shielded his eyes against the sudden glare and turned away, toward the dark hills to the east.

Moments later, he saw a serpentine line of bobbing torches wending its way from the highlands down into the sprawling camp. More torches and lamps blazed amidst the tents, and cooking fires blossomed from fresh wood pushed onto last night's coals; amber-haloed shadows danced across tent cloths and flattened grass, a dark army rising to greet the arrival of the sacred Ark of the Covenant.

The approaching line of torches reached the edge of the encampment and swelled to a surging mass of men studded with flickering, ocher flames. The entire camp was awake now, and men were singing and dancing before the procession as it made its way toward the command tents. Manoah was caught up in the press of soldiers, carried on a surging wave of bodies swept along by the lodestone pull of the Ark. He saw it, its shape shrouded in dark blue and purple cloths, borne slowly forward on poles that rested atop the shoulders of Levites from the House of Kohath. Walking ceremoniously in front of it were Deker and the sons of Eli. Hophni and Phinehas smiled and nodded to the crowds beneficently.

When the procession reached Deker's command tent, it came to a halt and Phinehas signaled for the Levites to set the Ark down. Raising his arms high above his head, the Priest invoked again the ritual words of Moses spoken at the safe arrival of the Ark to its destination: "Do return, O Jehovah, to the myriads of the thousands of Israel!"

The Israelite army responded with a deafening cheer; drums rolled and trumpet blasts shattered the waning night. Manoah felt himself caught up in the excitement despite his earlier reservations. The Ark of the Covenant had arrived!

Inside the walls of Aphek, the sound of the Israelite army roused the Philistines from their beds as well, and watch captains sent runners out into the slowly brightening darkness to determine the cause of the commotion.

In the most palatial house in the city, Sarnam eased from his bed, his head pounding with the after-effects of the beer he had imbibed the night before. He rubbed his bleary eyes and looked around, re-orienting himself as he recognized the room he was in, desecrated by the soldiers during their sack of the city—bloodstains splashed the doorway, and someone had hacked into the walls and table. He looked back at the bed, noticing for the first time the motionless forms of two naked women, still sound asleep. He had only the vaguest recollection of bringing them back to his room the night before, and he did not know their names. He lifted a clay jug of beer from the corner of the room and swilled some down, wrinkling his nose at the bitter, warm taste. He filled his mouth a second time and spat a stream of the brownish liquid onto the heads of the sleeping women. They shifted and moaned softly, but did not wake.

"It isss time to join your men."

Sarnam staggered in surprise at the sound of the voice to find Sihphil standing in the doorway of the room, his narrow eyes glimmering darkly from within the cowl of his robe.

Sarnam looked out the room's single window over the rooftops, squinting against the throbbing ache in his head. "What is going on out there?"

Sihphil took two measured paces into the room. "The Hebrewss have ssummoned a great magic from their temple. Thiss morning they have brought their god to the battlefield!"

Sarnam spat barley husks from the beer onto the floor. "We have faced gods in battle before. I have worn the blood of the holiest warrior-priests—it spills as redly as the blood of a slave."

"Hsss!" Sihphil stepped closer, his narrow, yellow teeth bared. "You of all peoplesss ssshould have causse to fear thiss god! You, who failed to defeat the armiess of Egypt! Thiss iss the god that wass the ssmiter of Egypt with plague and sslaughter! Thiss iss the god that ssent Pharaoh and the mightiessst of hiss forcess to the depthsss of the sssea!"

Sarnam frowned and shrugged, trying not to show how disturbed he was at the dark priest's words. "You are starting to sound like a common man, Sihphil. You and I both know that it is swords and spears that win a battle, not deities or demons."

"Fool!" hissed the priest. "Pray to whatever sspiritss you think may lissten to you! And while you are praying, you had better find a way to overcome the Ark of thiss Hebrew god!"

Gathering his black robes, the priest stormed out of the room. Sarnam tried to think of a clever, parting retort that would match his darkening mood, but his pounding head was too addled. Cursing to the paneled walls, he began to arm himself for battle.

38

The sun glowed sullenly through banks of grey cloud that loomed over the fields outside Aphek, shedding a colorless brightness that yielded neither warmth nor cheer to the Israelites who were assembling into battle lines there. This morning, their sun was a golden box, shrouded now beneath dark blue and purple cloths at the rear of the army, encircled by a solemn guard of ceremonially armed Levites, their spear-butts jammed in the ground to form a fence of polished shafts. The soldiers of Israel inhaled the presence of the Ark, and exhaled hope and expectation.

They had marched from Evenezer that morning at the break of dawn, singing as they followed the Levites transporting the Ark. From where Manoah walked, in the rearguard, the covered chest appeared to float, shoulder-high, just above the masses of men that flowed out of the valley toward Aphek.

The morning march had not been uneventful. Their route took them, unavoidably, through the site of the battle of three days before. The Torah forbade them from touching any corpse, and so they had picked their way gingerly through the bloated bodies of their countrymen, sending black clouds of ravens and crows noisily skyward. Mangy jackals and wild dogs bared their teeth and slunk away from their grisly feast, muzzles bloody. The marching soldiers tried not to look at the torn bodies, and failed.

But the presence of the Ark staved off the worst of the sorrow, or transformed it into an eager hatred, a hunger for vengeance that drove them forward like hounds chasing the scent of blood. The singing resumed; they passed by the Yarkon and once again found themselves upon the plain of Aphek.

Hophni and Phinehas strode among the troops like pagan kings, nodding imperiously and dispensing benedictions in response to the adulation that greeted them. Manoah noticed Deker's expression as he watched the Priests and thought he detected a hint of irritation in the big general's bearing. Perhaps Deker realized that many of the men were now looking to the sons of Eli for leadership.

A few moments later, Hophni and Phinehas met with Deker not far from where Manoah waited at the forefront of the Danite troops. "Summon the so-called priests of Dan," Phinehas commanded.

Deker hesitated, eyes narrowing. He disliked being ordered about before his army, but seemed to realize he could hardly challenge the authority of the newly appointed High Priest of Israel in front of his men. Scowling, he dispatched a runner to bring the priests of Dan to where he waited.

When they arrived, Hophni stepped forward without hesitation and, grabbing the collars of their *ephod*s, began ripping them in two. The priests tried to resist, stumbling backwards and screaming their indignant protest, but they found themselves ringed by Levite spears, forced to stand and endure while Hophni finished humiliating them.

"By the authority conferred upon me by my father, and my high office," Phinehas said, "I hereby order that these so-called priests of Dan be sent to the front lines of the battle."

"Priests are exempt from military service!" one of the Danites objected.

"You are not priests," Phinehas said coldly. "It is the tribe of Levi that was granted that exemption—not any man who calls himself a priest." He nodded to the Levite guards and they herded the Danite pretenders off in the direction of the city of Aphek, where the Zebulunites were forming ranks.

"You cannot do this!" one of them screamed.

"I could have you stoned for your presumptuousness" Phinehas shot back. "But I choose mercy. I will let you die as men."

Still screaming their protests, the Danites were prodded and dragged toward the battlefront.

Deker turned to Manoah. "Have you seen Lodan?"

Manoah shook his head. "Not since yesterday."

"He took a group of men scouting—he said something about going to the lip of the sea," Deker said. "I expected his return before now."

The grizzled general signaled his trumpeters, and a series of horn blasts sent the final contingents of the army shifting into place. In the vanguard, a bristling wall of spears jutted out from between the oiled, leather shields of Elon-tohr's Zebulunites, their faces grim and fell as they prepared to lead the charge against the enemy. Behind them, rank upon rank of

Naphtalites under Jahze'el of Hazor, Ephraimites under Deker, Judeans under Imri, and men of Manasseh under Asriel of Pirathon formed the main columns of the Israelite force, all of them bearing the long spears and tall shields and wearing the heavy scale-mail armor that was typical of those tribes. Scattered among them were the poorly armed Asherite fishermen and shepherds, and a few companies of the tribe of Reuben.

On either side of the main columns, Arod had positioned his Gadite hill-men, grizzled veterans in light, leather armor who would use their swiftness and mobility to protect Israel's flanks. On low rises bordering the Gadites to the north and south, the Benjaminite slingers and archers had found trees and rocks that would provide cover from which they could fire their missiles down on the enemy without exposing their own forces. Nearly half of Manoah's Danites were standing with them, many of them shepherds armed with slings or bows as well and prepared to use shield and sword to defend the archers if an attack swept their way.

At the back of the army, the rest of the Danites formed up as rearguard under Manoah, their ranks strengthened by any of Lodan's Issacharians who were not serving as runners, spies, or tacticians, or gone with him on his reconnaissance. Manoah looked at the intense, swarthy features of the men of Issachar and the wicked-looking, curved daggers tucked in their belts and was glad to have them beside him.

The blat of the ram's horns sounded again, two long blasts, and the Priests at the rear of the battle lines lifted the Ark onto their shoulders. Slowly, the army of Israel began lumbering forward toward the city of Aphek.

Just outside the city, the army of Philistia was likewise preparing to advance from the shadow of the walls toward their enemy. A scattered line of priests led by Sihphil gyrated at the forefront of the troop lines, their naked bodies shiny with oil, chanting and slashing themselves with obsidian blades until blood dribbled in crimson streaks down their bodies and legs.

Sarnam strode among them, his tall form made even more massive by his bronze plate armor and high, feathered helmet. The men cheered at his appearance—they knew him now as a leader who could take them to victory. He waved back to them, thinking through his carefully laid plans for the battle, and smiled grimly to himself. Dagon and Baal had chosen him for this purpose—to drive these Hebrew squatters out of the land of Canaan. They thought their greater numbers would save them. They thought their precious Ark would assure them victory. But he had not come this far by failing to know his enemy. They had brought their Ark—their god—to the battle. He had brought his own advantage, coming swiftly and in secret from the seashore.

He raised his arms and scanned the troops as they quieted. Word of the arrival of the Hebrews' Ark had spread among them, and in spite of their trust in him as a leader, he saw fear in many eyes. He despised their weakness, but it did not worry him. The gods of Canaan had already given them victory. When their swords fed on the blood of their enemies, his glory would be all the greater for their lack of confidence now.

"A man is proven by his courage," he yelled, his voice echoing against the city wall. "A man is proven by his power—by his control over lesser men! In Gibbethon, in Lod, in Aphek, the Hebrews you captured serve as your slaves, and by this you know you are strong. Think on those slaves—for it is their brothers who have dared to come against us today! Show yourselves courageous and prove yourself men, heroes of Philistia, that you may not serve the Hebrews, just as they have served you! Prove yourselves men, and fight!"

With a deafening roar, the Philistine army surged forward. Men on horseback and chariots quickly broke away from the infantry, thundering across the dead grass of the plain, the hooves of their mounts churning up clouds of dust behind them. In the midst of the running foot soldiers, Rephaim giants lumbered through the crowd, massive battle-axes cradled in their long arms. Some of the chariots bore the black-clad Gedhudhra, while other members of Sarnam's death-squad ran like shadows among the infantry, black swords raised, faces locked in a grimace of thirst for battle.

Elon-tohr's Zebulunites came to an abrupt halt at the top of a low ridge in the field, jabbing the bronze-capped butts of their spears into the dry soil, the front line dropping to one knee so that the longer shafts of the line behind them extended over their shoulders to form a bristling wall of shining, bronze points. The front rows placed their shields on the ground in front of them so that they protected all but their helmeted heads.

At almost the same moment, both Philistine and Israelite armies let loose volleys of arrows and sling stones, and the sky darkened with the hail of deadly missiles. Men and horses collapsed on both sides, some chariots tumbling spectacularly amidst the raging Philistine forces. Basar's Benjaminites sent wave after wave of arrows and stones into their ranks, but the Philistines raised their shields and came forward still, their progress barely dampened.

The leading row of chariots closed on the ranks of Zebulunites and on both sides, the men began roaring. The Zebulunite line drew together, as if the entire force had inhaled a great breath.

The two forces collided with a crash like a mighty wave clawing at a rocky shore, and the air filled with battle cries, the clatter of weapons against shields, the angry shrieks of horses, and the screams of the dying. The Israelite line held, and dozens of mounts and riders impaled themselves on the Zebulunite wall of spears. Elon-tohr's men hurled the bodies back into the Philistine ranks, but Sarnam's soldiers just climbed over their own dead and threw themselves recklessly against the Israelite line once more.

From either flank, the Gadites swept down into the tangled mass of men, horses, and chariots and began hamstringing every horse they could reach and shoving their thick spear shafts through the spokes of the chariot wheels. Basar's Benjaminites continued to rain stones and arrows down on the center of the Philistine force, where the soldiers massed so tightly that the missiles could hardly fail to find a target.

A series of horn blasts sounded from the hill where the grape-cluster banner of Ephraim identified Deker's command post: an order for the Israelites to advance! Screaming their anger above even the clash of battle, the Zebulunites pushed forward against their enemy, and slowly, the Philistine line began to crumple, first at either end, then in the middle. Israel forced Sarnam's forces slowly backwards.

The fighting intensified along the front lines, and as more and more Zebulunites began to die, the Naphtalites and Ephraimites behind them leapt forward to take their places.

From his position in the rearguard, Manoah could witness the destruction in the vanguard. Already, masses of bodies lay still and bloodied upon the field—the soldiers swarmed over and around them as if they were stones.

Saphold had made his way through Israel's ranks and was once again engaging in ritual duels with other Rephaim whenever he encountered them. Three times Manoah witnessed the bizarre challenges, as groups of Rephaim giants stopped fighting in order to encircle Saphold and another warrior, and each time Saphold quickly defeated his enemy and returned to the battle. The watching Rephaim would beat their breasts, chant "Dooom-aah! Doom-aah!" and return to the melee until the next challenge was made.

On a low rise at the back of Israel's forces, behind Manoah's rearguard, the Ark remained a silent presence, and Hophni and Phinehas watched the battle before them with grim satisfaction.

Israel continued to push the Philistine line back towards the city, building momentum now, and as the line spread out across the plain, more and more of the warriors on both sides were caught up in the fighting. Knots of Philistines had climbed the hills on either side of the army and were battling the Danites in an effort to reach the Benjaminite archers and stop their deadly hail of missiles. Dozens of chariots sprawled, overturned or broken, upon the field, the bodies of the horses that had pulled them flailing, tangled in their own traces.

A command of Philistine infantry made a furious charge against the Gadites on the northern flank, and managed to penetrate their line. Hundreds of them raced toward the Ark, and Manoah raised his sword and led his men in a fierce counterattack. For several minutes, he found himself at last face to face with the enemy, screaming and hacking wildly at everything that came within his reach.

In moments, the entire command that had penetrated the line lay motionless on the bloody grass, and Manoah looked quickly around to get his bearings. He realized that the fight had carried him and his warriors north of the main force, and he rallied them to him to return to position.

At that moment, he saw a solitary rider galloping furiously toward him from the open country behind Israel's battle lines, splashing through the swampy shallows along the Yarkon River. The rider was nearly lying across his mount's neck, and even from a distance, Manoah could tell that something was wrong by the way he leaned forward, hugging the horse's neck instead of holding the reins. The stallion, too, was making a valiant effort to keep up the pace the rider demanded, but it was limping as it cantered, favoring one hind leg. Manoah began running to meet the man, thinking that whether he was friend or foe, he would have to be dealt with.

When the rider drew closer, Manoah realized with a shock that it was Lodan the Issacharian. He reined in his frothing mount next to Manoah and tumbled from the saddle, collapsing to his knees in the dry grass. He pressed one palm against his right ribs, and both hand and the clothing beneath it were soaked in blood, to which yellow bits of dead grass were now clinging.

"Fall back!" Lodan whispered through gritted teeth.

"Lodan...What happened?" Manoah knelt and put one arm around him to try to help him to rise—he smelt of sweat and horses, and his mouth was full of blood.

Lodan pushed him away. "Fall back now! Give the order!"

Manoah glanced over his shoulder towards the fighting. His Danites had reformed the rearguard and were once again battling small groups of Philistines who had penetrated the flanks of the Israelite army in an attempt to reach the Ark. "What has happened?" he asked again.

"Army...lip of the sea..." Lodan hissed. "Ships at Joppa...We were caught..." He coughed and spattered flecks of blood across the back of his hand.

Manoah's mind raced. "An army? How many—when will they be here?"

Lodan grabbed the back of Manoah's neck with one hand, pulling Manoah's face closer to his own. "Deker!...fall back now!"

Manoah nodded, and gently lowering the bleeding Issacharian to the ground, raced toward Deker's position on a hill near the Ark. But even as he sped across the field, the thunder of many running feet rumbled from the north, and an army of Philistines, thousands strong, appeared from beyond the swamplands of the Yarkon.

39

The Philistines surged over the hills like a dark wave, raging towards Israel's northern flank with the wild confidence of fresh troops who know their appearance is a surprise to their foes. The thunder of their coming was so loud it broke through even the raging of the battle, and they poured down upon the field in a flood of flailing hooves and a cloud of grey dust.

Manoah tried to run faster, his legs already exhausted from the battle, and every gasped breath searing his throat and lungs. But within moments the soldiers of the rearguard and the commanders stationed with Deker on the hill saw, or heard, the new threat appearing from the north, and for a brief time confusion erupted along the back of the Israelite army as some soldiers turned to engage the approaching Philistines, and others continued battling those who were already attacking them.

Manoah reached his Danites moments ahead of the Philistines, bellowing orders to form a defensive line. His men responded just in time, and the fresh Philistine forces collided against them with a muffled crunch. The mass and momentum of their enemies pushed the Danites swiftly backwards against the main army, and Israel found itself sandwiched between two forces, and hemmed in by the Yarkon river and swamp on a third side.

The Philistines surged forward once again, and a fresh wave of arrows and sling stones fell among the Israelites. Hundreds of men fell under the onslaught, and in moments, the Israelite line collapsed. Manoah saw some soldiers begin to flee immediately, abandoning all hope of victory or even survival unless they escaped the battlefield.

Phicol, still bloodied from his struggle beneath his overturned chariot a few days before, led a charge of Philistine chariots into the crumbling defensive lines, and the heavy vehicles plowed through their ranks, scythed wheels leaving a trail of carnage behind them.

Manoah screamed at his men, trying desperately to reform their line, but his voice was lost in the cacophony, and the entire battlefield transformed into a writhing mass of soldiers fighting for their lives. Rephaim giants were deep inside Israel's ranks now, massive axes swinging, felling men in great arcs like stalks of wheat before a scythe. Manoah saw an Ephraimite hurl his spear toward one of the giants with stunning force, but its tip barely penetrated the Rephaim's massive breastplate, and the giant plucked it out and tossed it contemptuously into an Israelite nearby.

Then Sarnam's huge, black chariot began to descend the hill from which he had watched the battle, ringed by several dozen mounted Gedhudhra, raging down and through Israel's left flank. As their wedge formation sliced through the defenders, Phicol joined them on another chariot. Manoah's heart sank when he saw where they were headed.

The Ark of the Covenant.

Manoah called the Danites to him, struggling desperately toward the Ark's position. Somehow, he managed to assemble several score of his men and together they battled through the sea of Philistine soldiers that lay between them and the Ark.

Abruptly, Arod was at his side, his wild mane of hair flying, and together Danites and Gadites slowly pushed forward. Within moments, they were facing several ranks of black-clad Gedhudhra, and the death-troops stopped their charge and pushed them back.

Manoah heard himself screaming uselessly for Elon-tohr, knowing the Zebulunite was trapped in the front lines, trying to stop the chariots from destroying the vanguard. Arod was roaring like a lion, the veins on his neck bulging as he used both sickle-sword and shield as offensive weapons against anyone who came within reach of his long arms. But the Gedhudhra knew what they were about, and would not be baited, but maintained their line, locked tightly together, repulsing every attack that Manoah or Arod launched against them.

Then the Gedhudhra threw themselves against the Danites and Gadites with reckless abandon, their iron swords biting through the Israelites' bronze blades and easily shearing their light, leather armor. Manoah was face to face with them, and it took all of his skill and concentration to block the swift, furious sweeps and thrusts of his enemy's blades.

Sarnam's chariot and the Gedhudhra that followed it had reached the ring of Levite soldiers surrounding the Ark, and Manoah caught a heart-wrenching glimpse of the Levite novices trying desperately to defend the sacred chest and the Priests who stood beside it. Then something slammed into Manoah from behind and hurled him onto his face in the bloody grass, knocking the air from his lungs.

He rolled to his feet and saw quickly that what had hit him was the crumpled body of an Israelite warrior, one of several tossed like fallen leaves by the blow of a Rephaim axe. The giant was a few paces away, half again as tall as Manoah, his face scarred and his body encased in gore-smeared scale mail. He was roaring as he lumbered toward them with his weapon clutched in his knotted arms.

Arod leapt toward the giant, plucking a spear with a broken shaft from a body lying nearby. His leap brought him within reach of the Rephaim and he escaped a sweeping blow of the massive axe only by throwing himself over backwards to the ground at the last moment. Rolling over twice, he hurled the broken spear upwards from the ground; the blade slipped under the scales of the Rephaim's mail and buried itself in the giant's abdomen. His bellow was so loud it hurt Manoah's ears, and then he fell like a great tree, hurling his axe from him as he collapsed. The huge weapon spun twice, smashing men like stalks of stubble. The Rephaim hit the ground with a crash of armor, sending up a cloud of dust, and did not move anymore.

Manoah rallied his men and led another charge at the ranks of Gedhudhra, but failed once again to penetrate their defenses. Beyond the warriors he fought, he saw the death-troops effortlessly slaughter the Levite guards and surround Hophni and Phinehas. The two Priests were on their knees now, their backs to the Ark, their mouths moving in some unheard plea.

Then the young warrior without a nose stepped toward them, a short sword in each hand. Manoah watched in horror as the scarred Philistine did things to Hophni and Phinehas with his blades, things that made Manoah collapse to his knees, vomiting his revulsion onto the bloody grass.

When he managed to clamber to his feet again, he saw that the two Priests still lived—they were weakly trying to crawl away, pawing at the ground with what remained of their limbs, unrecognizable as the men they had been.

Now the ebon-robed priest with Sarnam stepped toward them and poured something from a clay pitcher onto their backs, some thick, yellowish liquid streaked with black. He raised his cowled head toward the sky, arms spread wide in an appeal to heaven. A lit torch appeared, as if by magic, in his clawed hands.

Manoah was now close enough that he heard one of the Priests praying: "Save us, Jehovah! Please, save us!"

The cowled priest's answer rang out even over the sound of battle. "Jehovah hasss abandoned you!"

For the briefest moment, as the two sons of Eli cast about for someone to rescue them, Phinehas' eyes met Manoah's. In that instant, Manoah saw in his eyes a recognition of the truth of the dark priest's words.

The priest tossed the torch casually toward them. It whooshed like a lamp guttering, but amplified hundreds of times, and Hophni and Phinehas disappeared in a blaze of flame. Over the tumult of the battle, Manoah could hear them screaming.

The press of fleeing men pushed Manoah back until he was unable even to reach the enemies driving at them. Greasy smoke swirled upwards from the sons of Eli, and behind the pall of ash, four of the Gedhudhra lifted the shrouded Ark onto their shoulders and began bearing it from the field, heading south, toward the cities of Philistia. A knot of the black-clad death-troops followed them, an undefeatable escort to bear the Ark away from Israel.

The tide of battle carried Manoah the opposite direction and pressed him abruptly against the enemy soldiers. He wept while he fought, unable to concentrate.

His mind filled abruptly with Naamah's beautiful face, and he was forced to confront the likelihood that he would never see her again. He was shocked to discover the anguish, the guilt, that he felt remembering that he had left her without telling her how much he loved her. He had given one of the people who cared the most about him reason to curse his name, and now that name was about to die out in Israel.

He stumbled on a body and fell, scrambling to his feet just as one of the Gedhudhra rushed towards him. He barely deflected the warrior's first attack with his shield, but then the Gedhudhra hacked furiously at the shield with his long, black blade, splitting the hide and wood into useless remnants strapped to Manoah's left arm. Manoah tried to retreat, but other men were battling behind him, and he had nowhere to run. The Gedhudhra came for him again, his dark face locked in a snarl, and Manoah parried his blows desperately. But the black-clad warrior was too fast, and his long sword slipped past Manoah's guard and slashed into his unprotected left shoulder. Manoah heard his own surprised yelp of pain, and saw as though all the world had slowed, the black blade falling towards him once again.

Then another dark shape, like a wisp of shadow, burst from the battling warriors all around them and landed with cat-like grace between him and the Philistine.

It was Elon-tohr.

40

Elon-tohr spun into the Gedhudhra like a dancer, his slender blade a blur of motion, his empty left hand extended behind him for balance. Within seconds he was battling half a dozen of Sarnam's death-squad, an impossible explosion of grace and skill, and all alone was still pushing them inexorably backward into their own forces. Spears hurtled toward him from the mass of men all around them, but he deflected them effortlessly, just one more step in his whirling dance of death, changing their courses with easy, elegant swipes of his blade; the spears careened with deadly precision into attacking Philistines.

Moments later, the rest of the Zebulunite vanguard joined him, coalescing into a bristling wall of sword- and spear-men that established a barrier between the Philistine forces and the Danites and Gadites. Manoah leapt to join the line of the battle, but Elon-tohr halted him. "Lead Israel from the field!" he yelled. "Organize the retreat!"

Arod led ranks of his Gadite hill-men to Manoah's position and together they reformed the rearguard, assembling into a broken line as trumpeters signaled the retreat. Soldiers began fleeing through the rearguard phalanx, like water draining from a pond; the Israelite army grew smaller and smaller, while Philistines poured in to fill the space they had left. Manoah stared in sickened awe as their departure revealed the bodies that littered the ground—thousands upon thousands of them, stacked atop each other, broken and torn by weapons, wheels, and hooves, motionless in the crushed, crimson-streaked grass.

Zebulunites, Danites, and Gadites tightened their ranks as the last of their brethren slipped past, presenting a wall of spears and shields to the

Philistine force. Manoah gave the signal, and slowly the rearguard began their retreat, measured and steady, yielding before the press of the Philistines but refusing to be driven into a rout.

Back they swept across the plains, quickening their pace as they went. The chariots and mounted Philistines pushed ever closer, and Manoah saw that his soldiers would never make it to the cover of the trees before the enemy cavalry cut them down. He sent a message by runner to Arod, and the wild-haired Gadite gathered his agile hill-men and led them in a series of furious counter-charges against the flanks of the mounted Philistines, pressing their attack only long enough to slow the progress of the cavalry, then dissipating like mist back into the Israelite rearguard before the Philistines could organize themselves.

Over and over, they repeated their attack, and each time, dozens of Gadites fell into silence. But their attacks hindered the Philistines just enough that the Israelite rearguard was able to increase the distance separating them, and Manoah led them swiftly towards the cover of the trees.

Manoah kept his pace steady as he walked, looking back over his shoulder more than he looked forward. At one of these moments, he tripped over something in his path, and looked down even as a wave of intense stench washed over him with sickening strength. He looked down and realized that the army had reached the site of the previous battle. What he had stumbled on was the bloated body of an Israelite man, his clothing and flesh torn by vultures and jackals. Fighting back nausea, he saw the corpses scattered throughout the field on which they stood, a mute and fetid testimony to the slaughter that had bloodied the ground several days earlier.

Choking back bile, he forced himself to keep moving, picking his way among the dead. By the time Manoah reached the tree line, he could see Israelite soldiers clambering up the scrub-dotted hills, fleeing in every direction. Here and there, captains were holding small forces together, but for the most part the units of the army were disintegrating as the soldiers realized the hopelessness of their position and began the journey away from the lost borderland and back to their homes and families.

A series of horn blasts sounded from somewhere in the Philistine ranks. From the cover of the scattered sycamores that spilled from the forest down the surrounding hills, Manoah turned and saw that, at last, the enemy charge had halted. Contented with their clear victory, the Philistine commanders turned cavalry and infantry back toward Aphek's walls; they had achieved their goal, and had no need to risk sending their foot soldiers into the cover of the forest where the chariots were useless. Calling his exhausted men to him, Manoah and the last of the Israelite rearguard melted into the trees.

By nightfall, the commanders had gathered in a narrow valley deep in the hills of the Shephelah. They met in the open air, clustered around a small, smokeless fire under a sky that showed neither moon nor stars. Basar the Benjaminite sat with his back against a tree, long legs stretched in front of him; Elon-tohr, Deker, Manoah, Lodan, Arod, and Asriel of Pirathon ringed the fire, the dancing light shadowing their grim faces. Jahze'el, commander of the Naphtalites, was conspicuously absent; he had fallen in the battle, crushed beneath the iron-bound wheels of a chariot.

Deker seemed lost. The grizzled commander paced restlessly, pulling at his beard and mumbling constantly to himself. "Thirty thousand dead!" he shouted at one point, to no one in particular. His eyes shone with orange firelight in their shadowed sockets.

"How many remain—how many have not fled back to their homes?" Lodan asked. Stained bandages wrapped his arm and chest, and he was still pale from loss of blood.

"We don't know—we are still waiting for the reports!" Deker answered, biting off the words. "A few scattered thousands. And more slip away every hour."

No one was surprised that the heart had gone out of the Israelite army. Manoah found himself struggling to find the motivation to stay and fight for a cause that everyone feared was already lost. If Deker's reports were correct, and thirty thousand of their brothers were silent on the fields of Aphek, then the greatest army they could hope to muster would still not be enough to counter the forces the Philistines had already shown themselves capable of throwing at them.

Besides, the Ark of the Covenant had been lost. Manoah knew that most of the Israelites shared his feelings about that loss—it felt as if their identity as a nation had been taken. Since its construction three hundred and forty four years before, no hands but those of the High Priest had touched the Ark. It had become their talisman, and they had carried it into battle stuffed to overflowing with their hopes. In a nation that worshipped without idols of any kind, Manoah had to admit that the Ark provided for many a tangible sign of God's presence—a crutch to support an ailing faith that sought concrete expressions of spiritual things. For those who relied on the visible to shore up their belief in the unseen, the loss of the Ark was tantamount to the loss of God's backing. After the carnage of Aphek, Manoah could hardly believe that the True God was any longer in their midst. And if the loss of the Ark meant that they had lost, also, Jehovah's support and backing, then their defeat at Aphek was the least of their worries. If Jehovah was no longer with them, then how long could they continue to exist as a nation? How long before their enemies closed in on them from every side and erased the name of Israel from the surface of the land?

"What has become of the Ark now?" Elon-tohr asked abruptly, as though he had been following Manoah's line of thought.

"The Philistines have made no secret of their movements," Lodan answered. "The Axis Lord of Ashkelon, this Sarnam, has returned south to Philistia. Most of the army follows him—he has left only sufficient force to hold Aphek and rebuild its fortifications. I am getting reports that small bands have made forays into Israel along the way, but apparently only to gather supplies and loot whatever cities are nearby. It seems for now they are content to have captured Aphek and the Ark."

Lodan shifted his bandaged arm, and winced. "But one commander—a scarred-faced young captain named Phicol, is leading a group of the Gedhudhra and other soldiers into the heart of Israel. It appears to be a terror campaign designed to cause our people to let their hands drop down. He is attacking towns and villages as he goes, but if the rumors my spies are hearing can be believed, his ultimate destination is more ambitious."

Lodan gritted his teeth—Manoah could not tell if it was in pain or anxiety. "He brags to our people in the towns he attacks—he says he is going to Shiloh, to burn the Tabernacle."

Silence settled over the group, and even the fire receded, appalled, into its darkening embers.

"I think that may not be so easy," Deker said. "Jehovah may fill the hand of High Priest Eli with power, and—."

"Jehovah has chosen to execute justice for all the wickedness that has been done in Shiloh these past years," Arod said. For once, the Gadite was not smiling. His hair was still matted with dried blood. "The young prophet, Samuel, was right. All his words have proven true."

"Then he is our hope now," Manoah said. "But without knowing it, the Philistines may take the heart out of Samuel as well, if they are not stopped. Between Aphek and Shiloh, one of the towns they are most likely to destroy is Ramathaim—Samuel's hometown, and the home of his family."

Deker stopped pacing. "This, then, is a task that we can do something about. Basar!"

The lanky Benjaminite stood smoothly and stepped into the circle. "My lord?"

"You are charged with carrying word of our defeat to Shiloh. Find Eli and tell him what has happened. Then get the Elders of the city to begin fleeing south, to a more defensible location. To Nob, perhaps. We need to get as many people as possible out of Shiloh before the Philistines get there. We will come with the army as quickly as we can."

Basar nodded slowly; it was obvious he did not relish the assignment.

"I am sorry to give you so grim a task," said Deker. "I would tell Eli of his sons' death myself, if my legs were as long as yours. But you are the fastest messenger I have that I can trust to get this warning to Shiloh. The lives of thousands depend on your reaching the city in time."

Basar nodded again. "I will leave immediately."

"Perhaps you should rest for a short time at least before starting out," Deker said.

"I will rest when my legs give out under me," Basar said, and loped silently away to the east.

They watched him disappear into the darkness of the forest, silent for a few moments. "I will gather whatever remnants of the army can be collected quickly," Deker continued afterward. "I will lead them to Shiloh and present what defense we can muster to enable as many to escape the city as possible. Asriel—you will command the rearguard and take over the supply lines; Lodan will continue to bring whatever intelligence he can to me.

"Elon-tohr—you are charged with evacuating the city of Ramathaim before the Philistines reach it. Take Manoah and Arod and however many men you think you will need. Get the family of the young Prophet safely to him in Shiloh."

"I would like to have the Rephaim Saphold come with us as well," Manoah said.

"Do it," Deker nodded. "You will need whatever advantage you can get to beat these cursed Gedhudhra."

The fire popped, and Deker pushed the unburnt end of a log into the coals with the toe of his sandal. "We must leave before sunrise. Get what rest you can until then."

Manoah dozed fitfully for a few hours before a watchman startled him awake in the cold hour before dawn. The sky was still dark, the morning's waxing light shrouded behind layers of heavy, grey storm clouds. He had been dreaming of Naamah.

"My lord—it is time," the watchman said to him, touching his shoulder gently.

Manoah rose and stretched. If anything, he felt more tired than he had when he had lain down to sleep. He strapped his sword belt on as the watchman padded among the other Danites, waking them.

Manoah joined the rest of the commanders. Elon-tohr wanted several dozen men each from the Gadites and the Danites—including a number of archers and slingers—and sent messengers to select them. The commanders blessed each other and Elon-tohr led his men off into the dark.

No horns marked their departure. They slipped quietly and swiftly down the forest's dark pathways, Arod and the Gadites in the lead, Manoah and a handful of his men taking the rearguard. Elon-tohr strode just ahead of the Danites, silent and enigmatic in the midst of the handpicked Zebulunites that accompanied him. Saphold lumbered along near Manoah, his broad face unreadable in the half-light.

Sunrise was a reddening of the eastern horizon, bleeding through the trees like a wound freshly opened. Gradually, the sky began to brighten, only to reveal how dark and thick were the clouds that had draped themselves overhead as far as the eye could see. Manoah wondered briefly if at long last they were going to get the rain they had been waiting for.

They traveled narrow pathways until they reached the road and turned to follow it, taking the quickest and most direct route toward Ramathaim. It was nearing mid-morning when the scouts returned and warned them that a small Philistine raiding party was not far ahead of them on the road, and approaching quickly. The Israelites melted into the trees on either side of the rutted track, drawing their sickle-swords or fitting arrows to bowstrings.

They heard the barking of the war hounds long before the raiding party reached them—less than five dozen men on foot, and three chariots. Half of the Philistines died in the first volley of arrows and stones released by the Danites, and in the moments of confused panic that followed, Elon-tohr led a charge against the remainder. Manoah let his rage swell and break against them as he fought, his mind filled with images of the destruction they had wreaked on Gibbethon, of the bodies of his brothers pinned to the gate of their home. In moments, the battle was over—Philistine soldiers, horses, and even dogs lay slaughtered on the roadway. Not a single Israelite had been killed.

Elon-tohr ordered them to leave the corpses where they lay. He sent the scouts ahead once more, and the little band of warriors hastened east along the road. The path climbed more sharply now, ascending through forests broken by great, wrinkled ridges of rock and camel-colored clay. For a time, the road took them along the edge of a steep, bare ravine that fell sharply away to the north, its bottom grooved and molded by the flash-floods that churned through it during spring rains. Leaving the ravine, they climbed over a tree-covered ridge, and then began to descend into the valley in which Ramathaim waited.

When they neared the outskirts of the town, Elon-tohr called a halt and waited for the scouts to return. They did not have to wait long—Manoah saw concern etched on their faces when they reappeared and conferred quietly with the grey-clad Zebulunite. Elon-tohr asked Manoah and Arod to come with him, and they followed the scouts through the trees, scrambling up a small hill that overlooked the valley.

When they crested the hill, they lay on their stomachs and looked down at the village nestled among the trees below them. Ramathaim was still and quiet—unusually quiet for the middle of the day. Nothing moved in the valley around the town, and no one was coming or going from the city. After a few moments, Elon led them further westward, to where they could get a better view of the gates.

When they reached their new position, hidden from view of the city behind a cluster of massive boulders half-buried in the roots of the sycamores, they could see clearly down into the town square. A large group of people—men, women, children, and old people—was gathered in a circle there.

They were ringed by black-clad Gedhudhra.

At the gates, a chariot shifted forward and backward as the horse harnessed to it tossed its head impatiently. Gedhudhra flanked it to either side, spears in their hands as though they were the guardians of the city.

In the chariot was a young man with a wild shock of blond hair, and a mass of reddened scar tissue where his nose should have been.

41

Only a few dozen of the Gedhudhra accompanied Phicol—obviously, the bloodthirsty, young commander had led a small group directly to Ramathaim after the battle at Aphek, guessing correctly that Israel would send a force to the city to try to save it.

Elon-tohr, Manoah, and Arod returned to their men and held a quiet meeting under the sycamores trees. "We cannot simply attack them," Manoah said. "Even if our numbers were greater and we felt confident of our ability to defeat the Gedhudhra, the Philistines would start slaughtering their captives as soon as they feel there is any chance of our entering the city."

"No doubt they have already killed many," said Elon-tohr. "The group huddled in the square is only a fraction of the inhabitants of this town."

"Let us hope the fraction includes the family of the young prophet, Samuel," said Manoah.

Thunder rumbled ominously somewhere to the west. "We need to find a way to draw most of the Philistine force out from the walls," Arod said.

"Our advantage is that we know something of our enemy," Elon-tohr said slowly. "Phicol's bloodlust will cause him to put his life in his hand to destroy us."

"Then let's give him something to destroy," said Arod. He knelt and swept yellowed leaves aside to uncover a patch of bare earth and began scratching a diagram in the soil with a broken twig. "Remember General Joshua's attack on Ai? If a small group of soldiers makes a convincing pretense of attacking the front gate, but then hastily retreats, as if overcome by the defenders—."

"Which we certainly will be," Manoah inserted.

Arod nodded, but continued drawing. "We can draw the Philistine force out from the city behind us. Let Phicol's hunger for blood be his undoing. Let him chase the attacking force into the wilderness. Meanwhile…" He drew a half-circle around his sketch of the city, an arc that ended at Ramathaim's back wall. "A second force—a small rescue group of hand-picked warriors—will enter the city from the rear. If they are swift enough, they may be able to overpower the warriors the Philistines have left behind to guard their captives and then lead the inhabitants out of the city."

All of them stared at the drawing in silence for a few moments. "It is a bold plan," said Elon-tohr. "Our decoy force will have to be convincing enough in both their attack and retreat—and that means that some of our men will be placing their lives into their hands."

He let the thought sink in before continuing. "And the Philistines will not leave their captives under the watch of only a few guards. In all likelihood, the rescue force will have to overcome a determined and powerful group—and overcome them quickly enough that the Philistines do not have time to kill their captives. This attack on the city has terror as its goal—a goal best accomplished by slaughtering our countrymen in front of our eyes."

No one said anything for a few moments. Manoah was trying to think of some improvement on the plan, but could not. Whatever action they took they needed to take soon—the Philistines could decide to slaughter the surviving inhabitants of Ramathaim at any time—they would not wait forever to close the jaws of their trap.

"I will lead the rescue group," Elon-tohr said at last. "I will take with me a few warriors from Zebulun and a few of the Danites—and I will take Saphold the Rephaim. Manoah—I would like you with me as well. Every man among us who can wield a bow or a sling will be under your command. Success will depend on our being able to dispatch as many of the guards as quickly as possible before they realize they are under attack.

"Arod—you will lead the decoy force. Your hill-men can melt into the forest as soon as you have drawn the Philistines far enough away from the city. My Zebulunites are not familiar with this terrain—they will need to follow your men's lead if they are to disappear under the cover of the trees."

Arod was grinning from ear to ear. "This is what Gadites are made for. The Philistines will reach for the sword that strikes them, and it will turn to water that runs between their grasping fingers."

Elon-tohr nodded once, a single curt movement. "So be it. May Jehovah be with us all."

Elon-tohr led the rescue force around Ramathaim, slipping silently among the trees and scrub until they attained a position on a rocky ridge at the rear of the city. Leaving the bulk of the men under the cover of the trees, he led Manoah forward to the edge of the embankment. They lay on their stomachs on the dry twigs and duff, peering through the grass at the city below them. They were high enough that they could peer over the squat city wall and see, between and over rows of houses, part of the town square and the gate. Phicol had gotten down from his chariot and was pacing back and forth in the gateway, like a lion guarding its kill.

Elon-tohr watched him for a moment and then silently gestured to Manoah to follow him back into the forest. When they had rejoined the waiting men, Elon gathered them all close.

"The Philistines who guard the people of the town are arranged in a circle around their captives," he whispered. "We do not know how many soldiers our enemies will leave behind when they take Arod's bait—but it will be several dozen at least. You archers and slingers will need to take out as many of them as possible before they have a chance to start killing their prisoners."

One of the Danite archers frowned. "If the Philistines are encircling our people, every arrow or stone that misses could kill one of our brothers!"

Elon-tohr raised one eyebrow. "Then you had better not miss."

The Danite shook his head. "My men are skilled—but how will we shoot true when we know that a single, unexpected movement from one of the Philistine guards will fill our hands with the blood of one of our brothers?"

"What if our archers and slingers do not attack first?" Manoah asked. "What if our foot soldiers rush at the guards, drawing their attention away from their captives?"

Elon-tohr's brow knitted, but he nodded. "They will break their circle around the captives and rush to meet us. We are their primary target—not the shepherds and farmers of Ramathaim."

Manoah nodded. "And as soon as they draw away from their captives, the archers and slingers can fire at them unhindered from their positions atop the houses on either side."

"Well done, Manoah," Elon-tohr said, and Manoah felt a flush of pride at the compliment. "Let us put our hands to it, just as Manoah has said."

The grey-clad warrior sent three of his Zebulunites down to secure the rear postern gate—one of them carried a slender pine tree cut from the forest, its branches lopped off to within a few inches of the trunk. Manoah watched the three warriors slink from the cover of the trees and lay the pine trunk against the wall. One of them shinnied quickly up it, using the stumps of branches like the rungs of a ladder, and disappeared over the top of the battlements. A moment later, the postern opened and the other two soldiers slipped inside as well.

Thunder rumbled again in the distance, and wind rustled the leaves of the trees overhead. The harsh cries of crows startled the silence, and Manoah glanced up to see several shadowy forms winging their way to the east. *Outrunning the storm*, he thought darkly.

Then a ram's horn's growling *blat* erupted from the forest's edge and the Israelite decoy force burst from the cover of the trees toward the gate. Arod ran at the forefront of his men, wild hair flying, a spear raised over his head and a freshly oiled, leather shield strapped to his left arm. Even the Gedhudhra were taken by surprise, scrambling to form a defensive wall; Phicol leapt into his chariot, cursing so loudly that Manoah could hear it from his hiding place in the forest.

The forces collided cacophonously, and Manoah felt the familiar itch in the palm of his sword hand as he watched, aching to leap from cover and strike a blow against the warriors who had destroyed his home and slaughtered his brothers.

Arod timed his attack brilliantly—it looked convincing even to Manoah. The Israelite line crumbled before the furious defense by the Gedhudhra, breaking into embattled knots of soldiers pushed backwards by their foes. Abruptly, the attackers broke and fled back down the road; the Philistines took the bait, chasing them into the forested hills. In a few moments, the sounds of their pursuit had faded.

Perhaps four dozen Philistines remained behind, encircling the citizens of Ramathaim herded into the town square. All of them were clad in black.

Elon-tohr led the rescue force down the hill and into the shadow of the wall; one by one they slipped through the narrow postern. Inside, they drew their weapons quietly, and crept through several alleyways that led them in the direction of the front gate.

Half of their force was archers and slingers—these, Manoah led up the stairs of any home that bordered the city square. Atop the houses, they found dozens of bodies of murdered Israelites, and more lay in pools of blood in the courtyards of homes all around them.

Grim-faced, the Danites tried to ignore the grisly sight. Silent as shadows, they slipped from rooftop to rooftop until they had arranged themselves into positions behind the parapets of the roofs closest to the town square. Swiftly, they strung their bows or removed the sling stones from the pouches slung over their shoulders. With stones in the palms of their slings and arrows nocked against bowstrings, they peered over parapets and waited for Elon-tohr's signal.

It came immediately. Without any battle cry or clash of weapons, the Zebulunite led the foot soldiers of the rescue force in a fierce charge towards the captured Israelites. As Manoah had predicted, most of the Gedhudhra leapt to meet the unexpected attack, leaving the captives, for the moment, unwatched. Manoah raised his arm, and as one the archers and slingers stood and released a barrage of missiles into the Philistines; the air hummed with the whirl of slings and the thrum of bowstrings. Half of the Gedhudhra fell to the ground.

But then the men who were among the Israelite captives raced forward, weaponless but filled with rage, attacking the Philistines with their bare hands. It was a brave but foolish decision—the Gedhudhra turned on them and began slaughtering them. Their screams of rage and pain echoed off the walls.

All around Manoah, his men looked for an opportunity to fire, whirling their slings overhead or standing poised with bows pulled back to their chins, but now the Philistines were among the captives and they could not shoot for fear of killing one of their own people—many of them women and children.

Elon-tohr raged into the mass of soldiers and captives, slender sword flashing. Just behind him, Saphold's massive form lumbered forward, his axe smashing anything that came within his considerable reach. Manoah watched as two Gedhudhra leapt toward the giant, swords and shields raised; but Saphold batted them aside with his axe, their broken bodies flying.

The battle lasted only a few moments, but in that time every archer and slinger on the rooftops was forced to watch the Gedhudhra slaughter Israelite men, women, and children. The soldiers of the rescue force were not spared, either—although they outnumbered the Philistine guards, the Gedhudhra fought like lions: swift, fearless, and deadly. By the time rescuers killed the last of them, two dozen Israelite villagers lay dead or dying in the red mud of the square. Almost as many of the rescue force were dead as well.

Elon-tohr instructed the men to arm themselves with the weapons of the dead Philistines. Manoah dropped his blunted sickle-sword and picked up one of their long, slender, straight black blades. Its weight and balance felt foreign in his hand, and after a moment, he picked his bronze sword up as well and slid it through the back of his belt. He would try to use this new, iron blade, but it did not hurt to have a back up.

A moment later, Elon-tohr led a couple towards Manoah. The man was tall and strongly built with a thick, full, beard. The woman's child-like face and large, brown eyes were wet with tears; masses of gently curling brown hair hung past her shoulders, and her full lips danced somewhere between a smile and a frown.

"Manoah, son of Ashnah," the Zebulunite said quietly. "This is Elkanah of Ramathaim, and his wife, Hannah. They are the parents of the child-prophet, Samuel."

"May Jehovah bless you men," Elkanah said, his lips quivering with emotion.

"His is the credit for this victory," agreed Manoah.

"We must go quickly," said Elon-tohr, gesturing towards the gate. "We do not know when the rest of the Philistines will return."

"Where are you taking us?" Elkanah asked.

"To Shiloh," said Manoah.

Elkanah frowned. "Shiloh is not a well-fortified city…"

"We do not go there for safety," Manoah said. "Even as we speak, the Philistines are marching on Shiloh to destroy it. We go to save it."

42

They fled from Ramathaim. Hannah gathered Elkanah's second wife, Peninnah, and all of their children, carrying only what they could pack in a few moments. The other families of Ramathaim did the same, and the shadows had barely lengthened before the entire group slipped through the gate of the city and disappeared from its view beneath the cover of the trees. They left to the sounds of children crying for the animals they had to leave behind, and of adults crying for the bodies of friends lying amongst the Philistine dead in the town square.

Elon-tohr took Saphold and a handful of Danites back to form a rearguard for their procession, instructing Manoah to keep them moving forward as quickly as possible. They had heard nothing from Arod, but hoped this meant that the fierce Danite was still leading the Philistines on a fruitless chase through the forests. Manoah sent scouts out ahead and to either side, hoping to prevent them from stumbling into Phicol's army by mistake.

Their pace was agonizingly slow. Most of the rescued citizens of Ramathaim were women, children, and the elderly; it took all of Manoah's efforts to maintain any sort of pace at all. He felt no frustration toward his charges—old men and women hobbling along, leaning on sticks and crutches, or mothers trying desperately to keep track of their wandering offspring. But he knew without doubt that every moment's delay increased the real danger that the Philistines would return and find them. Efforts by the mothers to keep their children quiet was likewise a failure: the young ones wept loudly when they were upset, shrieked when they were surprised or excited, yelled to each other across the mass of moving people.

The road wound through the trees, which began to thin as they traveled eastward, their path following ridges that meandered through the broken, wrinkled country, ascending in fits ands starts up the Judean highlands. The clouds darkened further until they shrouded the sun completely, and by mid-afternoon, it looked as though dusk had set in. To their right, Manoah could glimpse through breaks in the trees a broad valley, choked with dense clusters of sycamores and oaks surrounding untilled barley fields, orchards, and olive groves.

Flocks of sparrows rose from the fields like roiling, black clouds, darting through the sky in a carefully orchestrated dance, each keeping its place in the maelstrom of movement without any discernible communication with the other birds. Manoah watched them for a few moments, allowing himself to experience the measure of peace and joy that observing their carefree beauty brought to him. Each bird maintained its position in relation to the birds around it. Dipping and spinning in response to invisible stimuli in the air, the flock, hundreds strong, appeared to share a single mind. Their unity and coordination would have been the envy of any military general. He wondered for a moment what it would be like to be a part of such an army, to be so in tune with the people you served alongside that no words were necessary.

To the left, the land dropped away sharply into a long, broad defile that paralleled their course until some distance to the east, where the route of the road and the valley were split by a mountain peak jutting like a rocky spine from the forested slopes of the surrounding hills.

Manoah was about to suggest a brief rest when Arod and the Gadites burst from the trees to the right of the road, bloodied weapons still clutched in their hands. Their faces were flushed with exertion, and Arod had bits of leaves and twigs caught in his mane of hair. Manoah's heart sank when he saw how many of them now wore garments stained crimson by untended wounds.

Arod's irrepressible smile flashed at the line of refugees following Manoah. "They are not far behind us," he panted. "But it looks as though your mission was a success."

"Thanks to the bravery of your men," Manoah answered. "How many have you lost?"

Arod's smile dimmed. "It is not yet time to mourn our dead. Let us not speak of it until we find ourselves safe again."

Elkanah stepped forward. He was holding a finely forged, iron blade he had taken from the body of a Philistine, but he gripped its leather-wrapped handle as though it were a serpent that he was not sure was dead. "I am a Levite and of little use with a sword. But my father's fathers lived in these hills and valleys, and my sons and I know every footstep of them. If you men"—he gestured vaguely at Manoah and Arod—"can stand between us and our enemies when they appear, even for a few moments, we can lead you to pathways that the Philistines will find hard to follow—impossible, with chariots."

"So be it," said Manoah immediately. He sent a messenger back to inform Elon-tohr of their plan, and Elkanah and one of his sons took their positions at the head of the war band with Manoah. They had barely started moving forward again when the sound of hoof beats rumbled toward them from the east. Elkanah unhesitatingly turned south off of the road and plunged through the sycamore forest, clambering down a leaf-strewn slope toward the valley bottom. The refugees followed him while Elon-tohr, Saphold, and the Zebulunites and Gadites took up their positions on the road to wait for the arrival of the Philistines.

They did not wait long. Before the last of the rescued citizens of Ramathaim had slipped under the cover of the trees, the scarred, young warrior Phicol galloped into view, the Gedhudhra close behind him. They had abandoned or lost their chariots somewhere, and when they saw the Israelites on the road, they spurred their mounts forward savagely, screaming their battle cries as they came. Manoah heard Phicol's strange, wheezing voice above the others: "The sword reveals the heart!"

Manoah was well into the forest when he heard the clash of the soldiers behind him. He let Elkanah lead the people forward and loped back up the slope to get a view of the road. From his position, at a lower elevation, he could just glimpse Elon-tohr and Saphold, side by side at the head of the Zebulunites, slender sword whirling, massive battle-axe sweeping. For a moment, he considered joining them, but then thought better of it and returned to Elkanah's side.

For the remainder of the afternoon the pattern repeated itself. Elkanah led them onward through the twisted, broken valleys of the highlands. Sometimes their route took them through beautiful—albeit dry—forests, the yellowing leaves that carpeted the ground a gentle susurration beneath their sandals. Other times, they were forced to clamber over fallen trees and dead logs or slowly help the elderly up steep, rocky slopes. Always, the black-bearded Levite eventually brought them back to the road, and they would make good time for a while. Then the Philistines would find them again, a battle would ensue, and the refugees would disappear once more beneath the cover of the forest.

Phicol and his Gedhudhra tried to pursue them into the trees, but Elon-tohr and the rearguard always managed to hold their pursuers off long enough to give the refugees a large head-start, and then, more often than not, lead the Philistines off through a lonely, trackless part of the wilderness before themselves vanishing into the trees, leaving Phicol and his men cursing and yelling in some forsaken canyon or moldering grove.

When the sun began to set, it had been hours since Phicol had last caught up to them. Elon-tohr and the rearguard had returned to them some time earlier. They were traveling down the road again, and Elkanah suggested to Manoah that they turn into the forest and make camp at a spring not far from their position. The Levite led them down a short incline and through an area of dense pines, a wall of dark, thick-branched trees that screened them from the view of the road. Following landmarks visible only to his eyes, Elkanah guided them around a great mass of boulders, covered now with dry, browning moss, to a shadowed grotto that slept beneath its bed of gold and amber leaves.

The spring at the center of the grotto had all but gone dry; what remained were a stagnant pool and a muddy trickle across the forest floor that disappeared into a small, mucky section of ground a few paces away. A scattering of animal tracks pocked the soft earth around it, but any creatures that had come seeking water had long since vanished at the noise of the refugee's approach.

They set up a hasty camp. Having carried only a little food with them, small bands of men and women were sent out to scour the forest for whatever fruit or herbs they might find; a few of the Danites took their bows and slings in search of birds or game. They lit no fires yet, as much because of the unlikelihood of actually finding anything to cook as for the fear of the smoke being spotted by their pursuers.

Manoah watched Elkanah and Hannah helping their children arrange leaves into piles and cover them with extra mantles on which to sleep. The couple talked with each other in quiet tones, half of their words replaced with smiles, gestures, or subtle glances that comprised a sign language known only to them. They spoke, not to try to bridge a gap of understanding between them, but because the bridge was already there, and so wide that thoughts and words flowed effortlessly across it like the gentle ebb and rise of the tide. He watched them take hold of the tent cloths, one of them on each side, unfolding the stiff, black goat's-hair and walking sideways, hands moving in unison like dancers. Each seemed to know what the other would do before they did it, and without any explanation. He was struck suddenly by how much they reminded him of the sparrows he had seen in the fields earlier that day: a oneness of mind and of movement, a communication that went deeper than words.

He waited until their tent was erected and Hannah was settling into it with the children before he sought Elkanah out. "May I speak with you a moment?"

Elkanah finished wrapping the excess tent cordage around a broken oak branch. "What is it?"

"Samuel was Hannah's first child?" Manoah asked.

Elkanah nodded, but his brow furrowed in confusion. "Yes...She had been childless for many years before he was born."

Manoah opened his mouth, and then closed it again, trying to formulate the words to ask the question he hesitated to ask. "Your…relationship with her…How did you find that it changed when…when Jehovah opened her womb?"

Elkanah cocked his head to one side and his look of confusion deepened. "Changed? What do you mean?"

Manoah shrugged. "I just…I have seen what a powerful bond is created between two people when they produce a child together."

Elkanah stared at him for a few moments before speaking. "I will not say that we did not long to have children during those years before Samuel's birth. It was a constant strain upon Hannah—and a source of untold conflict in my household." He paused a moment and shook his head, as if remembering the frustration of those years. "But it did not change our relationship. I loved her before her vow, and I love her still."

Manoah felt his face reddening. "I beg your pardon, Elkanah. I did not mean to imply in any way that your love for your wife was lacking before…Of course you loved her. But didn't you find that when you learned she was pregnant—that Jehovah had answered your prayers, and that an heir would live to carry your name on in Israel—."

"'Sons are an inheritance from Jehovah,'" Elkanah quoted, interrupting him. His eyes narrowed, and he looked almost angry. "But I do not love my wife for what might come out of her womb. I love her for the beauty that flows from her heart. Were we childless to this day—were we to live until old age without sons or daughters, that love would not fail or falter."

They stood in silence a moment, and Manoah's shame deepened to a feeling far beyond that which caused a man to blush. He said nothing but suffered as though Elkanah had discovered him in the act of committing some great sin.

"In the grape harvest," Elkanah continued after a long pause, "we sing and we dance as we tread the grapes, and we celebrate the bounty of the land. We do not spend our days mourning that we have no wine. But on harvest day, we drink the juice of the vine, sweet and refreshing. Any man who stands with his feet buried in the press and can think only of wine…" Elkanah shook his head again. "When he has wine, he will find some other lack about which to complain. And that is no way for a man of Israel to spend his life."

Manoah could not look up from the ground, and after a few moments, Elkanah left and returned to help Hannah with the children. Manoah let his feet take him aimlessly away from the camp, wanting only to put some distance between himself and his memory of the moment that had just passed.

When he had married, his mother had taken up the common habit of asking each month to have the bloodstain of Naamah's cycle given her on a scrap of linen. Each time it was presented, his mother would begin to weep, then disappear for the day without a word, and Manoah would endure a lecture by his father on the necessity of producing an heir. In his mother's final days, she begged him to take a concubine or second wife that she might live to see the grandchild of her firstborn. He had refused. Even now, the thought of taking anyone but Naamah to his bed was inconceivable.

He missed Naamah. The realization, and the feelings it evoked, erupted within him like a long-pent flame. For so many days he had buried his feelings, choosing only to focus on his, and his family's, desire for children. Now, he looked inside himself and saw, with some astonishment, that behind his petty dissatisfactions hid a great wellspring of emotion. His loneliness for his wife had grown into an ache so great that his desire for sons paled into insignificance beside it. When he remembered how he had once felt that if she could not bear him sons he was better off without her as a wife, the memory sickened him. Naamah was beautiful, pure as the sun, radiant as starlight glimmering between the clouds.

Alone, under the trees, he fell to his knees and began to weep. He had abandoned her at Aijalon. Not by going off with the army to war—his abandonment had been deeper. When he had left Aijalon, he had left no part of himself with his wife. He had not even taken her with him in his thoughts.

43

Samuel strode slowly through the fields that bordered the road leading to Shiloh, enjoying a few moments to himself that Ahitub had granted him. From where he walked he could see the shadows deepening under the branches of the distant forest as the day progressed, and the squat, stolid shapes of a handful of stone watchtowers built by shepherds on the low hills.

It felt good to distance himself from the city. Even with Hophni and Phinehas gone off to the war, a tension ran through the populace that Samuel could not shake. Perhaps it was partly born of watching Eli escorted every morning to the Tabernacle gates where the High Priest sat on his chair, blind eyes staring to the west, looking older and weaker than Samuel had ever seen him.

At least Mara had left her self-imposed seclusion. Phinehas' wife had come out of her isolation since her husband had left for Aphek. She often waited with Eli near the gate, trying to comfort the old Priest in whatever way she could. Samuel watched her sometimes, the way her hand strayed constantly to her stomach, rubbing and caressing the swollen bump of her pregnancy. Buried in the signs of love and expectation that swept over her face at those times were equal signals of anxious dread.

Movement caught his eye; he looked down at the road and saw a man approaching Shiloh. The man jogged forward with the leaden, shuffling gait of a person who has pushed himself to the point of collapse. Samuel ran across the field toward him, feeling the slap of the dry grasses against his shins.

When he got closer, he saw that the man was a Benjaminite, long-legged and lanky, with his garments torn and dirt thrown on his head. Samuel's heart sank. *He comes from the battle.*

The Benjaminite saw Samuel nearing and stopped briefly to wait for him, his chest and shoulders heaving.

"You have word of the battle, my lord?" Samuel called as soon as he was near enough for the man to hear him.

The Benjaminite gave him a look of such anguish that Samuel knew the message he bore before he spoke a word.

"I must speak to the High Priest," the Benjaminite panted.

Samuel nodded and slipped the tall man's arm over his own shoulders to help support him as they began walking again toward the city wall. They had not even reached the gates before a crowd, led by the Elders who served in the square, mobbed them. Vermilion staffs clacked against one another as they pressed in close. "What news?"

"What has happened at Aphek?"

"What of the sons of Eli?"

The Benjaminite looked around at them with tears in the corners of his eyes. "Israel has been defeated."

A silence swept over the crowd like the passing of a dark thought, and then the people began to keen and wail.

"What of the Ark?" one of the Elders asked.

"And the Priests?"

The Benjaminite shook his head and raised his hands as if to ward off their questions. "I must go to the High Priest! Take me to Eli!"

The crowd started forward through the gates and toward the Tabernacle, the sounds of mourning spreading slowly through the city. After a few moments of walking, the Benjaminite turned toward the people. "Do not follow us! Shiloh is in danger."

The wailing, at least of those people near enough to hear him, quieted. "Gather what belongings you can carry," the Benjaminite continued. "An army of Philistines is on my heels. They are coming to Shiloh. Take what you can carry, and flee!"

He turned and began walking up the road toward the Tabernacle before the import of his words had truly made their impression on his listeners' minds. Within moments, the keening had reached new volumes, and all around them people began tearing their garments and throwing dirt or ashes on their heads.

It was the most surreal walk of Samuel's life. The sweaty smell of the man he supported filled his nostrils, and his head began to ache from the wailing all around him. Each slow step he took reverberated through his body as though he were falling more than walking, a fall that took him, pace by pace, closer to Eli and the revelation of what had happened. He stared at the road ahead of his feet as much as possible, because every time he lifted his head his eyes were overwhelmed at the nightmarish parade of images that surrounded him: faces whitened by ash, streaked with tears; children screaming at their parents' fear, families bearing bundles on their shoulders or atop some beast of burden fleeing hollow-eyed toward the city gate.

In spite of the Benjaminite's warning, dozens of people were still following them by the time they reached the gates of the Tabernacle. Eli sat there in his chair, dressed in the official garments of High Priest, his blind eyes casting about for the source of the mourning sounds he heard coming from the city below him. Tirzah stood to one side of him and Mara at the other, her hand resting on his thick shoulder. As Samuel and the Benjaminite arrived, Ahitub and a group of Priests appeared at the gate as well.

"Mara?" Eli asked, his blind eyes moving constantly. "Mara? Where is Samuel?"

Samuel slipped out from beneath the Benjaminites arm. "I am here, my lord," he said, taking Eli's hand in his own. It shook with palsy.

"What does this sound mean?" Eli asked.

The Benjaminite fell to his knees in front of the High Priest. "I am Basar of Benjamin, my lord. I am the one coming from—it is from the battle that I have fled."

Eli stretched out one hand toward Basar and touched his cheek. For a moment, the High Priest was silent as his fingers felt the tears that ran down Basar's face.

"What has happened, my son?" Eli asked, with the quiet deliberation of one who is unsure he wants his question answered.

"Israel has fled before the Philistines," Basar said in a rush, his voice cracking. "Tens of thousands of our brothers have been brought to silence on the field of Aphek."

Eli let out a great rush of breath and tears began flowing from his milky eyes.

"And your own two sons have—Hophni and Phinehas have been silenced!"

"Nooo!" The High Priest moaned, and his shoulders shook in silent sobbing.

"And...and the Ark of the True God has been captured!"

Eli's body stiffened in a lurch of shock and anguish at Basar's revelation, legs and arms straightening violently. The movement threw his chair backwards, and Samuel watched in horror as the Priest's heavy body teetered, then crashed to the road. He landed with a sickening crunch.

The crowd stared in shocked silence. One of the Levites knelt next to Eli, as if to help him up. But he did not touch him. Instead, he turned back toward the crowd, a stunned look on his young face. "He is dead!"

Samuel forced himself to take a step closer. The High Priest's head was twisted around at an unnatural angle, forced sharply sideways by the weight of his body pressing it against the soil. He was not breathing.

"Grandfather! Grandfather!" Ahitub lurched forward and fell to his knees, his hands hovering over the body as though unsure how to touch him.

"No!" Two Levites grabbed Ahitub's shoulders and pulled him backward; he fought them. "Do not touch the body!" one of them commanded him. Doing so would render Ahitub unclean and unable to serve in the Tabernacle until he had undergone purification.

Another Priest stepped forward and carefully removed the High Priest's jeweled *ephod*. Bowing his head, he handed it to Ahitub. "You are now High Priest of Jehovah's Tabernacle."

Ahitub shook his head, and his eyes did not leave Eli's still body. "No....no..."

Samuel heard the words as if in a dream, heard the anguished mourning of the crowd, saw Ahitub standing there, the *ephod* in his hands, and suddenly the memory of the words he had spoken to Eli swept through him like a searing heat. *Prophet of God*, he thought bitterly. *Doomsayer! The Ark is lost! What will become of us now?*

A choked cry from behind him caught Samuel's attention and he turned. Mara was clutching her swollen stomach in both hands, mouth open, eyes wide in pain and surprise. Tirzah was practically holding her up, her arms beneath Mara's arms. At her feet, a patch of muddy ground had formed and was slowly spreading out from her right foot.

Mara cried out again, her body curling in on itself in pain.

"Samuel!" Tirzah cried to him. "Help me!"

Samuel got under one of Mara's arms and the two of them helped her walk back through the gates, across the Courtyard, and toward her room. "The baby is coming!" Tirzah whispered to him as though it were a secret.

Samuel nodded. *Too soon!* he answered silently.

Mara's contractions were so intense that Tirzah and Samuel were carrying her by the time they reached her room. Both of them were panting with the effort and soaked with sweat. They entered and lowered Mara to the rug in the middle of the floor. The keening from outside pierced even the walls of the room, an eerie paean, like wind whistling through trees. A series of trumpet blasts sounded, and Samuel knew that the Elders were instructing the people to gather their belongings and flee.

"The baby is coming now!" Tirzah repeated as though she could not believe it. She pointed at one corner of the room. "The birthing stone!"

"He is dead!" Mara blurted out, her breath coming in panicked gasps. "My husband is dead! Hophni is dead! Eli is dead! The Ark..."

Samuel found the padded stone stool and dragged it over to the women. They helped Mara onto it; her slender arms were slippery with sweat. "I am here, Mara," Tirzah soothed.

"It is not time!" Mara murmured between gritted teeth, her hands pulling her belly toward her as if to stop the baby from coming.

"Get help, Samuel!" Tirzah whispered urgently. He nodded and leapt up, running to the door. He nearly bowled over two of the women from the Corps as they entered, carrying swaddling cloths, a pot of salt, and a vessel of clear water.

Samuel stood in the doorway as they went to Mara's side, unable to leave, feeling as though he were obligated to help in some way.

"It is coming!" Mara hissed, squeezing Tirzah's arm until the younger woman cringed with pain.

Samuel suddenly noticed pinkish fluid pooling on the rug. The birthing stool was already slick with it. He glanced up at Mara's face. Her skin was white and paling even as he watched.

Tirzah saw it, too, and for an instant she glanced at Samuel. In that anguished look he saw her thoughts as clearly as though she had spoken them aloud.

This was how she had been born.

She had told him once that her mother had bled to death giving birth to her—a guilt that Tirzah had carried with her all the days of her life.

A guilt that she was now reliving.

Time crawled by; Tirzah and the other women cradled Mara as she pushed, wept, bled and sweated. "It will be all right," Tirzah kept repeating, the trails of tears shining on her cheeks.

"Dead...they are all dead..." Mara panted between contractions.

"You are alive!" Tirzah was almost shouting. "Push, Mara! You are going to live! You are going to raise this child!"

Watching, Samuel felt strangely as though he, too, were trying to give birth—to a paroxysm of rage and pain that threatened to rip him apart.

Mara called out again, an explosion of sorrow, and screamed the baby into the world in a flood of blood. Tirzah lifted the child and one of the other women cut the birth cord with a knife of black obsidian. The baby was tiny, impossibly fragile, its limbs like twigs, half the size it should have been. *Only seven months*, thought Samuel. *It has come too soon.*

Blood and afterbirth covered the infant's translucent, bluish skin, but after a moment it wrinkled its red face and gasped, then began to cry, a thin, pitiful wail.

"Mara!" Tirzah said, failing to sound happy. "You have a son!"

Mara did not even look at the child. As the other women rubbed it with salt to turn it a healthy pink, she kept her face turned away. Her skin looked waxy under its sheen of sweat. "Let him be called Ichabod," she rasped weakly.

The name meant, "Where is the glory?" and it deepened Samuel's sadness. "He shall be called Ichabod," Tirzah answered, still holding the child out toward its mother.

"Ichabod," Mara repeated softly. "What glory is there now in Israel? It has gone into exile, for the Ark of Jehovah has been captured."

"Do not worry about that now!" Tirzah held out the wailing newborn, tears streaking her own cheeks. "Take your son! Here! He cries for his mother!"

But Mara did not respond. She lay still and silent on the rug, and with a rasp her breathing stopped and her body went limp.

And Tirzah knelt next to the dead woman in her room, her arms wrapped tightly around the naked body of the screaming child, and she bowed her head and wept.

44

The delegation that escorted the Ark of the Covenant followed Sarnam and the mage-priest Sihphil down the busy trade road from Aphek south toward Philistia. Sarnam sent teams of charioteers ahead of them into the countryside—not to attack or plunder (he would leave that to Phicol), but to announce to every village and hamlet that the Philistines had captured Israel's Ark of the Covenant and bore it as a sign of their victory back to the cities of the Axis Lords. Lod and Gibbethon were, of course, still in Philistine hands—Sarnam had workers repairing whatever was necessary in the cities to allow them to be used to house garrisons that could protect the trade route he now controlled.

Of course, he knew better than anyone did that their work was not yet done. Far to the north were a handful of Israelite cities that still exercised some influence on traffic on the road, and his army would have to capture them as well. A couple of them—Megiddo and Hazor—were even fortified and would likely require extended campaigns. Still—the Hebrews' defeat at Aphek had been complete. They would not have the heart or the military might to come against his army again. Thirty thousand of their warriors were being eaten by the crows outside the walls of Aphek—that was not a number they could readily replace.

When they saw Sarnam approaching down the road, convoys of traders burst into flurries of frenzied activity, herding wagons and animals off to either side and watching his delegation pass with wide, frightened stares. But most of all, their eyes went to the shrouded form borne on the shoulders of his Gedhudhra. When they saw the Ark, when they heard his criers proclaiming that Sarnam had captured it, he could see the terror and hopelessness that erupted within them. Sarnam was gratified to know that word of their victory would have spread from the mountains of Lebanon to the deserts of Edom before the week was out. He also enjoyed having so many Hebrews bowing before him as he went by.

They stopped for the night at the town of Jabne'el, a village conquered by his forces shortly after they had captured Lod. Within a few hours of their arrival, the Rephaim entered the city gates, dozens of lumbering forms, their huge axes now strapped across their backs. When Sarnam learned of their arrival, he immediately sought out their leader, a grey-bearded veteran named Gundar.

He brought several dozen of his Gedhudhra with him for the meeting. He did not truly feel threatened by the giants—they did not seem to Sarnam the kind of men who would break the terms of the agreement he had made with them. But it did not hurt to meet one's mercenaries with a show of force.

The Rephaim were sitting cross-legged, eating their evening meal when Sarnam found them. Gundar stood slowly at his approach. Sarnam did not waste time on pleasantries. "Your men were hired to fight for me! Why was one of them battling alongside the Hebrews? And why did I lose the help of a dozen or more of you every time you faced this rebel in battle?"

Gundar stared at him a long time before answering. "He was cast out of his *Metteh*. I cannot answer for him. But his presence constitutes a challenge of honor. We cannot ignore that challenge."

"Can you not? Every time this rebel appears, I am going to lose the aid that you promised to me while your men form circles and chant?"

The huge warrior's forehead creased. "These traditions are given us by the gods. We must respect their demands."

"The gods!" Sarnam spat. "The Hebrews were slaughtered wholesale! Is our record of victory not enough to prove to you the gods are on our side?"

"They are with us," Gundar said, "because we continue to live by our ancient ways."

"Do not your ways also include fulfilling the terms of your vows? What of your oath to support me in battle against our enemies?"

Gundar blinked slowly. "We brought you a great victory. We have fulfilled the terms of our oath. You have no reason to complain."

With that, the giant warrior turned away and sat once again among his men, picked up his bowl, and continued eating. Sarnam felt his rage boiling at this summary dismissal, especially in front of his Gedhudhra, but he knew better than to provoke the band of Rephaim. He allowed himself the comfort of deciding that he would find a way to betray the giant mercenaries sometime in the near future, to remind them that they answered to him, Sarnam, Axis Lord of Ashkelon. Until then he would bide his time and do whatever was necessary to retain their support through the campaign to come.

They left Jabne'el shortly after sunrise the next morning, continuing their journey south. Sarnam had half-expected Phicol to reappear during the night, but he had not. In spite of their successful campaign, the brutal young commander was intent on pursuing Hebrews who had nothing left worth taking. His thirst for blood had not yet been slaked. Sarnam doubted that it ever would be. The victory at Aphek had opened up an entire land to the scarred warrior's endless hunger. With the Gedhudhra Phicol had taken along and with the disorganized, defeated attitude he would find among the Hebrews, Phicol could create slaughter and mayhem for months—even years. At some point, Sarnam would have to summon him back—but he doubted if Phicol would come when he called.

By the afternoon of the second day, they arrived in the Philistine city of Ashdod. Sarnam had chosen it as their destination for several reasons. First, the Axis Lord of Ashdod seemed to be the most powerful of the Philistine leaders, and delivering this great war trophy to his city was a gesture of goodwill that Sarnam hoped would guarantee him the man's support in the future. In addition, Ashdod contained the largest temple to Dagon in Philistia, a massive structure visited by hundreds of their people every day. It had an entire hall for displaying trophies of war dedicated to the god. Keeping the Ark of the Hebrews in the temple would clearly demonstrate to the people Dagon's superiority over this Jehovah that the Hebrews worshipped. Nothing served to boost morale better than confirmation that the gods one served were mightier than the gods of one's enemies.

The Priests of Dagon were waiting for them at the gates of Ashdod when they arrived. Lord Ashdod ordered the opening of several kegs of wine and wheat beer, and before the delegation had even made it to the steps of Dagon's temple, a crowd of revelers, dancing and singing to the gods, engulfed them.

The Ark was carried inside by the Gedhudhra and placed next to the great statue of Dagon. When all was in place, the priests removed the cover from the Ark, and for a few moments, Sarnam and Sihphil stared in awe at the beautiful chest, gleaming and flashing even in the half-light of the lamps. Two golden cherubs arched upwards from its cover, wings outstretched towards each other, nearly as tall as the spread arms of the half-fish, half-human image of Dagon it confronted. The two icons faced one another: elegant golden Ark and dark stone idol. To Lord Ashkelon, the air in the temple tingled, as if a storm were about to break forth upon their city with violent fury.

After only a moment, a sense of dread began to overwhelm Sarnam, an unreasoning fear that caught the breath in his throat and sent his heart pounding in his ears, that weakened his knees and filled his mind with one thought: to flee as quickly as possible from before this golden chest that loomed silently in front of him. He looked over at Sihphil and saw the little priest was shaking, his lips curled back to reveal gritted teeth.

"Let usss leave!" Sihphil hissed, and both of them turned and exited the chamber as though death itself pursued them.

Outside the temple, the Priests of Baal used the opportunity to remind the people that Baal had not yet been convinced to copulate with Ashtoreth, as evidenced by the delay of the onset of winter rain, and that they must work the sympathetic magic to remind Baal of his duty. The inebriated crowd was quick to comply, and as night fell and the oil lamps flared to life along the city streets, their golden light played off the bare skin of hundreds of writhing, thrusting forms sprawled in courtyards and squares.

Nearer to Dagon's temple, the priests of Mot, god of death, comforted the families of those who had fallen in battle. In the darkened rooms of the squat, black temple of Mot, the two nearest relatives of each of the deceased were brought together and drugged with beer and herbs, then guided by the priests into sexual relations in order to appease the spirits of their slaughtered ancestors and to allow them to go to the underworld in peace, knowing that the loved ones they left behind continued to find comfort and fulfillment in their lives.

45

The Tabernacle's morning rituals had just concluded when Samuel, standing near the gates, heard the horns. At first they came from far off, from the hills or shadowed forests beyond the city, distant peals that hung in the suddenly still air above Shiloh like hunting raptors, invisible harbingers of doom. Moments later, the horns were echoed by the trumpets of the watchmen on Shiloh's towers, and the population exploded into motion.

What guardsmen there were began running toward the walls, shields bouncing against their shoulders, spears or sickle-swords clutched in white-knuckled fists. Merchants and farmers ducked into their houses and emerged with axes, knives, sickles, pitchforks, and other various harvesting implements, then rushed down the descending roads towards the city gate. Mothers herded their wide-eyed children together and disappeared into their houses or courtyards, many to reappear moments later on their roofs, shading their eyes and staring off in the direction of the sound of the horns.

People in the Tabernacle Courtyard around Samuel stopped what they were doing, and those not already involved in a sacrifice left quickly. Samuel studied them as they rushed past him, back out into the city: *arms held close to bodies; heads down, eyes wide.*

Ahitub appeared a moment later, his face ashen, eyes bloodshot from lack of sleep. Samuel knew he was trying to help to care for his newborn brother, Ichabod—who screamed with greater stamina than seemed possible for one so tiny—and to oversee the disassembling of the Tabernacle. When Basar had brought the news that the Philistines were closing on Shiloh, Ahitub had ordered the Priests to take down the sacred tent and pack it onto wagons for transport. Centuries before, the Israelites had disassembled the Tabernacle regularly, as they traveled across the wilderness of Sinai and spent decades battling the inhabitants of Canaan, before they chose Shiloh as the center of worship for the land. God had designed the structure, and Moses had built it, so that it could be readily taken apart. But, like the people of Israel, the Tabernacle had grown less flexible, less adaptable, with age.

The center of Israel's worship had once been a large tent, built of panels of cloth stretched over acacia-wood frames, and a fabric curtain-wall surrounding the Courtyard. But in the centuries since it had settled in Shiloh, the cloth curtain had become a wall of stone and wood, with towers and gate; the Courtyard expanded and then filled and become surrounded by storage buildings, residences, workrooms, and meeting halls. The Tabernacle itself had remained essentially as Moses had had it constructed, but centuries of immobility had taken their toll on the parts of the design meant to lend themselves to easy disassembly and transport. As the Priests and Levites began loosening the tent cords and taking apart the panels, they found that many tenon joints had frozen together; knots in support ropes had to be cut rather than untied, and some cloths, stiffened with age, tore dramatically when any unusual pressure was put upon them.

Now, the sacred Tent lay in pieces on the flagstones, and the Priests and Levites were struggling to load it onto wagons. At the sound of the horns they had stopped moving, too, staring as Ahitub was staring, as if they could somehow see the danger that approached outside the walls.

A moment later, a young man raced to the gate where Samuel, Ahitub, and a milling crowd lingered. "The army from Aphek is here!" he panted. "With refugees from across Israel—but the Philistines are at their heels!"

"I will tell the High Priest…" Ahitub began, and Samuel saw the look of pain and frustration pass over his face as he realized what he was saying. He took a deep breath, then turned to the captain of the Tabernacle guardsmen, standing near the gate. "Summon all of your men," he instructed him. "Take up your positions around the Curtain Wall."

He turned to Samuel. "Go with the messenger, back to the city gate. Tell the Elders of Shiloh that we stand ready to put our hands with theirs, whether for defense or evacuation. Bring back their words as quickly as you can."

Samuel nodded and followed the messenger down the descending streets toward Shiloh's main gate. All around him, fear and anxiety hung over the city like a blanket, its presence as tangible as mist against his skin. It emanated from every hollow-eyed face that peered from behind linteled doorways or over parapets; it lurked in the shadows of the empty shops, swallowed in unnatural mid-day stillness. Amidst the pealing of the horns, the wind's-rush of anxious voices, and the tramping of feet, he could still hear his own footsteps pounding in his ears. He felt suddenly incredibly alone and out of place. No other children were visible on the streets he passed through, and he struggled to keep up with the pace of the tall messenger he followed.

When they reached the gates, the guardsmen had already swung them nearly closed. A gap of a shoulder's-width had been left, and as Samuel arrived, soldiers were hurrying a haggard, travel-worn line of men, women, and children through it.

The messenger did not pause, and Samuel followed him, panting, up the mud-brick stairs that ascended the wall on one side of the gate. At the top of the broad bulwark, several of the city's Elders stood in a huddled mass, staring out towards the west. Samuel turned to follow their gaze.

Roiling dust cut a dirty, blonde swath across the near horizon; beneath it, like a giant swarm of locusts, an army of hundreds of infantry, cavalry, and chariots thundered toward Shiloh. The gap between the approaching Philistines and the tailing end of the line of refugees was narrowing rapidly, and Samuel saw immediately that not all of the refugees would make it through the gate. He watched in horror as the Philistine forces reached the line of fleeing people and began to slaughter them, swiftly and efficiently, following the string of refugees like a living path leading them toward Shiloh's gates.

Atop the wall, the thrum of bowstrings and whirling slings announced a barrage of Israelite missiles hurtling toward the Philistine ranks.

Beside him, Samuel heard one of the Elders shout an order down to the guards, and, pulling one more family through the opening, they shut the gate. Samuel understood why it was necessary—the Philistines were upon them, and they could not risk allowing one of them to lodge a chariot in the gateway, wedging it open. But Israelites stood just outside the walls still, screaming and pounding on the wooden planks. Samuel could see some of their faces from where he stood: men, women, and children, turning in horror toward the enemy troops closing on them.

The Philistine forces broke against the gate like an inflowing wave, slaughtering the last of the refugees outside the wall and then ebbing back to a safer distance from the fortifications.

Samuel glanced down into the town square just inside the gates where hundreds of people were milling in fright. His eyes were immediately drawn to an enormous, hulking figure that towered over the rest of the people gathered. It took him only a moment to realize that he was looking at a Rephaim giant, the first he had ever seen. He wondered what the man was doing inside the walls and scanned the crowd around him for some clue. It was then that he saw the tall, handsome Danite soldier who seemed to be the giant's escort and the family that stood just behind him.

Samuel ran down the steps and pushed his way through the crowd.

"Father! Mother!"

He shouldered past a huddled mass of frightened men and women and found himself staring at the knee of the Rephaim giant. He looked up, his heart racing with fear. It felt as though he were standing next to some great tree, or pillar. The man's thighs were thicker than Samuel's chest. The graying clouds outlined his shaggy head, but for just a moment, Samuel saw his eyes, deep-set, brown wells of light beneath heavy brows. He was surprised at what he saw there: *gentleness, kindness, and a deep, abiding sorrow.*

"Samuel!" He heard his father's voice and pushed past the Rephaim to his family. He was immediately engulfed in his mother's arms, then his father's. He looked around at his siblings and his father's other wife, Peninnah, and saw tears in their eyes.

His father said something to the tall, handsome Danite who stood next to the Rephaim and guided his family away from the crowd toward a less crowded alley that led away from the town square. Away from the loudest of the noise and chaos, Elkanah told him how they had been saved from Ramathaim and about the scarred Philistine warrior called Phicol who led the Gedhudhra and the army now attacking them. He told him about the courage of Manoah of Dan, Arod the Gadite, the Rephaim giant Saphold, and the enigmatic Zebulunite, Elon-tohr.

"After we escaped from Ramathaim," Elkanah continued, his voice hushed as though afraid others would hear, "this Phicol gathered thousands of soldiers from Philistia and pursued us here. The Princes think that Shiloh was his goal all along—that he has determined to destroy the heart of the nation."

Samuel's mind whirled. "We need to get to the Tabernacle, take what we can easily carry, and flee the city."

"Flee?" Hannah's brows knotted in confusion. "But aren't we safe within these walls?"

As if in answer to her question, a great boom thundered across the town square as the Philistines swung a battering ram of some sort against the city gates. Samuel looked at his father, and for a brief moment, as their eyes met, Samuel felt the rare wonder of knowing that he and his father were thinking the same thought, that for that moment they were united as father and son in a way that had never happened before.

"This city cannot withstand a siege or an attack," Samuel said to his mother; from the corner of his eye, he saw his father's nod of agreement. "We are not safe here for long."

Samuel told his family to wait and dashed back up the stone steps to the top of the city wall. The Elders were there, hunkered down behind the battlements. "I have come from Ahitub, the High Priest," Samuel said to them. "He asks for your instructions for the defense of the city."

"Have Ahitub gather whatever can be quickly transported from the holy site," an Elder said. "Tell him to be prepared to flee with the sacred utensils at a moment's notice. Have the Tabernacle guard armed and ready to defend the Curtain Wall with their lives in case the enemy reaches that far."

Samuel nodded his understanding and bounded down the stairs, skipping every other step. At the bottom, he found the tall, handsome warrior, Manoah of Dan, waiting for him. Behind him stood a lithe warrior dressed meticulously in grey. "You are the Prophet, Samuel," Manoah said.

Samuel nodded, internally bracing himself against what the man might say next. He studied the auburn-bearded face: *brow furrowed over narrowed eyes. Muscles knotting and un-knotting along the jaw. Nostrils flared.*

"I have heard that some women and children from Aijalon arrived in Shiloh a few days ago," Manoah said.

Samuel nodded again. "So I was told. Most traveled farther south, though—to Mizpah, or Nob."

"Have you seen my wife—she may have fled here from Aijalon? Her name is Naamah."

Samuel shook his head. "I am sorry, my lord. I have not--."

"She is tall, and very beautiful, with black, curly hair. She may have come here with other refugees."

Samuel shrugged. "I will let the Levites know you are looking for her," he offered.

Manoah nodded, his disappointment evident, and he and the grey-clad warrior strode away from Samuel into the city. Samuel watched them a moment and then joined his family waiting nearby. Together, they struggled through streets crowded with people, scurrying in panic, carrying their belongings. In contrast to Samuel's earlier trip down to the gate, it seemed now that no inhabitants were in their homes. Young men were making their way toward the gate, gripping spears, sickle-swords, and farming implements, the same look on all their faces: a determination that thinly masked their fear. Old men led women and children in the opposite direction, toward the Tabernacle and the parts of the city that lay beyond it.

When they reached the Curtain Wall, Tabernacle guardsmen were standing alertly on either side of the gate, spears clutched in white-knuckled hands. They looked expectantly at Samuel, as though hoping that the Prophet of Shiloh would give them some instruction or assurance. Samuel ignored them and passed through the gate into the Courtyard.

Inside, Priests and Levites wandered aimlessly or stood in groups near the gate talking in low tones while the sounds of battle came to them from the distance. Followers of Hophni and Phinehas were either dead with them or at a loss, unable to bring themselves now to accept Phinehas' long-hated son as their High Priest. More than one of them cast bitter glances in Samuel's direction as he passed.

Samuel found Ahitub near the great Altar, holding his screaming brother, Ichabod, in his arms. A nursemaid stood anxiously nearby. Samuel looked at his mentor's face as he approached, feeling anger and sadness well in his chest at what he saw. Ahitub's eyes were hollow with more than lack of sleep, and his expression was of a man defeated. His grandfather, father, mother, and uncle were gone, all lost to him in one day. Atop that burden, he was now forced to take on the weight of the High Priesthood, before he was ready for it. Ahitub stood still, but his eyes were the eyes of a man drowning.

Samuel gave him the message from the Elders at the gate. Ahitub stared at him a long time after he had stopped speaking, trying to digest his words. He opened his mouth as if to speak, then closed it again and looked down at the screaming infant.

At that moment, a thundering crash reverberated from the city below them, followed by screams of terror and pain. Ahitub's eyes snapped up to meet Samuel's, and they brimmed with desperation.

Samuel ran up the steps leading to the tower that squatted atop the Curtain Wall near the Tabernacle gates. The steps and the bulwarks were crowded with Levites and Priests; he pushed through them, but he knew the cause of the commotion before he reached the top of the wall. All around him, people repeated the words, first in whispers, then in frightened shouts: "The gate has fallen! The gate of Shiloh has fallen!"

He slid through the crowd atop the tower and peered over the battlements. He could see the gate, or what remained of it, clearly. The massive oak planks had shattered, splintering inwards, and Philistine Gedhudhra poured through the opening like a black flood.

So quickly! He thought. The gate should have held longer, especially defended by so many soldiers. But nothing at Shiloh was what it should be. For so many years the city and all that it represented had been neglected, until now everything had corroded from within—like the traditions that Israel was built on, like the Priesthood that was all that the nation had for leadership. What remained was a façade, without strength in its heart. The gates of the city were no longer a defense, only the appearance of one—an image of solidity decayed and corrupted within.

He watched as the Philistines filled the town square and people fled, screaming in every direction, through the city. Then a group of Israelite warriors burst into the square, wild-haired hill men, bucklers strapped to their left arms, spears clutched in their right. Just behind them came another group of soldiers, among them the towering giant, Saphold, his massive axe raised above his head.

Samuel felt a thrill run down his spine at the sight of the defenders. "Jehovah protect you!" he screamed toward them. "May He fill your arms with power!"

He leapt back to the stairs and raced down to Ahitub, who still stood near Samuel's family. "What should we do, my lord?" he asked breathlessly.

The High Priest jiggled the still-crying Ichabod in his arms, trying to quiet him. Finally, he spoke. "Tell the Priests to make sure all of the sacred utensils are accounted for. The Levites should collect whatever else they can easily carry from the rest of the grounds—from the storerooms. And tell the guardsmen to start escorting people out of the city."

Samuel nodded and went to his task. Within a few minutes, the wagons began to roll out of the Courtyard and disappear towards the back gate of the city, led, flanked, and trailed by guardsmen from the Tabernacle. With the wagons to follow, the people began to exit in a more orderly fashion. Samuel's family left as well, his father and oldest brother taking up positions as guards alongside one of the wagons. The Courtyard was nearly empty when the Priests on the tower shouted, "They have broken through the line! They are in the city!"

Samuel scanned the Courtyard in panic. The last wagons were gone, only a few people remained. Then he realized that all of them had forgotten one thing, one vital thing that must be taken with them.

The Eternal Flame.

Abandoned in the center of the Courtyard, the Great Altar smoldered silently, its copper plating gone dull under the shadow of the lowering clouds, a thin smudge of smoke still crawling skyward above its blackened grating. "Ahitub!" he yelled, and the High Priest looked over to him. "The Flame!" he said, unable to keep the panic from his voice.

Ahitub's eyes widened. "We need eight Levites from the House of Kohath!" he said. Another crash resounded from the city below them, as of a building collapsing, and all of them looked in that direction.

"Samuel!" Ahitub said urgently. "Eight Levites! Quickly! You must bring some from the guards around the wagons!"

Samuel nodded and raced out the gate and down the road, following the route that led toward the rear gates of the city. Smoke was rising in thick clouds from many areas below him now, and he could hear the crackling of flames as the city burned.

It seemed in those moments that he must be dreaming, caught in some horrific nightmare beyond the bounds of reality or imagination. The only sounds in his ears were the screams of people in fear or pain, the roaring fires, the clash of arms. He felt his own dread pushing all other thoughts and feelings from his mind and unconsciously looked toward the top of the city, where the Tabernacle had stood the day before, and every day before that for centuries. But there was no Tabernacle there now, and the Ark that had sanctified it was on its way to the cities of their enemies. Fighting back tears, he ran on.

Moments later, he caught up to the last of the wagons and breathlessly gave his message; the Levite guardsmen relayed it to the other wagons and within minutes he found himself leading a group of eight Levites of the House of Kohath back toward the Tabernacle site. Among them were his father and his oldest brother.

When they reached the Courtyard, Ahitub was unfolding and spreading the purple wool and sealskin coverings for the Altar across the flagstones. He had already located the long, copper-plated wooden poles that threaded through rings on the Altar's base as a means of carrying it.

Samuel retrieved a copper bucket and shovel from one of the storerooms—the room was partly emptied, but there had been no time to take everything. He raced to Ahitub's side and the High Priest scooped two shovels of glowing coals from the firebox into the copper bucket. Samuel layered white broom chips over it, and then Ahitub covered it with two scoops of ash from the Altar. Their eyes met a moment, and Samuel nodded and smiled at his mentor. The fire would smolder for many hours this way. The Eternal Flame would not be allowed to go out.

Ahitub took the shovel and scraped the remaining coals and ashes out of the firebox; they scattered across the flagstones and swirled feebly in the breeze. The High Priest and the Levites spread the wool cloth, then the sealskin cover, over the Altar, and the Levites took their places alongside the shrouded box, four on each side, and hefted the poles onto their shoulders.

A loud crash sounded outside the Curtain Wall, and Samuel looked up at the tower, half-expecting a guardsman there to tell them what was happening. But the tower had been abandoned, as had the rest of the Tabernacle.

Hooves pounded on the street just outside, and Samuel spun in horror, realizing that the gate to the Tabernacle stood wide open, and only a knot of Levites waited there, spears clutched in their sweating palms, their eyes wide with fear.

Three chariots exploded through the gate, crushing the Levite guards beneath scythed wheels and the flailing hooves of war stallions. Behind the chariots loped a dozen Gedhudhra, bloodied iron blades in their hands.

Samuel and Ahitub stood between the chariots and the Levites who bore the Altar. In the lead chariot was a young warrior with a wild shock of blonde hair and a mass of reddened scar tissue where his nose should have been. He looked at Samuel and leapt from his chariot.

"The seer?" he asked, his cold, blue eyes studying Samuel's face. He held his naked, black blade in his right hand and ran two fingers slowly along its bloody edge. "I am Phicol. I, too, see things hidden from others," he said, his voice a high-pitched wheeze. He nodded toward the sword he carried. "This shows me...The sword reveals the heart of a man."

He smiled then, a cold, reptilian grin, and raising the blade over his head, charged toward them, the Gedhudhra at his heels.

46

"I am sorry, my lord," the servant kept repeating, horrified at the thought of what punishment he would suffer for daring to approach Lord Ashkelon's bed. "But the priests of Dagon insisted! They demanded I wake you—they said you were needed immediately!"

Sarnam sat up slowly. His head pounded with the residual effects of the last night's beer. He scratched his beard and thought of killing the servant, but the man scurried off and disappeared, so he dragged himself out of bed, dressed, and went to find the priests.

The founders of Ashdod had built the city on a hill, terraced to capture and make good use of rain and runoff. As he made his way through the ascending, spiraling streets with one of his war-hounds, Groug, trotting obediently at his heel, he was forced to wind around the unconscious bodies of revelers from the night before, sprawled out wherever they had fallen, lying in pools of vomit and beer while the dogs licked them off dispassionately.

The final approach to the temple was a set of steep stairs. He arrived out of breath from the climb and leaned against the entrance pillars to rest a moment before going in. The view from the entrance was spectacular: the temple faced east, but to the west he could see the narrow strip of coastal dunes running like a tan border along the lip of the azure sea.

His reverie was interrupted abruptly. "Sssarnam."

He turned to find Sihphil staring up at him from beneath his dark cowl, his hands hidden in the folds of his robes. "My lord—you musst come insside."

The priest turned and led him into the cool interior of the temple. In the entrance chamber, the other priests and priestesses were whispering to one another with ashen faces. Lord Ashkelon handed Groug's leash to one of them; the dog barked twice and it echoed raucously in the stone room. Sihphil led Lord Ashkelon onward and into the temple proper.

He stopped as soon as he entered, stunned. There, before them, the Ark still stood, as it had the night before, in all its glory. But the huge idol of Dagon was no longer standing beside it. It now lay toppled, facedown on the dais, and by some strange chance, it had fallen so that its outstretched arms were spread towards the Ark.

"This has never happened, my lord," one of the priests said; he could not hide the fear in his voice. "Not even during the great earthquake. The base of the idol is broad, and it is heavy—."

"What does it mean, Priest?" Lord Ashkelon interrupted him.

Sihphil's pale face beneath the cowl was expressionless. "I do not know."

Lord Ashkelon stared at the fallen figure. No one could fail to notice that it *appeared* that the idol was paying homage to the Ark. *What god could do this?* He wondered silently. *What god is greater than Dagon, father of als— and in his own temple?*

"Have them raise Dagon back to his place," he growled to Sihphil. "Find out what is going on, priest! And tell no one what has happened here."

He left the temple and made his way quickly back down the winding streets, Groug trotting at his heels. People were beginning to wake now, the town coming slowly to life. A jerboa jumped across the road in front of him, long tail twitching, and Groug bounded futilely after it.

"Back, Groug!" he yelled at him. He realized abruptly that that was not the first jerboa he had seen that morning. Now that he was alert to it, he noticed more than a dozen others hopping through the city as he returned to his home. He had to hold Groug tightly to keep him from chasing the swift animals through the streets. Jerboas were not normally this common, and he did not like to see so many in the city. They carried fleas and bit people—especially sleeping people and children, and the wounds usually became swollen, red, and infected, and sometimes led to plague. He would have to order the priests to make sacrifices to Mot to slow down the rat's reproduction rates.

A frowning, dour-faced man in an embroidered, red robe met him at the gate of his home. "Lord Ashkelon?" the man asked, a trace of nervousness in his voice.

"Who are you?" Sarnam snapped.

The man raised one eyebrow at Sarnam's tone. "I am Tahom, grain overseer of Ashdod."

"What do you want, Tahom? I hope you don't bring me more bad news?"

The grain overseer's eyes widened. "Have you had bad news already this morning?"

Lord Ashkelon ignored the question. "What do you want, man?"

Tahom swallowed and raised his arms. In each hand, he was holding a dead jerboa by the tail. "It is a plague, my lord. The crops of Ashdod were devastated last night—they have been entirely eaten. The fields are overrun."

"Ashdod is infested with rats?" Lord Ashkelon was incredulous.

"The worst infestation I have ever heard of, my lord."

Lord Ashkelon spat out a curse and then regained control of himself. "This will cost us—that is sure. But we have plenty of grain laid up for the year in our storehouses—."

Tahom interrupted, shaking his head. "The storehouses were not spared, my lord. The rats have eaten everything. Not enough grain is left in the city for a month, let alone a year—and now the infestation is moving into people's homes."

Lord Ashkelon felt anger and fear rising within him. "What are you saying, man?"

"Unless some miracle occurs," Tahom responded, "Ashdod will need the grain from the other cities of Philistia to survive the winter."

Lord Ashkelon stormed silently into his house, leaving Tahom standing outside in the street. He cuffed the first servant who came close enough and then opened a barrel of beer and began to drink.

But the bad news did not end there. By the end of the day, messengers had come from Ekron and Gath, reporting that the plague of jerboas was not limited to Ashdod. The fields of those cities had also been destroyed, their storehouses emptied. The exultation of the night before began turning to fear.

Lord Ashkelon went to bed late that night, and his sleep was filled with nightmares of jerboas swarming over his body, their long, sharp teeth sinking into his skin in a thousand places.

He was wakened the next morning by another servant, his eyes red from lack of sleep, his face sweaty and white with fear. "The priests of Dagon insisted, my lord…"

He swatted the man aside and clambered from his bed. "What is it now?" he wondered aloud. He stood and a stab of fiery pain shot through him. He cursed and steadied himself against the cedar-paneled wall of his room. A terrible ache burned between his buttocks, as if he had sat on a hot poker. Fully awake now, he felt chilled and ached all over; sharp pains stabbed at his crotch, armpits, and neck. The servant was already leaving the room, walking with a strange, stiff-legged gait, and Lord Ashkelon noticed a trickle of blood running down one of his legs from beneath his short tunic.

He dressed painfully and ascended the winding streets again, each step agony. Everywhere he walked, jerboas bounded in front of him or stared at him from windowsills and low walls, their beady, black eyes mocking his inability to get rid of them. Already, their dead bodies, swarming with fleas, flies, and maggots, littered the gutters.

He arrived at the temple in a foul mood, fevered and faint. Sihphil ushered him inside, and Lord Ashkelon saw that the priests and priestesses were also sick and in pain, walking stiffly, faces pale and drawn.

When they entered the temple proper and saw what waited there, through his rage Lord Ashkelon felt the bitter bite of fear.

The Ark still gleamed, golden and flawless, in its place against the wall. But the great idol of Dagon, Father of the gods, had fallen once more. Only this time, it would not be raised again. It had shattered on the stone floor, its bearded head chipped and broken and lying in one corner of the room, its torso shattered into a dozen pieces, its hands resting, minus several fingers each, on the edge of the dais. Only the fish tail was whole, but toppled from its place into the dust on the floor.

"What is going on?" Lord Ashkelon bellowed at no one in particular. He glared at the Ark but was suddenly afraid even to approach it. The serene faces of the cherubs stared down at him, implacable, unafraid, daring him to touch again the sacred chest they stood guard over. Lord Ashkelon felt fear like a weight in his mind, an enshrouding fog that paralyzed his decision-making processes and made him want to go somewhere and hide until all of this was over. It was not a feeling he was used to, and it angered and frustrated him.

He and the priest left the temple and were greeted by throngs of people waiting at the base of the steep steps. One of the under priests ran up to them. "A plague has broken out in the city!"

"A plague? Oh, more good news!" Sarnam shook his head helplessly.

"What kind of plague?" Sihphil hissed from under his cowl.

"Piles…infections of the anus, O priest," the man responded. "And a burning fever…and great weakness…and stabbing pains throughout the body." He hesitated, waiting to see how his words were being received. When neither Axis Lord nor priest responded, he added, "In its final throes, it causes stomach convulsions so severe that people are vomiting up their own entrails. Death is sweeping the city."

By the time Lord Ashkelon made it back to his home, Sihphil at his heels, the city was descending into panic. He consulted with the magistrates and overseers and sent a message to the other Axis Lords to come to Ashdod immediately.

It took several days for Lord Eglon and Lord Gaza to arrive, and during that time Sarnam hardly moved from his bed, wracked with pain, fever, and weakness. He got up only to ease nature, and his bowel movements were excruciating and filled with blood. Fourteen of the household servants Lord Ashdod had assigned to him died during that time, and the city's activities ground to a halt. The heat intensified, so that even from within his inner room, Lord Ashkelon could smell the sickly aroma of the corpses that increased faster than they could be hauled away and burned.

Sihphil gathered and coordinated the efforts of the priesthood to try to overcome the plague. A near-constant stream of priests and sorcerers visited Sarnam's rooms: Exorcists and Purifiers who burned incense, chanted spells and shook rattles to expel evil spirits; ritual Lamenters who slashed themselves, dressed in sackcloth and performed ostentatious mourning rituals to appease any gods that had been offended; *Melachashim* who whispered and hissed incantations to drive away sickness.

When the other Axis Lords arrived, they made their way through the city, staring in appalled dismay at the horrific state of the people. News of what had happened to the image of Dagon had spread, in spite of Lord Ashkelon's warning to the priests, and even the Axis Lords were in a panic.

They gathered in Lord Ashdod's bedchamber. He was even more ill than Lord Ashkelon was—his servants had propped his head up with a pillow, and he looked out at the others weakly, sweating, pale, and wracked with pain and fever. "My lords, we have been dealt a blow…we are already facing a challenging year, as we will be hard pressed to get enough food, especially with so many of our men dead from…"

He convulsed with coughing, wincing with each lurch of his diaphragm. Then: "This infestation of jerboas…and this plague upon our city—it is without a doubt the hand of the god of the Hebrews upon us!"

Lord Eglon, a fat man with a pale, pocked face, looked at him with disgust. "You can hardly say your explanation is without doubt! There have been plagues before. If this Hebrew god had such regard for the Ark, he would not have allowed us to capture it."

"But the idol of Dagon!" Lord Ashdod shouted, and then was wracked again with coughing.

Eglon shook his head, his wattle jiggling with the movement. "The cycles of nature that Dagon initiated at times produce drastic aberrations! What we are experiencing now is nothing more than a part of that cycle."

"The question is: what shall we do with the Ark now?" Sarnam asked.

"My people, the people of the city," Lord Ashdod responded, "have made their wishes clear. They have demanded that the Ark be taken from here—and quickly! If you men do not fear this thing, let it go to one of your cities!"

There was a long pause as the Axis Lords looked at one another. Lord Ashkelon read much in those looks: None of them wanted to appear a coward. They especially did not want to appear to fear this Ark of a foreign god.

The Lord of Gath clapped both hands to his lap. "Very well then. I will take the Ark to Gath. I do not fear this Jehovah. The gods of the land are strong, and I will turn this Ark over to the priests of Dagon, Baal, Ashtoreth, Anath, and Mot. If they feel it is a threat to Philistia, we will consult with you men and destroy it!"

"It is the greatest prize we have ever taken in battle!" Lord Eglon protested.

"It is a prize I wish I had never seen!" Lord Ashdod responded.

"Thiss alone will not be enough," Sihphil hissed. "Though it may provide relief for thisss city."

"What do you recommend, priest?" Sarnam asked.

"Only one of the pantheon hasss the power to counteract ssuch a deadly plague," Sihphil answered, looking around him from beneath heavy lids. "Prince Resheph, god of Pessstilence, hass under hisss command a flying demonessss called Sha'taqat. She bearsss a wand with which sshe can cure any disseassse. Even the godsss at timesss require her ssservicesss."

"And can you summon this demoness?" Sarnam queried.

"Hsss!" Sarnam spat on the floor of the room and bared his teeth at the men around him. "We musst petition Prince Resheph for hisss aid." His clawed hands unfolded from his voluminous sleeves, palms up as if he was accepting some proffered gift. "It will require great sssacrificcce."

The next morning the priests who had accompanied Lord Gath covered the Ark again in its enshrouding cloths, bore it down the steep temple steps and placed it upon a wagon. With the Axis Lords watching, priests of Philistia offered five male infants on altars to Dagon and Baal, and Sihphil chanted and danced his petition to Prince Resheph for Sha'taqat's aid.

Oxen then pulled the wagon down the main avenue and out the gates, following the road toward Gath. The people of Ashdod watched it leave their city, but they did not have the strength to cheer.

Lord Ashkelon slept fitfully that night, his body still wracked with fever. He woke around midmorning and dragged himself out of bed, wincing and cursing.

A sweaty messenger from Gath waited outside his door. He had ridden from the city early that morning. "All of Gath is plagued—from child to old man!"

"Curse this Ark!"

The messenger cowered at his rage but was determined to see his message delivered. "It is worse in Gath than in Ashdod, my lord! Much worse! The people who are plagued--their rectums swell with infection until they protrude from their buttocks like a great boil, bleeding and putrefying in the heat! Even those who are not yet sick cannot sleep for the moaning of the victims!"

"What do the priests say?"

"They have instructed the people to fashion soft leather seats for their chairs with holes cut in the center to relieve the pain of sitting on the swollen piles."

"Leather seats? Do they have no...cure, no treatment?"

The messenger shook his head. "None, my lord."

By the next morning, another messenger from Gath arrived, this one pale and sickly himself. The uncontrollable vomiting had begun, and hundreds of the population of the city had died. The Axis Lord of Gath had sent the Ark to Ekron with a message: *Take the prize from me. I cannot bear to look at it. The power of God rests with this Ark.*

But when the bearers, two sickly servants riding upon a wagon, had arrived with the golden box shrouded in its dark coverings, they were met at the gates by a delegation of soldiers with lowered spears.

"Lord Ekron has ordered us to make certain the Ark does not come within our walls!" they announced to the anguished couriers. "Take it back to Gath, for we know you have brought it to us only to put us to death!"

The servants from Gath were not going to return to Lord Gath with the Ark still in their possession. Not knowing what else to do, they deposited it in a freshly plowed field just outside Ekron's walls.

By the next morning, plague had struck the city of Ekron. By the following evening, as the city walls cast their shadow upon the shapeless, brooding form of the covered Ark, sitting undisturbed and unattended in the field, hundreds in Ekron and the surrounding area were dead.

47

Watching Phicol bearing down on him, fear paralyzed Samuel. All thoughts of heroism and courage and even trust in Jehovah evaporated. In that moment, he forgot even about the Altar behind him and the Eternal Flame smoldering in the bucket in Ahitub's hands. He wanted only to run, to flee out of the Courtyard and away from these cold-eyed warriors and their black blades.

But there was nowhere to run.

Beside him, Ahitub fell to his knees and began to pray. Samuel found himself studying the look on Phicol's scarred face, a look further disfigured by rage and a frenzied madness that haunted the man's eyes. *What past creates such a man?* he wondered silently, even as another part of his mind closed itself off against the certainty of the pain and death that were descending on him.

Then movement atop the Curtain-Wall to Samuel's left caught his eye, and as he turned two men vaulted over the wall like cats, landing silently in a wide-stanced crouch on the flagstones, naked blades in their hands. One of them was a Gadite, his dirty blonde hair and beard framing his face like a wild mane. He was grinning from ear to ear. The other was dressed meticulously in grey. Howling, they launched themselves at the charging Philistines.

Swords crashed against swords, and the Courtyard echoed with the ring of arms, screams, and oaths. Instants later, a dozen Gadites followed their leader over the wall, as did Manoah and the Benjaminite Basar. The fighting became a maelstrom atop the flagstones, weapons whirling faster than the eye could follow.

Manoah grabbed Samuel's arm and propelled him towards the gate. "Follow me!" he yelled to Ahitub and the Levites.

A great, hulking form lumbered into the gateway: Saphold the Rephaim, his double-bladed axe in his hands. He charged into the fray like a bull gone mad, great axe swinging, sweeping men before it.

Manoah led Samuel, Ahitub, and the Levites through the gate, and the battling Israelites followed them, walking backwards, slowly giving way before the onslaught of Phicol and the Gedhudhra until only Elon-tohr and Saphold stood in the gateway. The Rephaim tore an ironbound wheel from an abandoned chariot and hurled it into the Philistines. It smashed through their ranks—those who did not dive for cover it swept away.

Elon-tohr rushed from the gateway and Saphold grabbed the outer handles with his massive fists and swung the gate closed from the outside. "Go!"

Led by Elon-tohr and the Gadites, they fled down the streets of Shiloh, listening to the furious pounding of the Philistines hurling themselves against the Tabernacle gates.

As they ran down the avenue that led them toward the rear of the city, Samuel could not help but stare over his shoulder at those gates, shielded now by the towering form of the Rephaim giant. Every day of his life since he was a son of three years, his hands had touched those handles, that polished, worn planking. But no more. His days as the Tabernacle's gatekeeper were done.

The screams of anger from inside the Curtain wall faded as they fled farther down into the city.

Smoke was roiling all around them now, burning their eyes and choking them as the building wind scattered ash and embers across the city. Flames erupted from windows and doorways of the homes they passed, and bodies, human and animal, littered the streets.

Samuel could not catch his breath, and it was more than the smoke-clouded air. He knew that nothing would ever be the same for him after this. A line had been crossed, a milestone on a journey that should never have been begun. There could be no going back for Israel now. There could be no going back for him.

He was surprised to feel the wetness of tears on his cheeks. *What kind of person am I?* he wondered. The Altar had been threatened. His father and brother, carrying it, had faced the peril of death. And he had stood, paralyzed by fear. It was just as the scarred warrior had said: the sword had shown what was in his heart. And now, he was fleeing in terror and furious at himself for his fear. He had lost more than a home this day, he knew. He had lost some final shred of his youthful self-confidence, his cherished belief that within him were noble qualities awaiting opportunity to be brought out.

He had been tested by fire, and, like the city he called home, he had not withstood that test.

They entered a portion of Shiloh not yet burning. A few people still scurried through the streets, fleeing in the same direction as they, but most were Israelite soldiers, loping back toward the sounds of battle, their eyes glimmering with the pale coldness of men who deal death.

After a few minutes, they reached one of the rear gates and exited it without pausing, moving as quickly as the pace of the men carrying the Altar would allow. They followed the well-traveled road that descended into the wilderness to the south, toward the lands of the tribe of Judah, the heart of Israelite territory.

After a few moments of travel, Samuel stopped and turned around to look once more on the city. Storm clouds hung heavy and angry in the sky, swallowing the billowing black columns of smoke. The drabness of the scene struck him—everything but the orange flames seemed painted in shades of grey, as though all color had been washed from the city. While he watched, flames erupted from a building on the hill, and in moments, it began to crumble before his eyes.

Like an earthenware vessel, he thought. Shiloh contained Israel's final sin offering. And now, appropriately, the container that bore that offering was shattered forever.

He turned back and continued moving. Thunder rumbled, ominously close, so that Samuel felt its power shake the ground at his feet. Just ahead of him, Ahitub stumbled forward, clutching the vessel in which the embers of the Eternal Flame smoldered, holding them close as though they were an infant child.

They descended into the cover of the trees. Samuel did not turn around again.

The city of Shiloh was lost.

48

Lord Ashdod died that night of the plague, ending his life in a bout of uncontrollable vomiting that virtually turned him inside out. Sarnam watched it happen, seated in a chair at the man's bedside. He would not admit it, but the sight filled him with terror.

The next day, he sent messengers to summon all the Axis Lords to the city of Ekron. He dared not ask them to come to him in Ashdod, since many of them were already blaming him and his capture of the Hebrews' Ark for the devastation their nation was suffering. Therefore, he chose a location that would require him to travel, as well, hoping to allay some of their resentment.

Lord Ashdod's household servants, at Sarnam's instruction, fitted a wagon with a bed of linen cushions and down-stuffed bolsters, and erected a tent over the bed. Sarnam led them to believe that the structure was to shield him from the weather, which was growing increasingly threatening, with dark clouds massing overhead and wind building from out of the west. But even more important to Sarnam than being sheltered from the threat of rain was his desire not to be seen in his humbled condition by his subjects.

Lying on the bed of cushions as they traveled, every jostle of the wagon was agony. His body ached, weakness and daggers of pain stabbing out from his groin, his armpits, his neck, and—especially—his buttocks. Sihphil hovered over him the entire trip, like some pale, black-shrouded nursemaid, but in spite of his constant mumbling and hissing, he seemed unable to do anything to alleviate Sarnam's misery.

The strange priest had himself become only slightly ill, a fact that made Sarnam angry and suspicious. He wondered if there was not some undisclosed spell or concoction that Sihphil was secretly using for himself. It was more likely, he knew, that the priest was simply so imbued with the dark powers he studied and cultivated that they protected him from whatever spirits were causing the disease. Still, the knowledge that he was at the mercy of the sorcerer just added to the misery he was already feeling.

They arrived at Ekron near the end of the day. As they passed through the city gate, Sarnam shifted in order to peer out through a gap in the tent cloths, wincing with pain at the movement. Between the swinging, linen curtain, he could see a sliver of the city square, and in one corner of it an idol of Ekron's patron god: Baal-zebub, Lord of the Flies. As he watched, two priests were smearing handfuls of moist dung over the idol. He had heard of the practice before, although this was the first time he had seen it. The dung drew a cloud of flies, swarming and crawling over every surface of the idol. From a few paces away, it appeared that the stone carving was moving, brought suddenly to life. Baru-priests, trained in the interpretation of signs and omens, would listen to the buzzing of the insects and out of the sounds extract a message from the god. Sarnam knew that this day they were pleading with Baal-zebub to free them of the effects of the plague. He also knew somehow that their efforts would be useless.

The wagon bore him through the city streets until they arrived at the meeting hall that fronted the palatial home of Lord Ekron. There, Sarnam's servants carried him on a litter through the wrought-bronze gate, across a flagstoned courtyard and through a pillared entry into the hall. Inside, the Lords of Gath, Gaza, and Ekron were waiting for him, reclining on piled cushions, pale and sweating. Each had brought their chief priests with them—they, too, were obviously ill, though some tried to dab cool water on the foreheads of the fevered Lords they served. Servants, themselves wracked with pain and fever, stood all around the hall with clay or copper bowls in their hands. At an urgent gesture from a priest or lord, they would scurry forward from time to time and catch their vomit, then carry it outside and dump it into a furnace kept burning in the courtyard.

As Sarnam settled into his position, he heard the rain outside begin to thrum on the roof, a wild, driving rain that whipped against the building in gusts of wind. *At least we have that to be grateful for,* he thought. The drought was ending. The crops they had planted would finally begin to sprout.

"Our land is devastated," Sarnam began, bringing the room to a hush. He gestured weakly toward Sihphil. "Our priest's appeals to the gods are going unheeded."

"Hsss!" Sihphil bared his teeth. "We mussst give it more time! The demonesss Sha'taqat hass been ssummoned! Sshe will come, and there iss power in her wand to cure any disseasse!"

"We cannot know the ways of the gods!" Sarnam snapped back,

pain making him impatient even with the dangerous priest. "It is obvious that whatever gods or demons you are appealing to are impotent in the face of this Jehovah!"

"We have drawn his ire down upon ourselves by taking this Ark," Lord Gath said.

"Dagon iss the great El, father of all other godsss—." Sihphil began.

"Then Dagon has abandoned us!" Sarnam snapped.

The two men faced each other in silence. Outside, the rain drummed against the walls and roof. Sihphil's eyes had gone flat and cold, like chips of obsidian glimmering darkly from beneath his cowl. Sarnam knew he was doing himself no good by alienating the priest, but he had no patience left, no more willingness to wait on the inconstant will of the gods. If Dagon wanted him to conquer the land of Canaan and drive out the Hebrews, then Dagon would need to do something to overcome the plague that was keeping him bedridden and slowly killing off his army.

Finally, one of the other priests in the room shifted, wiping at his tired eyes. "There are other gods we can appeal to. We have not yet made sacrifices to the gods of Egypt, who are acknowledged to be the greatest healers in the world."

"Egypt?" Sarnam said. "Have you forgotten that the god of this Ark humiliated the deities of Egypt, one by one? To which of them would you appeal? Isis, queen of heaven, who could not cleanse her own sky of gadflies and gnats—though the Hebrew camp was free of them? Ptah, who could not heal his own people of a plague of boils? Ra and Horus, sun gods who could not pierce the darkness that descended over all the land at the word of Jehovah?"

The gathered priests scowled at him, but they could not argue the truthfulness of what he said.

"We must appease Jehovah," Sarnam continued, "or our entire nation will be destroyed. Egypt was spared for one reason only—they let the Hebrews go."

Lord Ekron shook his head. "But we do not have them held captive—at least, not many of them."

"We hold captive their Ark!" Sarnam shot back at him. "But we cannot just send it back. It has to be done properly to be sure we placate Jehovah."

He turned to face the priests, wincing with the effort. "What is the procedure for doing such a thing?"

The priest who had spoken earlier sighed. "It will be necessary for us to study the matter, and inquire of the gods. Ancient traditions from Caphtor may apply, and we know a little of the way the Hebrews worship their one god. It will take some time to discover what is proper."

"Very well," Sarnam said. "Find those answers! We dare not make a mistake in this, but I want this Ark out of Philistia as soon as may be. And in the meantime, we must recall our remaining forces from the territory held by the Hebrews or risk further retribution from Jehovah."

"It is your mad dog Phicol that is still there!" said Lord Gath. "The rest of our armies have returned to their homes."

Sarnam scowled, but the man was right. And he knew if he tried to send a message to the Gedhudhra ordering them to return, Phicol would find a way to destroy the message or otherwise circumvent him if he wanted to. The young warrior would not hesitate to simply kill the messenger and continue with his slaughter. Sarnam did not deceive himself for a moment into thinking that he could control Phicol. Nothing controlled Phicol, except for the hatred that burned inside of him, that drove him to commit the endless acts of savagery that made him so useful to Sarnam.

"Dispatch a messenger to the Rephaim encamped at Gath," he said. "Tell Gundar to send a party of his mightiest warriors into the heart of Canaan. Tell him that they must find Phicol and the Gedhudhra and bring them back to Philistia. Tell him to make sure the Gedhudhra know that the order comes directly from me, no matter what Phicol may say. They will listen. But warn the Rephaim—Phicol himself will have to be carried away bodily."

"In that case," said Lord Gaza, "I am glad that it is the Rephaim who are being sent to do the task."

49

Like an insatiable, ethereal predator, the storm was hunting them.

The roiling clouds swallowed the western horizon, blotting all else from the sky. Glancing over his shoulder, Samuel could see the streaks of grey above the near slopes of the hills, and closer, where rain had begun falling in curtains across the thirsty land.

A few days ago, that promise of rain would have meant hope for Israel. It would have been the wet guarantee of crops that would sprout in the spring. But on this day, as the group of weary refugees struggled slowly south, retreating from their enemies, hope was not something hiding among the other baggage they carried strapped to their bodies or piled atop their creaking wagons. Hope was something they had not brought with them. Hope had been left behind, in the cooling ashes of Shiloh.

It seemed to Samuel that they had lost everything that made them, the nation of Israel, what they were: the Ark, their High Priest, their holy city, and their confidence in Jehovah's protection against their enemies. They traveled now grasping onto all that was left of the *idea* that was Israel, a belief cobbled together from the tangible remnants they carried—the sacred implements, acacia panels, and piles of cloth that could be rebuilt into the Tabernacle; the great copper Altar; the smoldering embers of the Eternal Flame. The refugees clung to these miscellanies as a drowning man clings to the flotsam of his sinking ship. But looking around him as they traveled, Samuel wondered if these fragments were enough to keep them afloat in the face of the tempest that pursued them.

They were a somber group. From time to time, the Levites bearing the Altar set the burden down and a new shift of men took over, pausing only long enough to heave the gold-plated carrying poles onto fresh shoulders. Samuel followed in their footsteps, shuffling forward in stunned silence, unbroken even by the weeping of the women or the screams of the children who were too far south for them to see or hear.

They walked with the overwhelming sense that they had neither destination nor point of origin, that they were like a boat, cut adrift in the heart of the sea, caught by some mighty wind and borne south upon it, burdened with the looming expectation that the next wave would swamp and sink them.

Spread out in front, on either side, and behind, Israelite soldiers escorted them, appearing and disappearing in the landscape like shadows. Samuel had learned that the legendary Elon-tohr was out there somewhere, as was the Danite Manoah and the giant Rephaim Saphold who traveled with him. He had heard men discussing a celebrated Gadite chieftain named Arod. He supposed it was a comfort to know they were guarded. But in spite of the soldiers' presence, he no longer felt safe anywhere.

To Samuel, even the landscape had changed. The smothering clouds gave everything a grey, pallid look, one that matched the ashen faces of the people around him. Spring's leaves and blossoms remained tightly locked away from sight still, and the hills and valleys they passed were a sullen, dull brown. Tree and shrub stretched skeletal arms toward the sky, as though they, too, prayed for rain.

They followed the Great Road south, heading towards the territory of Judah. What they would find there, Samuel did not know. He did not think anyone knew. The extent of their planning had been to escape, carrying what they could of their faith with them. It made Samuel think of stories he had heard shepherds tell about hunting lions who would roar to frighten their prey into fleeing into the mouths of another pride lying in wait among the tall grass. He felt uncomfortably like a fleeing sheep at the moment, running away with an indistinct hope of safety as their only destination, and no map or trail that they knew would take them there. He wondered whether they were running into even greater danger than that which they had left behind.

The group sustained a vague sense that if they could reach the territory of Judah, they would be safer than at any other place in Israel. Judah was the largest tribe, and its lands contained more fortified cities, and more Israelite soldiers, than any other territory. Perhaps the Philistines pursuing them would be hesitant to enter Judah. Besides, at the border of Judean territory, next to the road, the city of Jerusalem rose above the surrounding countryside. The Jebusites inhabited it, a warrior-tribe who protected their territory so fiercely that they continued to hold their city even after it had become, hundreds of years before, an island in a sea of Israelite land. Now the Jebusites traded warily with Israel, and on that basis a fragile peace lay between them. Samuel was sure they would let Israelite refugees pass their city unhindered, even as they did for caravans of merchants every day. The Philistines had no such arrangement, though, and so might not want to come near Jerusalem with an army and risk provoking the Jebusites.

It was a weak plan, at best, he admitted to himself and wondered if the men with him were plagued by similar doubts.

As darkness fell, Ahitub called a halt to their march. They had not heard or seen any sign of the Philistines since leaving Shiloh, and it was possible that Phicol and the Gedhudhra had decided not to pursue them or had raided into another area of Israel. They were not far from the Israelite city of Nob, less than an hour's march from the shadow of Jerusalem's walls. Exhausted, the Levites set down their burdens, including the shrouded Altar, and huddled in small groups wherever they could find a place to sit or lay.

The thunder continued to rumble somewhere to the west, but the rain had not yet reached them. Samuel sat across from Ahitub as darkness swallowed more and more of the land all around, softening the lines of distant trees and hills, settling over everything like the stillness of a funeral crowd at the moment that the widow stands to speak. Samuel respected the silence. He did not say anything, even to Ahitub, but watched as the bereaved Priest wept.

Between the two of them, on a patch of rocky soil, rested the pot in which the coals of the Eternal Flame smoldered. Samuel resisted the temptation to remove the layer of ash that covered it and feed twigs into the flames. He knew fire. He knew that uncovering the flame would cause it to flare up, quickly consuming the wood they had, and that the dry twigs that could be found nearby would not add anything meaningful to its lifespan. They would turn quickly, and uselessly, to powdery ash, and drift toward heaven on a winding pathway of smoke.

So, instead of feeding the flame, he merely sat across from it, watching the copper pot as though he could keep the fire alive by his willpower alone. Across from him, Ahitub wrapped a grey, wool cloak tightly around his Priestly robes and kept his eyes fixed on a spot of ground a few paces in front of him. Samuel studied his care-lined face: *muscles slack, lips slightly open, brows knitted, eyes shining with tears.* Samuel tried to imagine how his mentor must have been feeling. To have lost his grandfather, uncle, father, and mother all at once—it was more than Samuel could comprehend.

But Ahitub had lost even more than that. History would remember him as the High Priest under whose leadership Shiloh had been destroyed. Samuel tried to picture what the city must look like now—the crumbling buildings, the smoldering hilltop of embers and ashes where once all Israel had looked for guidance, comfort, and stability.

His imaginings led him on to another thought, an abrupt and

devastating realization that these events would be forever bound to people's memory of him, as well. Samuel, the Prophet of Shiloh. Samuel, during whose service as Prophet the Ark of the Covenant had been captured, and the holy city at the heart of Israel lost to Philistine dogs.

"We will need wood for the fire soon." Ahitub's voice, husky with emotion, interrupted Samuel's thoughts.

"How much longer before we can restore the Flame to the Altar?" Samuel asked.

"I do not know. We are near Judah now—somewhere in Benjamin's territory."

"Where are we going?"

"South. Maybe to Nob. Maybe farther."

Samuel was trying to frame his next question when the sound of heavy footsteps interrupted his thoughts. He craned his neck and saw the giant Saphold lumbering out of the darkness toward them. Manoah walked beside the Rephaim, and the expression on the Danite's face was one of utter sorrow.

When he reached Samuel and Ahitub, Saphold gingerly lowered his massive bulk to the ground, sitting cross-legged a few feet from the pot that contained the Eternal Flame. Seated, his head was still nearly as high as Manoah, standing quietly behind him. Samuel and Ahitub looked at him inquisitively, but for several long moments, the giant said nothing, just stared at Samuel with quiet sadness in his eyes.

"He asked to speak to the Seer," Manoah said.

Samuel was taken aback and felt overwhelmed at the thought of the expectations this foreigner might have for him. Whatever Saphold was hoping to get from the famous Prophet, Samuel knew he would be disappointed with the truth of what he found.

"You have spoken with the God Jehovah?" Saphold rumbled quietly.

"I have heard Him speak, but only our greatest Prophet, Moses, carried on conversation with the True God," Samuel answered carefully.

"He is different from the gods of my forefathers," Saphold said.

Samuel nodded. "Your people's gods are many, and are idols of wood and stone—gods who can be injured, imprisoned, and even destroyed. Jehovah our God is One, the Creator, Invisible, and He cannot be contained in anything made by the hands of man."

Saphold looked puzzled. "This Tabernacle you are transporting—it did not contain your god?"

"No."

"This Ark, which the Philistines have captured—it did not contain your god?"

"No."

"And this light that burned over the Ark, this—." Saphold struggled to remember the word Manoah had taught him.

"The *Shekinah*."

"Yes—this *Shekinah*. Was it not the presence of your god?"

Samuel started to answer immediately, then caught himself and paused, thinking carefully about how to word his response. "It was a sign of His presence—just as the shadow of a man tells you of his being there, even if you do not see him yourself."

"Then, with this light now extinguished, your god is gone?"

Samuel looked over at Ahitub, hoping for help. But his mentor was staring at him with something akin to longing in his deep-set eyes. Samuel turned back to Saphold and shook his head. "No. Jehovah may have left...He may have...He has removed himself from Shiloh. But He is not gone. No place can contain the True God—and no place can exclude Him, if He chooses to inhabit it."

"If his army is defeated, his light is gone, his Tent is torn down, his holy city is burned, then how do you know he is still present, this invisible god?"

"Moses, our greatest Prophet, wrote of our forefather Abraham: 'And Abraham put faith in Jehovah, and Jehovah considered him righteous.'" Samuel gestured at the men gathered around them. "We have Abraham's faith, and it allows us to see that which is invisible."

"With your faith you can see god?"

Samuel smiled a moment, remembering Eli at the Tabernacle gates in the morning. It seemed like years had passed since those days. "I knew a blind man who saw Jehovah as clearly as you and I see...well, perhaps as clearly as you and I see the wind."

Saphold glanced at the treetops on a ridge to their west. They were swaying gently, and as they watched, the breeze reached down and brushed over the top of a field of baca bushes that bordered the forest, rustling and whispering through the stiff leaves.

"All Canaan knows of the wonders your god performed on behalf of your people," the giant said, nodding. "In freeing you from Egypt, and delivering much of Canaan into your hand."

"He promised this land to the children of Israel," Samuel answered. "And he will not fail to fulfill that promise."

"The Creator of all things," Saphold breathed.

"Do you not see His handiwork all around you?" Samuel asked.

Saphold looked back at him for a very long time before responding. "So that is why they call you the Seer."

Samuel felt a lump in his throat, feeling that in spite of the truthfulness of the giant's words, he had overstepped some boundary of propriety. He wondered abruptly that he himself had never thought of the connection before—that a Seer was, truly, one whose faith must be greater than that of other men. He felt again the crushing sense of his own inadequacy for this high honor. He could not even confirm the Rephaim's words aloud—to do so was too much like boasting.

But he did not need to. Saphold nodded slowly, and Samuel thought he glimpsed a smile beneath the black beard. "A god that can never be captured, never destroyed."

"Never hidden from those who know how to see Him," added Samuel.

"Then He is here, even now?"

The wind picked up, whistling through the dry tree branches, soughing across the dead grasses on the hills, stirring whirlwinds of dust on the road near where they sat. Samuel glanced at the clouds and felt a spattering of raindrops against his upturned face. "He is here," he answered softly. "He can be found wherever His true worshippers are, for them He will never abandon."

Lightning forked to the west and the whole group flinched. A roll of thunder followed the flash, so loud it shook the ground upon which they sat.

Ahitub rose to his feet. "We had better get moving."

The rest of the group were rising when lightning struck again, twice, so close that Samuel could hear it sizzle and snap through the air. The thunder's crash hurt his ears, and the rain was suddenly a downpour, soaking through Samuel's linen *me'il* and *ephod* in seconds.

Ahitub lunged forward and scooped up the bucket that carried the Eternal Flame; the layer of ashes on its top was already darkening under the rain's onslaught. He wrapped a fold of his traveling cloak over it and blinked water out of his eyes. "We have to find cover!" he yelled over the sound of the rain.

The group drew together unconsciously, as if by clustering nearer each other they could somehow escape the downpour. Samuel hunched his shoulders and, glancing to his left, saw the shadowy form of Elon-tohr, standing perfectly still at the edge of the group. He was staring into the greyness beyond their encampment. *Water dripping down furrowed brow. Jaw tight. One hand resting on the hilt of his sword.*

Samuel followed his gaze. At that moment, lightning flashed once more, over the trees to the southwest, and in the light of the forking white branches, a group of shapes was outlined. Samuel saw them for only an instant, a huddling of dozens of indistinct forms. But in that instant, the brilliant white light gleamed off raised swords.

A long, slender blade appeared in Elon-tohr's hand.

The shapes slid closer, emerging like spirits from the shrouding cover of rain and darkness. They were men, dozens of black-clad soldiers, a feral light gleaming in their eyes. At their head was a young warrior with a shock of blonde hair, plastered now against his forehead by the rain.

"The sword reveals the heart!" he yelled over the downpour.

Raising their blades and screaming out savage battle cries, Phicol and the Gedhudhra charged towards them.

50

Splashing muddy water with every step, Elon-tohr, Manoah, Arod, Saphold, and the Gadites hastily formed a defensive line between the Levites and the charging Gedhudhra.

The two forces collided in a cacophony of arms and battle cries, all rendered strange and unearthly to Samuel's eyes by the torrents of rain. He crouched next to Ahitub, staring, every muscle in his body urging him to flee.

The Gedhudhra outnumbered their defenders at least three to one. For several moments, it seemed that all the world had disappeared except the two lines of warriors, slinging arcing droplets of water from the ends of their swords with every swing.

It was when Samuel saw the first Gadite die, just a few paces in front of him, that he was jolted from his stupor. The man appeared to fall so slowly, his bare, muscular arms thrown wide in shock, his hair, stringy and matted with rainwater and blood, stuck to his cheeks and forehead. He collapsed backward onto the muddy earth, and his sickle-sword, shaken from nerveless fingers, slid across the ground to land near Samuel's feet.

Lightning illuminated the scene again in a cold, hard flash of brilliance, and the thunder rumbled its way through Samuel's chest. He grabbed Ahitub, standing frozen and wide-eyed next to him, the Eternal Flame clutched in his arms.

"Ahitub!" Samuel screamed, but his voice was lost in the clamor of the battle and the echo of the thunder. Ahitub did not look at him, in spite of the fact that Samuel was now tugging on the High Priest's arm.

Samuel kept pulling, wanting desperately to lead his mentor away from the battle. "Ahitub!" he screamed again.

This time, the High Priest looked down at him, his eyes wild. "We are finished!" he said, in such a hush that Samuel saw the words on his lips rather than heard them.

A hand-axe whistled past Samuel's head and he flinched away, letting go of Ahitub's arm. Not fifteen paces distant, Elon-tohr and Arod stood back to back in a closing circle of black-clad Philistines. Elon-tohr's slender black blade was whirling in front of him so fast that Samuel saw it only as a blur of dark movement. From three sides, Gedhudhra lunged and hacked at the Zebulunite, a dozen attacks coming at once, but somehow his blade was always in place in time to counter every slash, to parry every thrust. His mouth was open, his eyes wide as a man in the throes of ecstasy, an exquisite dancer performing his flawless masterpiece. At his feet, half a dozen bodies already lay, forever silenced, in the mud.

At his back, Arod fought with an oiled-leather buckler and a short spear with a thick shaft of fire-hardened oak. He was grinning from ear to ear, whipping the spear's bronze head around him like a madman. Already, one black Philistine blade, torn from the hand of some Gedhudhra who had underestimated the Gadite's strength, jutted from his shield like a black, metal branch.

Similarly surrounded by a knot of Philistine warriors, Manoah and Saphold fought a few paces away. Bellowing as if he had caught some of the thunder's roar in his own lungs, Saphold swung his mighty axe at any who dared come within reach of his arms. Two warriors lay dead at Manoah's feet, but those who were struck by the massive Rephaim were hurled back into their own ranks with such force that they bowled other men over like a landslide flattens trees.

Then Arod—still smiling—slipped on the muddy ground and went down. He instantly disappeared beneath the mass of Gedhudhra that surged forward. Elon-tohr leapt to try to rescue him, but the legendary Zebulunite was now surrounded on all sides by his enemies, and even he could not defend against all of them at once while saving his fallen companion. Samuel thought that Arod was lost, but suddenly, the wild-haired Gadite burst free of the mass of soldiers, screaming and tossing men off him, his face covered in matted hair and watery blood streaming from a wound over his left eye.

Saphold's bellow rose above the tumult, and Samuel spun to see that someone had at last pierced the giant's defenses. A spear was buried in his shoulder, its bronze tip just protruding from his back.

"No!" Manoah yelled, lunging forward, desperation carving his features as he redoubled his efforts to keep the exultant Gedhudhra from overwhelming the giant Rephaim. Saphold grabbed the spear shaft in one massive fist, just where it disappeared into his shoulder, and jerked it free.

For a moment Samuel thought the huge warrior was going to faint—he took two stumbling steps backward, his eyes rolling up in his head as blood poured down his breastplate and dribbled into the mud forming at his feet.

Then, just in front of him, a one-eyed Gedhudhra landed a crippling blow against Manoah's left arm. At the sound of Manoah's yelp of pain, Saphold bared his teeth and, screaming, crushed the one-eyed man with a single swing of his axe.

Four more Gadites went down before Samuel's eyes. Several of the Gedhudhra died as well, but their companions did not slow—they just stepped on the bodies of their dead comrades as though they were nothing but dirt and pushed toward the unarmed Altar-bearers.

"Men!" Elkanah shouted above the tumult, gesturing toward the shrouded Altar. He led the unarmed Levites as they hefted the Altar onto their shoulders again, and began moving as quickly as its weight would permit them, away from the fight and down the road. After only a few paces, Elkanah left his place under the Altar and, drawing his own sword, threw himself into the fray near Manoah.

Samuel tugged on Ahitub's arm again. "Please! Please! We have to go!"

Ahitub looked down at him, still hesitating.

"The Flame!" Samuel yelled, and, at last, the High Priest seemed to come back to himself. The Altar could be rebuilt; the sacred implements could be forged again. But the Flame must be protected; the Flame must endure.

Ahitub turned from the battle and, with Samuel still clinging to his arm, ran toward the road, following the Levites bearing the shrouded Altar. The dark cloths draped over its surface were soaked now, making the burden even heavier as the Levites slogged forward through the mud. After only a few steps, one of the bearers slipped on a patch of slick ground and fell to his knees. For a moment, the whole group looked in danger of falling, the Altar listing to one side precariously, the wet cloths that covered it dragging their hems on the muddy ground.

When they recovered their footing, the bearers hurried forward toward the road once again. Behind them, over the hiss of the rain, Samuel could still hear the angry clash of arms, the screams of injured men. He forced himself not to turn around, worried that even a glance over his shoulder would undo him were he to see his father injured. His heart pounded wildly, and the single thought of escape screamed through his mind.

Just as they reached the edge of the road, Samuel saw something moving ahead of them, a mass of shapes approaching through the rain and darkness. In moments, the shapes coalesced out of the gloom, monstrous, towering forms, a massive wall of soldiers that stood between them and escape.

Samuel, and the Levite bearers, and Ahitub, stopped in their tracks, frozen with fear.

An entire contingent of armored Rephaim giants lumbered down the road towards them.

A huge fist gripped Samuel's insides, a crushing force of terror or anguish, or perhaps it was the sudden departure of his will to live, a void left in him by the certainty that, at this moment, death would be more desirable than what remained of his life.

He knew with chilling certainty that even if Elon-tohr and all those who fought with him could break free of the battle they now waged, they would be unable to stop the wave of huge, lumbering forms that bore down on Samuel and the Levites. The approaching Rephaim were like a force of nature, powerful beyond belief.

Samuel heard his own voice, praying aloud for protection and help, his throat tight with weeping. But even as his mouth formed the words of the prayer, his mind struggled to believe the truth of what was about to happen. In his most cynical moments, he had not imagined that his life would end this way or that Jehovah their God would allow His people to fall into such a state, to suffer the loss of everything in Israel that was holy and sacred.

The Levite bearers stood stunned in the roadway, staring at the approaching giants, rain running unheeded into their eyes.

Beside him, Ahitub fell to his knees, incomprehensible words of prayer forming on his lips, both arms wrapped tightly around the copper pot clutched against his chest.

When the Rephaim were only a few paces away, Samuel looked up into their faces, into their dark, deep-set eyes.

He realized with breathless shock that they were not looking at him.

They were not looking at Ahitub, or the Altar, or any of the Levites.

They were looking beyond them. Though they cradled their huge battle-axes in their arms, they did not raise them as they closed on Samuel.

Almost as soon as he realized he was not about to die, the giants swept past him, and Samuel, the Levites, and Ahitub all turned in stunned surprise to watch them lope toward the embattled warriors.

Manoah saw, too, the Rephaim giants closing on them, and with the sight, what little hope that remained in him died. He had dared to believe that somehow the unreal skills of Elon-tohr and Arod and the superhuman strength of Saphold gave them a chance against the Gedhudhra. It was a slender chance, a delicate thing that he had kept sheltered deep inside himself, lest the madness all around him snap it apart.

But the sight of the giants shattered that hope in an instant. They were pinned now between two superior forces. There was no escape this time for the heroes of Israel.

He saw Saphold turn to look at him. A strange look haunted his sad, deep-set eyes. "Farewell, Manoah of Dan," he heard him say. "Jehovah has saved you."

Then Saphold grabbed his axe by the end of its handle and spun in a great arc, sweeping away a dozen Gedhudhra in one blow, sending bodies flying in every direction. Raising the axe above his head, he thundered from Manoah's side toward the approaching giants. As soon as the Rephaim saw him, they beat their chests and bellowed out the now-familiar challenge in their guttural language. Stopping their rush forward when they reached Saphold, they formed a circle with Saphold in the middle, his axe still raised above his head.

While the Gedhudhra nearby untangled themselves from the bodies of their companions, Manoah stared in stunned disbelief. A single Rephaim stepped forward, a huge, scarred warrior nearly as large as Saphold. He raised his axe above his head.

But then Saphold suddenly flipped his own axe upside-down, placing the top of the blade against the sodden ground. He looked at the champion opposite him and nodded once.

Manoah leapt toward the circle. "No!"

The scarred champion swung, and half the head of his axe disappeared in Saphold's chest. Convulsing, Saphold fell backwards into the mud.

The Gedhudhra were all around Manoah once more, and as he spun to defend himself, he heard the familiar chant from behind him, a booming "Doom-aaah! Doom-aaah!" from the Rephaim. His arms and shoulders ached as he struggled to keep fighting, fighting just to stay alive, knowing that his survival now depended on the skill of Elon-tohr and the Gadites. But with Saphold gone, the Gadites began to die more quickly, slaughtered by merciless Gedhudhra, tumbling into the mud all around Manoah.

Then the Rephaim rushed forward once again, still shouting "Doom-aah" as they came. They swept past the Israelite defenders and, holding their axes horizontally in front of them, pushed back the Gedhudhra from the Israelites. Two of them grabbed Phicol by his arms, lifting him bodily, and began running west toward Philistia. They were shouting something to the black-clad death-troops, but Manoah could not make out what it was. But in moments, the Gedhudhra broke off the fight and began loping away, following the giants who were carrying a screaming, struggling Phicol from the battle.

For a single moment, Phicol freed one of his arms from their iron grip. In the instant before the giant grabbed it again, Phicol drew one of his axes from his belt and hurled it furiously toward the Israelites.

As if the entire world had slowed, Samuel watched the axe whirl toward them, illuminated by a great flash of lightning, slinging rainwater as it spun, hurtling past the piles of the slain, past the exhausted warriors.

Hurtling toward Ahitub.

Samuel screamed and lurched forward, knowing already that he was too late.

The axe smashed into Ahitub with devastating force. But instead of burying itself in his ribs, it hit the pot of embers clutched in his arms. As Ahitub fell over backwards, the axe struck the Flame from his grasp, and it tumbled, spinning, towards the wet ground.

Still screaming, Samuel dove for it.

51

Samuel landed on his side in the mud, arms outstretched to catch the tumbling pot. He missed, and the copper vessel landed in the muck next to him, bounced once, and spinning, threw ashes and embers in an arc that passed over the wet ground, across Samuel's torso, and then again onto the other side of him. Some of the coals found their way past his *ephod* to his skin—he felt them burning and he lurched upright, brushing wildly at his chest and stomach with his muddy hands.

The pot bounced once more, spun in the air, and then landed solidly—upside down. Samuel, on his knees now, reached for it, knocking it away to reveal a pile of embers already soaking up the water from beneath them. Rain poured down onto all the ash around him as well, darkening it instantly to the flat, grey color that told him it was emptied of life. He reached out and tried to scoop all the ash together into a pile, but everything he touched was wet, and even the heat of the embers began to dissipate in seconds.

"Ahitub!" he cried, knowing all the while that the High Priest could do nothing to help him.

He scanned the ground desperately, already sure that he would never find what he was looking for. In the darkness he would have quickly spotted any glowing ember, any spark of life that remained among the ashes.

The Flame was extinguished.

He, Samuel, had let it die.

A moment later, the rain stopped, as suddenly as it had begun. Thunder continued to rumble somewhere off to the east, and occasional flashes of distant lightning glowed against the body of the clouds over the

Jordan valley.

Samuel remained on his knees scanning the ground around him, hot tears on his cheeks. All was truly lost now. The Flame, their last living connection to Israel's sacred past, was extinguished.

A great muscle of cloud flexed somewhere above him, allowing dusky moonlight to paint details on the scene of the battle. A few paces away from him, the Levites stood with wide eyes, peering through the darkness at the spilled ashes, still supporting the Altar on their shoulders. Almost within Samuel's reach, Ahitub slowly sat up from the mud, looking from his empty hands to the copper pot as if unable to comprehend what had happened.

Samuel glanced to the right, where his father stood alongside Elon-tohr, Manoah, Arod, and the Gadites amidst the silent, mud-spattered bodies of the fallen. Blood ran from their rain-soaked bodies in moonlit, pink rivulets. Several of the Gadites sank to their knees in exhaustion, still staring off confusedly in the direction that the Rephaim and Gedhudhra had disappeared.

Manoah stood next to the largest of the corpses, brow knotted in disbelief as he looked down at the fallen form of the giant Saphold. At the sight of the Rephaim, memories flooded back to Samuel of their conversation that evening.

"A God that can never be hidden from those who know how to see Him," he had said to the giant.

But looking around him, Samuel could not see his God. He found no sign of Him in the scene of devastation in which the group stood, alone on the muddy road, bereft of the sacred city they had called home.

He looked back at the wet ashes and then gently brushed them with his fingers. They had become thick and pasty; oily swirls spread out from them into the mud and pools of standing water all around him.

What do you see, Samuel? He heard the voice of Rohgah asking.

He closed his eyes as if by not looking, he could make the horror around him disappear. For a moment, thoughts of their losses consumed him: the Ark, the *Shekinah*, Eli, the Tabernacle, Shiloh, and now the Flame. Was this not what made Israel a nation? Was it not these things that set them apart as a Chosen People? He had grown up believing in these defining accoutrements serving at the heart of true worship on earth, proud to be there amidst all the ancient traditions, these iconic trappings and symbols of his people's role in God's purpose. He had believed these things would always be there—even as it had seemed that Eli would always serve as High Priest, that Israel would always conquer their enemies, that Samuel would start every day of his life opening the gates of the Tabernacle in Shiloh.

Waves of emotion buffeted him: confusion, anger, fear, doubt. He reached down and scooped a double handful of the wet ashes, cupping his hands around them tightly. Clutching them to his chest, he raised his eyes toward the moonlit sky above him.

"Jehovah!" he pleaded. "Please! I cannot see what to do! I cannot see it!"

Unnoticed, the wind stirred across the muddy field.

He squeezed his ash-filled fists until he felt his nails biting into his palms.

"Heavenly Father!" he implored. "Do not abandon us! Please! Show us what to do!"

The wind leapt through the night, and Samuel smelled it as it blew over him, changing the fragrance of the air, blowing tendrils of his long, wet hair into his face. He was sure for a moment he smelled salt air, as from the sea, then the dank, earthy odors of the shadowed places under dense trees, then the sweet, perfumed dampness of river valley jungles, then the crisp, dry smell of fields of ripened wheat. His skin goose-pimpled as the wind passed through his soaked garments and he shivered, suddenly aware of the cold, muddy ground on which he knelt.

But in the midst of the chill he felt something else—a warmth on the left side of his chest, a warmth that steadily grew to an uncomfortable burning sensation. He let the soaked ashes he clutched drop back to the earth and, grabbing his collar with both dirty hands, pulled the cloth away from his chest. Looking down his coat, he felt the warmth of his own breath against his damp skin. He breathed again, slow and steady.

Something glowed, dark crimson, in the fabric of his *me'il*.

From a few paces away, he heard Ahitub's voice: "What did you find, Samuel?"

He did not answer. Instead, he pulled his cloak off and then drew his coat, the linen *me'il* his mother had woven for him, over his head. It was not entirely wet—his cloak had shielded much of it from the downpour. Holding the linen garment away from the mud, searching its folds, he found a charred circle that had rested over his heart, no bigger than the end of his thumb.

Drawing it toward his mouth, he gently exhaled again, feeling the air flow from his lungs and out past his dry lips, a part of himself given to his task. He could almost see his breath brush the charred spot on the garment, and when it did, a crimson ember blossomed in the linen, burning a hole that slowly spread, while tendrils of white smoke swirled past his bowed head.

The people were all gathering now, drawing around him in a tightening circle of anxious faces and curious eyes. When they saw the smoke rising, white in the moon's white light, they gasped as one, and Ahitub crawled across the mud to Samuel's side.

Samuel looked up sharply. "We must get the Altar to Nob!"

He stood, cradling his bundled *me'il* in his arms. Ahitub stood as well, and Samuel heard orders being yelled, felt his feet carrying him to the road and then down it, rushing southward, surrounded by a swarm of people who appeared and disappeared from the darkness around him like shadows. Together they rushed forward, but Samuel's eyes were on the bundle of cloth in his arms, his mind struggling to make sense of what had happened, to believe that it could actually be so.

Every step took them closer to Nob, to the city that was, by now, waiting for their arrival, to a city where they could find dry fuel to feed the Flame. But Samuel was no longer afraid they would not reach that destination. At the moment that he had discovered that the Flame was not extinguished, Samuel, in some deep corner of his heart, had also realized that it could not be.

That tiny, growing circle of crimson and black slowly consuming his *me'il* was every answer he had been looking for. Israel was a holy people, a chosen people—not because of the Torah, or the Tabernacle, not because of the Ark that sat within its Holy of Holies, not even because of the Eternal Flame. They were who they were because of something deep inside each one of them, a flame that no man, and no circumstance, could extinguish, a flame that was passed on from father to son since the days of Abraham, a burning faith that one day, God would fulfill His promise to make Israel a kingdom eternal. Like the *Shekinah*, this flame came from Jehovah himself, and nothing outside their own hearts could extinguish it.

Samuel saw it now.

That flame was what he needed to preserve.

That flame existed even when it was invisible, when only eyes of faith could see it. It burned in the heart of every faithful servant of the True God. He had seen it in Tirzah, in Ahitub, in Rohgah. He had seen it ignite in the Rephaim Saphold.

And he knew now that it burned also in him—in Samuel, the Prophet of Israel.

It burned in him.

A god that can never be captured, never destroyed, Saphold had said, and Samuel had answered him: *Never hidden from those who know how to see Him. He can be found wherever His true worshippers are, for them He will never abandon.*

He wondered that the words could have been his. They expressed the faith that he had always wanted, the faith that Rohgah had tried to awaken within him. He had said them to Saphold, but perhaps only now did he truly understand them. Some things he could not see with human sight, no matter how many details he noticed, no matter what his eyes perceived that others might have missed. Samuel had witnessed it in the eyes of faithful, old men who came to the Tabernacle, their eyes fixed on something that he thought he could never see.

Eli had known.

Some things were seen best by men who were blind.

The group struggled onward through the night, pushing themselves to their physical limits. The forced march may have taken hours, but the time passed for Samuel in a blur. He cradled the smoldering *me'il* in his hands and watched as the embers slowly consumed it. He realized that the person he had been the day before would have worried that the garment would be spent before they reached the city. But that person was gone.

As dawn drew near, in some part of his mind he was aware of the walls of Nob rising up before them, outlined by the lightening sky to the east. Predawn brushed everything around him with the red of blood, of wakening coals. He could hear the building volume of voices crying out, words of greeting, of welcome, of concern.

The group rushed forward, through the open gates of the city, heedless of the anxious faces all around them, staring, or the questions and greetings thrown at them in the waning darkness. Outstretched hands brushed his arms, bodies crowded close, but he did not stop moving.

They passed through the gate and into the city courtyard. There, the stumbling Levite bearers set the Altar down heavily, slumping to the flagstones in exhaustion. Samuel rushed forward and pushed the smoldering, blackened handful that remained of his *me'il* into the firebox. Levites summoned from somewhere in the city brought dry slivers of cedar, and Ahitub placed them, crisscrossed atop each other, over the garment. Kneeling before the firebox door, the High Priest blew on the embers until a flame blossomed, leaping exultantly through the kindling.

More fuel was added; bone-dry pieces of cypress and white-broom wood until the flames streamed skyward, popping, snapping, and thrusting back the lingering shadows from the courtyard.

Smoke wreathed its way toward the dissipating clouds, bearing with it glimmering sparks, the sweet aroma of cypress oil, and the silent prayers of the gathered Israelites, faces upraised, all around the Altar.

The first sharp rays of dawn broke over the hills, piercing a narrow gap between the deep purple of the mountains and the grey-black of the clouds. A shaft of golden sunlight speared across the walls of Nob.

A Levite stood in the shadow of the gates, staring in wonder at the Flame, his trumpet held loosely in his hands. The shine of dawn glowed off the Altar's burnished surface, wet and gleaming from the rain, reflecting yellow light onto the man's face. Samuel rushed toward him. "Blow your trumpet! Blow! A new day has dawned in Israel!"

The Levite looked at him for only a moment, then, turning, lifted his silver trumpet and blew a single, piercing note, and its sound echoed off the walls all around them, echoed from the hills beyond the walls, echoed from the highlands of the Shephelah all across the brightening land. For a moment, the entire city stopped and turned, listening to the sound of that paean of hope singing its way into every anxious heart.

The courtyard blurred in Samuel's vision, but he did not brush the tears away.

What he needed to see could not be found by his eyes.

Eli had been right.

No one could hide the dawn.

52

Manoah wandered from the courtyard down one of Nob's streets, crowded now with people gathering at the sounding of the Levite's horn. For a few moments, he was a fish struggling upstream, brushing shoulders with the flow of excited Israelites passing him on their way to the gates. Women and children hung their heads out second-story windows or leaned over the edge of roof parapets, calling out, trying to learn the meaning of the commotion. Everywhere Manoah looked, he saw people, but he had never felt more alone.

Saphold's death had affected him in ways he could never have imagined. He was haunted by the memory of the giant standing, arms spread wide, the Rephaim champion's sword buried in his massive chest. Saphold had made no effort to defend himself—unlike every other time that the giant had come up against warriors from his people. "Jehovah has saved you," Saphold had said. The words played themselves over and over again in Manoah's memory, and yet he was no closer to making sense of them.

The answer to the riddle hovered somewhere in his mind, just beyond his ability to grasp it. His thoughts were crowded with so many other emotions and memories he could not sort them out. He wanted to go somewhere quiet, away from the press of people that surrounded him, somewhere he could sit, holding Naamah in his arms, and think…

At the thought of his wife, the ache of his loneliness increased abruptly into a physical pain that tightened his throat and chest until it was difficult to breathe. He stumbled sideways on the road and slumped against the damp, packed-earth wall of a building. He could feel the chill of the moisture absorbed by the wall during last night's rains soaking through the shoulder of his tunic.

He did not even know where to begin looking for her. Was she still at, or near, Aijalon? Had she fled south and east, as so many had, and come to Shiloh? Had she been in the city when it was attacked? Or had she fled with others farther south, into Judah's territory?

Standing still exacerbated his anxiety, and so he pushed away from the wall and let his feet carry him deeper into the city, escaping the crowds and walking with long strides down the muddied roads. On either side of him, houses loomed over their packed-earth walls; women labored atop the flat roofs, patching damage done by the previous night's downpour. He passed the houses without looking up, just listening to the women's voices and the gentle sounds of their work. He found comfort in walking away from the hubbub at the gate, concentrating on the rhythm of his own footsteps and the way the gates of the houses slipped past him on either side as he walked, a slow, steady measure of his progress.

"Jehovah has saved you," Saphold had said. His last words had been a statement of his newfound faith in the True God. The scene played itself out in Manoah's mind: the fall of Arod, the knowledge that they were being overwhelmed by Phicol and the Gedhudhra, the thundering wave of approaching Rephaim warriors, the sudden confrontation with Saphold...

And, abruptly, he understood.

Saphold had seen immediately what Manoah had missed: that the Rephaim had come, for some reason Manoah could not fathom, to *stop* Phicol and the Gedhudhra, not to aid them. But when they had seen Saphold, their mission had taken second place to their ancient traditions—namely, their imperative to challenge this warrior whom they had banished from their tribe. Saphold had realized that if he had fought the champion who stood against him, then while that battle raged, the Gedhudhra would likely have defeated the Israelites. At the least, Manoah and many of his countrymen would have died while the Rephaim set their primary mission aside to fulfill the dictates of their ancient traditions.

Saphold had known that every moment that passed while he defended himself against his giant countrymen would cost the lives of Israelites—and would, possibly, have meant the destruction of High Priest Ahitub, the Prophet Samuel, and the Altar—and even the Eternal Flame.

The Rephaim had sacrificed himself to save that which made up the people of Israel.

Manoah suddenly remembered the night before the battle of Aphek, sitting in the darkness next to a small fire talking about the kind of God Jehovah was. In his mind, Manoah heard his own words to the Rephaim: *"For the sake of His great name, and for the sake of His purposes, I will give my life. His purpose is served by our living, but if it is necessary for me to die to secure that purpose for others, then I will gladly do so."*

His sadness deepened, thinking that his words could have been, indirectly, the cause of the giant's death. Yet how could he mourn such a sacrifice? Would he not have done the same, were he in Saphold's place? Would he not have done so gladly just days before, longing for a noble death that would free him from the burden of his childlessness, of Naamah's pain?

But those thoughts were anathema to him now. Memories of his wife conjured longing, and loneliness, and a love so deep that it breathed hollowness through his soul. He could not lose her. If his journey was ever to end, that end had to be with Naamah.

He pictured her in his mind: the way her black curls framed her face, the shocking beauty of her wide, intense eyes. In his memory, those eyes were wet with emotion and her wide, full lips sharply down-turned. For so long she had lived with loss and disappointment. He tried to picture her smiling and could not, and the failure opened a great chasm deep within him.

He sensed, rather than heard, a movement behind him and turned to find Elon-tohr following him.

The grey-clad warrior stared at him a moment, and Manoah saw something akin to sadness in his eyes, a pathos that he had not seen in the warrior since the night they had spoken in the Forest of Hereth. "Come with me," Elon-tohr said.

Manoah was about to question the command, but the Zebulunite was already gliding swiftly up the street. Manoah hurried after him, and they wound through several alleys, making their way across the hill on which Nob was built.

"Where are we going?" Manoah asked once, but Elon-tohr only glanced silently over his shoulder.

They stopped next to a wooden gate in a packed-earth wall surrounding the courtyard of a simple home. Manoah scanned the courtyard, and the street, looking for the reason Elon had led him to this particular home.

"I told you that I had a wife once," the grey-clad warrior said, almost in a whisper. Once again, his head was lowered, like a man ashamed but angry at being so.

Manoah nodded.

"Of all the losses I have suffered—friends and relatives fallen in battle, fathers and grandfathers slipped away in death, neighbors and countrymen succumbing to disease—of all the losses I have suffered, the loss of my wife is the one I have never recovered from."

Manoah's mind raced, trying to puzzle out what the Zebulunite was trying to tell him. "Are you afraid I have lost my wife?"

"I am afraid, unless you decide otherwise today, she may have lost you."

Elon-tohr bowed, then turned and disappeared without another word down a nearby alley. Manoah was left standing alone, wondering at the warrior's words, but unable to convince himself that he did not understand them. He had wondered many times why the Zebulunite had remained so close to him throughout both battles and the journeys before and afterward. He had even considered asking him about it but could never find the words. He had contented himself with silent gratitude for Elon-tohr's presence, deciding to accept it as a blessing without searching too hard for an explanation.

But the enigmatic warrior had seen him and Naamah together at Gibbethon and in the days after. He had somehow become aware of the tension between them and in his own way determined to see both of them through it.

Manoah turned toward the house he stood in front of, wondering why the Zebulunite had brought him there. Then the gate swung into the road right in front of him. Two women burst through it, cradling baskets of food—bread, date cakes, dried fruit—in their arms. They stopped in surprise when they saw Manoah standing there, and he met the eyes of the woman closest to him, just an arm's length away.

It was Naamah.

It was impossible, but there she was, standing, flushed and beautiful, her eyes wide with surprise at seeing him, and...

She was smiling. That smile, perfect and beautiful, filled a hollow space in his recollection, and suddenly he found his memory of the joy that had been theirs for the first years of their marriage. It flooded back over him with such power that he felt light-headed; he reached out and grasped the opened gate to keep from falling over.

He hesitated only a moment, then wrapped his arms around her so abruptly she dropped the basket she was carrying, scattering fruit and loaves of bread into the dust at their feet. He held her against him so tightly that he could feel every curve of her body pressed against his own. Her arms wrapped around him, and she squeezed him tightly back.

"I was so afraid I had lost you," she whispered into his ear.

"You almost had," he whispered back. "But you will never lose me again."

53

Months later, the arguing in Philistia was over. The nation was all but broken, thousands upon thousands dead from the scourge that had swept their territory in the Ark's wake, their grain stores destroyed by jerboas, their spirit shattered.

In the end, they had no choices left. Sihphil and other priests had danced and prayed and slashed themselves until several of them had died, either from plague or blood loss.

Some among the Axis Lords stubbornly resisted the course of action the others proposed. Lord Gaza in particular, his territory least affected by the plagues, tried to reason with his fellow leaders. "My priests tell me that the gods, at certain revolutions of time, engage in great conflicts which we mortals are unable to witness. The powers released by these struggles can produce mutations in the bodies of men and of animals, in the soil of the earth, and in all things that grow in that soil. It is their opinion that we are experiencing just such a time."

A group of Elders was assembled, among them priests, chanters, diviners, and mages of all kinds—those who had been assigned to learn, by whatever means, the proper procedure for returning the Ark to the land of the Hebrews. Presiding was an ancient, wrinkled priest by the name of Gahan.

"The god of the Hebrews is a god who demands sacrifices of apology," Gahan said, "and offerings to soften his face. Unless we return the Ark with such an offering, his hand will not turn away from us."

"What kind of offering are you talking about?" Lord Eglon asked.

Gahan looked at him gravely. "It must correspond to the guilt of the five Axis Lords in taking this Ark from the Hebrews."

"Guilt!" Lord Gaza looked as if he would have struck the man, but he did not have the strength to raise himself from his chair. "How dare you talk of guilt! This man should be flayed alive!"

"You may do as you wish to me," the old man responded calmly. "But unless you heed the words of this counsel, the plagues will continue until all Philistia lies in ruins, its cities emptied, and its fields destroyed."

The room quieted again. Gahan continued, "Some of us still remember the ancient traditions of our people from our days on Caphtor. Many lifetimes ago, we suffered a plague brought on by angering a foreign god. The priests of Caphtor used a sacred ritual to appease that god. I suggest we do the same.

"We must, therefore, fashion five golden piles and five golden jerboas," Gahan continued. "These will demonstrate our acknowledgement of the power this god has shown over us. We must send them with the Ark back to the land of the Hebrews."

Lord Eglon spat on the tiled floor in disgust. "Are the Axis Lords of Philistia truly to make ourselves servants to this rabble? Our people wrested this land from the inhabitants with our swords! The gods of the land accepted our worship, and none has ever driven us out because Dagon and Ashtoreth, Baal and Ashdod, Anath and Mot are with us! Our gods will bring us victory over this kingless mob!"

Argument broke out in the room again; many of the young men there agreed with Eglon. After a moment, Gahan raised his voice above the din. "Men! Men! These plagues are the work of their god, Jehovah! Have you so quickly forgotten what he did to mighty Egypt? Will you be unresponsive to his plagues, as Pharaoh was, only to have his entire country destroyed, his firstborn annihilated, his army washed up lifeless on the shore of the Red Sea?"

The room quieted; they had not forgotten. "Remember," Gahan continued, "once the Hebrews left Egypt, the plagues upon that country stopped. Likewise, when the Ark is returned to Israel—with the proper offerings—their god's hand will lighten against us."

Lord Gath sat almost upright on his divan, his bushy red beard fanned out across his barrel chest. He had such large bags under his pale, green eyes that they quivered as he spoke. "What is the procedure, priests, if we do as Gahan advises? We cannot march these offerings to their temple in Shiloh. How will we present them to their god?"

The chief priest from Gaza bobbed his head in acknowledgment. "We have discussed this and consulted our ancestors with sacred rites. We must put our offering into a box and place it and the Ark onto a new wagon. We must hitch two cows that have never been put in a yoke before onto this wagon, and lead it to the edge of the territory of the Hebrews."

Lord Ashkelon cleared his throat. "If this god is truly the one responsible for our woes, he will also respond to our efforts to return his Ark. Let us use this opportunity to make a test of this. Choose for the wagon two cows that are giving suck to new calves and separate them from their young. Then hitch them to the wagon and see where they go. If they begin to lead the wagon north, towards Beth-shemesh, into the territory of the Hebrews, then we will know it is this Jehovah who leads them, and it was he who caused us all this calamity. But if they wander elsewhere, or if they return to their calves, then we will accept that these events have been part of the normal cycle of nature and the struggles of the gods."

Sarnam scanned the room; there were no more arguments. He was not surprised: with the priests and the wise men ready to back the plan, the other Axis Lords were unlikely to disagree. For two of them, he suspected, anything that got the Ark out of Philistia was acceptable—and the more quickly it happened, the better.

Craftsmen, carpenters, and goldsmiths were found, and a wagon was quickly constructed. The goldsmiths made wax figurines of their bulbous piles and of the jerboas, poised on their hind legs as if ready to jump. These wax images were gently packed in clean, new clay with a single, hollow tube, made from a dried reed, leading from the top of the image to outside the clay mold. After the clay had dried, the mold was turned upside down over the coals of a wood fire, and the wax within melted and dripped out of the reed tube. When all the wax had been melted, the molds were righted and molten gold was carefully poured into the tubes. In a few moments, it had hardened, and the clay was broken and rinsed away. An hour of polishing with handfuls of fine sand and horsetail stalks left them with ten gleaming images.

These they loaded into a box and placed it onto the wagon. Fetching two cows, their udders heavy with milk, they led them, lowing mournfully, away from their bleating calves. The cows, not unexpectedly, resisted the men bringing them; they nearly had to drag them away from their young. But as soon as they were hitched to the wagon by yoke, they lowered their heads and began to rush forward headlong, following the broad road as it led them east, toward Israel, lowing as they went.

Israel received their Ark back, but it was not the end of the matter for Sarnam. When the delegation that followed the wagon returned to Philistia and reported on its reception, the Axis Lords summoned him to face them in the court of Ekron.

"Our priests, necromancers, and diviners are all in agreement," Lord Ekron pronounced, speaking for the Axis Lords. "Our suffering began when you arrived. Many signs that the gods are displeased with us have marked your presence here. Thus do the Axis Lords of Philistia declare:

You are hereby banished from Philistia."

Sarnam could do nothing. His Gedhudhra would have fought for him, if he ordered them to. But a civil war against all the armies of Philistia was not what he wanted.

"I will go," Sarnam conceded. "But I will return. Remnants of our armies are still scattered throughout Egypt and Libya. I will collect them from wherever they may be found. And when I return, you will welcome me back, and we will ride together against the Hebrews, and this time, they will fall to our swords."

"Do not try to dictate to Philistia what we will do," said Lord Gaza. "You are no longer an Axis Lord."

By the time the sun rose in clear skies the next morning, Sarnam, Sihphil, Phicol, and the Gedhudhra were once again on their ships in the harbor of Ashkelon. Watched by a grim army stretched along the beach, they rowed out of the harbor and then unfurled their sails to catch the wind that sprang up as the sunshine warmed the air. With no fanfare—no trumpets blown, no drums pounded, Sarnam the one-time Lord of Ashkelon and his army sailed onto the waves of the Great Sea. From the perspective of those watching on shore, they slowly shrank in size, until they disappeared into the horizon line far to the west.

54

On the tenth of the month of Ethanim, in late summer of the year following the destruction of Shiloh, Ahitub presided over Israel's celebration of the Day of Atonement.

It was not done at Nob. When the Philistines returned the Ark of the Covenant, it arrived on a new wagon, pulled by two young cows and accompanied by an assortment of unusual, golden figurines. The cows stopped their journey, seemingly of their own volition, in the field of a Priest named Joshua outside the walls of the city of Beth-shemesh, in the territory of the tribe of Benjamin.

Some of the inhabitants of the city chose to ignore the commandment forbidding any to look upon the uncovered Ark, and seventy people were instantly struck dead for their presumptuousness. After that, the citizens of Beth-shemesh begged Samuel and Ahitub to have the Ark removed from their territory.

After a lengthy and volatile assembly of Priests and tribal chiefs was convened, the decision was made to allow the Ark to remain in the territory of the tribe of Benjamin. It was to Benjamin that Jehovah had delivered the Ark, and so, at least until the Tabernacle was reconstructed, it was decided that the Ark should remain in Benjamin's land.

In harmony with the assembly's decision, a procession of Priests and Levites transported it to the nearby city of Kiriath-jearim, the nearest fortified hill-town, safely away from the Philistine plain and the borderlands of the Shephelah. There, the Priests deposited it in a room owned by a righteous, old man by the name of Abinadab. Ahitub sanctified Abinadab's firstborn son, Eleazar, to guard and watch over the Ark, and Eleazar's brothers, Uzzah and Ahio, were assigned to assist him.

So it was that, in the rolling around of the year, when the Day of Atonement once more drew near, Jehovah came again to Samuel in the night and instructed him that the ceremony was to be performed, not at the Tabernacle's construction site at Nob, but at Kiriath-jearim, in the courtyard of the home of Abinadab. Ahitub, along with the rest of the Priests and Levites, once more bore the Altar of Burnt Offering and its Eternal Flame across Israel and set it up temporarily in the courtyard.

The entire nation appeared to be gathered in the valley that spread before the hill upon which the city sat, many of them already living in the tents that the people would be required to inhabit for the weeklong Festival of Booths that followed the Day of Atonement. Princes, Chieftains and family heads were summoned into the city itself to watch as High Priest Ahitub slaughtered bull and goat, and ceremoniously carried the blood through the heavy screen that hung over the door into the room that now served as the Holy of Holies.

Samuel, watching every movement from the courtyard where the Altar of Burnt Offering had been erected, wondered what Ahitub would find when he entered that sacred room. Would Jehovah, in effect, have taken up residence there? Would the *Shekinah* be shining over the arched wings of the cherubs poised atop the Ark's golden lid?

When Ahitub emerged, Samuel saw the wonder in the High Priest's widened pupils, the awe that quickened his breathing and spread goose bumps across his arms and scalp. Ahitub did not speak, but there was no doubt in anyone's mind what he had seen within the Holy.

The *Shekinah* was burning once again.

The rest of the ceremony passed for Samuel in a blur. When a chosen man left Kiriath-jearim, leading the goat for *Azazel* down the long road, lined on either side by tens of thousands of hushed observers, Samuel felt a palpable sense of relief at the realization that the sins of his entire nation were being carried away in Jehovah's eyes. This Day of Atonement, freed from the corruption of Eli's sons, fulfilled the longings felt by the people of the nation for years. It was, truly, a fresh start for Israel.

Tirzah led the Women's Corps in a rousing chorus as the music of the orchestra swelled. Samuel let his eyes play over the crowd, finding his own feelings reflected in the faces of those watching. Elon-tohr, Manoah, and Naamah stood near each other, and Manoah's arms were wrapped tightly around his wife's shoulders; both were smiling. Even the haunted, grey-clad Zebulunite seemed more at peace than Samuel had ever seen him.

Not far from them, on the other side of the road, a group of Elders including Lodan the Issacharian, the lanky Benjaminite Basar, and the wild-haired Gadite, Arod. Arod's grin was so wide it made Samuel want to laugh out loud.

When Ahitub had placed the final offering of the ceremony on the Altar grating, a man eased his way through the crowd to Samuel's side. Samuel turned and found himself staring into a pair of piercing, blue eyes, as bright and sharp as a bird's.

It was Rohgah.

"Well, Prophet of Israel," he said to Samuel, his eyes sparkling. "What will you do now?"

Samuel smiled, remembering the last time Rohgah had asked him that question—it seemed as though an age had passed since then. He looked around at the Priests and Levites serving under Ahitub, at the sense of unity, purpose, and faith that Jehovah had restored to Israel. A High Priest whose heart was fully toward Jehovah was once again leading the people in true worship. The Tabernacle would be rebuilt, to become, as it had been for so many years in the past, the heart and soul of the nation.

"I will go home," Samuel said at last. "I think that my work is done at Nob."

"And what waits for you at home?" Rohgah asked.

Samuel smiled crookedly. "Houses to be restored. Lives to be rebuilt. My family, and the people of Ramathaim, will need all the help they can get to remake what the Philistines destroyed."

"And then?" Rohgah pressed, sensing there was more.

Samuel looked over the fields spread out below the city, visible through the gate of Abinadab's courtyard. The last grain harvest had already been brought in for the year—a good harvest, and the storehouse s were stuffed with barley and wheat. Bordering the fields, olive, fig, and date trees still sagged under the weight of their crop, as if to make up for the year before, and fat cattle and sheep wandered in the shade of their branches. "Someone must go out into the land," Samuel answered finally. "Someone must travel throughout Israel, to see the truth of what we have become, to find that which still ails us as a people, and to heal it."

Rohgah nodded slowly, but his bright eyes never left Samuel's own. "And what of your assignment from Eli, as the Gate-opener of the House of God?"

Samuel looked at the old man in silence for a moment, and something more than words passed between them, a sense of their place in Jehovah's arrangement, an understanding shared by two vastly different people who had both heard the Voice of the True God.

Samuel knew the answer Rohgah was waiting for. And it was the only answer Samuel could give. "That gate is open, my lord. It will not be closed again while I live."

Rohgah's smile deepened the wrinkles etched around his eyes and mouth. "Then you have, indeed, learned to see at last."

Only a few paces away, Ahitub spread his arms wide above his head, standing between the gathered watchers and the Altar's Flame. Samuel and Rohgah turned to watch as the High Priest of Israel, outlined by the roaring flames and whirling smoke spiraling behind him, pronounced the Benediction on the cleansed nation. "May Jehovah bless you and keep you. May Jehovah make His face shine toward you, and may He favor you. May Jehovah lift up His face toward you, and assign peace to you."

And Samuel and Rohgah faced each other again, and along with the thousands of Israelites gathered in and out of the city, chanted the *Shema* with one voice: "Jehovah our God is One."

The Appendices

Appendix A: **Glossary of People, Places, and Things**

Appendix B: **Bibliography**

Appendix C: **The Two Eternal Thrones**

Appendix D: **In Defense of Artistic License:**
On Decisions Made by the Author in Matters On Which the Holy Scriptures are Silent or Unclear, Conflict with Jewish Tradition, or reflect authorial suppositions and deductions

Appendix E: **Chronology**

APPENDIX A:
GLOSSARY OF PEOPLE, PLACES, AND THINGS

Aaron	First High Priest of Israel; brother of the prophet Moses
Abihu	Son of the first Israelite High Priest, Aaron. Abihu and his brother, Nadab, were executed by Jehovah for disrespecting their office
Abinadab	A holy man of Kiriath-jearim in whose home the Ark of the Covenant was kept following its return from Philistia; his sons were Eleazar, Uzzah, and Ahio
Abraham	Patriarch and forefather of Israel and all other Semitic peoples
Ahimelech	Firstborn son of Ahitub, and grandson of Phinehas
Ahio	One of the sons of Abinadab of Kiriath-jearim, who assisted in caring for the Ark of the Covenant after it was moved to their home
Ahitub	Firstborn son of Phinehas, son of Eli
Aijalon	Valley and fortified city in mountains of Judah; site of Joshua's famous victory during which the sun stood still over Gibeon
Almodad	Father of the Prophet Rohgah
Ammonites	An exceptionally fierce, cruel people whose lands bordered Israel to the east, and who warred with Israel in the days of Judge Jephthah
Amorites	Hamitic people inhabiting Canaan prior to Israel's conquest of the land; ruled by the kings of Og and Sihon, east of the Jordan
Anat	Canaanite goddess; Baal's sister, daughter of El/Dagon, goddess of war, the hunt, and savagery; known for her cruelty and bloodlust
Anatolia	Present day Turkey and ancient home of the Hittites
Aphek	Fortified city in Ephraim; site of two battles with the Philistines and the capture of the Ark of the Covenant
Aram	Syria, bounded on the East by Mesopotamia, to the West by the mountains of Lebanon, on the north by the Taurus mountains, and on the south by Palestine and the Arabian desert
Ark of the Covenant	The sacred, gold-plated, acacia chest located in the Holy of Holies of the Tabernacle and associated with God's presence
Arod	Gadite military commander
Ashdod	One of the cities of the Philistine pentapolis; the religious center of the nation and worship of Dagon
Asher/Asherites	One of the twelve tribes of Israel
Ashkelon	One of the cities of the Philistine pentapolis, and their most important port on the Great Sea
Ashnah	Father of the Danite prince, Manoah
Ashtoreth	Canaanite goddess; the wife of Baal; goddess of war, the hunt, sex, and fertility; often portrayed as a nude female with rudely exaggerated sex organs
Assinu priests	Homosexual priests of Canaan who performed or presided over aspects of sex worship in the rituals of Canaanite religion

aurochs	Extraordinarily giant bull, now extinct, but once known from India to Britain for its size, intractability and power
Axis Lord	Translation from a Philistine loanword *seranim*, which seems to combine the word for "prince" with the consonants of the word for "axles"; One of the five principal rulers of the Philistine nation in Canaan
Azazel	"The Goat that Disappears" or the scapegoat; a goat used in Israel's Atonement Day ceremony to symbolically carry away the sins of Israel into the wilderness
Azor	Judean prince and commander of Israel's armies at the battle of Aphek
Baal	Dagon's son, "Prince of the Earth"; god of fertility, lightning, and thunder; often portrayed bearing a lightning bolt, his chosen weapon, and wearing a horned helmet, showing his connection with the bull, a fertility symbol. The god Mot's annual victory over Baal was believed to bring on the dry season; Baal's liberation and his mating with his wife, Ashtoreth, were believed to result in the coming of the rain and to ensure fertility in the coming year. Baal was the primary deity of Canaan
Baal-zebub	"Lord of the Flies"; the Baal worshipped by the Philistines at Ekron. The stone idol of Baal may have been smeared with animal dung and the buzzing of the flies this drew interpreted by priests
Babylon	A mighty city and kingdom of Mesopotamia, built along the great river Euphrates in present-day Iraq
Baru-priest	Canaanite diviner, seer and interpreter of omens and signs, including oil on water, smoke of incense, casting of dice, livers of sacrificial animals, flight of birds, stars
Basar	Benjaminite military commander
Bashan	Forested region in the north of Israel near the Sea of Galilee; traditional territory of the Rephaim
Benarza	Conductor of the sacred orchestra and singers at the Tabernacle in Shiloh
Benjamin	One of the twelve tribes of Israel, known for their skill as slingers, archers, and shepherds
Beth-horon	Two towns, Upper & Lower Beth-horon, built on hill-tops along the ancient route from the maritime plain over the Shephelah through the Valley of Aijalon to key inland cities of Israel
Beth-shemesh	A priest's city on the northern boundary of Judah's territory
Canaan	The Promised Land, the Levant; the land given to Israel by Jehovah, running from Dan on the border of Lebanon in the north to Beersheba in the south, and bordered on the west by the Great Sea and on the east by the Arabian desert
Caphtor	Ancient name for the island of Crete, whence the Philistines emigrated
Chanter	Canaanite psalmist or sacred poet who chanted or sang the myths during rituals, to invoke the help of the gods and remind them of their abilities and previous assistance to mankind
Chaser & Driver	Magical swords of Baal, forged for him by the smith-god Chuosor
Chousor	Canaanite craftsman/smith god also called Kothar-and-Khasis (skillful and clever); identified with Ea or Ptah of Egypt and with the city of Memphis
Dagon	Also called El; "Creator of Creatures", and "Father of Mankind"; grey-bearded, drunkard lord and father of all other Canaanite gods, the god of wheat, inventor of the plow; depicted as having a human torso, head, and arms but with the body and tail of a fish
Dan/Danites	One of the twelve tribes of Israel, primarily composed of shepherds and herdsmen who serve as the traditional rearguard of Israel's army
Day of Atonement	The most important of Israel's holidays, celebrated on the 10th of Ethanim with several sacrifices, and climaxed by the High Priest's once-annual entry

	into the Holy of Holies to sprinkle the blood of sacrifice before the Ark of the Covenant; the ceremony concluded with a "goat for *Azazel*" being led into the wilderness to die, metaphorically carrying away Israel's sins of the past year with it
Dead Sea	Terminus of the Jordan River in Canaan; also known as the Salt Sea; devoid of life due to high concentrations of mineral salts
Deker	Ephraimite commander of Israel's military forces
Edom/Edomites	A land east of Canaan inhabited by the descendants of Esau, Jacob ben Isaac's brother. A long-standing enmity existed between the Edomites and the Israelites
Ekron	The northernmost city of the Philistine pentapolis
Eleazar	Third son of Israel's first High Priest, Aaron; Eleazar became High Priest himself just before the Israelite conquest of the Promised Land began
Eleazar, 2	Firstborn son of Abinadab of Kiriath-jearim, who was anointed to watch over the Ark of the Covenant after it was moved to that city
Eliab	Young Levite serving at the Tabernacle in Samuel's day
Elkanah	Father of the child-prophet, Samuel, and husband of Hannah and Peninnah
Elon-tohr	Zebulunite warrior reputed to be more skilled in battle than any man living at the time of the battle of Aphek
Enlil	Father of the Judean Prince, Azor
Ephod	An apron-like priestly garment with a belt, or girdle
Ephraim	One of the twelve tribes of Israel
Forest of Ephraim	A dense and deadly forest east of the Jordan, near Mahanaim
Forest of Hereth	A forestland in Judah
Gad/Gadites	One of the twelve tribes of Israel
Galilee	A mountainous region of Naphtali and including the territory of Zebulun, known for its abundant springs, fertile soil, variety of crops and trees
Gath	One of the cities of the Philistine pentapolis, located east of the Philistine plain
Gaza	One of the cities of the Philistine pentapolis, Gaza was the location of a famous temple of Dagon
Geshur/Geshurites	An Aramaen kingdom bordering on the Argob region of Bashan, east of the Jordan
Gezer	A Kohathite Levite city on the Palestinian coastal plain
Gibbethon	A Levite city in the territory of the tribe of Dan, located on the edge of Philistia
Gibeonite	Proselytes to Judaism from the city of Gibeon who were responsible for gathering the wood and water used for sacrifices at the Tabernacle
Gilead	Mountainous region in Israel located east of the Jordan and north of the River Jabbok
Great Sea	The Mediterranean
Gudhudhra	The death-troops of Sarnam, Axis Lord of Ashkelon; trained in the long war against Egypt, then chosen for their unquestioning loyalty and fierceness in battle
Gundar	A Rephaim commander
Hannah	Mother of the child-prophet Samuel and wife of the Levite, Elkanah
Hazor	A major city in northern Canaan
Heber	Brother of the Danite prince Manoah and husband of Leah
Hittites	A Hamitic people descended from Heth, who inhabited the mountainous regions of present-day Lebanon, Syria, and Turkey, and were famous for their production of iron and exceptional chariots
Holy	The primary, and larger, room within the Tabernacle, containing the golden

	Altar of Incense, the Table of Showbread, and the Menorah
Holy of Holies	Also called the Most Holy; the secondary and smaller room within the Tabernacle, a perfect cube containing only the Ark of the Covenant with the supernatural *Shekinah* light shining miraculously above it; the Most Holy could be entered only once per year, during the Day of Atonement, by the High Priest
Hophni	Second son of High Priest, Eli, and brother of Phinehas
Horus	A member of Egypt's most popular triad of gods, along with Isis and Osiris; Horus was a falcon-headed sun-god
Ichabod	Youngest son of Phinehas and his wife Mara; Mara died giving birth to him
Ileah	Wife of the Judean commander, Azor
Imri	Prince of Judah and commander of Israel's armies at the second battle of Aphek
Isaac	Son of Abraham and a patriarch of the nation of Israel; father of Jacob, who was renamed Israel
Isis	A member of Egypt's most popular triad of gods, along with her consort Osiris and her son, Horus; she is credited with healing abilities
Issachar	One of the twelve tribes of Israel
Ithamar	One of the sons of Israel's original High Priest, Aaron, from whom the Priests of Israel descended
Jabne'el	A Judean city located near Israel's border with Philistia
Jacob	Also known as Israel; Patriarch of Israel, son of Isaac and grandson of Abraham
Jebusites	A mountain-dwelling Canaanite people who held the city of Jerusalem in Samuel's day
Jericho	One of the most ancient Canaanite cities and the first one conquered by the Israelites under Joshua
Jeroham	Father of Elkanah and grandfather of Samuel
Jonathan	A young man who became a priest to the tribe of Dan
Joppa	An ancient seaport of Canaan located in the northern part of the territory of Dan
Jordan River	The main river of Canaan and the natural division between East and West Canaan; it drains Hula lake, flows through the Sea of Galilee and terminates in the Dead Sea
Joshua	The leader of Israel and General of its armies during its conquest of the Promised Land
Judah	The largest of the twelve tribes of Israel
Judea	A territory of the land of Israel south of Samaria, north of Idumea, west of the Jordan and east of the Shephelah
Judge	Men raised up by Jehovah to lead or deliver His people prior to the period of Israelite kings
Judge Gideon	Judge of Israel who led his people to victory against the Midianites and Amalekites with an army of only 300 men, armed with torches, horns, and water jars
Judge Jephthah	Judge of Israel in the days of Samuel's childhood; he led the Israelites to victory against the Ammonites and sent his only daughter, Tirzah, to serve in the Tabernacle
Kenites	A semi-nomadic people known for their metal-working skills who were hired by the Egyptians to work their mines
Kiriath-jearim	A hilltop city in the territory of the tribe of Judah to which the Ark of the Covenant was taken following the Battle of Aphek and the sack of Shiloh
Kohathite Levites	Descendants of the family head Kohath, one of the three sons of Levi. The sons of Kohath (who included Moses and Aaron), were assigned to

	Tabernacle service with the responsibility to transport the Ark of the Covenant, the screen that shielded the Most Holy from view, the Table of Showbread, the Menorah, the Altars, and the utensils.
Korah, sons of	Descendants of the rebellious Israelite prince, Korah, who did not follow their father in his rebellion and later became known for their psalms and musical compositions
Laish	A northern Canaanite city destroyed by the Danites, who later rebuilt it and gave it the name of Dan
Leah	Wife of Heber, sister-in-law of Manoah and Naamah
Lebanon	Region bordering the land of Israel to the north, famous for its lush forests and mountains
Levi/Levite	One of the tribes of Israel. Typically, the term is applied only to the members of the tribe that were not descendants of Aaron (who made up the Priests). Levites served as the assistants to the Priests. They were divided into three families: Gershonite, Kohathite, and Merarite, each with duties exclusive to that family. Most Levites took up their duties at age 25 or 30 and served at the Tabernacle for only a few weeks each year. They were supported by a tithe collected from the other tribes and were exempt from military service (although they were not excluded from the distribution of spoils). They had no territory of their own but rather were given forty-eight cities scattered throughout the Promised Land
Levite cities	Cities distributed throughout Canaan that were given to the members of the tribe of Levi as their own (although, typically, members of the tribe whose territory the city was in resided there as well)
Lod	A city in the territory of Benjamin
Lodan	Military commander of the tribe of Issachar, responsible for military intelligence and strategy
Makkedah	A city in the Shephelah; home of Manoah
Malediction	Collectively, the evils that would result if the nation of Israel rejected Jehovah and the Torah, as outlined at Deuteronomy 28 and other places; contrasted with the Benediction, or blessings that result from obedience
Manasseh	One of the twelve tribes of Israel
Manoah	A prince of Dan, husband of Naamah, and father of the Judge and hero Samson
Mara	Wife of the corrupt Priest Phinehas, mother of Priests Ahitub and Ichabod (whom she died giving birth to)
Mark of Cain	Metaphoric expression based on Genesis 4:15; likely a well known solemn decree that simultaneously identified Cain as a criminal and protected him from execution for his crimes
Megiddo	A strategically vital city in the Plain of Esdraelon (valley of Megiddo) controlling the major trade and military routes that intersected there. Site of many decisive battles and assigned to the tribe of Manasseh, who conquered the city and put the Canaanite inhabitants to forced labor
Melachashim	Canaanite sorcerer-priests who whispered or hissed to cause or avert evil or sickness
Micah	A man of Ephraim who installed a Gershonite Levite as a priest for his household; this led to the line of "Danite priests"
Midianites	A people descended from Abraham's son Midian; they became nomadic tent-dwellers who oppressed Israel at various times in history
Mizpah	A city in the territory of Benjamin
Moses	Ancient leader of the nation of Israel; mediator and recorder of the Torah, greatest of Israelite prophets

Most Holy	*See* Holy of Holies
Mot	Canaanite god of death, dissolution, evil, sterility and the Underworld. Sits on a pit for a throne in the city of Miry in the Underworld, holding a scepter of bereavement and a scepter of widowhood. His jaws and throat are of cosmic proportions. Canaanites believed the waxing of his power brought on the dry season
Mycenae	Greece
Naamah	Wife of Manoah of Dan and mother of Judge Samson
Nadab	Firstborn son of High Priest Aaron, who was executed by Jehovah for offering illegitimate fire
Naphtali	One of the twelve tribes of Israel
Nazirite	One who has been set apart for special service by a vow, either their own or that of their parents before their birth. Nazirites could partake of no products of the vine, could not touch a dead body, and were forbidden from cutting their hair for as long as their vow was in force
Noalah	Concubine of the Judean Prince Azor
Nob	City in the Jordan Valley in the territory of Judah, south of Jerusalem, to which the Tabernacle was moved following the Battle of Aphek and the sack of Shiloh
Og of Bashan	A famous Amorite king of the Rephaim in Bashan, a giant whose sarcophagus was 13.1 by 5.8 feet
Peninnah	Second wife of Elkanah, the Levite of Ramathaim
Phicol	Philistine captain under Sarnam; leader of the famed Gedhudhra
Philistia	Region of Canaan along the coast of the Mediterranean south of the Sorek river, comprised of very fertile plains, wide, sandy beaches, and scattered lowland forests
Phinehas	Firstborn son of High Priest Eli, husband of Mara, and father of Ahitub and Ichabod
Phinehas, 2	Anciently, the son of Eleazar, a High Priest famous in Israelite history for his zeal for pure worship
Phoenicia	Country along the Mediterranean coast between Israel and Syria and bordered to the east by Lebanon. The people of Phoenicia were the greatest mariners of the Middle East
Priests of Dan	Group of Priests falsely claiming to lead the tribe of Dan in worship of Jehovah, but in fact acting in opposition to and in competition with the true Priesthood in Shiloh
Prince Resheph	Canaanite god of pestilence
Ptah	*See* Chousor
Pugnit	A Philistine Axis Lord of the city of Ashkelon
Ra	Egyptian sun-god
Rabbah	Capital city of the nation of Ammon
Ramathaim	Home town of the Prophet Samuel and his parents, located in the mountains of the territory of Ephraim and later known as Arimathea
Rameses	Traditional name of a family of Pharoahs of Egypt
Rephaim	A race of giants who once inhabited portions of Canaan, in particular Bashan and the forests of Ephraim
Reuben	One of the twelve tribes of Israel
Rohgah	A prophet in Israel during the days of Jephthah and Samuel
Salt Sea	*See* Dead Sea
Samuel	Son of Elkanah and Hannah and dedicated to Tabernacle service as a Nazirite from before his conception by his mother, Samuel became a prophet at the age of twelve

Saphold	A Rephaim giant banished from his tribe
Sarnam	A Philistine general and veteran of the Philistine wars in Egypt who became the Axis Lord of Ashkelon and led Philistia in their campaign against Israel in the days of Samuel's childhood
Sea of Galilee	A freshwater lake in northern Palestine also known as the Sea of Chinnereth, the Lake of Gennesaret, and the Sea of Tiberias; it is fed primarily by the Jordan River and is the site of a thriving fishing industry
Shapshu	Canaanite sun-goddess who often acts as a messenger for Dagon and has dominion over ghosts. She is said to be under Mot's influence when Baal is preoccupied with his palace and the weather turns hot and dry
Sha'taqat	A flying demoness of the Canaanite pantheon who possesses a wand with magical healing powers
Shekinah	The miraculous, supernatural flame that burned above the lid of the Ark of the Covenant in the Holy of Holies in the Tabernacle and was a symbol of Jehovah's presence with Israel
Shema	Israelite declaration of faith: Hear, O Israel—Jehovah our God is One
Shephelah	A region of low hills situated between the mountains of Judah and the plains of Philistia
Shiloh	Religious capital of Israel; site of the Tabernacle
Sihphil	The Canaanite magician-priest who supports and accompanies Sarnam, Lord of Ashkelon
Simeon/Simeonite	One of the twelve tribes of Israel
Sinnishat zikrum	Literally, "the female male"; lesbian, cross-dressing Canaanite priestesses who served during certain sex-rituals
Tabernacle	The tent of worship that served as a mobile temple for the Israelites during their sojourn in the wilderness and continued that function at various locations until the building of Solomon's temple. It was surrounded by a Courtyard that contained the Copper Basin of washing water for the Priests and the Altar of Burnt Offering; it was divided within into two chambers, the Holy and the Holy of Holies
Tahom	Grain overseer of the Philistine city of Ekron
Teraph	Idols representing family gods
Timnah	A city on the border of Judah and Dan's territories, located along the torrent valley of Sorek
Tirzah	Daughter of Judge Jephthah, dedicated by her father to Tabernacle service; she was honored by all the women of Israel during a special festival held each year
Torah	The Law of Moses, the divine commandments and guidelines given to the nation of Israel by Jehovah through the prophet Moses and which served as the guide for all aspects of life
Troy	Ancient city famously conquered by the Mycanaean Greeks
Tyre	The principal Phoenician seaport, located north of Israel
Ugarit	Major Hittite city destroyed by the Philistines and their allies in the 12th century BCE
Uzzah	A son of Abinadab of Kiriath-jearim, who assisted his father and brothers in caring for the Ark of the Covenant after it was moved to their home
Yamm	Canaanite god of seas and rivers who lives in a palace under the sea, can take the form of a dragon and whose battles are considered responsible for rough winter sea-storms
Yarkon river	A river flowing into the Mediterranean from the Plain of Sharon
Zebulun	One of the twelve tribes of Israel
Zelophehad	A man of the tribe of Manasseh who died leaving only daughters; his

inheritance was divided among his daughters and provided a precedent for future cases under the Mosaic Law

Zorah   A city in the Shephelah inhabited by the tribe of Dan; the birthplace of Judge Samson

APPENDIX B:
BIBLIOGRAPHY

- *A History of Ancient Egypt*, by Nicolas Grimal, 1988; Blackwell
- *All Scripture Is Inspired of God and Beneficial*, Watchtower Bible and Tract Society of Pennsylvania; 1990 Watchtower Bible and Tract Society of New York
- *Ancient Egypt*, General Editor: David P. Silverman;
- *Archaeology of the Bible: Book by Book*, by Gaalyah Cornfeld; David Noel Freedman, Consulting Editor, 1976; Harper & Roe
- *Atlas of Ancient Egypt*, by John Baines & Jaromir Malek, 1980; Les Livres De France
- *Battles of the Bible*, Chaim Herzog and Mordechai Gichon; 1997 Greenhill books, Lionel Leventhal Limited
- *Bible Almanac*, Edited by James I. Packer, Merrill C. Tenney, William White, Jr.; Thomas Nelson Publishers, 1980
- *Canaanite Myths and Legends*, by John C. Gibson, T. & T. Clark Publishers, 2004
- *Dictionary of Deities and Demons in the Bible*. K. van der Toorn, B. Becking, P. W. van der Horst, editors. William B. Eerdmans Publishing Company. Grand Rapids, Michigan. 1999.
- Essays On Geology Cowen, Richard (for his upcoming book "Exploiting the Earth" John Hopkins University Press) ; available for viewing at www.geology.ucdavis.edu/~cowen/~GEL115/index.html
- *Everyday Life In Bible Times*, National Geographic Society 1967
- *Geographical Companion to the Bible*, by Denis Baly, McGraw-Hill Book Company, Inc., 1973
- *Great Events of Bible Times*, Doubleday & Company, Inc., Garden City, New York
- *Great People of the Bible and How They Lived*, Principal Adviser and Editorial Consultant G. Ernest White; 1974 The Reader's Digest Association, Inc.
- *I & II Samuel: A Commentary*, Hertzberg, Hans Wilhelm (trans. J.S. Bowden), The Westminster Press, 1964, Philadelphia
- *Insight On The Scriptures*, Watch Tower Bible and Tract Society of Pennsylvania 1988; Watch Tower Bible and Tract Society of New York

- *Middle Eastern Mythology*, by S. H. Hooke, Dover Publications, 2004
- *Nelson's 3-D Bible Mapbook,* Simon Jenkins; 1985 Lion Publishing
- *People of the Sea: The Search for the Philistines,* Dothan, Trude & Dothan, Moshe, Macmillan Publishing Company, 1992, New York
- *See The Good Land*; 2003 Watch Tower Bible and Tract Society of Pennsylvania; Watch Tower Bible and Tract Society of New York
- *The American Heritage Guide to Archaeology*, Warwick Bray and David Trump; 1970 American Heritage Publishing Company
- *The Bible As History,* by Werner Keller, William Morrow and Company, New York, 1956
- *The Complete Temples of Ancient Egypt*, by Richard H. Wilkinson, 2000; Thomas & Hudson, Ltd.
- *The Dictionary of Ancient Egypt*, by Ian Shaw & Paul Nicholson, 1995; Henry N. Adams, Inc., Publishers
- *The Harper Atlas of the Bible*, Times Books Limited, Harper & Row, Publishers, 1987
- *The Historical Geography of the Holy Land*, George Adam Smith, 1894 Hodder & Stoughton, Ltd, London
- *The Holy Land Satellite Atlas*, ROHR Productions
- *The House of David*, by Jerry M. Landay, 1973 by George Weidenfeld and Nicolson; published by Saturday Review Press, E.P. Dutton & Co., Inc., New York
- *The New Bible Dictionary*, Organizing Editor J.D. Douglas; 1979 WM. B. Eerdman's Publishing Co.
- *The New Manners & Customs of Bible Times*, by Ralph Gower, 1987; Moody Press
- *The Oxford Companion to the Bible*, Edited by Bruce M. Metzger and Michael D. Coogan; 1993 Oxford University Press
- *The Oxford History of Ancient Egypt*, by Ian Shaw, 2000; Oxford University Press
- *The Temple*, by A. Edersheim, 1874
- *The Westminster Dictionary of the Bible,* John D. Davis and Henry Snyder Gehman, The Westminster Press, Philadelphia, 1944.
- *The Works of Josephus: New Updated Edition*; Translated by William Whiston, 1987 Hendrickson Publishers, Inc.
- *The Works of Philo Judaeus*, translated by Charles Duke Yonge, London, H.G. Bohn, 1854-1890.
- *The World of the Bible*, Roberta L. Harris; 1995 Thames and Hudson Ltd, London

BIBLE TRANSLATIONS CONSULTED

- *New World Translation of the Holy Scriptures*, Watchtower Bible and Tract Society of New York, Inc., International Bible Students Association, Brooklyn, New York, U.S.A.
- *The David Story*, by Robert Alter, 1999; W.W. Norton & Company, Inc.
- *Good News Bible with Deuterocanonicals and Apocrypha (Today's English Version)*, American Bible Society
- *The Bible in Living English*, translated by Steven Byington, Copyright 1972 by Watch Tower Bible and Tract Society of Pennsylvania; published by Watchtower Bible and Tract Society of New York, Inc., International Bible Students Association, Brooklyn, New York, U.S.A.
- *The King James Version*
- *The New Jerusalem Bible*
- *The Holy Bible, New International Version*, Copyright 1984 by International Bible Society, Colorado Springs, Colorado
- *The Old Testament, Douay Version*, Copyright 1949, Catholic Book Publishing Co., United States and Canada
- *The Holy Bible, New American Standard*, Foundation Publishers, 2005
- *The Holy Bible, the Contemporary English Version*, American Bible Society, 2000
- *The Holy Bible, American Standard Version*, Thomas Nelson and Sons, 1929
- *Young's Literal Translation of the Bible*, Robert Young, Greater Truth Publishers, 2004

APPENDIX C:
THE TWO ETERNAL THRONES

I grew up reading books.

Like most boys, I went through phases in my reading choices: mysteries, adventure novels, historical fiction, fantasy, science fiction, classical literature. But two genres were always present in my life: the Bible and Bible literature, and Arthurian literature, in all its various forms. My religious upbringing and my own convictions explain my continued interest in the Bible, but I have no meaningful explanation for the draw of the legends of Britain's most famous king. Perhaps it was simply a boy's love of adventure, honor, chivalry, and the endless rescuing of fair maidens. Perhaps it was that, even back then, I instinctively sensed what I would consciously discover only years later: that the accounts in the Bible and the famous legends of King Arthur are, in fact, connected.

I am not the first to notice this correlation, but it has received very little attention in our times—a shame, I think, since the last two decades have seen a revival of interest in the Arthurian stories. I have read dozens of novels (and viewed several films) that attempt to present an "historical" version of the tales, setting them in Celtic or Roman Britain, presenting Camelot or Camlann as an early iron-age mud fort and Arturius as a Celtic horse-lord battling the forces of Rome or the tribal disunity that gripped the islands of the United Kingdom in ancient times.

But the true story of the origin of the stories of King Arthur and the Knights of the Round Table—or at least what I am convinced is the true story—is an even more fascinating one. As long ago as the late medieval period, writers and collectors of Arthurian tales recognized—and, likely, augmented—their similarity to a famous period in the history of the ancient nation of Israel.[1]

---

[1] For further information on the subject of this essay, I refer the reader to "The King's Sin: The Origins of the David-Arthur Parallel." By Guerin, M. Victoria. (IN Sharpe, William and Christopher Baswell (eds.)) and *The Passing of Arthur: New Essays in Arthurian Tradition.* (New York: Garland, 1988). and "The Alliterative *Morte Arthure*: The Story of Britain's David." Shoaf, R. A. *Journal of English and Germanic Philology.* Champaign, IL. 1982 Apr., 81:2, 204-226.

The writers and compilers of Arthurian stories had to make the fictional character of Arthur into a real person, a leader worthy of being remembered for thousands of years. This required that he not only inspire loyalty in people who had never met him, but also that he have his flaws, that he be "achievable" as an exemplar for the medieval man. To accomplish this, they fell back upon previously established models of what a great king should be. For the people of the medieval period, and much of the Renaissance, the greatest model of kingship was to be found in the religious traditions in which they had been steeped: in the story of King David of Israel.

David was remembered as the greatest king of Israel, the one who united the twelve-tribe kingdom into the greatest military and social power of its day[2]. David was a pious man, but he was also a sinner. He was chosen by God, but had to fight in order to hold onto his throne. David was the progenitor of the one who would—in the future—save Israel, and the world. David was the ideal model for King Arthur as a military hero-king.

The parallels between David's time and Arthur's were many, even on a socio-political level. Though their reigns took place thousands of years apart, each of them ruled their nation during a time of religious change: David saw Israel make the transition from rule by Judges and Priests to a solidified monarchy, and the transfer of worship rituals from the Tabernacle to the Temple in Jerusalem; Arthur (so the story goes) aided Britain in its (only marginally successful) transition from pagan worship to Christianity. Both of them helped take their nation from a loosely collected, and sometimes violently disunited, group of tribes to a single, united kingdom. Both lived during a time of great technological change, a key chapter in the slow but inexorable switch from the Bronze Age to the Age of Iron, with all the environmental, military, and socio-economic repercussions that accompanied it.

Ancient historians, as I have mentioned, saw these parallels. Geoffrey of Monmouth, one of the most famous Arthurian (pseudo) biographers, stated specifically that he intended to portray Arthur as the one who would make Britain "a new Israel."[3]

Our modern-day versions of the Arthur story are so many and varied and based on such diverse sources that we can hardly look at them as any kind of a unified whole. The reality is that many poets, historians, clerics, bards, and rulers were each putting together their own versions of

---

[2] In 2 Chronicles chapter 34, written around 460 B.C.E., almost six and a half centuries after David's reign, Jehovah is still referred to as "the God of David" (34:3) and David was still the touchstone by which the quality of the kings of Israel were measured (34:2).

[3] Geoffrey of Monmouth's *Historia Regum Britanniae,* 16-21.

the Arthur story at around the same time. Some of them presented themselves as genuine historians; others were more forthright in their admission of literary, rather than historical, aspirations. What resulted was a fascinating jumble of accounts that at times overlap and at times contradict one another. In the late Renaissance, this mass began to be distilled into "official" versions, the most famous of which is probably Sir Thomas Mallory's *Le Morte D'Artur*.

Let us take a look, then, at some of the elements of these "distilled" versions of the story.

Nearly all of them start with Merlin. There is little agreement as to who or what Merlin was, except that he came into his powers at a young age, that he had abilities beyond that of ordinary men (usually including prophetic vision), and that he was responsible in some way for the enthronement of Arthur and, in some versions, Vortigern. He was often known for his biting sarcasm and fearlessness in confronting powerful rulers. He also served as an advisor to the king for many years, and it was after his death that Arthur fell into decline.

All of these salient details fit the Biblical character, Samuel ben Elkanah. He, too, became a prophet at a young age (twelve, according to Josephus)[4], manifested other powers, and was responsible for the enthronement of Saul and David. He is presented in the Scriptures as a person of biting wit, fearless in the face of powerful rulers[5]. He, too, served as an advisor to David until his death, after which David's kingdom began to fall into decline.

Saul and Vortigern present yet another set of parallels. Both were threatened by outside invaders (Philistines and Saxons), and both failed in their charge to defeat their enemy by having mercy on the opposing people: Saul allowed the king of the Amalekites to live, and Vortigern allowed the non-Christian Saxons into Britain.

Mallory's story of Uther and Igraine is clearly patterned after the Biblical account of David and Bathsheba. Uther saw Igraine and immediately desired her; she was married, so he had her husband (the Duke of Tintagel) killed and slept with her, conceiving the next king of Britain, Arthur. Later in the story, when Uther becomes ill, he gives his blessing for his son to become king.

Correspondingly, David saw Bathsheba and immediately desired her; she was married, so he had her husband (Uriah the Hittite) killed, and slept with her. Though the child of this union dies, their next son, Solomon, becomes the next king of Israel. Later, when David becomes ill, he gives God's blessing for Solomon to become king.

---

[4] *The Antiquities of the Jews*, Chapter 10:4
[5] For one of several examples, see his sarcastic responses to Saul in *1 Samuel* 15:14, 28.

The Book of Ruth describes David's origins—in fact, it is likely one of the primary reasons for the book's inclusion in the Holy Scriptures. It highlights David's somewhat spotted ancestry—illegitimacy through his ancestor, Perez, and Moabite blood from Ruth[6]. Matthew's genealogy of Jesus[7]—depicted as a "greater David" in Scripture[8]—traces him through Perez, and mentions only four women: Tamar, the would-be prostitute, Rahab the prostitute, Ruth the Moabitess, and Bathsheba, alluding to yet another sordid episode.

Arthur's conception was also illegitimate, and this fact, as well as further sexual sins, feature greatly into the story of Camelot.

The next infamous element of the Arthurian story is the account of the Sword in the Stone. There are kings ruling in Britain, but also a great deal of conflict as to who will succeed and who has the right to rule as High King. According to Mallory's version, the Archbishop of Canterbury announces that the challenge of the sword in the stone was a way for God to indicate his choice of king. In most versions, it is Merlin who has placed the sword in the stone, or at least had some share in doing so. The leaders of Britain are all gathered around the stone, so the choice can be made before them all.

This event is mirrored in the scene in 1 Samuel chapter 16 in which Samuel is told to anoint as king the one that Jehovah indicates to him. The gathering of Jesse's sons parallels the gathering of leaders around the sword in the stone.

But the symbolisms of this scene run deeper still. The sword, again according to Mallory and some French sources, is plunged through an anvil which sits atop a block of stone[9]. Withdrawing the sword from the stone, through the anvil, would seem to be a clear metaphor for the production of weapons-grade metal from ore, or rock. This was a major development in Arthur's time, when the Celtic peoples and their successors the Saxons made the transition from bronze weapons to iron. Entire books have been written about the mysticism, superstition, and wonder that surrounded the forging of iron for centuries. For our purposes, suffice it to say that the making of

---

[6] *Ruth* 4:18-22
[7] *Matthew* 1:1-17
[8] See *Psalms* 89:20, 27; *Ezekiel* 34:22, 23; *Revelation* 22:16
[9] *Le Morte d'Arthur,* The Tale of King Arthur, Chapter 1: "...a marble block into which had been thrust a beautiful sword. The block was four feet square, and the sword passed through a steel anvil which had been struck in the stone, and which projected a foot from it." (Translation by Keith Baines)

iron was a technological achievement of such complexity that historians are still in awe that ancient peoples were able to accomplish it at all.[10]

Interestingly, the transition from bronze to iron in Palestine took place in David's day. Only in the Biblical account, the events surround, not David's coronation, but the event which solidifies his claim to the throne: his confrontation with the giant, Goliath.

In Geoffrey of Monmouth's version of the Arthur story, a young King Arthur battles a giant, incapacitates it with one blow of his sword to the giant's brow, then tells Sir Bedivere to cut off his head and carry it into the camp. The true story is much more fascinating. David, likely still in his teens, uses a sling to kill the Philistine champion, a Rephaim giant called Goliath. The feat is accomplished by a single blow to the giant's brow. David then cuts off the giant's head and carries it into the camp of Israel (transporting it to his capital, Jerusalem some years later). Once again we see reflections of key symbolic elements in the two stories: both involve a giant; a unique sword; a stone; and an unknown, young, heroic contender for a disputed throne.

The swords of both kings deserve mention as well. Of course for Arthur, his magical sword Excalibur, received from the religious figure the Lady of the Lake, played a key role in his early conquest and his final battle.[11] David takes Goliath's sword for his own. Nowhere is it suggested that the sword has magical powers; however—imagine the size of a sword wielded by a nine-and-a-half foot tall champion! Not only would it have been huge, but it would no doubt have been of the finest quality metal that the Philistines had available to them—iron, even, possibly, steel forged from meteor-ore. (Two centuries earlier, Egyptian Pharoah Tutankhamen was buried with a very fine steel dagger lying on his chest. Archaeologists have concluded that the dagger was made of meteor-steel, likely forged by Hittite smiths. The Philistines conquered the Hittites less than a century before David's time, and shortly thereafter, iron and steel begin to appear in the archeological record in Palestine). Only twice in the entire canon of the Hebrew Scriptures are real specifics given about a particular weapon. David makes a comment regarding Goliath's sword that finds no parallel anywhere else in the Bible. When it is returned to him at the hands of the religious figure, High Priest Ahimelech, the future king says, "There is no other like

---

[10] See, for example, the excellent notes made by Dr. Richard Cowen for his upcoming book *Exploiting the Earth* (John Hopkins University Press), that can be viewed at www.geology.ucdavis.edu/~cowen/~GEL115/index.html

[11] See *Le Morte d'Arthur*, The Tale of King Arthur, chapter 1 "Merlin", wherein Merlin informs Arthur that the scabbard of Excalibur prevents its wearer from losing any blood in battle (and which also describes its bestowal on Arthur by the Lady of the Lake)

it."[12] In both Arthur and David's cases, the possession of an extraordinary sword is one of the indications of a divinely-approved ruler. What would David have looked like as he charged into battle with an enormous (possibly two-handed for him) sword, fighting enemies who typically carried blades less than twenty-four inches long?

King Arthur follows up his coronation by gathering the greatest warriors of his kingdom into an extraordinary fighting unit, the Knights of the Round Table. It includes a threesome of valiant brothers, Gawain, Gaheris, and Gareth. David, too, collects together his *gibborim*, his "Mighty Men." Both Mallory and Nathan the Prophet (author of 2 Samuel) devote considerable time to the development of the back-stories of these knights and the amazing—even supernatural—achievements that brought them to the king's attention. The *gibborim*, too, include a threesome of valiant brothers: Joab, Abishai, and Asahel, the sons of Zeruiah.

Toward the close of his reign, Arthur decides that being a successful warrior is not enough. He desires to accomplish something less military with his life, something that will have meaning for future generations. Thus is the Grail quest conceived, and Arthur will spend much of the rest of his life trying to find the holy chalice. In the end, he is unworthy to do so, and the privilege is enjoyed by a knight more pure in heart, Sir Galahad.

In David's waning years, he, too, decides that his military accomplishments are not sufficient. Seeing that the place of worship of the True God is a simple tent (the Tabernacle), he determines to build a true Temple for Jehovah—a more noble and spiritual goal[13]. But David, like Arthur, is found unworthy to do so, and the privilege is enjoyed by a king with less blood on his hands: David's beloved son, Solomon.

At the heart of the Arthurian story is a tragic love-triangle: Arthur, Guinevere, and the Round-table knight, Lancelot (who is a foreigner). An illicit relationship between Lancelot and Guinevere proves to be the undoing of Arthur's kingdom. While rescuing Guinevere from execution for adultery, Lancelot inadvertently kills Sir Gareth. When Arthur's son, Mordred, wages war against his father, Gawain and Gaheris' desire for vengeance on their brother's killer force Arthur to remain alienated from Lancelot, and drive the nation into a full-scale civil war.

As mentioned earlier, a love-triangle haunts the life of David as well. In this case, it is King David who falls in love with Bathsheba, the wife of one of his *gibborim*, a warrior named Uriah the Hittite (a foreigner). Their illicit relationship results in Bathsheba's conceiving a son. David conspires to have Uriah killed, then takes Bathsheba as his own wife.

---

[12] *1 Samuel* 21:9
[13] *2 Samuel* 7:1-16

Earlier in the David story, King Saul's battle-chief and uncle, Abner, is forced to kill Asahel during a battle.[14] For the rest of David's life, Asahel's brothers refuse to rest until they have executed vengeance for this crime.[15] They, also, force David into battle when he would rather avoid it. They are directly involved when David's son, Absalom, revolts against his father, and Joab murders Absalom against David's direct orders.[16]

David and Arthur are both plagued by their sins for the majority of their lives. But Arthur's sin has greater repercussions for him and for his nation than David's does. Because of Mordred, the result of his sins, Arthur never accomplishes the mission he is set to—and so, in British lore, is destined to one day return. David did complete his tasks, and was able to have one of his descendants—Jesus of Nazareth—rule Israel for all eternity.

Interestingly, Christ Jesus had the mocking accusation "King of the Jews" hung over his head at his death. But the Scriptures assert that he was, in fact, destined to return to fulfill all that he was set to by God. This is the hope that the authors of the Arthurian legends also hold out for Arthur.[17]

To the medieval audience for whom these tales were originally written, Arthur represented a unique leader—one who was loved by his subjects, who had human weaknesses and faced human trials. Arthur is presented as a re-incarnation of the values that King David has always been known for. Although Arthur's life ended in disgrace and destruction, the authors express their confidence that he, like Jesus the Messiah, the son of David, will return and rule again with all the traits that made him great.

For this reason, David is called by Jewish rabbis "the first and the last of the Jewish rulers." Among British historians and bards, Arthur is named "the once and future king."[18]

---

[14] *2 Samuel* 2:18-23
[15] Beginning with Joab's cold-blooded murder of Abner (*2 Samuel 3:26-27*)
[16] *2 Samuel* 18:9-15
[17] For example: "In some parts of Britain it is believed that King Arthur did not die and that he will return to us and win fresh glory and the Holy Cross of our Lord Jesu Christ…" (*Le Morte d'Arthur,* Le Morte d'Arthur, chapter 4 (translation by Keith Baines)
[18] *Shitah Hadashah* and the oft-quoted "*rex quondam, rexque futurus*" (Shoaf 209)

APPENDIX D:
IN DEFENSE OF ARTISTIC LICENSE—
ON DECISIONS MADE BY THE AUTHOR IN MATTERS ON WHICH THE HOLY SCRIPTURES ARE SILENT OR UNCLEAR, CONFLICT WITH JEWISH TRADITION, OR REFLECT AUTHORIAL SUPPOSITIONS AND DEDUCTIONS

The Divine Name: Jehovah
"One of the most fundamental and essential features of the biblical revelation is the fact that God is not without a name; he has a personal name, by which he can, and is to be, invoked."—*The New International Dictionary of New Testament Theology* (Volume 2, page 649)

God's personal name in Hebrew is written יהוה. These four letters are called the Tetragrammaton, and are transliterated into English as YHWH or JHVH. This name appears more often in the Scriptures than any other—almost seven thousand times in the Hebrew and Aramaic texts of the so-called "Old Testament." The name is a form of the Hebrew verb *hawah*, which means "to become." The name itself signifies "He Causes to Become"—a designation of the One who fulfills all his promises and unfailingly realizes his purposes.

There can be no doubt that the divine name was commonly used in ancient times. Many archaeological discoveries bear this out. For instance, in a burial cave southwest of Jerusalem, a Hebrew inscription from the second half of the eighth century B.C.E. contains statements such as "Jehovah is the God of the whole earth."[19] Pottery fragments discovered in Arad from the second half of the seventh century B.C.E. included a private letter that began, "To my lord Eliashib: May Jehovah ask for your peace" and ends, "He dwells in the house of Jehovah."[20] In 1975-6, a collection of Hebrew and Phoenician inscriptions were discovered in the Negeb that included the Tetragrammaton in Hebrew letters. Just outside Jerusalem's walls, a small, rolled-up strip of silver was excavated and dated to before the Babylonian exile. It had the name of Jehovah written on it in Hebrew.[21] The Lachish Letters, written on potsherds and found in the ruins of Lachish, appear to be communications from an officer at a Judean outpost to his superior during the war between Israel and Babylon toward the end of the

---

[19] *Israel Exploration Journal*, Volume 13, No. 2.
[20] *Ibid*, Volume 16, No.1.
[21] *Biblical Archaeology Review*, March/April 1983, page 18.

seventh century B.C.E. Seven of the legible letters begin their message with a salutation that uses the Tetragrammaton; it appears in the messages eleven times.

No one today knows how the name of God was originally pronounced in Hebrew. Superstition caused the Jews to stop pronouncing the name in the 1st or 2nd centuries, and eventually its proper pronunciation was forgotten. (As an example of this change, in Jerusalem's Israel Museum one fragment of the Greek *Septuagint* that has been dated to the first century C.E. has God's name four times in Zechariah 8:19-21 and 8:23-9:4. Four hundred years later, the Alexandrine Manuscript was written, and in this copy of the *Septuagint* God's name had been replaced in those same verses by abbreviations of the word *Kyrios*, or "Lord").

When the name was written by superstitious Jewish scribes, the consonants were marked with the vowel points for the word *Adhonai*, or "Lord." (They apparently deemed it too holy to write accurately, although Moses clearly would not have agreed with them). From this came the spelling Iehouah, which eventually became Jehovah in English. Most modern scholars feel that "Yahweh" (or some variation thereof) is a more accurate representation of the ancient pronunciation.

Should we, therefore, abandon the pronunciation "Jehovah" because we know that it is not the ancient Hebrew pronunciation? Of course not. If we did, we would have to abandon "Jesus" in favor of "Yeshua" or "Yehoshua"; Jeremiah in favor of "Yirmeya'hu"; Timothy in favor of "Timotheus". In fact, we would have to change the pronunciation of virtually every name in the Bible. But we don't. Even when we are sure of the pronunciation of an ancient name, we typically replace it with the recognized, English version. After all, we do not fault the Italians for calling Jesus *Gesù*, or the Greeks for calling him *Iesous*. This is the nature of translation—we use the most commonly recognized version of a particular word in our own language. To abandon the name entirely—to, in fact, replace it with less meaningful titles like "Lord" or "God" is an absurd notion with absolutely no grounds in scripture or logic.

In the words of John W. Davis, a missionary in China during the 19th century: "If the Holy Ghost says Jehovah in any given place in the Hebrew, why does the translator not say Jehovah in English or Chinese? What right has he to say, *I will use Jehovah in this place and a substitute for it in that?* . . . If any one should say that there are cases in which the use of Jehovah would be wrong, let him show the reason why; the onus probandi rests upon him. He will find the task a hard one, for he must answer this simple question,—*If in any given case it is wrong to use Jehovah in the translation then why did the inspired writer use it in the original?*"—*The Chinese Recorder and Missionary Journal*, Volume VII, Shanghai, 1876, italics added.

Many translators and scholars have recognized this truth:

- "From this point onward I use the word Jehovah, because, as a matter of fact, this name has now become more naturalized in our vocabulary and cannot be supplanted."—*Theologie des Alten Testaments* (Theology of the Old Testament) by Gustav Friedrich Oehler, second edition, published in 1882, page 143.
- "In our translations, instead of the (hypothetical) form *Yahweh*, we have used the form *Jehovah*...which is the conventional literary form used in French."—*Grammaire de l'hebreu biblique* (Grammar of Biblical Hebrew), by Paul Jouon, 1923 edition, page 49.
- "That they [the Jews] now allege the name Jehovah to be unpronounceable, they do not know what they are talking about...If it can be written with pen and ink, why should it not be spoken, which is much better than being written with pen and ink? Why do they not also call it unwriteable, unreadable, or unthinkable? All things considered, there is something foul."—Martin Luther, 1534

Strangely, however, most modern Bible translators still choose to remove the name wholesale, or nearly so, replacing it with the title "LORD" or "GOD" in all capitals. Most of them cite reasons identical or similar to the following:

- "In this translation we have followed the orthodox Jewish tradition and substituted 'the Lord' for the name 'Yahweh' and the phrase 'the Lord God' for the phrase 'the Lord Yahweh.' In all cases where 'Lord' or 'God' represents an original 'Yahweh' small capitals are employed."—J.M. Powis Smith and Edgar J. Goodspeed, 1934 edition.
- "For two reasons the Committee has returned to the more familiar usage of the King James Version [that is, omitting the name of God]: (1) the word 'Jehovah' does not accurately represent any form of the Name ever used in Hebrew; and (2) the use of any proper name for the one and only God, as though there were other gods from whom he had to be distinguished, was discontinued in Judaism before the Christian era and is entirely inappropriate for the universal faith of the Christian Church."—Preface to the *Revised Standard Version*.

No other gods from whom Jehovah had to be distinguished? There are millions of gods! The Bible itself attests to this fact. (1 Corinthians 8:5; Philippians 3:19). The Old Testament is filled with references to gods; the Hebrew word *'elohim* is even used by Bible writers to refer to Israelite men in positions of authority. (Psalms 82:1, 6; Exodus 4:16; 7:1). The fact that Jehovah is the *almighty* god does not alleviate the need to distinguish him from the thousands—millions today—of other gods.

It is astonishing to me that Bible translators, supposedly men who revere the book that they are translating, would decide that a name that the Bible itself uses nearly 7,000 times is "entirely inappropriate" for Christians! It should be noted that they do not raise these issues as regards any other name in the Scriptures, including that of Jesus Christ himself, although many of them consider him Almighty God incarnate.

Interestingly, the same translators that insist on removing the divine name from their works do so only when the name stands alone. The name of God is one of the most common elements of Biblical Hebrew names, appearing prominently in Ahijah, Elijah, Irijah, Isshijah, Jahzeiah, and many, many others—not to mention the oft-quoted "Hallelujah". Almost every Biblical name that ends in "-ah" or "-iah" is, in fact, derived from the name "Jehovah." None of these translators has changed Elijah's name to Eliyahu, or some other more accurate Hebrew equivalent. Nor have they replaced the "Jah" in his name with "Lord" or "God", capitalized or otherwise.

Thankfully, many modern translators have recognized that their responsibility lies, not in amending the divine text in accordance with Jewish tradition or their own opinions, but in reproducing the words of the original writers as accurately as possible. Thus the translators of the *American Standard Version* of 1901 wrote in their preface: "[The translators] were brought to the unanimous conviction that a Jewish superstition, which regarded the Divine Name as too sacred to be uttered, ought no longer to dominate in the English or any other version of the Old Testament . . . This Memorial Name, explained in Ex. iii. 14, 15, and emphasized as such over and over in the original text of the Old Testament, designates God as the personal God, as the covenant God, the God of revelation, the Deliverer, the Friend of his people . . . This personal name, with its wealth of sacred associations, is now restored to the place in the sacred text to which it has an unquestionable claim." Similarly, Steven T. Byington wrote regarding *The Bible in Living English*, "The spelling and the pronunciation are not highly important. What is highly important is to keep it clear that this is a personal name. There are several texts that cannot be properly understood if we translate this name by a common noun like 'Lord,' or, much worse, by a substantivized adjective." J. B. Rotherham wrote of his *Studies in the Psalms* (1911): "The employment of this English form of the Memorial name (Exo. 3:18) in the present version of the Psalter does not arise from any misgiving as to the more correct pronunciation, as being Yahwéh; but solely from practical evidence personally selected of the desirability of keeping in touch with the public ear and eye in a matter of this kind, in which the principal thing is the easy recognition of the Divine name intended."

I have chosen, therefore, to use the name "Jehovah" in this novel, the common English translation of the name that would have been used in Samuel's day. If by this usage readers become aware of the bizarre and unjustified removal of the divine name from so many versions of the Bible, it would be for me a great reward for my efforts in taking on this project.

The Eternal Flame

As specified in Leviticus 6;12, 13, the Torah required that the fire on the Altar of Burnt Offering never be allowed to go out. Jewish tradition holds that the Altar fire was originally miraculously kindled by God. However, the account at Leviticus 1:7, 8 indicates that Aaron or his sons lit the original flame in the Altar, and it was only later (Leviticus 8:14-9:24) that a miraculous flame sent from heaven was joined to that which had already been ignited. Thereafter, the Eternal Flame would no doubt have been a mixture of the natural and the supernatural flames. I have chosen to emphasize the Flame's divine origin both because it is commonly held in Jewish tradition, and because it better serves the story. It is, of course, beyond debate that the explanation in Leviticus is the accurate one.

Samuel, son of Elkanah

Samuel's childhood assignment in Shiloh is clearly delineated in Scripture, namely, as a gatekeeper of the Tabernacle in Shiloh. It was the job of the Priests to light and to feed the Eternal Flame burning in the Altar, and Samuel was not a Priest. It was the job of the Levites to assist the Priests in their duties, and it is likely that Samuel had some share in these tasks. As for the gathering of wood, this was done (or at least overseen) by the Gibeonites, whose story is recorded in Joshua, chapter 9.

Samuel's direct association with the Flame is entirely my own invention, chosen for metaphoric reasons rather than historical ones. In describing his activities during this time in Israelite history, I have tried not to contradict anything stated in Scripture. If the reader feels I have overstepped, I sincerely apologize.

Tirzah, daughter of Judge Jephthah

Determining the chronology of the book of Judges is an extraordinarily challenging task. I do not believe that anyone can claim to have definitively outlined it, since there are too many variables that the Scriptures fail to clearly explain. A primary problem is that we cannot know if the terms of office of the various Judges overlapped or occurred concurrently. The book clearly does not travel linearly through time, making extensive use of flashbacks especially in the final chapters.

The subject of chronology is addressed more completely in Appendix E. In the context of that information, the following facts informed my decision to place the (Biblically unnamed) daughter of Judge Jephthah in the Tabernacle during the same period during which Samuel served there: At Judges 11:26, Jephthah, at the start of his term of office, refers to a period of "three hundred years" during which Israel had controlled lands east of the Jordan. Using the year 1473 B.C.E. as the date of Israel's crossing the Jordan and the conquest of Jericho, the start of Jephthah's six-year term of office would begin at around the year 1173 BCE. Samuel's birth and death can be approximately placed using contextual information (such as the date of Saul's coronation, Samuel's death, etc.). Since Josephus (*Antiquities* Book 5, 10:4) tells us that Samuel became a prophet at twelve years of age, reasonable inferences as to the date of his death place his time of service at Shiloh concurrent with the Judgeship of Jephthah. Certainly, other conclusions can be arrived at; this is the one I have adopted for the purposes of this story. (See also *Insight on the Scriptures, Volume II, p. 26*, published by The Watchtower Bible and Tract Society).

The language in Judges 12 through 16 seems to suggest a chronology much more definitive than other portions of that book. After mentioning Jephthah's death in 12:7, verse 8 reads "*After him*, Ibzan of Bethlehem led Israel." Verse 11 follows with, "*After him*, Abdon, son of Hillel, from Pirathon, led Israel." After Abdon's death in verse 15, Chapter 13 verse 1 begins "Again the Israelites did evil..." and proceeds to introduce the judgeship of Samson. (All italics mine). The use of the phrase "after him", which is not used in introducing the leadership of previous judges, seems to indicate a continuous chronology, rather than an overlap or simultaneity of judgeship.

Songs and Rituals

I have included various songs, rituals, and practices that are found in post-exilic sources, including the *Mishnah*. These are, for the most part, associated with the Temple of Jesus' day rather than the Mosaic Tabernacle. Certainly many, if not most, of them were unknown to Israel in the tenth century B.C.E. However, they are the only information we have regarding the details of how the ceremonies of the Torah were practiced, and it seems likely that the descriptions in the *Mishnah* are based on ancient traditions, some of which may be reflections of what went on in the early monarchy or period of the Judges. It is my hope that the reader will forgive this anachronism on the grounds that the artistic license taken is based on the best and most accurate information that the author had at his disposal.

Phinehas, Son of Eli

In *The Antiquities of the Jews* by Flavius Josephus, the author writes in Book 5, Chapter 11 that "Phineas already officiated as High Priest, his father having resigned his office to him, by reason of his great age" at the time of the Battle of Aphek. Though this cannot be confirmed by Scripture (and allowing that in some other areas, Josephus has proven himself somewhat unreliable as a historian), it seemed to me to be not wholly unlikely since the book of 1 Samuel informs us that Eli was, indeed, blind at the time of the battle and, as a blind man, would have been unable to fulfill the requirements of the Day of Atonement. For this reason, I have chosen to include the installation of Phinehas as High Priest in the story.

Rohgah, son of Almodad

An unnamed Prophet served Israel in the days of Jephthah (Judges 10:11-13). Very shortly thereafter, an unnamed Prophet came to Shiloh to reveal Jehovah's condemnation of Eli's sons (1 Samuel 2:27-36). Since these two events occurred near each other geographically and chronologically, and since there was apparently no abundance of Prophets in this period of Israel's history, I have made the two characters one and the same.

Malediction

The Hebrew word translated "malediction" is *qelahah*, and is derived from the root verb *qalal*, which literally means "be light", but when used metaphorically means "call down evil upon" or "treat with contempt." (The English "malediction" is a translation from the Latin "to speak ill of). The Malediction is a theme that runs through the Hebrew Scriptures, and its prophetic description in Deuteronomy 18 (as seen in Rohgah's vision) is fulfilled over and over in the trials faced by Israel throughout its history until its final manifestations in the destructions of Jerusalem by the Babylonians in 607 B.C.E. and again by the Romans in 70 C.E.

Even a cursory reading of Deuteronomy 18 will quickly establish that the disgusting and violent contents of Rohgah's vision are no exaggeration of what was foretold.

The Philistines

Most modern scholars consider the Philistines of the Bible to have been one of the "Sea Peoples" that traveled south, probably originally from Mycenae, Cyprus, and surrounding lands, conquering territories as they went, finally arriving in and being defeated by Egypt. Enough investigation has been done into their culture, including a lengthy and on-going archaeological dig in the city of Ashkelon, to provide us with a fairly good guess as to the life and times of these ancient people.

It is the records of Egypt that provide us with most of the extra-biblical literature available. The Egyptian records call the "Sea Peoples" by the names of their individual tribes. The "Peleset," likely the Biblical Philistines, seemed to have originated in Mycenae; the "Lukka" perhaps from the Lycian region of Anatolia; the "Ekwesh" could have been Achaean Greeks; the "Denen" probably Danaean Greeks; the "Sherden" possibly Sardinians; the "Teresh" perhaps Tyrrhenians Etruscans, or Taruisians from Anatolia; and the "Shekelesh" may have been Sicilians.

Homer's famous story of the Trojan War was a battle involving the Mycenaean Greeks of this time period. It is entirely possible that Odysseus and the warriors who sacked Troy were the forefathers of the Philistines who eventually settled in Israel.

The Denen, Lukka, and Sherden probably began their migration as early as Akhenaten's reign. Rameses II reports that the Lukka, Sherden, and Peleset served as mercenaries in his army at the Battle of Qadesh. Rameses had earlier been forced to defend himself against the Sea People's attempts to establish a chain of forts to the west of Egypt. About 1176 B.C.E., he wrote: "No land could stand before their arms...they desolated its people, and its land was like that which has never come into being...Their confederation was the Peleset, Tjeker, Shekelesh, Denyen, and Weshesh..." Archaeologists now feel that the Sea People were probably part of a greater migration of people who were displaced by widespread crop failures and famine. In fact, Pharaoh Merenptah recorded shipments of grain sent to the Hittites during this period to prevent their starvation.

After wreaking havoc in Mycenaean Greece, they destroyed the Hittite empire, ransacking its capital Hattusas, and sacking Ugarit in Syria and the Cyprian capital, Enkomi. Traveling down the coast, they appeared to have assisted smaller groups of Philistines already settled on the Philistine plain to conquer the city of Ashdod. A burnt layer in the ruins of that city in the 13th century B.C.E. may mark their violent arrival.

The Sea Peoples continued south, arrived on the Nile Delta coast and joined with the Libyans to create a force of about 16,000 soldiers (if the Egyptian records can be trusted).

They entered Egypt, accompanied by their wives and families, carrying their possessions in ox-drawn carts that moved along the inland roads, paralleled by flotillas of ships sailing down the coastline. Their first attack on Egypt was during the fifth year of Pharaoh Merenptah, and it took him by surprise. But he recovered, killed more than 6,000 and routed the rest, finally settling the captives in military colonies on the Nile Delta.

In the 8th year of Rameses III, they returned to Egypt by land and sea. Rameses defeated them on land. The Philistine navy continued toward the eastern Nile Delta, but Rameses lined the shore with archers who kept up a continuous volley of arrows into the enemy ships whenever they attempted to land. Rallying, the Egyptian navy launched a counter-attack, using grappling hooks to haul in the enemy ships and defeated them in a brutal hand-to-hand battle.

Egyptian records indicate that the Pharaoh allowed some of the Sea Peoples to return north, giving them the territory we now call Philistia to settle in.

It is at this period in history that the Philistines suddenly become a significant problem for the nation of Israel. Starting with the Battle of

Aphek, Israel faced off against the Philistines repeatedly, throughout the life of Samuel and the Judgeship of Samson, and continuing through the reigns of Saul and David.

One other detail of Philistine culture played rather prominently into the Biblical narrative. In the book of 1 Samuel, Chapter 13, Samuel records that the Philistines had completely taken over the business of smithing in Israel. I will discuss this development further in future books. For the purposes of this story, it is worth noting that this detail likely refers to the Philistine mastery of *iron* working—a conclusion that is supported by the archaeological discoveries from the time period. If this is true, the Philistines must have learned the skills from the Hittites, whom they had conquered years before.

"Philistine" has entered into the English vernacular since the seventeenth century as a synonym for boorish or uncultured. Archaeology in recent decades has in many ways debunked this notion. The Philistines achieved high levels of artistic sophistication and a deep appreciation for aesthetic values. The fact that these qualities existed in a culture that also practiced child sacrifice, ritualized sex rites, and barbarous military methods is not surprising when one considers the obvious parallels in "advanced" cultures in the world today.

Manoah of Dan

Manoah of Dan, in this story, is *the* Manoah of Dan, father of Judge Samson. If this seems anachronistic or confusing to the reader, I refer you to the heading "Tirzah, daughter of Judge Jephthah" in this Appendix and Appendix E for an explanation of why I have placed the birth of Samson after the battle of Aphek. I have based the character of the man on the comments Josephus makes about him in *Antiquities*.

Priests of Dan

Judges chapter 17 records the account (apparently taking place early in the period of the Judges, perhaps shortly after Joshua's time) of the Ephraimite man Micah. This Micah stole 1,100 silver pieces from his mother; when he returned them, she had them made into an "*ephod*, a carved image, and a teraphim," or household god. Micah then installed one of his sons as a priest, violating several requirements of the Torah (Exodus 20:4-6, Deuteronomy 12:1-14). Later, Micah hired the Gershonite Levite Jonathan to serve as his priest, apparently feeling that by replacing his son with a Levite, he was acting more acceptably. (Judges 17:7-13). As the account continues, spies from the tribe of Dan spend the night in Micah's house and receive a prediction of success for their mission from the Levite Jonathan. When this prediction came true, the Danites convinced Jonathan to accompany them and become the priest to a tribe and a family instead of for just one man. Jonathan agreed and went with them, taking along the *ephod*, the teraphim, and the carved image.

When these Danites conquered the city of Laish and renamed it Dan, they installed Jonathan and his son as priests. According to Judges 18:27-31, this arrangement continued in the tribe of Dan "all the days that the house of the true God continued in Shiloh." This places the conclusion of the sacrilegious service of Jonathan's descendants at the general time of the Battle of Aphek. I have made their downfall one of the direct results of that battle—as much because it served the interests of the story as for any other reason.

Canaanite Worship

Much has been written by archaeologists and historians regarding the vulgar, licentious, and violent religious practices of the ancient people of Canaan. So that the reader will not feel that I have exaggerated the situation, I include the following quotes from reliable sources:

"At its worst, . . . the erotic aspect of their cult must have sunk to extremely sordid depths of social degradation" (*Archaeology and the Religion of Israel,* W. F. Albright, 1968, pp. 76, 77).

"Excavations in Palestine have uncovered piles of ashes and remains of infant skeletons in cemeteries around heathen altars, pointing to the widespread practice of this cruel abomination" (*Archaeology and the Old Testament,* Merril F. Unger, 1964, p. 279).

"Temples of Baal and Ashtoreth were usually together. Priestesses were temple prostitutes. Sodomites were male temple prostitutes. The worship of Baal, Ashtoreth, and other Canaanite gods consisted in the most extravagant orgies; their temples were centers of vice. . . . It seems that, in large measure, the land of Canaan had become a sort of Sodom and Gomorrah on a national scale....Just a few steps from this temple was a cemetery, where many jars were found, containing remains of infants who had been sacrificed in this temple . . . Prophets of Baal and Ashtoreth were official murderers of little children...Another horrible practice was [what] they called 'foundation sacrifices.' When a house was to be built, a child would be sacrificed, and its body built into the wall...enormous quantities of images and plaques of Ashtoreth [have been found] with rudely exaggerated sex organs, designed to foster sensual feelings. So, Canaanites worshiped, by immoral indulgence, as a religious rite, in the presence of their gods; and then, by murdering their first-born children, as a sacrifice to these same gods" *(Halley's Bible Handbook,* Henry H. Halley, 1964).

"On a high and lofty mountain you have set up your bed; and thither have you climbed to offer sacrifice. Behind the door and the side posts you have set up your phallic symbol; and apart from me have you stripped and gone up, you have distended your parts; you have bargained for those whose embraces you love; and with them have you multiplied your harlotries, while gazing on the phallus"(Isaiah 57:7, 8, *An American Translation*).

"Didst make thee images of the male, and didst act unchastely with them?"(Ezekiel 16:17, *Rotherham*)

"The references to Anath in the Ras Shamra texts give some indication of the degraded conception of the deities that the Canaanites undoubtedly shared with the Syrians. Anath is described as the fairest among Baal's sisters, but as having an extremely violent temper. She is depicted as threatening to smash the skull of her father, El, and cause his gray hair to flow with blood and his gray beard with gore if he did not comply with her wishes. On another occasion Anath is shown going on a killing spree. She attached heads to her back, and hands to her girdle, and she plunged knee-deep in the blood and hip-deep in the gore of valiant ones" (*Ancient Near Eastern Texts*, edited by J. Pritchard, 1974, pp. 136, 137, 142, 152).

"[Images that] feature a goddess with emphasized genitals, holding up her breasts...probably represent... Asherah." (*The Encyclopedia of Religion*)

"The Ugaritic epic literature has helped to reveal the depth of depravity which characterized Canaanite religion. Being a polytheism of an extremely debased type, Canaanite cultic practice was barbarous and thoroughly licentious...The brutality, lust and abandon of Canaanite mythology was far worse than elsewhere in the Near East at the time. And the astounding characteristic of Canaanite deities, that they had no moral character whatever, must have brought out the worst traits in their devotees and entailed many of the most demoralizing practices of the time, such as sacred prostitution, child sacrifice, and snake worship. . . . The character of Canaanite religion as portrayed in the Ugaritic literature furnishes ample background to illustrate the accuracy of . . . Biblical statements in their characterization of the utter moral and religious degeneracy of the inhabitants of Canaan" (*Archaeology and the Old Testament*, Dr. Merril Unger).

"Excavations in Palestine have brought to light a multitude of A[starte] figures in all forms; . . . most of them are small, crude figures, an indication that this deity was chiefly used in home worship, perhaps worn by women on their person or placed in an alcove in the house. . . . The sensual nature religions of A[starte] and Baal appealed to the common folk. Of course, serious injury was inevitable; sexual perversions in honor of the deity, voluptuous lust, and impassioned exuberance became a part of worship and later moved into the home" (*Calwer Bibellexikon* (Calwer Bible Lexicon)).

"Religious festivities became a degraded celebration of the animal side of human nature. Even Greek and Roman writers were shocked by the things the Canaanites did in the name of religion" (*The Lion Encyclopedia of the Bible*).

"Of Canaanite religious practices, mention will only be made here of the sacrificing of children, for excavations have directly verified this. In Gezer as well as in Megiddo, the way corpses of children are immured . . . speaks conclusively . . . for this practice" (*Die Alttestamentliche Wissenschaft* (Science of the Old Testament)).

"In no country has so relatively great a number of figurines of the naked goddess of fertility, some distinctly obscene, been found. Nowhere does the cult of serpents appear so strongly. . . . Sacred courtesans and eunuch priests were excessively common. Human sacrifice was well known . . . The aversion felt by followers of YHWH-God when confronted by Canaanite idolatry, is accordingly, very easy to understand" (*Recent Discoveries in Bible Lands*).

"Acts in imitation of the deity were regarded as service to the god. . . .Ashtart had a number of men and women ministrants who were described as consecrated persons . . . They consecrated themselves in her service to prostitution" (*The Religion of the People of Israel*)

"Feasts…were celebrated in the family tomb or at burial mounds with ritual drunkenness and sexuality (possibly involving incest) in which the deceased were thought to participate (*International Standard Bible Encyclopedia*)

(After discussing the Ugarit text, in which Baal copulates with a heifer) "…If it be argued that Baal assumes the shape of a bull for the act, the same cannot be said for his priests who re-enacted his mythological career" (Archaeologist Cyrus Gordon).

The Hittites

The Hittites originated from somewhere beyond the Black Sea, occupying central Anatolia and then northern Syria. They built their military around their heavy chariotry (ridden by the landed nobility) and their infantry (comprised of soldiers of lower status), but they were not above using mercenary troops who were paid in booty. Their chariots, built with iron axles strong enough for three-man crews, dominated the battlefield, almost unstoppable by infantry. They were masters of strategy. By around 1590 B.C.E. they had ended the Amorite dynasty in Babylon. Their expansion ended (as did the expansions of so many ancient empires) with Egypt: in around 1300 B.C.E. they fought Rameses II at the battle of Kadesh, on the Orontes. The results of the battle were indecisive, but from this time forward, there are records of marriage treaties being made between the Egyptians and the Hittites.

Syria was the crossroads of world commerce. Products from the Aegean, the Mediterranean, and as far as Britain, entered the Near East by ports like Ugarit. The Hittites capitalized on this and for a brief period of time became a major trading power.

It was sometime around 1193 B.C.E. that the fortunes of the Hittites really changed. At around this time, the Sea Peoples swept through Anatolia, coming by sea and land. Internal strife and governmental instability prevented the Hittites from dealing with the threat, and they were conquered. Many cities of Anatolia and Syria were destroyed, including the Hittite capital.

But the Hittites, in their time as a middle-eastern power, had made one of the most significant contributions to the region in all of history: they initiated the iron age. How they discovered the secrets of iron smelting is a matter of conjecture, but a possible explanation is as follows:

Iron, unlike the noble metals, is almost never found as an element, but always as an oxide. The temperatures achieved by normal, wood-burning forge fires of ancient times (1,000-1,100 Celsius) are not hot enough to melt iron ore into a liquid state, and some kind of catalyst is required at all but the highest temperatures.. But early Hittite smiths had access to a unique sand from the shores of the Black Sea, a sand that contained both iron ore and the slagging materials required to melt it at lower temperatures. With charcoal fires and bellows, they could produce iron bloom—iron particles mixed with iron oxide, slag, and charcoal reside. Already master metal-workers, they developed techniques to wring the iron from this bloom by folding it at high temperatures.

It was the Hittites who brought iron to the Middle East. This advancement would shape the next thousand years of history in the region: its environment, its warfare, its industry, and its politics.

Rephaim

The fervor of the ongoing arguments as to the historicity of the races of giants mentioned in the Bible (Rephaim, Anakim, and Emim, as discussed in Deuteronomy 2:10, 11) is well-illustrated by the number of web-pages one can find by doing a search on the subject. (Admittedly, most of the pages seem to be the work of conspiracy theorists with access to photo-editing software and too much time on their hands). There is very little physical evidence that could be used to prove the existence of these races of giants that are clearly described in the Bible. However, possible support can be seen in some of the gargantuan dolmans, or standing stones, set up in the Bashan region where the Rephaim were supposed to have lived. Also, in the southern part of Israel, it has been reported that giant battle-axes (over 8 feet tall, with heads weighing thirty pounds each) were discovered and are now kept in the National Museum in Baghdad, Iraq. Archaeologists almost universally consider these to have been ceremonial weapons. For the author, the clear statements of reliable witnesses, such as

Joshua, Moses, and Samuel, are sufficient to establish that the Rephaim and other races of giants did, truly, exist.

The Aurochs

The Hebrew word *re'em*, accurately translated "wild bull" (*urus* in Latin) refers to a now-extinct creature known to have inhabited southwest Asia, northern Africa, and Europe until the seventeenth century. The name "aurochs" comes from the German *Auerochs*, meaning "original ox." Skeletal remains have revealed that this amazing bovine stood six feet or more at the shoulder, stretched to ten feet long (not including the tail), and weighed over 2000 pounds. Its horns could span more than six feet. When Julius Caesar saw the aurochs in Gaul, he wrote: "These *uri* are scarcely less than elephants in size, but in their nature, colour, and form are bulls. Great is their strength, and great their speed: they spare neither man nor beast when once they have caught sight of them." In the Scriptures, the creature is noted for its strength and intractable disposition (Job 39:10, 11) as well as its swiftness (Numbers 23:22; 24:8).

The Tribes of Israel

I have made reference in a number of places to the specialized roles that the various tribes of Israel fulfilled in battle. This fascinating detail is based on the wonderful text *Battles of the Bible*, by Chaim Herzog and Mordechai Gichon (1997 Greenhill books, Lionel Leventhal Limited), and I refer the reader to chapter five of that work for further information. A careful reading of 1 Chronicles 12 will provide most of the scriptural basis for their conclusions, which seemed to me to be very sound (and, frankly, convenient for the story which I was developing).

Shiloh

Modern archaeologists locate the ancient city of Shiloh at Khirbet Seilun, about 9.5 miles north-northeast of Bethel. During most of the period of the Judges, the Tabernacle remained at Shiloh. But when the Ark was captured at the battle of Aphek, Jehovah never allowed it to be returned to Shiloh. In fact, Jehovah had forsaken Shiloh, as pointed out in Psalms 78:60, 61 and alluded to in Jeremiah 7:12, 14 and 26:6, 9.

Archaeological evidence at the site supports the Jewish tradition that following the battle of Aphek, the Philistines continued their conquest and captured the city, burning it to the ground. This, of course, necessitated the moving of the Tabernacle—and, indeed, the next time the Tabernacle is mentioned in the Scriptures, it is located at Nob (1 Samuel 21).

The Plague on Philistia

Various theories have been put forth regarding the specifics of the plague that overwhelmed Philistia after they captured the Ark of the Covenant. The account in 1 Samuel 5 and 6 tells us that the plague included an infestation of jerboas (*Septuagint*) and was marked by piles (Heb. *bapholim*). This word in Hebrew is associated with the human anus, and the Masoretes pointed the word with the vowels for *techorim*, or "tumors." This was likely a show of modesty on their part, but it could very well also provide us with further information as to the nature of the disease. The Latin *Vulgate* (ClementineRrecension, S. Bagster & Sons, London, 1977) adds the detail that "their rectums protruding began putrefying. And the people of Gath took counsel together and made themselves seats of skins."

Josephus adds: "…they died of dysentery and flux, a sore distemper, that brought death upon them very suddenly…they brought up their entrails, and vomited up what they had eaten, and what was entirely corrupted by the disease." (*Antiquities of the Jews, Chapter 11*).

To many modern researchers, these clues add up to a divinely originated bubonic plague. The "piles" could easily have been the "buboes," and the infestation of jerboas, carriers as they are of fleas, could have been responsible for the spread of the disease. The high death rate, the rapidity of the spread of the contagion, and the agonies experienced by the dying all fit the pattern of bubonic plague—albeit a particularly virulent and violent strain. I have chosen to accept this conclusion for the purposes of this story.

Whether or not the lack of buboes on other areas of the victim's bodies is due to a unique manifestation of the disease or to the focus of the writers of the account is unknown.

APPENDIX E:
CHRONOLOGY

"Anyone approaching the study of ancient history for the first time must be impressed by the positive way modern historians date events which took place thousands of years ago. In the course of further study this wonder will, if anything, increase. For as we examine the sources of ancient history we see how scanty, inaccurate, or downright false, the records were even at the time they were first written. And poor as they originally were, they are poorer still as they have come down to us: half destroyed by the tooth of time or by the carelessness and rough usage of men." (*The Secret of the Hittites*, by C. W. Ceram, 1956, pp. 133, 134).

"The purpose of this book is to present, in series, the chronologies of various contiguous areas as they appear in 1964 to the eyes of regional specialists. Despite the new information, the over-all situation is still fluid, and forthcoming data will render some conclusions obsolete, possibly even before this volume appears in print." (The Foreward (p.vii) to *Chronologies in Old World Archaeology*, edited by Robert Ehrich, 1965).

Bilblical chronology is a subject to which many volumes have been devoted, all of them written by sharper minds than mine. Unfortunately, these volumes tend to be consistent in only one thing: their disagreement with one another. The reality is that, while the overall framework of Biblical chronology has been firmly established for some time, the details of certain time periods (i.e., the book of Judges) are still unclear. There is simply not enough information given in the Scriptures to be definitive on the subject. This has required the author to make certain decisions, not on what I believe to be true, but on what I believe could possibly be true. My conclusions are conjectural and, as such, will be (appropriately) contested by some, roundly denounced by others.

The following is an effort on my part to provide the barest outline of Biblical chronology that may help to inform the novice of the reasoning that has informed my choices in this story. For those who desire more information, I refer them to the excellent article on "Chronology" in the encyclopedia *Insight on the Scriptures*, listed in Appendix B.

The following chart gives the basic scriptural foundation upon which the chronology I have used in this story is based.

	Event	Date B.C.E.	Years between events
The 1,656 years of this period are clearly described in Genesis 5:1-29 and 7:6. The figures given are based on the Masoretic text, well established as more accurate than the Greek *Septuagint*.	From Adam's creation	4026	
	to the birth of Seth		130
	to the birth of Enosh		105
	to the birth of Kenan		90
	to the birth of Mahalalel		70
	to the birth of Jared		65
	to the birth of Enoch		162
	to the birth of Methuselah		65
	to the birth of Lamech		187
	to the birth of Noah		182
	to the Flood	2370	600
This era is described in Genesis 11:10-12:4. The year that Terah died was also the year in which the Abrahamic covenant was validated, and Abraham entered into Canaan.	to Arpachshad's birth		2
	to the birth of Shelah		35
	to the birth of Eber		30
	to the birth of Peleg		34
	to the birth of Reu		30
	to the birth of Serug		32
	to the birth of Nahor		30
	to the birth of Terah		29
	to the death of Terah	1943	205
These figures are based on Genesis 12:4, 21:5, 25:26, 47:9, and Gal 3:16, 17.	to the birth of Isaac		25
	to the birth of Jacob		60
	Jacob's entry into Egypt		70
	to the Exodus	1513	215
1 Ki 6:1 gives 480 yrs from the Exodus to temple construction. Deut 2:7, 29:5, Ac 13:21, 2 Sam 5:4, 1 Ki 11:42, 43, and 12:1-20 give the basis for these calculations.	to Israel's entry into Canaan	1473	40
	to Saul's reign	1117	356
	to David's reign	1077	40
	to Solomon's reign	1037	40

In the midst of this tidy timeline we must insert the problematic period of the Judges.

Judge	Term of office	Reference
Othniel	40 years	Judges 3:9-11
18 years of oppression by Moabites		Judges 3:14
Ehud	80 years	Judges 3:12-30
Shamgar		Judges 3:31
20 years of oppression by Canaanites		Judges 4:3
Deborah/Barak	40 years	Judges 4:1-5:31
7 years of oppression by Midianites		Judges 6:1
Gideon		Judges 6:2-8:32
Abimelech and Jotham		Judges 9:1-57
Tola	23 years	Judges 10:1-2
Jair	22 years	Judges 10:3-4
18 years of oppression by Philistines, Ammonites		
Jephthah	6 years	Judges 10:6-12:7
Ibzan	7 years	Judges 12:8-10
Elon	10 years	Judges 12:11, 12
Abdon	8 years	Judges 12:13-15
Forty years of oppression by Philistines		Judges 13:1
Samson	20 years	Judges 13:2-16-31

We can establish the overall length of this period, even though it is not directly apportioned in Scripture: We have several periods of known length (the time spent wandering in the wilderness, the rules of Saul and David, and the years of Solomon's reign leading up to the building of the Temple) that total to 123 years. Subtract that from the 479 years between the Exodus and the beginning of Solomon's fourth year, and we are left with 356 years from Israel's entry into Canaan in 1473 B.C.E. until the start of Saul's reign in 1117 B.C.E.

But totaling all of the terms of office of the Judges gives us a sum of 410 years! Obviously, then, some of these terms of office were served concurrently, rather than successively. Indeed, the descriptions of Judges Ibzan, Elon, and Abdon give no indication of their taking any military action at all during their terms. Did they judge Israel during the 40 years of Philistine occupation (Judges 13:1)? We must make educated guesses, but the Scriptures provide no basis for any degree of certainty. It is noteworthy that Judges 13:2 does not begin "After him..." as does 12:8, 12:11, and 12:13. Samuel, the author of the book, deliberately wrote "Meanwhile..." This seems to me to indicate that the events of chapter 13 are happening sometime during the 40 year occupation. This wording also allows for the possibility that the reigns of Judges Ibzan, Elon, and Abdon took place during this 40 years. Having this kind of overlap provides one explanation for the chronological difficulties of the book of Judges. It also places the reigns of Ibzan, Elon, Abdon, and Samson during the lifetime of Samuel—which, in turn, matches the political situation between Israel and the Philistines during this time.

Using the information of these two tables, however, it is not difficult to extrapolate many other dates, often to a precise degree, and sometimes (as in the case of the periods of the various Judges) to an approximate degree. A timeline can be constructed, then, that might look something like this:

DATE	EVENT
4026	Adam's creation
3896	Cain slays Abel, Birth of Seth (Gen 4:8, 25)
3791	Brith of Enosh (Gen 5:6)
3701	Birth of Kenan (Gen 5:9)
3631	Birth of Mahalalel (Gen 5:12)
3566	Brith of Jared (Gen 5:15)
3404	Birth of Enoch (Gen 5:18)
3339	Birth of Methuselah (Gen 5:21)
3152	Birth of Lamech (Gen 5:25)
3096	Death of Adam (Gen 5:5)
3039	Enoch taken (Gen 5:24)
2984	Seth dies (Gen 5:8)
2970	Birth of Noah (Gen 5:28)
2886	Enosh dies (Gen 5:11)
2791	Kenan dies (Gen 5:14)
2736	Mahalalel dies (Gen 5:17)
2604	Jared dies (Gen 5:20)
2490	120 year pronouncement by God (Gen 6:3)
2470	Birth of Japheth
2468	Birth of Shem
2375	Lamech dies (Gen 5:31)
2370	Death of Methuselah, **The Great Flood** (Gen 7:11)
2369	Rainbow covenant (Gen 9:12, 13)
2368	Birth of Arpachshad (Gen 11:10)
c.2335	Birth of Sargon the Great
2333	Birth of Shelah (Gen 11:12)
2303	Birth of Eber (Gen 11:14)
2269	Tower of Babel; Birth of Peleg (Gen 11:1-9, 16)
2258	Egypt enters First Intermediate Period
2239	Reu born (Gen 11:18)
2207	Serug born (Gen 11:20)
2177	Birth of Nahor (Gen 11:22)
2148	Birth of Terah (Gen 11:24)
2134	Beginning of Middle Kingdom of Egypt
c.2100	Ur-Nammu founds final Sumerian dynasty
2030	Death of Peleg (Gen 11:17)
2029	Death of Nahor (Gen 11:25)
2020	Death of Noah (Gen 9:29)
2018	Birth of Abraham (Gen 11:26)
2008	Birth of Sarai
2000	Gilgamesh epic written; Hittites settle Anatolia; Mycenaeans conquer Greece
1977	Serug dies (Gen 11:23)
1950	Elamites destroy Ur
1943	Abraham crosses Euphrates; beg. of 430 years to Law (Gen 12:4, 7; Ex

12:40; Gal 3:17
1933 Lot rescued, Abram and Melchizedek (Gen 14:16, 18; 16:3)
1932 Ishmael born (Gen 16:15, 16)
1930 Arpachshad dies (Gen 11:5)
1919 Covenant of Circumcision; Judgment of Sodom & Gomorrah (Gen 17; 19:24)
1918 Birth of Isaac; Beginning of "450 years" (Gen 21:2, 5; Acts 13:17-20)
1913 Weaning of Isaac, Ishmael banished; beginning of 400 year affliction (Gen 21:8; 15:13; Acts 7:6)
1900 Shelah dies
1893 Abraham attempts to sacrifice Isaac
1881 Death of Sarah (Gen 17:17; 23:1)
1878 Isaac and Rebekah married (Gen 25:20)
1868 Death of Shem (Gen 11:11)
1858 Birth of Esau and Jacob (Gen 25:26)
1843 Death of Abraham (Gen 25:7)
1839 Eber dies
1830 First great Babylonian Dynasty
1818 Esau marries Hittite wives (Gen 26:34)
1800 Hammurabi rules in Babylon--end of Sumerians; Stonehenge built
1795 Death of Ishmael (Gen 25:17)
1781 Jacob flees to Haran (Gen 28:2)
1774 Jacob marries Leah and Rachel (Gen 29:23-30)
1767 Birth of Joseph (Gen 30:23, 24)
1761 Jacob returns to Canaan; wrestles angel, renamed Israel (Gen 32:24-28)
1750 Joseph sold into slavery (Gen 37:2, 28)
1738 Death of Isaac (Gen 35:28, 29)
1737 Joseph made Prime Minister (Gen 41:40, 60)
1728 Jacob's family enters Egypt (Gen 45-47)
1711 Death of Jacob (Gen 47:28)
1700 Hittites form old kingdom with capital at Hattusas
1668 Hyksos invasion ends Middle Kingdom of Egypt
1657 Death of Joseph (Gen 50:26)
b.1613 Some time before this date was Job's trial
c. 1600 Egypt becomes first world power (Exo 1:8)
1597 Birth of Aaron
1593 Birth of Moses (Ex 2:2, 10)
1570 Start of New Kingdom in Egypt
1560 Birth of Joshua
1553 Moses kills Egyptian, flees (Exo 2:11, 14, 15; Acts 7:23)
1531 Hittites destroy Babylon, Hammurabi dynasty ends
1514 Moses at the burning bush (Exo 3:2)
1513 1st Passover, Exodus, Red Sea; end of 400 year affliction, 430 years period;
Law covenant made; Bible writing begun by Moses (Gen 15:13, 14; Exo 12, 14, 24; Gal 3:17; John 5:46)
1512 Tabernacle completed; priesthood installed; Exodus, Leviticus completed (Exo 40:17; Lev 8:34-36; Lev 27:34; Num 1:1)
1500 Aryans conquer Dravidians in India; Hinduism originates in Indus
1474 Death of Aaron
1473 Job, Numbers, Dueteronomy written; Moses dies; Israel enters Canaan (Num 35:1; 36:13; Deut 29:1; Deut 1:1, 3; Deut 34:1, 5, 7; Josh 4:19)
1467 Major conquest completed; End of 450 yrs (Josh 11:23; 14:7, 10-15;

	Acts 13:17-20)
1450	Book of Joshua completed; Death of Joshua; Hittites conquer Asia Minor (Josh 1:1; 24:26, 29)
1447	Benjaminites mass sex sin
1437	New generation of Israel subjected to Canaanites
1436	Othniel raised as Judge, subdues Canaan; 40 years of peace
1424	First Jubilee celebrated
1396	Israel subject to King Eglon 18 years
1395	Judge Ehud raised up, delivers Israel; 80 years of peace
1365	Amenhotep IV and Nefertiti rule Egypt
1348	Tutankhamen rules Egypt
1316	Judge Shamgar kills 100 Philistines
1317	Israel subjugated to King Jabin of Hazor
1318	Judge Barak, Deborah defeat Sisera; 40 years of peace
1279	Judge Gideon defeates Midianites with 300 men; 40 years of peace
1278	Midianites devastate Israel
1274	Hittites battle Egypt at Battle of Kadesh
1239	Gideon dies, Abimelech usurps power
1238	Judge Tola judges 23 years
1215	Judge Jair judges 22 years
1200	Sea Peoples devastate Hittite empire; Archaic period of Greece begins
1185	Fall of Troy at the hand of the Mycenaean Greeks
1181	Jephthah driven out; Hannah makes vow at Tabernacle
1180	Samuel born
1179	Rameses III conquers the coalition of Sea Peoples under Sarnam
1177	Samuel brought to Tabernacle, registered as a Levite & Nazirite
1176	Ahimelech born; Libyans and allies invade Egypt
1174	Israel repents of false worship due to oppression by enemies
1173	Jephthah becomes Judge and Leader of Israel
1172	Jephthah battles Ammon; Tirzah sent to Shiloh
1171	Jephthah defeats the tribe of Ephraim
1168	Samuel becomes Prophet; Defeat at Aphek; Death of Eli & his sons; Sacking of Shiloh and move of Tabernacle to Nob
1167	Ark returned to Israel; Ibzan becomes Judge; Angel visits Manoah
1166	Samson is born
1162	Samuel marries
1161	Judge Ibzan dies
1160	Elon becomes Judge
1158	Egyptian workers strike when Rameses III fails to pay them
1157	Saul born; Harem conspiracy in Egypt, Queen Tiy attempts assassination
1156	Rameses III dies of injuries during trial of conspirators
1155	Rameses IV sends expedition to gold mines in south of Egypt
1151	Joel born to Samuel; Judge Elon dies and is buried at Aijalon
1150	Abdon becomes Judge; Rameses IV dies of smallpox
1149	Abijah born
1142	Abner born; Judge Abdon dies; High Priest Ahitub dies; Battle of Mizpah; Samuel becomes Judge of Israel
1141	Samuel's circuit begins
1138	Samson begins judging Israel
1137	Jonathan born to Saul
1133	Ishvi born to Saul
1131	Malchishua born to Saul

1130	Doeg the Edomite born
1128	Abinadab born to Saul
1127	Nathan the Prophet born?
1126	Merab born to Saul;
1125	Armoni born to Saul
1124	**JUBILEE YEAR**
1123	Mephibosheth born to Saul
1121	Ish-bosheth born to Saul; Samson captured?
1120	Joel and Abijah sent south with wives
1119	Samson killed
1117	Saul anointed; Samuel's sons corrupt (1 Sam 10:24; Acts 13:21)
1116	Attack by Nahash
1115	Defeat of Nahash--confirmation
1114	Army grows-Philistines ally with Rephaim
1113	Battles of Michmash and Migron
1112	Ishvi, son of Saul, dies accidentally; Michal born
1110	Kish dies
1107	David born (1 Sam 16:1)
1100	Book of Judges completed; Phoenician traders settle on Iberian Peninsula (Judg 21:25)
1095	Saul defeats Agag--Condemned!
1092	David anointed by Samuel; plays for Saul
1091	Battle of Elah; David made war chief
1090	Book of Ruth completed (Ruth 4:18-22)
1089	David marries Michal
1088	David and Samuel at Naioth
1087	Mephibosheth born to Jonathan; David in Nob, Achish
1086	Doeg kills priests
1085	David saves Keilah--is pursued
1084	Samuel dies; Nabal; David's flight to Philistia
1083	David in Philistia
1082	Battle of Mt. Gilboah-Death of Saul, sons
1078	1 Samuel completed (1 Sam 31:6)
1077	David becomes king of Judah (2 Sam 2:4)
1076	Ishbosheth installed as king by Abner
1075	Battle of Helkath-hazzurim; Death of Asahel
1074	Absalom born to David
1073	Abner defects to David; Joab kills him
1072	Ishbosheth killed
1071	Zion taken by David
1070	David King of Israel & Judah; conquest Jerusalem; moves Ark (2 Sam 5:3-7; 6:15; 7:12-16)
1069	David builds house with Hiram
1067	Battle at Baal-perazim
1066	Battle of Rephaim
1065	David brings Ark; plans temple; gets covenant
1064	David conquers Philistia, Moab
1063	David conquers Zobah, Syria; Edom
1062	David honors Mephibosheth; conquers Ammon/Syria
1061	Seige of Rabbah-sin with Bathsheba
1059	Child David and Bathsheba dies.
1058	Solomon born; Rabbah taken.
1057	Rape of Tamar

1055	Absalom kills Amnon, flees
1052	Absalom recalled; Revolts! David flees
1051	Hushai; Athitophel's suicide
1050	Civil War! Absalom killed and mourned
1049	David returns to Jerusalem
1048	Sheba's revolt; Amasa killed
1047	Three year famine
1045	Sons of Saul exposed by Gibeonites
1044	Wars with Philistia--Mighty men
1040	Book of 2 Samuel completed (2 Sam 24:18)
1037	Solomon becomes king (1 Ki 1:39; 2:12)
1034	Temple construction begun (1 Ki 6:1)
1027	First Temple completed (1 Ki 6:38)
1026	Temple dedicated by Solomon
1020	Song of Solomon written (Cant 1:1)
1000	Ecclesiastes completed (Eccl 1:1)

Obviously, the apportioning of events between the years of 1450 B.C.E. and 1117 B.C.E. are supposition on the part of the author. This is also true of most of the events between 1117 B.C.E. and 1037 B.C.E. This timeline is one way in which the information in Judges and the books of Samuel and Kings can be rectified. It is by no means the only way. Many readers will no doubt recoil in horror at the suggestion that Samson was alive in Saul's day, or that Samuel could have been serving as a Judge at the same time that Samson was. I do not assert that this outline is accurate, or even highly plausible. It is one possibility, one which seemed to me to fit the information available in the Scriptures and to serve the story I was attempting to tell. Perhaps by the time the next volume of this Chronicle is published (deo volente!), I will have re-written this timeline to reflect discoveries uncovered in my continued research on the subject.

ABOUT THE AUTHOR

Since the tender age of 7, Timothy Wilkinson has been a writer of fictions. An avid sailor and a teacher of history and literature, author of volumes of poetry and plays for screen and stage, he spends his days in the rainless gray of Washington State's Olympic Peninsula with his wife Chelsey. His latest endeavor, the *Eternal Throne Chronicles*, of which *Prophet Of Isreal* is the first installment, is the fruit of nearly a decade of re-writes, abandoned drafts and a cavalcade of research.

-Jordan Avery